From Dusk to Dawn

By
Niambi Brown Davis

Parker Publishing LLC

Noire Passion is an imprint of Parker Publishing LLC.

Copyright © 2008 by Niambi Brown Davis
Published by Parker Publishing LLC
12523 Limonite Ave., Ste. #440-438
Mira Loma, California 91752
www.parker-publishing.com

ISBN: 978-1-60043-036-7
First Edition

Manufactured in the United States of America

Cover Design by Jaxadora Design

From Dusk to Dawn

By
Niambi Brown Davis

For Tex

Chapter 1
❧

A stab of pain jerked Ayo Montgomery awake. Peering at the clock through slits of barely opened lids, she dragged herself to a seated position. This pale orchid room had always been her sanctuary but today it was a fragrant, steamy prison. She reached out, groping for last night's glass of water and two red and white capsules. Before tossing them down her throat, Ayo grimaced. She eased her head back against the mound of pillows. Shifting again, she drew her knees to her chest. The phone rang, disturbing her short-lived relief. That morning, the soft tones sounded like shrill clanging. Glancing over at the caller ID, Ayo squeezed her eyes shut, picked up the handset and jabbed "talk."

"You know why I picked up this phone? Just so I could hang up on you!"

"Whoa, Ayo! Are you still pissed?"

"Pissed? Pick one reason, Justine—the oiled-up blubber belly or the scrawny scarecrow?"

"Come on, Ayo—I told you last night that I'm sorry!"

"You ought to be." Ayo's snarl eased into a low chuckle. "Just teasing. I'm not pissed, I'm in pain. It's my never-ending female problems." She sighed, twisting to press her side against the pillows bent into a wedge of firm support. "But back to last night–I let you drag me to your cousin's book club, but why did the discussion end up with two broke-down, cut-rate strippers? Where'd they get those g-strings? A ten-pack from the dollar store?"

"Stop!" Justine Lewis-Randall giggled. "Elmira decided it was a fitting finale to the discussion of Erotique Noire."

"She did, huh? Then Elmira should stick to selecting books and leave the selection of man-candy for somebody else. The only thing I wanted to do after seeing those two erotically-challenged jokers was laugh. And that skinny one—ole boy should have been dancing to 'Hungry Like a Wolf.' Besides, if I want to, I can get my own half-naked sweaty man."

As soon as the words left her mouth, Ayo dropped her head in one hand. Too late. It was just the opening her best friend needed.

"Oh you can? According to my recollection, you've only been out with two men in eighteen years."

"Then you must have been sleeping with Rip Van Winkle instead of Nick Randall," Ayo shot back. "Besides, men our age want a model just off the showroom floor. And I'm not nipping, tucking or sucking anything out of my body to please some old dude who'll need a blue pill before I'll need K-Y jelly! And I'll be damned before I turn into a cougar!"

"Cougar? Ayo, I don't know *what* you're talking about, but I can't wait to find out."

"Don't worry," Ayo chuckled. "I'm not going "Animal Planet" on you—besides you've already got your man." Ayo teased. "But for your information, a cougar is an older woman on the prowl for younger men. According to the woman I saw on TV there's a whole movement out there. But this one looked like a dried up stick of beef jerky with lots of hair and a wrap-around grin. They should have picked a better spokes-kitty to represent them," Ayo giggled.

Justine gagged on the laughter stuck in her throat. "Ayo, you are so wrong. I do not believe you said that!" she croaked out.

"It's true! Anyway if the time is right, the man will find me, he'll have to because I'm sure not looking. But I've got to get myself up and ready for an appraisal. You remember my mother's collection of pottery and glass? I'm certain they're worth more than I thought."

"So who did you get to do the appraisal?"

Finally something to veer Justine off the track of her relentless matchmaking. She meant well—in the thirteenth year of her own happy marriage, she wanted something close to that kind of life for Ayo. But Ayo's life didn't need fixing—she was finally at a place of peace, and although it *might* be nice, she didn't need a man to make her life complete.

"His name is Bilal Abdul-Salaam. Eileen recommended him. He's done some work for her gallery and he was at the top of her list. Anybody who's alright with her is more than good enough for me."

"What a strong, masculine name—is he a Muslim?"

In slow motion, Ayo pushed herself off the crumpled sheets, pulling the damp t-shirt away from her sticky skin. "I don't know, but it's hot and my whole body is crying for mercy. I want as little fabric as possible touching me, so whatever he is, he'd better be prepared to see some skin."

Justine was too genteel for a full belly laugh—her chuckle escalated into as much of a guffaw as she could muster. "So what do you think he's going to do? Run out of the door at the sight of your bare arms?"

"At $100.00 an hour, he shouldn't care if I'm flaunting a fur-trimmed see-through and three-inch heels. Some Muslim men have a problem with a woman not being covered, but if he's one of them, he'd better walk with some blinders."

"Ayo, give the brother a break," Justine giggled. "Besides, this Mr. Abdul-Salaam might be interesting..." She let the sentence trail off into an unspoken suggestion.

In spite of her pain, Ayo burst out laughing. "You don't give up, do you, Miss Matchmaker? You're hopeless; at the rate you're going, any man who can get the subject and verb to agree might be interesting. Right now the only man I want to see will be toting a toolbox and a container of Freon. But I love you anyway," she chuckled. "And I'll talk to you later."

Ayo didn't feel like it, but just before two o'clock, she pulled on a simple orange shift and slipped her feet into matching flat sandals. Although her cramps had all but disappeared, what she really wanted was to drape herself in the shapeless bag of a Hawaiian print house-dress that barely touched her skin. She pulled her fingers through her hair. The light brown twists fanned out, brushing the tops of her shoulders. A pale tinted gloss was the only makeup she could bear to touch her face. Out of habit, she reached for "Ayo's Ambrosia", the signature scent she created for herself. But she set the vintage atomizer back on the dresser. One spray would be a return invitation for the headache she'd finally gotten rid of.

At two o'clock the brass pineapple knocker struck the door. When Ayo swung it open she couldn't keep her eyes from rolling. *Not today! Here we go again...*"

"Yes?" The word unfurled like the sneer it was intended to be. Why couldn't these street ball players follow one simple sign? The public courts were only one more block down the street. *Look at him—vanity, thy name is baller.* A pretty boy at that, posed at her door like the prince of the city.

Nothing was out of place on this man, not even a drop of perspiration on a day that was a preview of hell. The dove-gray linen shirt and charcoal pants fit as if each thread had been woven over his body—but she didn't know what kind of ball he planned to play in that GQ ensemble. He was clearly lost, but he was wasting her time.

"Mrs. Montgomery?" When he leaned back to stare up at the

numbers above the brass knocker, the cool gray fabric flattened against his broad chest. "I'm Bilal Abdul-Salaam."

Ayo's mouth dropped open. She was glad he didn't extend his hand because hers was stuck to her side. "You can't be!" The haze of annoyance cleared, and Ayo's stomach took a slow somersault. *Good Lord*! He was nothing like the picture she had formed in her mind—the one in which Bilal Abdul-Salaam would be an academic, no-nonsense, righteous right-on brother. Instead she stared up into eyes the color of dark maple syrup. His face brought to mind a magnificent tribal mask—eyes like chips of dark amber, high cheekbones and lush, full lips. Could skin really be that color? His was ebony brushed with a hint of amber and gold. A slender mustache rimmed his mouth and chin, blending into the fine beard that dusted a strong jaw line. Each coil of his immaculate locks flowed past broad shoulders, tied back by two pencil-thin pieces of his own hair. He was over 6 feet of primal, yet refined masculinity. If *Gladiator* had been filmed south of the Sahara, this man could have been its star.

Damn! As stupid as she looked, he probably thought he'd been paid to appraise a collection of wall-mounted singing fish and wide-eyed puppies painted on velvet.

Ayo scrambled to regain her composure, unaware that Abdul-Salaam's brows had knitted together into a frown. He speared her with a sharp glance. "Since we made an appointment for today at 2:00, who else could I be?"

Ayo's head jerked up. Fine or not, he'd better check himself. Better yet—she'd do it for him. "Since you didn't show up wearing a name tag, I had no idea who you were. I saw a man standing on my porch with a duffle bag. For all I know you could be a baller or a burglar!"

Abdul-Salaam raised one thick, silky eyebrow. "Then you must be familiar with a better class of burglar than the rest of us. I've never heard of one who knocked on the door and introduced himself."

Ayo's patience unraveled. The heat flushing her body had nothing to do with the cloying humidity that left the entire city gasping for air. It was a warning, a Beware-of-Ayo sign: look out, because whatever came to her mind would come flying out of her mouth like a poisoned dart.

But not this time. Especially not in front of her next-door neighbor who had just come out onto his porch and was paying more attention to her and Bilal Abdul-Salaam than the circulars crammed into his mailbox. Besides, she *had* started the drama. Even more, she needed the appraisal. He was number one on Eileen's list; how long it would take to get an appointment with number two? This man must be a damn good appraiser, but he needed a client relations intervention—

quick, fast and in a hurry.

Sighing, Ayo gave in. "Okay, look; we're both wasting time, bickering outside in this heat." And the sooner he got to work, the sooner he could be out of her house and on his way to whatever cave he called home. "Since we've solved the identity crisis and I've already paid my deposit, let's put an end to the verbal sparring so you can earn your money!" Ayo gestured to the open door. Bilal's jaw clenched. She expected him to turn on his heel and stalk away without a word. Instead, his gaze swept over her bare arms and the expanse of skin exposed by the scoop at the top of her dress.

"Oh, good Lord," Ayo groused to herself. "What's next? A speech on modesty? If I'd known the jihad squad was coming, I would have answered the door in crotchless panties!"

A long low whistle snapped her out of a mental recitation of words synonymous with Neanderthal. "*Man*…this is beautiful!" Next to him, Ayo's eyebrow raised. She gave a smug snort. The room had that effect on first-time visitors. Against walls the color of pale butter, a marble topped mahogany console held her collection of barware. A large armoire with carved pineapple columns sat between two windows hung with curtains of sheer white batiste. It was the smaller version of rooms found in great houses of the eighteenth century Caribbean. This room, in fact her entire home, paid homage to the skill of West Indian cabinetmakers.

"Beautiful," he repeated, murmuring his praise in a late-night "Quiet Storm" voice that made Ayo think of a rainy night in front of a fire with a man like him. But as gorgeous as he was, he'd waste the romantic opportunity to deliver a stern lecture on the sins of the flesh. When he stopped in front of the gleaming teakwood table, Ayo squashed that thought and replaced it with a fantasy of his hand on her flesh, the same way Bilal's long fingers stroked the dusky rose Weller vases arrayed on the long gleaming table. Slowly, he circled, paying the same loving attention to the Roseville Pottery, gleaming cobalt blue stemware, and the butterfly perched on the shoulder of bisque Piano Baby in mint condition. For the first time since his arrival, the furrow between his brows disappeared. "You have some lovely pieces here." He looked up at Ayo and her breath hitched. It was the smile—it transformed him from scowling to spectacular. This time the heat that flushed her body had nothing to do with anger or the weather and everything to do with the slow, sensuous movement of his hand. Ayo willed away the sharp and unexpected attraction to the man whose face she wanted to slap just seconds before.

"Thanks," she murmured, lowering her eyes in case they beamed her erotic thoughts straight out into the room. She gestured to the card table that could hold his laptop and camera. "If you need anything else, I'll be in the kitchen. It's through that door." She pointed to the golden mahogany door, painted from top to bottom with a graceful, curving palm tree. The word "welcome" was etched above it in stenciled script. His lush lips turned up into a smile. "Beautiful and creative." In spite of the heat, she welcomed the warmth that surged through her body. *Maybe I misjudged him.*

Ninety minutes later, Ayo pushed away from the table, intending to head for her home office. Instead, she stood rooted to the spot, unable to tear her eyes away from the sight that greeted her. Bilal stood with his back to the door. His long legs were spread apart. Dark gray fabric cupped his sculptured butt like the palms of a lover. A roadmap of veins stood out in the lean, muscular arms raised high over his head. He arched his neck, and the luxurious locks fell like a curtain of velvet around his broad shoulders. It was just a stretch, to work out kinks that must have come from an hour and a half of bending, photographing and cataloging, but from him it was an erotic, primal celebration of masculinity. Ayo felt a sharp pull in her solar plexus, and lower; the sweet tightening that a woman never forgets, no matter how long the dry season has lasted. Baby, baby, *baby!* A play list of suggestive song titles slid into her brain like a sexy slow drag. No doubt this man did more with his body than sit at a desk, poring over books on glassware and pottery. She slipped back into the kitchen, glad that her bare feet made no sound. An involuntary, sensual smile curved her lips. What a waste! A man so mouthwatering had no right being a puritanical zealot.

≥▲

Bilal pulled a paper towel from the roll stashed in his duffel bag, swiping it across his forehead and inside the collar of the shirt that stuck to his back like wet tissue. Shaking his head, he looked up at the ceiling fan and over at the floor model in the corner. Every piece that adorned the pale yellow walls and gleaming hardwood floors bore the grace of Ayo Montgomery. Like its owner, the house was beautiful. But today it was as hot and steamy as a sweat lodge! At least the final picture of each piece and its markings had been taken. He placed the digital camera and tripod back in the duffle bag, glad he could complete the rest of his valuation in the cool comfort of his air conditioned home. Bilal stood and stretched again. Right now what he needed was a tall glass of cold ice water.

When he knocked on the half-opened decorative door, Ayo Montgomery twisted around.

"Oh! You surprised me, Mr. Abdul-Salaam. Can I help you?" She stood quickly, tugging at her dress with one hand and pressing the other against the skin at the base of her throat. Bilal's head jerked up. He fixed a stare on the green and yellow stripes on the kitchen curtains; anything but the bare skin of the woman in front of him.

"May I have a glass of water, please?"

Her expression changed from surprise to chagrin. "Oh, I'm so sorry! I know it's boiling in here. I should have brought you something to drink a long time ago. Every air conditioning repairman in the city must be on call. I guess that's why I can't get one of them to show up here." When she smiled, he noticed a dimple that ended just below the constellation of three tiny moles on her right cheek.

While she filled a glass with crushed ice and water from the door of the refrigerator, Bilal looked around the room. In the bright yellow kitchen, a blend of aromas wound around one another. The sharp, tangy scents of pineapple and lemon were laced with coconut and softened by another fragrance with a similar, richer scent. Through a window over the sink, the green length of a luxuriant back yard was visible. Although the high heat of summer had driven most of the blooms into hiding, the graceful weeping willow, ornamental grass and wildflowers made the garden an urban oasis.

"Here you are. This should bring you back to life." Without its earlier sharp bite of anger, her voice spread over him like cook silk. When she offered him the cold, sweating glass, Ayo Montgomery was close enough for him to breathe the clean, orange-blossom scent of her hair. He stood frozen like a display window mannequin.

"Mr. Abdul-Salaam?" she repeated, holding the glass out further. "Oh, sorry," she exclaimed, plucking a green-bordered cloth napkin from the table and wrapping it around the damp surface. Her fingers brushed his hand. Bilal flinched and stepped back, as if the cool drink had suddenly transformed itself into a hot poker.

Ayo blinked. A fleeting glimpse of confusion crossed her face before it morphed into a mask of controlled anger. She banged the glass down, sloshing icy water over the striped table cloth. "You know what? You Taliban wanna-be's piss me off, trying to prove you're more Muslim than the Grand Ayatollah himself! I touched your hand, Mr. Abdul-Salaam; I didn't grab your crotch!"

Bilal's eyes flashed a stormy dark brown. A muscle twitched in his clenched jaw. His voice was cold as the slushy liquid he didn't get to drink. "Well check this out, Mrs. Montgomery—I wouldn't let you close enough to grab my crotch! First you treat me like I'm a home invader; make me work in that sauna without a drop of water, and now this? You're just like those other Bible-beating Crusaders—instant experts on Islam after hearing a five-second sound bite by a gang of know-nothings. You have no idea of what you're talking about, but

I'm not surprised!"

Ayo spun around and turned her back, tossing the last words over her shoulder. "Here's what I do know—if you weren't finished in there, you are now! Don't bother to come back with your report. Mail it along with your bill. And you can see yourself out!"

Chapter 2
🍸

If Bilal could have kicked himself and driven at the same time, he would have done it right there at the intersection of North Capitol and Riggs Road. Let the passengers under the crowded bus shelter see what a complete fool he had been. If every man, woman and child on that block laughed at him, he deserved their scorn, on every count—from his curt response to Ayo Montgomery's startled greeting all the way to the disastrous end.

Next to him, the thumping bass of D.C.'s homegrown go-go blared over his XM Radio's spoken word. Four young women rocked in the red Mustang convertible, hunching their shoulders back and forth to the beat. The driver glanced over and reared back in her seat, spearing Bilal in a stare of frank, seductive appraisal. "Oooh, baby, you are *foine!*" she shrieked, twisting her glossy red mouth around the word. The light changed, but before he was out of their sight, she and her passengers turned to deliver a rapid-fire flurry of kisses in Bilal's direction. There had been a time when their attention would have inflated his head like a hot air balloon, but those days were long gone. Bilal raised one hand to give them a distracted wave.

Grabbing his cell phone from the seat beside him, he punched in a speed dial digit. It rang five times before clicking over. "I've got something for you and something to tell you," he replied to the soft-voiced invitation to leave a message. "I'll be over tomorrow."

🍸

Ayo waited until she heard the door slam. She scraped her chair away from the table, hard enough that it tipped backward, nearly sending her sprawling to the floor. "Damn! If I break *anything*—this chair or my behind, I'm suing his ass!"

She grabbed the handle of a wicker basket in one hand and flung open the kitchen door with the other, letting the screen slam shut behind her. Her fury equaled the heat of the day. Instead of her usual, careful unpinning and smoothing them into perfect squares, Ayo yanked the lilac sheets from the line and tossed them into a heap inside the basket. Clothespins hit the plastic container like a shower of hailstones, except the few that missed their mark and ended up like abandoned stick figures in the velvety green grass.

It became a gerbil-on-a-wheel kind of afternoon. Round and round, but getting nowhere. Ayo scowled and stomped around the house, wanting something to kick. Never a real live dog, but if she owned a stuffed canine, by now it would have been reduced to fake fur and fluff. There was plenty to do, but she couldn't keep her mind on any one task, leaving an unfinished list, a half-read article and the beginnings of a meal behind her. She finally gave up and headed for the coolest room in the house, thanks to the windows facing the shady side of the yard. She jerked the cord with such force that the bamboo blinds slapped down hard against the sill. Ayo stripped to her underwear. She tossed her dress on the back of a chair and sprawled on the daybed, letting her anger and the heat claim her.

That night, the temperature and her ire went down with the sun. After a long, cool shower Ayo stretched out on her bed, freshly made with sun-sweetened sheets. Overhead, the blades of an art-deco ceiling fan blew away the remaining heat of the day. A glass of Pinot Grigio and a tray of honeysuckle-scented candles sat on her bedside table. The pale yellow tapers sent a fragrant, calming glow out into the room. After the first sip of wine she sighed, feeling a little more in control of her runaway emotions. Reaching down, she searched through a bedside basket of magazines. Ayo's lips curved up into a smile when she pulled out a copy of *Yellow Silk*. It was one of her favorites; she loved the sensual and literary collection of erotic poems and stories from around the world. Halfway through the first exquisitely written story, Ayo tossed it down. Was the moon full? Maybe that was why she let that knuckle-dragging chauvinist turn her into a raving lunatic. When the phone rang, this time she was glad to hear Justine's always-cheery voice. She could make a simple greeting sound like a warm-up for the prize behind door number two.

"Hey, Ayo, when is Kedar due back from Canada? Do you want me to pick him up from the airport?"

Ayo shook her head, even though she knew Justine couldn't see her. "He came back early. He wanted to have more time with me and go over to Annapolis, too. There's only a few days left before he heads back down to Florida."

Justine hesitated. "Isn't that the same day you have a doctor's appointment?"

Ayo's mouth twisted. It wasn't Monday, and it wasn't soon enough. The heavy bleeding had increased and the cramps that came along felt like muffled hammer blows. "No, it's two weeks away. Probably a waste of time. I've been to every doctor in DC and nobody can figure out what's wrong. This time I'm going to Baltimore to another specialist. Hopefully he can give me some answers."

"I hope so, too. Anything that puts you in bed two days a month needs to be named and healed. But Ayo—"

So much for the welcome relief–lawd, have mercy, here we go, Ayo sighed. "Yes?" She took a deep swallow of wine to buy some time.

"Don't give me that 'yes.' You know I can read you like a tarot card. So what else is wrong?"

"What do you mean?" Even though she knew it was futile, Ayo played the innocent.

"You know what I mean. As my eloquent and scholarly husband says, 'I can tell when you've got a wild hair up your butt. So come on with it'."

Ayo stripped the residue of anger from her voice and in a monotone, recounted the lowlights of the afternoon.

"I know I started it. He just wasn't at all what I expected, and when he showed up on my steps looking like a gorgeous, modern-day warrior king, I didn't know whether to throw him out or drag him inside and ravish him in the hallway." Ayo's frown deepened. "But the man's a spawn of the Taliban. Looking at me like I was the whore of Babylon—in my own house, at that! And when I accidentally brushed his hand, he jumped back like I was poison!" The longer Ayo spoke, the higher her voice rose, until it lurched into an indignant halt. Her hand swept in a wide arc, back and forth across the smooth fitted sheet.

"Justine, are you there?" The silence surprised her. At any other time, Justine would have interrupted her rant with a string of non-stop observations.

"Yes, I'm here. Just waiting for you to wind down so I can tell you what I think."

"No kidding. So what else is new?"

"Ha!" Justine retorted. "There you are! I was wondering where my friend Ayo had gone. For a minute I thought one of your weeping willows had broken a window and taken over your body."

Ayo bounced back against the pillows. For the first time since early that day, she let loose a genuine laugh. "Save your way with words. You need each and every one to make that trifling councilwoman look good!"

"And that's why my clients pay me big bucks. But my dear, the only way you can escape is to hang up. And I know you won't," Justine retorted.

"Don't test me," Ayo threatened through a wine-induced giggle. She raised her half-empty goblet. "I'd better drink the rest of this wine, because I'm sure going to need it!"

"Trying to take the edge off the truth? Forget it, and don't say another word. Now I know I wasn't there, but I think the both of you misjudged the other. You've already admitted that you treated him like a Saxon invader. The man's not a mind reader; he probably thought you were crazy. And as far as him being a religious fanatic, how do you know? Did he give you the Muslim equivalent of the 'you need Jesus' spiel?"

"Well, no…" Ayo mumbled.

"Then you're missing the whole point. Ayo, he walked into the house of a good looking woman in a short dress. He might be a Muslim, but he's still a man. And what man is not going to look? He wasn't offended by you, he was attracted to you!"

"Calling me a Bible-thumping Crusader is a weird way of showing it."

A burst of choking laughter bombarded Ayo's ear. "Oh my goodness! Now I know exactly what's going on." Justine launched into an off-key, whispered version of Barney theme song. "You like him, he likes you, now what the hell are you gonna do?"

"Shut up, Justine! I have never met a man I disliked more!"

Ayo's indignant declaration fell on deaf ears. "Go ahead—keep on fooling yourself, but the truth will out."

"Justine, the truth has *been* out. I'd rather join a convent than look in that man's direction."

"So you're going to put him on your no-fly list?" Justine chortled. "I'll bet if he knocked on your door right now, you'd give him a round-trip ticket, boarding pass and first class seat."

"You know you're getting on my nerves, don't you?"

"Yes I do, and I hope it's your last nerve, too. Because you're in deep denial, my sister," Justine giggled. "Oh," she exclaimed, "you and this foolishness almost made me forget to ask. Do you have plans for Saturday night?"

She didn't give Ayo a chance to answer. "I know how mopey you get when it's time for Kedar to go back to school. So listen—Bernard White is having a reception to introduce the Thomas Day exhibit before it's featured at the National Gallery. Nick and I know you'd love to go and we want you to come with us. And here's the sweet part—one of the smaller pieces will be on display! So—"

Ayo sat straight up. She cut Justine off in mid-sentence. "Oh, I'd love to! I had planned to see the exhibit when it opens, but I would kill to see one of Day's pieces up close." Years ago, in her other life as a researcher, Ayo had gathered an extensive amount of information on Day, a supremely talented man from a family of free African Americans. He was one of the largest furniture manufacturers in eighteenth century North Carolina, with work commissioned by two governors. The only piece of information that dampened Ayo's strong admiration for this extraordinary man was that he himself had been a slave owner.

"Good," Justine exclaimed. "For a minute I thought you were going to give me some trouble. No sense in you sitting in that house brooding."

"That's what Kedar tells me all the time. Don't worry–no moping," she chanted in a parody of the cheery song.

Long after their phone call ended, Ayo drew her knees up to her chest and laid her head on crossed arms. A toothy news anchor droned from the television, but Ayo paid him no attention. She may have brushed off her friend, but she couldn't ignore the little voice that never failed to tell her the truth, even when she wanted to duct-tape its mouth shut. It made her admit why she'd tossed down the magazine. She couldn't finish the story because the end of each erotic sentence was punctuated with the face of Bilal Abdul-Salaam.

૨ৡ

The remnants of his botched, pre-dawn meal sat on the cream and coffee-colored granite counter. His attempt to scramble an egg in a new non-stick frying pan failed miserably; it clung so hard to the bottom that Bilal gave up, tossing out the egg and the pan along with it. He tried to salvage the soggy cereal by dumping more flakes into the bowl. When it turned from cornflake pudding to something resembling wet paper mache, Bilal gave up and fed it to the disposal, even though his next meal wouldn't come until after sundown.

At one-thirty, he stood with an international gathering of Muslims in the beautiful blue and white tiled Islamic Center on Massachusetts Avenue. The *ahdan*, the call to prayer, filled him up, winding its way into his soul as it never failed to do, each time he heard its plaintive beauty, especially at Ramadan. For some, fasting between dawn and sunset for an entire month seemed an extreme sacrifice. But to him it was a beautiful, spiritual time. A time to reflect on his faith, his blessings and his family. And since he had set the goal, a time to put his personal life in order.

A half-hour later Bilal strode up the steps to the Carroll Avenue Victorian like a man on a purpose. In his haste, he brushed against one of the tall terra cotta planters on either side of the door. He caught the wobbling container before it spilled red flowers and potting soil onto the porch's painted floor.

A woman came to the door, gliding like a graceful swan set on crystal-clear waters. A high-crowned knit hat covered her head, framing smooth skin that was a canvas for almond eyes and a lipstick-model mouth. More than once she had been compared to a younger, sable-brown Phyllis Hyman, but Zahirah Ahmed was the identical, female version of her brother.

"As-Salaam-Alaikum, sis." They gave each other the greeting of peace, planting kisses on each other's cheek. "Here's the book you wanted. I finally found it online. It's used, but in pretty good shape." He looked behind her to the arched doorway. "Where's Kalil? And the baby girls?"

"Oh thank you!" she exclaimed, already thumbing through its fragile pages. Zahirah loved black folk tales and this was a 1947 first edition. "Kalil's on the road already. He's taking the girls over to Mama. But what's up with you?"

They walked through the colorful room, decorated in modern Moroccan style and done in shades of blue, gold and ivory. The rich fragrance of Zahirah's rose-scented rock incense wafted from an ornate gold burner in the corner. Next to a pile of large, tasseled pillows, Bilal slouched in a Haitian cotton chair, under a framed print of elaborate blue, gold and black calligraphy. His head rested against the chair's ivory headrest, sending a fall of locks over its back. "I messed up, big time." He stretched one leg out, bouncing out a staccato beat with his heel.

Zahirah smiled, even as she wagged a warning finger at her brother. "Tell me about it, but stop banging up my floor!"

"Sorry, Z!" Bilal straightened, jerking up his khaki-clad leg.

Zahirah raised one eyebrow. "Something's got you worked up—so what happened?"

"I met a woman."

The huge smile didn't surprise him, but he didn't expect Zahirah to sit up and clap. "Does that mean you finally got rid of Katherine?"

Bilal gave a dry laugh. It was no secret that Katherine Hall was not his sister's favorite person. "I don't know what you see in her," Zahirah admonished him after a few encounters with his former girlfriend. "She's okay on paper—attractive, well-educated, carries herself well. But if you're looking for wife material, that lawyer lady will be in her office more than in your bed."

"Aw, come on, Zahirah," he chuckled. "Getting rid of sounds like killing her and stuffing her body in a cooler. Although I'm sure the thought crossed your mind," he admonished with a tease and a raised eyebrow.

She grinned and stuck out her tongue. "Whatever you call it is fine with me. You know that relationship was a waste of time."

Bilal nodded, steepling his fingers under his chin. "True—and I thought she might be the one, but when I found out she didn't want to have children, that curtain crashed down. Just goes to show—what you meet isn't always what you get."

Bilal and Katherine met at Heaven, the latest magnet for DC's young hip glitterati. His client was part-owner and asked Bilal to meet him there to discuss the restoration of an antique desk he bought at auction. In the swirl of women spilling from swatches of fabric covering as little of their skin as possible, Katherine's cool understated elegance stood out. Wherever he found himself in the club, she moved to place herself in his sight and kept her eyes on him, cradling a goblet of amber liquid in one French-manicured hand. Their introductory tango ended at the bar when he turned to find her standing beside him holding her empty glass. He bought her another drink, found a secluded table for two, and asked her to wait until his meeting was over. Just as quickly, the relationship fizzled.

"That's true, and I know it's only my opinion, but I wish you and Hasina could have made it work. She was warm, intelligent, funny as heck and crazy about you. And not that it matters, but she was Muslim, too. You didn't have to break her in." Zahirah's mouth turned up into a puckish grin.

Bilal snorted out a short burst of laughter. "You're crazy! But Hasina wanted to go back home to Guinea and I wanted to stay here. For us, there was no meeting in the middle. However, my smart-mouthed sister, I didn't come here to rehash the past. There's someone that has my full and undivided attention."

"Uh-oh? You mean the mighty Bilal Abdul-Salaam is smitten? Now this I want to hear, but you've got to tell me quickly. I have to be at a CVS in Rockville today. Their regular pharmacist is on leave, and I'm filling in for two weeks."

Bilal leaned forward, dangling his clasped hands between his knees. One corner of his mouth lifted. The whole encounter rolled like an old-fashioned eight millimeter through his brain. Ayo Montgomery's sensuality and her formidable anger were a potent, intoxicating combination. "I did an appraisal yesterday for a woman who was a referral from Eileen Waring. Eileen told me her friend had a decent collection that she'd inherited from her mother. So I go over there, expecting to meet a pleasant, middle-aged woman. But when Ayo Montgomery opened the door, she blew me completely and totally away like a leaf in high wind." He didn't mention Ayo's effect on his body. That was too much information, even for a sister with whom he shared almost everything.

Zahirah's eyebrow arched. "Uh-oh, she must be some woman. But what went wrong?"

"You know how it is—a brother can admire a woman who looks good, but he shouldn't be gaping like a wild dog in a meat house."

His sister bolted up in her chair. "Bilal Abdul-Salaam! No, you didn't!"

Bilal jerked his head up. A small frown wrinkled his smooth brows. "You know I didn't! Like any other man, I enjoy the sight of a beautiful woman. But I try to do it without my tongue dragging the ground. Anyway, she thought I was somebody else, and I used her confusion to go on the defensive, to cover up my attraction to her." Bilal looked up at his sister. "I was a fool." The frown pleated into deeper lines. "But it gets worse. I asked her for a drink of water, and when her hand brushed against mine, I jumped back like she was a leper. Man, she was *furious!*" A rueful smile tugged at his lips. "But that sister is no pushover. She gave me as good as she got. After the water fiasco, she put me out." Bilal chuckled. "Told me to mail the bill and report and carry my butt on out of her house. But I'm going to see her again, and even if she comes to the door with a pot of boiling oil, we're going to talk."

Zahirah studied her brother. "Is that the only reason? Just to talk?"

Bilal shook his head, remembering Ayo's lush curves, those never-ending legs, and the scent of her hair. "Oh, *no*, my sister. *Insha'Allah*, God willing, that conversation will be our beginning."

Chapter 3

"I almost forgot to call you!" Justine heaved like a neophyte runner at the end of a marathon. "But I was on my way—"

Ayo's eyes narrowed. Her grip on the five-page document creased it into something resembling a kindergarten craft project. She cut straight across Justine's breathless explanation. "You won't believe what that man did! It must be his mission in life to piss me off!"

"Whoa, Ayo! What man are you talking about? Whoever he is, I hope he's wearing body armor."

"Bilal Abdul-Salaam—that's who!"

Justine's laughter bubbled like spilled champagne. "Uh-oh—the drama continues. What did he do this time?"

"I told him to send me the report and his bill. The last page requires my signature—don't you know he left it off? What kind of professional is he? Now I'll have to talk to him again!"

"And I'll bet that just burns your biscuits, doesn't it?" The bubbling turned into a full belly laugh, one which Ayo had trouble appreciating.

"Justine, I don't see anything funny at all. I told you I never wanted to see his butt again."

"Yes, you do. You want to see more than his butt. And that's why you're hollering louder than one of those masked anarchists in front of the World Bank. To paraphrase the Bard, 'The lady doth protest too much'."

"You know what? You're supposed to be my best friend, and you're no help at all!"

"Ohhh, I thought you didn't want my help!" Justine snickered. "But we'll have to take this up later—and we will. Can you be ready at six-thirty?"

"Yes, Justine, but the question is—can you?"

"You know Nick doesn't do late. I'll be ready on time, believe me. And I'm so glad you're coming. Who knows—since you insist that you

can't stand Mr. Abdul Salaam, which by the way is a complete crock—
you might meet another who really catches your eye."

I should grab a man off the street just to shut her up.

"So you think I'll find my dream lover tonight?" Ayo chuckled.
"Just like that?"

"No, but you might find a suitable prospect! Anyway, we both have
got to get ready. And you know how long it takes me."

Wrapped in a cream, waffle-weave bathrobe, Ayo padded barefoot
into the bathroom. Spider plants and ferns formed a green canopy in
the cream and terra cotta tiled retreat. She ran warm water in the tub,
adding a splash of rich amber oil to sweeten her soak.

An hour later, Ayo pored through the closet, pushing back hanger
after hanger until she found it, flattened between two other dresses.
Accented with sea green foam that splashed out from the center, the
slim, coral peachskin was perfect. Too bad there would be no one to
admire her legs in the strappy coral sandals, peeking out from the
knee-length slit. But it was okay; the ego boost that came with looking
good was sufficient in itself.

In spite of her long and elaborate grooming routine, Justine and her
husband pulled up at six-thirty on the dot. At six feet tall and one
hundred and ninety pounds, Justine left nothing to chance. "As big as
I am, I can't afford to look sloppy," she insisted when Ayo teased her,
calling her "Glamourene." Justine booked standing appointments to
keep her corkscrew curls, her hands and feet well-groomed. Once a
month facials kept her cinnamon skin smooth and glowing. Justine's
dazzling dimpled smile was her calling card; she made sure her teeth
were always perfect pearls.

"Hey, you two." Ayo patted Nick's shoulder as she slid into the
back seat of his Toyota SUV.

"Hey, yourself." Nick smiled over his shoulder. Silver began at his
temples and crept through his thick black hair, ending in a half-dollar
patch at the top of his head. It contrasted against skin his wife called
midnight velvet. "Okay, you know the drill—I have to make my usual
spiel. I know you're doing big business with your soap-making, but
can I convince you to come and give me some help, even just a little
bit?"

The three of them had a long history together. Nick Randall had
been her professor of African American history when Ayo was a
student at University of Maryland. Right away, she impressed him
with her zeal and knowledge. At eighteen, and in the second semester
of her sophomore year, Ayo became a part-time research associate at
Randall, Cooke and Associates where Justine had a contract for public
relations services. Ayo's mouth tightened. "Are you kidding? Even if I

considered it, it would never be while Margaret's there. I've got a long memory, Nick."

"Oh, you haven't heard?" Smiling broadly, Nick regarded his wife. "You didn't tell her? Now that's a first." He gave his wife a playful pat on her arm.

Tossing her cap of glossy curls, Justine raised her nose in the air. "It was useless information." Her eyes flashed, but two deep dimples creased her perfectly made up face.

"She's no longer with us," Nick told Ayo. "Margaret took a job a couple of months ago with the District Government in the Historical Preservation Division."

Ayo arched one eyebrow. A hint of disdain crept into her voice. "Instead of a reference letter, you should have sent them a sympathy card. Or maybe some holy water, a stake and a rope of garlic."

Margaret Charles had been her immediate supervisor and daily nemesis. From the first day Ayo showed up with her cornrows, youthful enthusiasm and uncommon talent, Margaret tormented the younger woman. Her subjugation lasted for a year until the day Ayo flew into the woman's office like a heat-seeking missile, taking her by surprise with a blistering resignation that still caused Nick to laugh out loud.

"Margaret's ears must be burning! I'll bet they've been on fire for twenty-three years—since the day you finally laid her out." Nick's hand slapped the steering wheel. "Girl, I choked on my coffee when I heard you ask her 'where's your pointy hat and cat!'" At a stop light, Ayo watched Nick's shoulders shake. "And when you told her to take that broom she'd been riding and sweep that mess out of her office, I thought I would have a heart-attack from laughing."

That day had been one of the worst of her life, but time and the joy that followed her meltdown made it insignificant. Now when her red-headed former nemesis came to mind, she could laugh. Five minutes later they pulled up in front of a house set on the side of a hill deep inside Rock Creek Park. Every window of the grand colonial was lit up. After Nick parked, Justine hurried around to the driver's side, waiting for her husband to lower himself from the driver's seat. "I'd love to have a little red Corvette," he quipped. "But with my leg, it's easier to climb down than up." Outside, he leaned on a carved cane topped with a lion's head. Nick's service in Vietnam earned him a purple heart and a leg wound that still ached. He carried the cane whenever he'd be standing more than a few minutes.

At the top of the curving stone walkway, and framed by the light behind him, Bernard White's six-foot, five-inch frame filled the entire doorway where he stood, greeting his guests like a serene, self-assured monarch. A wide, white smile contrasted against skin the color of sun-baked clay. The two men exchanged a brief masculine embrace.

"Glad you could make it," White continued, turning to Ayo. "And who is your friend here?"

"This is Ayo Montgomery. Years ago she was my best researcher. Now she owns Maracas Bay, an herbal body care business." Nick's eyes twinkled with merriment. "But I still keep trying to lure her back."

"That's high praise, my sister, coming from Nick Randall. He's a most worthy heir to the legacy of Carter Woodson."

"You're right about that." Ayo nodded her agreement at the man who cultivated her thirst for the who, what, when, why and where of history. "He was my teacher, mentor, and the person who gave me my start when I was green as grass."

Nick winked at Ayo. "So come on back," he teased. "You owe me."

❧

Bilal stood next to a brick mantle, topped by a magnificent arrangement of fresh tropical flowers. Around him, the stylish representatives of DC's political and arts community ebbed and flowed in a colorful tide. Many of them were his clients for appraisals or for the restoration of fine pieces of furniture. He spotted Mrs. Henderson, one of his blue-haired, Gold Coast clients. She could never get her eyes past his hair or pronounce his name correctly. Bill Sollum, she called him. But she loved his work, and as a frequent buyer of antiques for her showpiece home, she was one of his best customers. Right now, he didn't feel like hearing his name mangled. It was time to go, anyway. And when he spotted red silk poured over a lush, familiar figure linked arm in arm with one of his father's colleagues, Bilal knew it was past time.

He took a hurried, admiring glance at the row of iron sculptures from the west coast of Africa, and headed towards the door. Near a room off the foyer, he spotted his host with a small group. Laughter spilled from the circle where they stood. Suddenly, Bilal's legs locked in place. His plans for a Tivo'ed viewing of The Boondocks was replaced by a wave of overwhelming gratitude and resolve. "*Al-Hamdu-Lillah*, Praise God," he whispered out loud, suddenly oblivious to everyone else. Nothing could make him leave now. Moving quickly through the crowd, he passed a medieval altarpiece that, under other circumstances, would have held him captive by its beauty. This time the beauty that made him hold his breath was sheathed in coral.

Her back was to him. She stood with one leg turned slightly out, giving him a knee to ankle look of one of the gorgeous legs he'd seen that day in her house. Covered, she was even more alluring, but he'd never forget the sight of her skin, glowing from a thin sheen of perspiration that coated her like dew. And her hair—just like that day, the tiny twists hung to her shoulders in a light copper curtain. She moved away from the group toward a server. Bilal quickened his pace.

࠰

"Mrs. Montgomery."

Ayo stiffened. That voice—it caressed her like a lover's warm lips down the center of her spine. She wanted to bolt through the crowd, but some deep-seated masochistic impulse drove her to turn. Facing him, Ayo forced down the sigh that threatened to escape from her lips. Tonight his luxuriant mane hung free. A flawless ecru raw silk shirt and chocolate slacks draped Bilal's taut muscular body. He must have a tailor and valet on standby. No man could look that good all the time. He smiled, and one side of his luscious mouth curved up a little higher than the other. Ayo flushed, imagining the feel of those lips on hers, being wrapped in his arms, molded against the length of his long, strong body. He stood close; not enough to invade her space, but enough for her to breathe in the intoxicating blend of jasmine, sandalwood and citrus warmed by sheer masculine heat. Ayo's pulse raced. At that moment, an ice cube would turn to steam against her skin.

Across the room, Justine's head lifted like a lovely deer at the edge of the woods, sniffing the air, but not for danger or for nourishment. Her man/woman radar detected the exquisite tension between Ayo and the man whose aura obviously held her spellbound. There was no escape now. Ayo groaned inwardly. Where was a trap door when she needed one?

With nowhere to hide, Ayo made the introductions, speaking in a flat, matter-of-fact tone. She hoped it would cover up the nervous excitement that skittered through her like hermit crabs on their way to the sea.

"Nicholas and Justine Randall, this is Bilal Abdul-Salaam." Ayo peeped over at Justine and looked away. Justine's gaze darted between the two of them. Her coral-painted lips formed a rounded O.

Bilal greeted the couple, smiling at Justine and leaning forward to clasp Nick's outstretched hand. "Pleased to meet you, Mr. & Mrs. Randall."

"If you're a friend of Ayo's, you have to call me Nick." Suddenly, he winced, leaning more of his weight on the cane. Justine's attention shifted from the unfolding drama to her husband. She moved closer to his side, linking her arm through his. "Nick, I think we should go now."

"I guess so, baby," Nick sighed. "Right now my leg feels like somebody kicked me with a steel-toed boot."

"Then let's get you home." Turning to face him, Justine brushed her free hand over her husband's arm. Her friend's delicious drama took second billing to Nick's discomfort.

Before Ayo had a chance to react, Bilal spoke up, favoring her friends with the unforgettable smile she'd seen only once during their unfortunate first encounter.

"I'll see to it that Mrs. Montgomery gets home. I have some business that I need to discuss with her."

As focused as she was on her husband's comfort, Justine's head whipped around. "Why, thank you, Bilal," she chirped. Ayo wanted to choke her. *In a minute she'll applaud.* No one but Ayo caught her friend's swift, furtive grin. "We certainly appreciate it." Looping her arm through his, Justine walked away as quickly as she could without dragging Nick behind her. "Come on baby," she crooned. "I'll get you home and comfortable in no time." From near the door, she turned, sending Ayo a triumphant farewell wave.

It happened so quickly. Here she was, in the last place she expected it, face to face with the man she both hoped and feared to see again. He stood with both hands crossed behind his back. His smile warmed her like a roaring fire and a shot of cognac. Relaxed and charming, Bilal was nothing like the rude judgmental man she'd practically thrown out of her house.

"Surprised that I'm not swinging a scimitar and bringing down jihad on crotch-grabbing infidels?"

Ayo's eyes stretched wide. "What?" Her choked response had none of the snap she'd normally toss back to make him eat every sarcastic word.

Bilal was enjoying himself far too much for her taste. The smile he stifled was about to become full-fledged laughter. Ayo's face flushed; she felt like she'd fallen down a rabbit hole on her way to meet the Mad Hatter.

"Don't you remember? I think you made your point quite well."

"Oh, Lord," she muttered. But enough was enough. He'd had his fun and it was about to be over. Ayo lifted her chin and looked straight into eyes that brought a twinge to her gut and moist heat between her thighs. "Mr. Abdul-Salaam, I hope your volunteering to drive me home wasn't to make some kind of point or to deliver a reprimand. Because I have one of my own." Ayo leaned forward slightly and tilted her head, causing the beaded earring to lie against the curve of her neck. "You didn't mail the signature page. Maybe if you'd spend less time chastising "infidels"—two fingers wagged a quotation mark—"and more on your business you'd—"

"Please." He held up one large hand. The command in his voice clamped Ayo's mouth shut in surprise. Who did he think he was talking to? But his reply came before she could demand an answer. "Not to reprimand you. But as you say, to make my point. Actually, there are two." A small smile tugged at one corner of the mouth that built a slow fire in Ayo's body. "First of all, I've been a Muslim for all of my thirty-two years." His voice softened and grew serious. He moved one step closer to Ayo, bringing more of his masculine heat with him. The eyes that looked down at her were pools of dark honey. "And as far as the signature page—well, let's just say I knew exactly what I was doing."

Ayo inhaled a sharp breath. Her small grasp on control disappeared completely.

"What's the matter? Cat got your tongue?"

Ayo lowered her lashes. "I'd say it was more like a big old mountain lion." She couldn't remember being so completely flustered by a man.

His eyes mesmerized her, flashing like a kaleidoscope of dark precious stones. "I love a woman with a good sense of humor," he spoke softly. "And I'm grateful that you didn't bang me over the head with one of Bernard's sculptures. So can we put our unfortunate beginning to rest and start again?"

Bilal gazed down at her, moving closer. With a gallant half-bow, he crooked his arm. "If you're ready, your chariot awaits." So much had happened so quickly. She couldn't believe it herself, when instead of giving him part two of the heated tongue lashing she began that day in her house, they left the reception with his hand placed protectively at her back. When he seated her like a chivalrous dark knight in the immaculate Fifty-seven Chevy, Ayo was already high on the beauty of the evening and the man beside her.

Inside her house, the scent of vanilla laced with orange blossom met them at the door. A low light bathed the living room in soft amber. Ayo dropped her keys and purse on a Balinese end table and gestured to a lyre-shaped settee backed with plump, palm-print pillows. "Please, make yourself comfortable. I promise, this time you won't suffer from heat or thirst." Their smile conveyed the memory of that day. "And speaking of thirst, I have some lemonade that my cousin describes as delicious and down-home. Would you like some?"

Bilal leaned back and crossed one leg over his knee. The intense gaze he trained on her was like a slow, warm caress. He spoke softly. "With that description, how can I refuse?"

While Ayo fixed their drinks, Bilal stood in front of a table of family pictures arranged around an antique satin glass lamp. Each frame had been softened by gently worn gilt. The little girl with thick braids standing between a smiling couple had to be Ayo. And there she was again, surrounded by a group of grinning people, this time in a cap and gown. In another she posed with one hand on her cocked hip, wearing a straw hat, tube top, and white painter's pants. The man with his arm around her had to be her late husband. His face was the same as the handsome young man in the next picture. But there was one that held his gaze the longest. A very pregnant Ayo looked directly into the camera. Her husband must have taken it himself. No one else could have inspired such an expression of serene bliss and pure love. *Insha'Allah, God willing, one day that's the way she'll look at me.* He turned when she came back, bearing two glasses on a rattan tray.

"These pictures are wonderful. But you're even lovelier now. Except in this one." Bilal pointed at her pregnant photo.

Time had softened the sharp, sweet nostalgia into a collage of beautiful memories. "Thank you," she murmured. "It was the most joyous time of my life. Full of my baby and real happiness." It was a time when nothing could take away her bliss. But she brought herself back to the present and the man who might make her feel that joy again.

Ayo placed the tray on a small rattan table beside them and sat beside Bilal, steeped in the ultra-female awareness that covered her in his presence. "Here you are," she murmured, offering him a frosted glass wrapped in the same kind of napkin she'd handed him that turbulent day. When their fingers touched, this time instead of pulling it away, his hand enveloped hers.

"What a difference a night makes," he spoke softly, turning again to Ayo's photo collection. "Your son looks just like his father."

"He does." Her smile was wide-open with maternal love and pride. "Kedar's in Annapolis right now, but soon he'll head back down to the sunshine state for another year of college."

Bilal leaned forward. His eyes widened. "Kedar? How did you choose that name? In Islam, Kedar was the second son of Ishmael, and an ancestor of the Prophet Muhammad, peace be upon him."

"We chose it from the Song of Solomon. *I am black, but comely, O ye daughters of Jerusalem, as the tents of Kedar.*"

"A Biblical choice. Are you a regular churchgoer?"

Shaking her head, Ayo couldn't stop the spread of a wide grin. And she couldn't resist a good-natured poke. "No, I'm not a Bible-thumping Crusader," she chuckled.

Bilal bowed in her direction. "Touché." A small smile tugged at both corners of his mouth.

"But I do have a strong belief in God. I learned it up close and personal years ago. It's been my foundation ever since."

"Aside from a strong faith, I see there's something else we have in common," he told her, keeping her in his unwavering eyesight. Everything in her that was female rejoiced.

Ayo tilted her head. "And what is that?"

"A love of beautifully made furniture. This was done by a master craftsman." Bilal ran his hand over the back of the love seat. "Your pieces are wonderful."

The sensual motion pulled her attention. Flushed by the sight of his hand stroking the wood like a lover, and by the praise he gave her, Ayo wanted to run the cool glass over her heated skin. And his.

"My sister would love this room. She's a pharmacist, but Zahirah has quite an eye for design." Bilal turned his attention from the fine workmanship to the woman in front of him. Unlike his first time in Ayo's house, he didn't restrict his gaze to the space above her head or a spot on the floor. He didn't have to. When she leaned against the loveseat with one silky leg tucked under the other, his gaze was bold and uncensored. In the amber light behind her, Ayo's hair was a bronzed halo of swirls, spirals and coils. Coral fabric glowed against skin the color of dark clover honey. Beautiful, and completely at ease in the fragrant sanctuary she created for herself, Ayo shimmered with sensuality.

"Is she your only sibling?"

"Yes, she is—and my twin."

"A twin! She must be beautiful!"

"Ah, now, is that a roundabout compliment?" There was certainly nothing hidden in the lowered lids, and the sensual half smile he bestowed on Ayo.

It was too late for a botched, stammered cover-up. "A direct and truthful observation," Ayo chuckled in a voice softened by the exquisite tension swirling around them. "And now that I've revealed how handsome I think you are, I hope you'll answer a question."

"With that revelation, you've earned the right to ask me anything,"

He could make a living off that voice, Ayo thought, imagining a collection of adult bedtime stories. "Was our unfinished business the missing signature page? Did you leave it off on purpose?" The words came out in a soft rush.

"Mea culpa, on both counts," he murmured, reaching over to cradle one of her hands in his larger palm. Gently, he stroked the lifeline with the pad of his thumb. "Because I wanted to see you—no, I had to see you again. And I was prepared to do whatever I had to do. By any means necessary. But fortunately for me, Plan A worked." Bilal chuckled softly.

Ayo's eyes widened. "You had a Plan B?"

Bilal's lips curved up. "Oh, I had a Plan Z." Once again, his lips grazed her hand. "Have you ever been somewhere or seen something and got that 'bingo' feeling, in one instant you've found everything you've been looking for?"

Ayo blinked. She had been so wrong about this man. On all counts, it seemed. Puritanical, religious, a zealot? Bilal was anything but her stereotypical misjudgment. She nodded, too full of swirling emotions to speak.

"Since the day I walked through your door, you've been that 'everything' to me. And when I saw you tonight, I wanted to fall on my knees and give thanks, but you would have gotten away before I could get up again."

It was what everything Ayo had hoped for, even during the fit of anger when she hated to admit that she couldn't get him out of her mind. She hesitated, trying to arrange the words so that they left her mouth making sense.

"Bilal, I mean…I know you're asking a simple question, not for my hand in marriage or anything, but I'm not trying to be an Old Miss Young, bragging about my young lover to anyone who will listen."

Bilal stared. "Did you just say "Old Miss Young?" He threw back his head, letting loose a belly laugh that eased into a slow, rolling chuckle. Ayo loved the sound and the look. The hair cascading around his shoulders raised Bilal's sensuality quotient to the infinite power. "Now that's a brand new one! But listen," he spoke softly again, cupping her face in his strong, warm hands. His lips were an inch away from hers, melting her like soft candy in the sun. Ayo's whole body throbbed from his touch and the heat in his words. "When a man is captivated by a woman, her age is the last thing on his mind."

She let out a soft sigh. "But I've been out of the relationship game for a long time."

He put a finger over her mouth. "You know what? Those beautiful lips are moving too much. This is not a game, and I'm definitely not playing. All I want is to hear you say yes."

It was all she wanted to say. She wanted to grab him. She wanted to be Meg Ryan in *When Harry Met Sally*, and scream "Yes! Yes! Yes!"

Instead she uttered the word in a voice so soft he had to bend to hear her. "Yes," she murmured.

Bilal's smile was like the sunrise. He drew her into the warm circle of his arms, grazing his bearded jaw against her cheek. "Tomorrow I leave for a week in North Carolina. And the next week I'll be in New York for a professional conference. But when I come back, we'll finish this conversation. In detail. I promise," he murmured, brushing his thumb over her full bottom lip. "We'll have a lot of catching up to do."

He was ten years younger, but as Satchel Paige famously pointed out, neither of them minded, so it didn't matter. He was the first man in years that made *Natural Woman* roll through her mind. Every verse. In a relationship with each other, they both would win. The last of her defenses crumbled. *The man will find me,* she had told Justine. It appeared that he had.

He left her smoldering. Later, under the canopy of her planter's bed, Ayo replayed every word. But wait a minute—he was certainly not the spawn of the Taliban. But he was a Muslim, and progressive or not, was he celibate? He couldn't be—not from the way he touched her, and the sensual implication of his promise. He'd better not be!

Chapter 4
❧

*T*herapy, solace, livelihood—soap making was all these things to Ayo. She was in her element in the bright, aromatic kitchen, immersed in the alchemy of soap. No food had ever been cooked in this room, outfitted in stainless steel and dedicated to the creation of Maracas Bay's luxuriant line of products. The scent of pineapple and coconut permeated the room as she transformed lye, water, and oil from raw, incompatible ingredients into the beginning of bath-time bliss.

Ayo pushed the protective goggles up into her hair, sighing with deep pleasure at the view outside her window. The previous night's storm wrung every drop of humidity from the air. In place of the sooty gray, Mother Nature handed D.C. a peace offering of a turquoise sky, white clouds and golden sun. Her mood was a bright as the perfect weather. She pulled off one rubber glove with her teeth and dialed, stirring in a hypnotic rhythm while she talked.

"Hey, Magda, I've got some news for you. I wish I could see your face when I tell you, but Verizon will have to do for now."

"I hope it's the answer to why your periods are suddenly so heavy."

"No," Ayo sighed. "Not that. Dr. Randolph said he couldn't find anything. It's not fibroids, so it just might be something related to perimenopause."

"You've got to be kidding! What do you mean he couldn't find anything?"

"That's what he said. The man probed so high up in my insides I felt like a Thanksgiving turkey ready for stuffing. I wanted to ask him if all those diplomas plastering his wall really came from Dr. Buzzard's Mail Order Medical School."

"Huh," Magda snorted. "That might be funny if it wasn't so serious. You need to see another doctor. And don't interrupt. I know you've seen three already, but there is something wrong with any woman who's confined to bed and bleeding like the Red Sea!"

Magdalene Mansfield Malone was the rock on which her family rested. At the death of the last of the elder Mansfields, Magda assumed the role of family matriarch and guardian to 17 year old Ayo, sweeping her under wide and loving wings. Ayo came to live with Magda and her husband Buck. She helped Ayo settle her parents' estate. When Ayo returned from Trinidad and finally graduated from the University of Maryland, Magda and Buck stood and clapped like the proud parents they had in fact become. Since then, she lost no opportunity to cluck, hover and sometimes admonish like a mother hen. She and Ayo were ten years apart and their relationship shifted, depending on the situation; sometimes almost mother and daughter, but mainly older and younger sister. They were a lot alike: stubborn, generous, slow to anger, but certain to explode when pushed too far. The two women loved each other unconditionally and if she had to, one would go to war to protect the other.

"I know. My friend Eileen has a client who raves about her doctor. She got the number and passed it along to me. I decided to wait for this latest set of results, but pretty soon I'm calling in the big guns."

"You better," Magda warned. "So what's this news?"

"Before I tell you, I want to know about Buck, Jr. I hear he has high hopes for the Naval Academy. He told Kedar he couldn't wait to put on those midshipman whites."

"He's doing just fine," Magda replied. "His grades have always been good, so I'm sure he'll be okay. And our congressman put in a good word for him. I know one thing—if he doesn't get in I'm going over there and burn a cross right in front of John Paul Jones' crypt!"

Ayo let loose the boisterous laugh she kept indoors and saved for close friends and certain family members. "Oh, I can see it now. Your snooty, Severn River neighbors would say 'see, that's what happens when you let them in.' They probably think you bought the house with five winning numbers and the Powerball."

"A few of them know about Buck's construction company. And when I catered the governor's affair, suddenly I was the best little colored girl in town. Money or not, I'll bet there's more than one hood and sheet stashed in the trunks of those luxury cars. But forget them. What's this news that's got you sounding like Mata Hari?"

Ayo tapped the big stainless steel spoon on the counter's edge. "Did you hear that drum roll? Are you ready for the grand announcement? Do you want to hear what I have?"

Magda shot back at the silence on the other end. "Come on, Ayo. Stop playing."

"A man, baby; a man!"

"Say what?" When the shock wore off, Magda's jubilation set in.

"Well, alright now. Lord have mercy, it's about time! At the rate you were going, or not going, actually, I thought you were going to have to close up shop before you got a chance to see if your goods still worked!"

"I'm about to find out," Ayo whooped.

"See? What have I been telling you all along? I know you loved Maurice more than life, but it's been twenty-two years! You're still young, and Kedar is practically grown. You did a wonderful job raising him alone, but now it's your time. So tell me about this man. He must be something else if he brought you in out of the cold!"

"Now that he is, Magda, believe me..."

Ayo ladled raw soap into the shell-shaped molds, ticking off each point for her cousin while she worked. "He's D.C. born and raised; he owns his own business—he's an appraiser of fine arts and collectibles and a furniture restoration specialist—he graduated with a degree in Economics and Business Administration, but he went back to the University of Rhode Island to become a certified appraiser. Oh, and you should see that sweet Fifty-Seven Chevy—he restored it himself! He's Muslim, and has a twin sister." She hesitated for dramatic effect. "And, he's thirty-two years old."

"Well, well, well, from famine to feast." Magda's low, sexy chuckle signaled her admiration and approval. "You don't do anything halfway, do you? And a Muslim, huh? A Farrakhan Muslim or a mainstream brother?"

"Mainstream, Magda," Ayo chuckled. "And it's been a longtime since I've been with a man who can cause women's tongues to drop out and drag the ground."

"Oh, really?" Magda queried. "Even if he's a strict Muslim, at thirty-two years old, I'll bet he hasn't been hiding in the bathroom playing with himself. Does your instinct tell you he's a womanizer?"

Ayo shook her head. "Quite the contrary. And this is the month of Ramadan, when Muslims fast between sunup and sundown. I almost shot myself in the foot with what I didn't know about Islam, so I'd never ask him, but I wonder if they abstain from sex as well. It's been a looong time for me," Ayo chuckled. "So I can wait a few more weeks. Especially for a man like him."

"If he doesn't want to wait, you don't have to. Refraining from sex is only required between sunup and sundown, just like fasting."

The soap ladle hung in her hand, suspended over a tray of empty molds. Was she the only one living in the dark ages? "Wait a minute! How do you know so much?"

"Surprised you, huh?" Magda chuckled. "Sometimes I cater affairs that require halal meat. It's meat that has been butchered according to the rules of their religion. The best way I can describe it is as the Islamic equivalent of Kosher. Anyway, I have a supplier in Silver Spring. He's from Pakistan, and he and I have long conversations when I go to his shop." Magda chuckled. "He calls me Mag-a-da. He says 'Magada, if I see one more imposter with a bad accent playing a terrorist on TV, I will turn them in to Homeland Security myself!'"

"Oh, wait until I tell that one to Bilal!" Ayo exclaimed. "He'd like that very much."

"You sound like you like him very much. And I am so glad for you, baby, really glad. And now that you've gotten your love life back on track, let me tell you how to keep him. You ready?" A slow chuckle rolled up from her chest.

"Uh-oh," Ayo snickered. "Hold on a minute. I know I need to be sitting down for this one!" With the last of the shell-shaped molds had been filled and covered to sit undisturbed for twenty-four hours, Ayo grabbed a Coke and continued the conversation on a short walk to her home office. The oversized monitor displayed an open spreadsheet program. Ayo leaned forward, sliding her mouse across the pad to save and close the spreadsheet she had been toiling over since forever. *Excel for Dummies*—it must have been written with her in mind. "I'm afraid to ask—but go ahead anyway."

"Granny said to put a piece of bacon in your drawers, wear it all day, and then cook it for his breakfast the next morning!"

Ayo choked. She ducked fast. The geyser of Coke exploded inside the trashcan instead of all over her keyboard.

"Magda!" Ayo croaked out.

"Magda, what? I'm telling you that's what she said! Girl, you didn't know Granny like we did because you were only nine when she died. But let me tell you something—that old girl was a pistol. Oh, and one more thing about the bacon. In your case, it would have to be turkey bacon!"

After she hung up, and before she could stop laughing, Ayo heard footsteps thudding towards the kitchen.

"Mami!" Behind her, Kedar Montgomery burst into his mother's home office, unraveling strings of gooey cheese from a super sized slice of pepperoni pizza. "You sound like you got locked up in a comedy club or you're going crazy in here by yourself. What's so funny?" He grinned, and deep dimples creased each side of his apple butter brown face. A white do-rag protected the intricate whorls and loops of his freshly-braided hair.

"It's your Cousin Magda—need I say more?"

Kedar laughed himself. "Uh-uh, no you don't. She had me laughing the whole time I was there." He bent his six foot one frame over to plant a greasy kiss on Ayo's cheek, but she ducked, tugging loose the ties of her son's headgear. "Ha! You missed."

"Oh yeah?" Kedar stuffed the pizza between clenched teeth. Before she could stop him, he pushed hard on one arm of the chair and sent her spinning like a dervish.

"Kedar, stop!" Ayo stuck out her foot and stopped the spin, but Kedar lunged forward and grabbed her tight. She tried to slap him away, but she was laughing too hard.

"You can't handle this!" Kedar bellowed, raising his arms wide and strutting like a barnyard rooster. A swift, hard pound to the center of his chest followed his youthful declaration of machismo. His bragging sputtered into laughter when Ayo rolled her eyes up to the ceiling. Kedar fell onto his mother, draping half his lean muscled body across her shoulders. Ayo twisted her neck to look up at him.

"Behave yourself and tell me about Canada! Did you go to any pre-Caribana parties?" Every country with a sizeable population of Trinidadians had its own version of the spectacular pre-Lenten bacchanal.

"You know I did. 'Get some'tin and wave," he chanted, snatching the shiny white fabric off his head and flinging it over his head in time with the refrain. With his other arm, he clutched his mother even tighter. Ayo giggled and struggled to get away.

"Stop fighting me, woman—I'm a *man*!"

Ayo fell back, too weak from laughing to fight him any longer. She pointed one finger up at her son. "You know what? You think your name is spelled M-A-N, but it's really B-O-B."

Kedar cocked his head. "B-O-B?"

A smirk tugged at the corners of Ayo's mouth. She jumped up and poked him in the same spot where his fist had struck. "Big Old Baby!"

Kedar hung his head. More laughter broke away from the edges of his make-believe pout. "Aw, see now, Auntie Karen and Auntie Avril didn't make fun of me like that."

"Sure they didn't. I know those two took turns spoiling you rotten. They probably met you at the airport with a twenty-one-gun salute and had thrones set up for you—one in each of their houses," she teased. "You should be used to it by now, and if it makes you feel better, they did the same thing to your father. He was the baby and only 'boy chile,' so they all treated him like a prince. Now you're the boy king—the last living link to their brother and the last male to carry the Montgomery name."

It was Kedar's turn to roll his eyes. "I know, I know, but oh *man*, Mami. They hugged and kissed me from the time I landed in Toronto until I got back on the plane! You know how it is—'oh gosh, dah-

ling...' he mimicked. "They even pinched my cheeks in public! Hey, you know what? One time me and Auntie Avril ran into this man who took one look at me and said "boy you is Maurice Montgomery in print! Yuh have to be his son!"

"Really? Did he tell you his name?"

"No; seeing my face was such a shock that he kept talking nonstop. But I know he worked at the television station. He said "de whole place grieve when yuh faddah die. But ah glad to see dat he chile grow up big an' strong!"

Kedar's expression softened. He hopped up on the edge of Ayo's desk to face her, sliding all but one of the silver-framed family pictures out of the way. "Look at you, Mami." He gazed from her youthful image back over to his mother. "I like this picture," he said softly. The dimpled grin held its usual mix of tenderness and admiration. "You still look the same."

Twisting around he turned, taking a long look at an eight by ten, black and white that captured an alley lined with small shacks covered by galvanized tin roofs. Two men faced each other in combat, both faces contorted by anger. Near them, another man stretched one arm behind his back to hurl a huge stone. The photographer captured the man's angry, open-mouthed grimace and the rock soaring toward its target.

Ayo's lips curved into a small smile. "I'm so glad I was able to get his cameras back. That picture was the last one on the roll. Maurice never saw it, but he would have been so proud of the impact it had in the region, even more than the awards it won. This picture was on the front page of every paper in the Caribbean."

"My father sure had talent," Kedar murmured. He was hardly ever without a smile, but the emotional connection to the father he never knew had a strong hold on his heart. "I wish that he'd been alive to see it."

Kedar jumped down from the desk, searching under the rattan coffee table until he found the thick scrapbook Ayo used to document the pictorial history of their family. He flipped through the pages until he found the picture. "This one is my favorite." Kedar rubbed his thumb across the image. In it, his young parents stood on the steps of their Caribbean hillside home with their arms wrapped around each other. "I wish he had lived, for us to be together as a family. But it's been you and me, Mami, for all these years. And nothing or no one will ever come between us." Kedar looked at the picture and the mischievous grin resurfaced. "You was kinda fly back then," he winked. "But you know what—you still are."

"And you know fly, don't you," Ayo winked. Time to lighten the mood. As it was, this time of year was always bittersweet. She was proud of the young man her son had become, but the day he left for school was the saddest day of each year. As much as she fussed about them, she missed the greasy pizza boxes, half-empty cans of soda and mildewed swimming trunks left in his laundry basket. "I love you, Kedar."

"You know I love you, too." Kedar snatched a tissue from her desk and bent to wipe away the smear of pepperoni grease left by his kiss. Then he smacked a louder, cleaner kiss on each of her cheeks. "That's why I'm glad you finally got out of the house the other night. But it's been so long, you probably didn't know how to act."

"Shut *up*, Kedar!" Ayo tried to frown, but laughter pushed it out of the way.

"Gotcha!" Kedar pointed at his mother and burst out laughing. "Hey, is there anything you need for me to do before I head downtown? There's a photo exhibit on Jacques Cousteau at the National Geographic. You know I got to check out my boy."

The year Kedar turned thirteen, by way of National Geographic's Explorer, he became a Cousteau fanatic. That same summer, Ayo signed them both up for an undersea explorer's camp on one of California's nearby islands. After that week, Kedar knew his life's work would center on the sea. He joined his school's swim team and became a strong, competitive swimmer. Time in the water and weight training had turned her baby boy into a sleek, muscular young god. He turned his love for the water and all its inhabitants into a marine biology major at a Florida university and to his mother's dismay, he earned a Master Scuba Diver certification from the Professional Association of Diving Instructors.

Ayo's eyebrow arched. "Sure, sonny," she cackled, rubbing her hands together in an exaggerated expression of glee. "Right after you move these tubs into the soap kitchen. I've got an order to work on, but this is as far as I could convince the deliveryman to bring them. Told me his job was to deliver, not lift and tote." For Ayo, everything had its place, and the big white five-gallon tubs interfered with the calm of her cool, plant-filled oasis with its sea grass club chairs cushioned with green and red hibiscus print pillows.

"What? You mean you didn't bribe him with food?" Kedar teased, grabbing the handle of each tub. He came back, straddled a chair and slumped over the back. Catching Ayo's eye, he began to sing in broad broken English, "tote 'dat barge…"

Ayo grabbed a crumpled ball of paper and threw it at his head. When it struck his forehead, she jabbed her finger in his direction. "Listen *Old Man River*! You didn't tote anything."

"Yes I did. All you did was point and say 'put that here, put that there.' I felt like ole' Jim on the plantation!"

"Oh yeah?" she challenged. "Well let me find my belt and I'll try to make it real for you."

Kedar leaped out of the chair. He scrambled backwards with his hands held high "I give, I give," he sputtered. Like an actor deftly changing characters in the middle of a scene, Kedar dropped his hands and stretched his eyes wide, giving Ayo his "baby boy" face. "Now since I've been so helpful, can I take your truck?"

"See that? A bribe. But who can resist that face?" She pulled a key ring from her top desk drawer and handed it to him. "Here, you can take it, but, wherever you go, keep the doors locked and your phone on. These days, people will carjack you even in front of the White House."

"Naw, Mami, they only want Escalades and Navigators. And besides, the Sequoia ain't got no rims."

"Kedar, if you're riding and they're walking, twenty-four inch rims or tin-can hubcaps, they'll take your car and throw you out on the street—or worse!"

He leaped up and planted another kiss in the center of Ayo's forehead before he disappeared around the corner, jingling her spare set of keys. "Thanks. I'm out, Mami!"

"See you later, frogman."

"Ribbit!" he tossed over his shoulder.

The day she dreaded had finally arrived. Kedar slapped both hands over his face and twisted his head back and forth. "Oh, lawd, mi boy chile gon' *again*," he wailed, before pitching his voice to a lower register. "But ah done tell she a' ready ah comin' back jus' now!"

Ayo couldn't catch her shrieks of laughter before they exploded through the long corridor. Ducking her head, she peeped up to see how much attention her outburst had attracted, or if a squad of Transportation Safety Authority officials were bearing down, ready to eject them from Reagan National Airport. Kedar pulled his arm from her waist and bent over, shaking and snorting with laughter. When he spoke in patois, few people could tell that he hadn't grown up in Trinidad. Kedar owed his perfect delivery to the recordings he'd found of Paul Keens Douglas, comic extraordinaire, and his father's favorite. When they could finally speak without bursting into fresh laughter, Kedar leaned down to kiss his mother's cheek.

"I'm glad we could laugh this time, because I hate sad farewells. And don't forget. I'll be home for a long weekend in the middle of October. It'll be here before we know it." Ayo and Kedar lingered; one of his long arms draped across his mother's shoulders. He looked down at her. "You're doing well, Mami. This time you only sniffled instead of boo-hooing all over the airport."

She gave him a playful pinch. "Mr. Man, I have never boo-hooed in this airport and you know it."

"Yuh *lie*," he teased her, easing back into patois. Kedar hung back, letting a few straggling passengers move ahead of him at the checkpoint. When he could wait no longer, he joined the end of the line. At the point of no return, Kedar blew his mother a kiss. Her resolve crumbled, and choking back a sob, she raised one open hand to catch it. Ayo drove slowly through the city, wrapped in a blue fog. And it didn't help that her side throbbed like a stadium during Battle of the Bands.

The year he left her nest had been brutal. It brought back too much of the depression she'd suffered when her Maurice died. After his death, Ayo associated change with loss—sunset, the end of summer, the last day of the year. Gradually, she worked her way out of the tight fist of melancholy. Now, instead of fighting it, she gave in to her sadness at his leaving. "Okay, you've got one day to mope and then it's over," she told herself in what had become a yearly mantra. At home her ration of moping began. She glanced at them, but the invoices she needed to record might as well have been written in Sanskrit. At eight o'clock she put down her book and let the television watch her until it was time to sleep. On her way to her own bed, she wandered into Kedar's room. Standing at his desk, she smiled at the picture of her grinning son, encased in a wet suit with scuba tanks strapped to his back. Next to it were pictures he'd taken of the sea in its many faces—calm, stormy, blue and bursting with foam. Smiling, she brushed her fingers across the frames. Turning to look at his bed, she burst out laughing.

"Now look at that." Kedar was a first-class slob, but today was one of the rare times that almost everything was in its place. It was his farewell gesture of love. But in spite of his best efforts, a few old T-shirts lay balled up at the foot of his bed. Ayo sat down on the turquoise comforter and folded them, needing an excuse to linger in his space. The next morning she woke to find that the perfectly folded shirts had become a damp pillow. Instead of in her own room, she slept through the night, fully dressed and sprawled across her son's bed.

❧

Even in the unforgiving mid-morning heat Ayo hummed. This time, when she took her clothes off the line, each piece was folded neatly and not one clothespin left abandoned in the grass. On her way back inside, the tune to "What a Man" chimed from her pocket. Ayo smiled; she'd programmed the song to ring when Bilal called.

"I can't wait to see you next week," he told her in that beautiful baritone that made her feel dipped in dark, warm chocolate. She loved his voice; out of his mouth, her name always sounded like a love poem.

"I'll be there as soon as the plane touches down. There are only two stipulations." She wasn't sure—did she hear a tease in his voice? A small frown crinkled the smooth space between Ayo's brows. Two? "What kind of stipulations?" *Ah, here it comes—break out the burkha time.* In her head, Ayo rhymed the words to Howdy Doody's theme song. Did he have some kind of Muslim hole card to spring on her?

"That day in your kitchen, I saw a bowl of something that made my mouth water. Let's make a deal–your signature page for some good home cooking." He forged ahead; she couldn't get a syllable out, much less a few well-placed words... "And wait a minute—before you fly off the handle, it's not a statement about a woman's place," he chuckled. "It's an admission—I can barely cook and I don't mind begging."

He had done it again! Before she could spear him with a pointed remark, Bilal knocked Ayo off the high horse she was ready to climb. His comeback was swift, smooth and more than a little endearing. Her shoulders heaved, but she kept the giggle under wraps.

"But I'll have to come at sunset. It's Ramadan, and we break our daily fast after the sun goes down."

Ayo let her laughter break free. What a man, for real. "Since you confessed so nicely, how can I refuse? I'll see you at sunset."

Chapter 5

One cold Coca Cola later, the hammering in Ayo's side had dulled to a muted throb. Now she stood in front of an oval, floor length mirror and smirked at herself. "Look at you, a more than grown woman with a stomach full of butterflies waiting for a man like a girl on her first date." Earlier that day, the clouds opened up, sending down a driving, slanted downpour that didn't let up. A few minutes later, the weak sun finally peeked out, teasing her with a broken promise before hiding again behind the slate colored clouds. Ayo planned to wow him with a sunset meal on her back porch, but the weather put an end to all except the wow factor. Toasting herself with a half glass of smoky Shiraz, Ayo turned for a full view of herself. The factor was in full force. A sheer, long-sleeved, hip length cream-blouse covered a camisole of the same color Rather than clinging, it floated over her curvacious body. Bell-shaped sleeves floated over her. Ayo hated her hips until the sand shifted, as her mother described the transformation. Then the rest of her body caught up, dipping in and out in just the right places. Under it she wore black capris and black mules with a high, corked wedge heel. A sliver of silver decorated with tiny silver bells circled her left ankle. Ayo pulled up her twists, clasping them in place with a silver hair clip.

When the phone chimed, she grabbed it up on the first ring. "I'm at the airport, and I'm counting down the hours. I can't wait to see you. Are we still on?"

"Oh yes indeed we are." The sky was still the color of an old bruise, but Ayo didn't care. Bilal's voice covered the dreary day with a layer of sunlit gold. "And you'd better show up with your stomach on 'E' for empty."

"Ah, just wait," he chuckled. "You'll find out that my stomach is like the Seven-Eleven—open all day and night."

It had been a long time since Ayo cooked for a man she really cared about. But here she was, kneading a mixture of flour, yeast and sugar. Soon the beginnings of her mouth-watering homemade rolls sat rising from the warmth of the stove top, giving off the peculiar perfume that signaled home, comfort and contentment. While she chopped onions, tomatoes and cucumbers for spicy gazpacho, Ayo hummed to the rhythms of Cuba's legendary Buena Vista Social Club and smiled, thinking back to the day when she and Bilal went at each other like dueling verbal assassins. If anyone had told her a few weeks later she'd be waiting for him like a schoolgirl, Ayo would have sent them a gift certificate for a straight jacket.

A knock on the door set the butterflies in motion. Walk, don't run, she breathed. He can probably feel the heat from here all the way through the front door. Everything she wanted was on the other side of that door, and as Magda said, it was time to come in from the cold.

When she opened the door, it was like seeing him for the first time. The slow appreciative smile grew as his gaze rested on her hair, her lips and followed the length of her body. Ayo's lids fluttered briefly before she could look him in the eye and absorb his magnificence. She was like Icarus, whose waxen wings melted when he flew too close to the sun. And like the mythical character, she was falling; not into the sea but into the sweet, heady air that surrounds new lovers. He moved first, stepping forward to draw Ayo into the warm space inside his damp jacket.

"You're beautiful," he whispered against her hair. Holding both her hands, he stepped back, giving her a full-length appraisal that moved over her body like a lover's touch. "And I do mean beautiful." Ayo sighed.

The few butterflies had grown to a thousand in her stomach. Against his strong warmth, she inhaled the unique heady blend of sandalwood and his clean male scent. He was black power personified in an ebony jacket and black cowboy-cut jeans whose fit paid homage to the strength in his thighs. A gold ankh dangled against the black silk tee stretched across his broad chest, lending a cultural touch to the classic look. A few drops of water glistened against the dark-brown coils falling free around his shoulders. With the fingers of one hand entwined in her hair, Bilal drew her face to his, brushing his mouth across her lips and the center of her forehead. Her mind, her heart and her body responded to the man who had hardly been out of her thoughts.

Slowly, reluctantly, he let her go and they moved inside. "Can you hold this for me?" She reached for the jacket, but he had already shrugged it off with one hand and was shaking it out through the open door.

"Not that," he smiled down at her. "This is what I want you to hold." Bilal's eyes crinkled at the corners. So caught up in the sight of him, she didn't notice the shopping bag. Inside the protective plastic was a pale blue tote, with gold tissue paper stamped with dragonflies spilling over the sides.

"It's beautiful!" Ayo exclaimed, gently fingering the luxurious paper.

"Nothing less for you." The fluttering in her stomach had turned to full riot. She was grateful for the sudden, distracting growl that rumbled from his midsection.

Chuckling, he looked down and patted his flat belly. "The scent of that good cooking has my hungry beast riled up and ready to go."

Ayo tilted her head up. "Isn't that what you came for?"

Bilal's tilted his head, responding to the soft sensuality of her challenge. Giving her a repeat of the slow, bold stare his hooded gaze had taken earlier, he stepped close enough to breathe in her fragrance. "For now."

Heat flooded her body; it was as if he'd touched her. If a look could ignite her, what would happen when later came? Because it would come. And when it did, she would be more than ready. Ayo's voice caught; when she spoke, it was soft and husky. "So if we want to hasten that day, we should take care of first things first, shouldn't we?"

"Indeed we should," he murmured, drawing her close to his side for the short walk to the kitchen.

In the bright room, the aromas of good home cooking met them. Bilal settled back in the green-striped upholstered chair, giving his long legs space to stretch out. Ayo blinked, dragging her gaze away from his powerful thighs and the place below his belly where they joined. Couldn't let him think she ready to pounce, although her hot flashes had nothing to do with menopause and everything to do with the long-dormant desire of a woman for just the right man.

Instead, Ayo pored gently through the soft decorative tissue. "This is too beautiful to tear," she murmured, finally withdrawing the coffee-table sized book from its decorative nest. "Oh, Bilal." Ayo spoke his name softly, holding the book to her chest and smoothing her hand over the glossy cover of Caribbean Elegance "Oh," she repeated. It came out again in a whisper of wonder. Already the evening was like a dream sequence created from middle of the night fantasies. Instead of flowers, Bilal brought a gift that spoke directly to her heart. "This looks just like my house in Trinidad—the porch, the plantation shutters, the garden–everything!"

Pleasure softened his voice. "I was in a bookstore, and when I saw it, there was no better gift for you. I'm glad you like it." Ayo looked up; their eyes locked until a buzz from the stove pulled their gaze away from each other.

With the moment broken, Ayo jumped up to punch an icon on the stove's digital panel. "Can't burn up the first meal I cook for you, now can I?"

Ayo stood. "So, as my son used to say, come on and eat up." She gestured to the counter arrayed with a variety of food and drink. "Over here we have homemade rolls, and paella." She held up a squat pitcher full of lemon slices floating in pale liquid. "And more delicious down home lemonade, of course."

"You took me seriously about my appetite, huh?"

"Oh, yes I did, but there's more!" Ayo chuckled, imitating a Food TV host and brandished a large serving spoon, posing in front of the stainless steel refrigerator. "I've shown you the protein and carbohydrates, but I'm sure you know that a balanced meal also consists of fruit and vegetables." Wearing the same mysterious smile, she withdrew the bowl of cool, spicy gazpacho and another filled with dark red strawberries. "Go ahead and pile that plate as high as you like." Bilal didn't need a second invitation. By the time he had loaded up his plate, another spoonful of anything and it would overflow.

Leaning forward, he took a slow look around the room that whispered welcome to him. "Being here feels so good." His gaze skimmed the yellow striped tea-towel curtains and the wood-and-metal baker's rack brimming with pots of herbs and small plants. "In this kitchen, seeing your domesticated side…"

Ayo's head jerked around. "What did you say?" In slow motion, she set down the serving utensils and turned her body to face him. A deep frown pleated her brows. She folded her arms across her chest, and when she finally spoke her earlier warmth dropped to subzero. "Domesticated? You mean like a house cat instead of a female lion?"

Bilal stiffened. Squeezing his eyes shut, he pressed both hands over his face. "Oh no," he groaned. "I don't believe I said that!" Bilal was half out of the chair. He scraped it back, ready to make yet another disastrous retreat from this very same room. When he looked up, instead of a woman ready to throw him out, he saw Ayo's shoulders shaking and a hand over her mouth. He sat down hard in the chair, raking one hand through the hair that had fallen into his face when his head slumped forward. "Oh man!"

"I'm sorry," she gasped. "I knew exactly what you meant. But your expression was priceless." Ayo giggled again. "I had to keep it going for just a little while longer!"

Bilal narrowed his eyes in a show of mock offense. "So you let me hang, huh?" He shook his head and laughed. "You saw me get up, didn't you? I just knew you were ready to put me out—again! Now what I was trying to say was this—and let me get it right–you have a knack for making a house a home. That's it!" he exclaimed, slapping his hand on the table. "My tongue just got ahead of my brain."

"Didn't it now? A few years ago I would have jumped all over you," Ayo confessed. "I would have read you the riot act from the feminist manifesto, and if it didn't exist, I would have written that book on the spot." She grabbed a paper towel and swiped at her eyes. "But now it's time to eat and drink." Ayo poured the drink into a glass garnished with a half-circle of lemon. "Besides if your mouth is full, you can't stick your foot in it!"

"No lie," Bilal exclaimed, shaking his head. "If my sister or my mother had heard that, neither of them would ever let me live it down!"

Ayo filled her own plate and sat across from him. "Really? Muslim women?"

Bilal's fork was halfway to his mouth when he set it down on the plate and pulled his expression back to neutral. Leaning forward, he rested his chin on steepled fingers and gazed at Ayo. "Yes, really. Do you think because they're Muslim women that they're meek, mild and one step behind their men?"

Ayo blinked. "Well, no, not exactly, but–"

"But what?" He spoke softly; still Ayo was uncomfortable under his piercing gaze.

"The Muslim women I knew would never dare challenge a man on a woman's role."

Bilal gave a short laugh. "You don't know Adilah Abdul-Salaam. She taught my sister well. Both of them are the epitome of grace and femininity, but their tongues have never been tied by our faith." Bilal shook his head again. "After a steady stream of half-truths, there are people who believe that all Muslims have harder hearts than their brothers and sisters of other faiths. They see women getting beat or who are afraid to speak. They see men who've committed atrocities or children carrying toy guns shouting 'death to the infidels.' And with no other information than a news clip they make up their mind that what they've heard about Islam must really be true." Bilal's forefinger tapped the table. "There are about a billion Muslims in the world— and most of us are going about our business being *good* Muslims and good citizens. But the word is that we're all ignorant, oppressive tyrants." Now all ten fingers of his hand drummed the table.

"But what about those women sweltering in the heat of summer all cloaked up in black with nothing but their eyes showing while their men stroll around cool as a cucumber? That's just crazy! You mean to tell me they'd dress that way if they had a choice?" Ayo took a quick breath and plunged ahead. "And I had a friend in college. She married a Muslim who would make the Puritans seem like Animal House frat brothers. The woman couldn't breathe without his permission. And her face always pops into my mind when I think of a Muslim woman."

"And his when you think of a Muslim man?"

Ayo nodded.

"So what about me?" Bilal bit into a warm buttery roll while he waited for her reply.

"But you're different."

"You mean like a regular brother instead of a scowling fanatic ready to issue a fatwa against everybody who doesn't think like me?"

"Oh Lord," Ayo's head dropped down on her folded arms like a bag of cement. "My foot in mouth trumps yours hands-down. But how come your family is so, uh, progressive? Was everybody in your family born Muslim?"

"No, in their twenties, my parents joined of the Nation of Islam. According to them, everybody hung together back in the sixties—the political nationalists, the cultural nationalists, the Black Muslims. Anybody with 'black' anywhere in the name of their organization. In that mix of people, it was hard to be anything but open-minded. But when Elijah Muhammad's son broke with his father's brand of Islam, my parents followed. Before Zahirah and I were born, they became what people refer to as "orthodox" Muslims. We're Sunni." Bilal laughed again. "My mother swears that in spite of his unorthodox brand of Islam, Elijah Muhammad was really a conservative Republican in disguise. As far as my family, my brother-in-law, Kalil is from India, and he's been a Muslim all his life. Believe it or not, there are more people like us than you think. Trust me on that. My parents are cool people; you'll see."

His shoulders slowly relaxed. Bilal sighed and leaned back in the seat. "But you know what—I didn't come here to give you a lecture on Islam 101. I came here to see you."

"Even though I almost ran you out with my ignorance?" Ayo looked up and felt her own surge of relief. The heart-stopping smile was back. Bilal reached across the table and covered Ayo's hand with one of his.

"Are you kidding? Don't you know that food trumps ignorance anyday? Especially where my stomach is concerned!" His mouth twitched. They both burst into laughter that cleared the air of all their misspoken words.

Ayo stared at the clean plate that not long ago had been piled high.

"You weren't kidding about your appetite," she smirked. "I'm afraid to offer you some dessert—it might kill you." Ayo looked into his eyes and gave him a softer smile. "But I'm so happy that you chose to break your evening fast with me. And that you enjoyed it."

Bilal cupped her face in both hands. "Ayo Montgomery, you have no idea how much I enjoyed this evening. But I promise to spell it out in exquisite detail. Very soon. But right now, before I forget it in the face of your beauty and this exquisite meal, I'd better have you sign the elusive signature page."

She was glad when he changed the subject, before she embarrassed herself by melting into a pool of female flesh at his feet. Instead, Ayo covered by punching him on his arm. "I ought to get a copy of this piece of paper and frame it. If I hadn't shown up at that reception, it would have been the only reason for you and I being together right now."

It had been so long, Ayo had stopped considering the possibilities. Now, not only did she have a man, but one who never lost sight of what he wanted and how to claim it. She smiled, a secret, sexy smile that went out like a light when he stared down at his watch and back up at Ayo.

"Oh, no!" he exclaimed, "I didn't realize it was so late. I should have been in Takoma Park a half-hour ago. I'm about to be dead meat!" Ayo hid her sharp disappointment with a bright smile that she hoped didn't appear to be forced.

Bilal placed the papers in a folder in his briefcase. "I can call on the way over. I promised Zahirah I'd baby-sit the twins so that she and Kalil can have a night out." He shook his head and smiled. "It'll be fun. Those munchkins are the most precious little people on earth."

Ayo exhaled. It wasn't the loose ends of a previous relationship that called him away; it was him being a good brother, literally and figuratively. And, as she could tell by the affection in his voice, a doting uncle.

"That's so good of you. And I know you can't be late, so I'll put my mouth-running to rest and walk you to the door. Sometimes my welcome wagon has a hard time rolling to a stop. Along with a cooking gene, I inherited the gift of blab," Ayo told him with a laugh. "As far as that gene is concerned, I got mine and another that must belong to some poor short-changed family member."

Bilal burst out with deep, rich laughter. "And their sense of humor, I see."

Ayo shook her head. Her mouth curved into a half smile. "No, we all got our fair share of that one," she chuckled. "And before you go, there's one more thing, since you're from the 'microwave or die' school of cooking."

"Is it that obvious?"

"Yes, it is. And you as much as admitted it," she chortled. "Take this food with you." Ayo held the bag out to him, waving it like a pendulum over her forefinger.

"Oh man!" Bilal exclaimed, peering down into the fragrant offering. "I won't have to cook." He turned and raised one eyebrow. "I mean microwave—for a week!"

It was an exceptionally warm night. Ayo could hear faint strains of Carter-Barron's last summer concert. It was an old-school group of rhythm and blues crooners—a real date-night show. Ayo smiled. This is how it's supposed to be. The beauty of the evening—their conversation, shared food, a greater understanding—perfect for a man and a woman finding their way together. Bilal grasped both her hands and held her out from his body. His gaze traveled from the top of her head to the toes she had polished with great care. "I love your welcome wagon—this warm and beautiful home, your fabulous food, the way you look. But what I love most is the way I feel when we're together."

She was going to be with him, in every way. Of that there was no doubt. To be with him meant knowing all that made him Bilal Abdul-Salaam. The next morning Ayo passed the soap kitchen and took her coffee into the office. Before the age of the internet, research meant long searches through card catalogs and stacks of books in libraries and research centers. The scent of a room full of books, the feel of handwritten works in her hand was a great part of research that she loved. This morning she put together that love and her skills with twenty-first century technology. It led her to a book written by a black woman,who was both scholar and college professor. She was also the first woman to lead a mixed-sex group of Muslims in Friday prayer. Ayo was astounded to learn that the president of the Muslim Association of North America was a Canadian woman. By noon, she understood that the rift between Shia and Sunni had to do with the line of succession from the Prophet Muhammad. And that Islam's belief that God had no offspring and needed no intermediaries spoke to her own belief.

Chapter 6

❧

"*S*top laughing at me!" Ayo stomped her foot, jostling loose the phone's earpiece. From the mound of silk on her dresser, she plucked a sheer scarf swirled in shades of sienna and cream. It suited her wide-legged amber slacks and matching long-sleeved blouse. "You know how special tonight is; otherwise I wouldn't be asking all these questions. And Lord knows, I don't want to say or do the wrong thing."

"You mean like asking for a poke chop or a shot of Wild Turkey?"

"Bilal!" Ayo sputtered out his name. "And what do you know about "poke chops."

"I went to school in the South, baby," he chuckled. 'Poke' was everywhere. But I want you to calm down. My family is definitely not a scowling, sour-faced clan. Besides, it's after sundown. They've eaten, so they won't bite!"

Ayo burst out laughing. "If you're trying to persuade me with humor, it worked!"

He laughed softly. "Good. So don't worry about it and *please* don't wrap yourself from head to toe in a bed sheet," he teased. "You can even show some skin if you want to."

"If you say so…"

"I do," he insisted. "And listen, we both have to get ready. So I'll see you soon. And without the butterflies. Okay?"

Bilal was half-dressed when the phone rang again. Mark Forrester's number glowed from the screen. The friendship began in their freshman year; two boys from Northeast DC who had never met until they arrived on campus. After college, they both returned to the city. Mark began his career as chief financial officer of an independent boy's school located on Eleventh and M Streets, NW, where uptown began its merge into downtown. His world took an unexpected turn when Mark realized that much more than overseeing the financial affairs of the institution, he wanted to provide the best education money didn't have to buy for the fifty boys of Midtown Prep. He became a student himself, going back to add a BA in education to his Bachelor of Science in Economics. He didn't stop there; he was currently a night school student in the Masters of Education program at Georgetown University.

"Salaam, bro. What's up?" Bilal switched to speakerphone so he could continue to dress.

"Peace back at you, B. You busy?"

"I'm dressing—just trying to make sure I get my clothes on right," he chuckled. "I put you on speaker." He sat on the side of the bed, pulled on his socks, and stood again. "Can you hear me?"

"With that space-age phone of yours, I can read your mind." The speaker magnified Mark's boisterous laughter as it erupted through the room. "And what's this about getting your clothes on right? You're the only man I know who can make an old T-shirt and shorts look like they just came from the cleaners."

"You exaggerate and you know it," Bilal shot back, laughing along with his friend's good-natured but accurate observation. "Hold on a minute." He stepped inside the elaborate cedar walk-in that he'd built himself. With shelving and racks for everything from belts to his black knee-length cashmere coat, the fragrant room rivaled a small menswear boutique. "So what's happening with you?"

"Just checking back with you. The day you called, I was in the process of calling Arlena on the carpet for getting too friendly with the UPS driver—I did my frat brother a favor by letting her intern with us, but man, she is too much! But later for her."

"You know Arlena–if it can't be done on her back, it can't be done. About time," Bilal snorted. "Anyhow, you will not believe this. I still can't believe it myself! Remember when I told you about the sister on Manchester? How we butted heads? I had another rabbit to pull out of the hat, but when I saw her at Bernard's reception, it was a gift. I didn't know if she would curse me out, but I couldn't let her get away. This time, instead of fighting, we connected. And every second after that has been perfect. Tonight I'm taking her to meet my family."

"Well, alright! So I guess she's the lady in your life?"

"You better believe it."

"And how does this fit in with the rest of your plan?"

"You mean the marriage-and-family plan?"

Mark snickered. "You know it. Ever since you turned thirty, you've been on a mission. Every woman you came across had to pass the potential wife test. I know you love kids—that's why you're so good with my boys at the school and with your sister's twins. But what's your rush?"

"Simple. I'm ready to be a family man, with a wife and children of my own. Just like my father. You know he and I have had big run-ins. But for me, Latif Abdul-Salaam is still the best example of what it means to be a good Muslim and a real man."

"I know," Mark laughed. "Your dad has his ways, but his love for your family can't be denied. I remember the first time I met him. Hanging judge was the first thing that came to mind. I felt like he could see right through me to all the dumb-ass things I'd ever done."

Bilal laughed out loud. "You're not the first person to say that, believe me."

"So what's the next step?"

"One thing I'm not going to do is beat around the bush and follow some arbitrary rules. She's forty-two and has a twenty year old son, none of which matters to me. I know that relationships take time, and *Insha'Allah*, we'll get there. And when we do, nothing or nobody will keep me from loving Ayo Montgomery."

"So, my brother—tell the truth. You want this to go all the way down the aisle and into the delivery room?"

Even as he contemplated the question, it didn't take long for the answer. "Yep. Just like that. The other day, a group of us were talking after Friday *jumah* prayers. One of the brothers has been married for a year, and says it was the best thing that has happened in his life. He said his wife was his other half and that he was hers. He loved coming home to completeness. Now I know what he means."

Mark's reply took a little longer; he was obviously searching for the right words.

"But have you considered at her age, and with a son she's already raised, that she might not want to be a mother again? Or that she can't?"

⁊⋆

For five full minutes after it ended, Bilal's pep talk eased her mind. Then the doubts came back, clamoring full force in her head. Ayo shut them out by putting together a gift basket of Maracas Bay soaps for his family. The beauty and fragrance of her handiwork soothed her mind; she chose amber and frankincense for his father, coconut and pineapple for his mother and sister and clear cotton-candy bars embedded with bright yellow ducks for the four-year-old twins.

She tied a pale green ribbon at the top of the basket, trying to control emotions that hovered between fear and elation. Maybe by the time Bilal picked her up, her wild imaginings would have settled somewhere in the middle. How bad could it be? Parents who raised a man like Bilal had to be warm and decent people.

Just as Ayo bent to set the big basket into an oversized shopping bag, she heard Bilal's knock. She swung open the door and leaned into his warm and now familiar strength. When she pulled back, Bilal took one of her hands and twirled her in a circle, examining her from head to toe. "You look good, baby. Not too plain, not too sexy. See?" He kissed the center of her forehead. "All that worry was for nothing."

"You don't look half-bad yourself," Ayo murmured. Blue was Bilal's color; he was immaculate and casually elegant in the collarless dark teal shirt and matching pants.

She leaned up to brush her lips across his. "And since I've passed your muster, I know I'm ready to meet your family."

In front of her house, Ayo eased into the Chevy. A flame of pain flared in her side. She winced, allowing her head to loll back against the soft leather headrest.

Alarmed, Bilal tossed the bag on the backseat. Ayo heard the contents jostle against one another but at that moment couldn't get her mouth open to protest. He frowned, rushing to kneel in front of her at the open door. "Ayo, what's the matter?"

Of all the nights to have cramps! Ayo tried to smile but grimaced instead. "My mother used to call it 'female trouble.' I don't think it's anything more serious than that. And I have some medication that I take for it." She brushed the back of his hand and touched his face. "Don't worry," she teased. "It comes with being womanly and domesticated."

Her attempt at humor didn't sway him. His jovial mood disappeared. Bilal stood, reaching back inside to help her from her seat.

"Let's go back in the house. We can cancel with my family tonight. They'll understand. I don't want you suffering for something that we can do another time."

"Oh no," she protested, even as another wave of pain rose and fell like childbirth contractions. "I've been looking forward to this all day. I'll take one of these horse pills, and by the time we get there, I'll be on the way to feeling better." Another deep breath blunted some of pain's sharp edge. She fished around through a jumble of keys, tissues, and makeup until she found the amber bottle of gigantic capsules. Reaching over for the bottled water in Bilal's cup holder, she uncapped it and tossed one of the pills into her mouth, followed by a long gulp.

"Ah," she burped and giggled. "I'll be okay soon. These big boys attack pain like a sledgehammer. Please, let's just go." She'd put too much emotional energy into the day, alternating from anticipation to apprehension and all the emotions in between. She could deal with the pain. Besides, his parents and sister were probably just as eager to meet the woman he cared for enough to bring home.

Bilal's brows furrowed. He looked at her long and hard before starting the Chevy. "Okay, but if I see you grimace one more time, we're coming back here and I'm putting you straight to bed!"

"No worries, baby," she promised, patting his arm and easing back against the seat. "Besides, I love this time of day. It'll be good for what ails me." It was right after sunset and just before the street lights flickered on. A constant stream of cars traveled both sides of the street. Families took after-dinner strolls. People whose pets had become their children walked their animals in the grassy areas fashionably known as dog parks.

Latif and Adilah Abdul-Salaam's gabled home sat on top of a shady hill in the Brookland section of D.C. Like a magnet, the screened porch drew Ayo's eye to furniture upholstered in splashes of muted green and yellow blossoms. A Florida room, her mother would call it. More casual furniture took up the rest of the space—a couch and low table on one side and at the other end, a round cafe table and four matching chairs.

Inside the foyer, Ayo stopped to exclaim at a collection of photos. The most striking depicted a convocation of brown skinned women. Proud and regal, they were all dressed in white, wearing the iconic head covering of women of the Nation of Islam.

Suddenly high-pitched voices grabbed her attention. "Unca B!" Two identical, nut brown girls clattered down the hall, dragging two adults behind them. Ayo was right, Zahirah Ahmed was indeed beautiful, and as poised and lovely as Ayo had imagined. The thigh-length version of a classic white blouse over tailored black slacks heightened her lovely grace. A bold black-and-white patterned scarf covered Zahirah's hair and ended in an ascot tucked in at the top of her blouse.

"The face gives me away." She pointed at herself with a laugh that was low and musical. "So you know who I am. It's so good to meet you!" Zahirah turned with twinkling eyes at the man held firmly in the two-handed grip of one of his little girls. "And this is my husband, Kalil." Dr. Kalil Ahmed stood an inch above his wife, with skin the color of coffee laced with cream. His dentist could have used that perfect white smile as advertisement. A Georgetown Hoya bulldog grimaced from his t-shirt and the baseball cap he wore over straight, jet black hair that brushed the back of his neck. "I'm happy to meet you," he replied in a voice that held the lilt of India. "I would love to stay longer, but I must look in on a patient this evening."

"No, Daddy!" One of the twins protested. She hung onto her father as if her toddler-sized strength would be enough to hold him there.

"We don't want you to go! Can you please tell your sick people to talk to the nurse? Nana is a nurse and she talks to sick people at her work. Don't they have nurses like Nana?"

The adults laughed together at her sincere determination. "And these two are our daughters, Kamla and Kamilah." Ayo recognized the soft maternal smile that came natural to most mothers. A beautiful blend of Africa and India met in the twin girl's wide brown eyes, full lips and in the froth of kinky, curly hair that framed their faces. *Dougla,* Ayo thought, recalling the Trinidadian slang for that particular racial mix.

"Come on babies," Bilal grinned. "Let Daddy go to work. He'll be back before you can say 'Baby Bop.'" The girls became a giggling duo when their father bent to kiss each of them. They were surrounded by love, Ayo noted. And it was obvious that the men of the family were wound tightly around the fingers of their two precious girls.

Bilal kneeled down to scoop up the girls, and with four little arms wrapped around his neck, the three of them resembled a moving totem pole. He turned clockwise and then counterclockwise in a slow circle with the giggling children clamped on each side of his chest. When he tried to set them on their feet, they tightened their grip and wrapped their legs around each of his.

Almost unable to move, he shuffled toward Ayo, sending the twins into fresh bursts of laughter. "See what I have here? Kamilah and Kamla, this is my friend, Miss Ayo. Ayo, these are my baby girls." He had said they were the most precious little people in the world and their love for him was clear as day.

"Salamma-laykum," they chimed in unison. The greeting of peace became one word in their four-year-old mouths.

Kamla reached up to pat Ayo's arm in the rapid, urgent insistent way of children who are bursting with something to say. "Did you bring your children? 'Cause we have toys to play with!" She waved an open palm in the direction of a jumble of brightly colored blocks. A pair of soft cloth dolls sat propped up next to the Sesame Street crew of Ernie, Bert, and the Count.

Ayo pointed at the caped character and then back to the twins. "Ah, ah, ah," she laughed, mimicking the Count's exaggerated Transylvanian accent.

Four sets of eyes opened wide. Then the girls clapped and burst into shrieks of laughter. Ayo reached out to twirl a spiral of each girl's hair.

"When my boy, Kedar, was little, he loved The Count. Now he's nearly as tall as your Uncle B."

Kamla looked up at Bilal and back to Ayo. "He is? But he can still play," she insisted. "Unca B plays with us all the time. We ride on his back, but we have to take turns. If Kay-dar comes to play, me and my sister can ride at the same time."

"Oh no!" Bilal bent his head, groaning like a man in pain. Kamilah grabbed one of his hands and shook it back and forth. "Unca B, what's the matter?" Both girls looked ready to burst into tears.

"That means I won't be lead horsy anymore!"

"Unca B!"

The commotion brought two other adults to the hallway. Ayo looked up and held her breath. *All hail the king.* Latif Abdul-Salaam could have been a pharaoh, a general, a captain in another life. He stood straight, almost at attention, like a man used to giving orders and getting what he wanted. Instead of salt-and-pepper gray, the thin mustache and slender beard that circled his face were silver, a striking contrast to skin the color of dark, aged rum. The slate-gray collarless shirt and matching slacks draped in perfect fit over his more than 6 foot frame. Like father, like son.

"As-Salaam-Alaikum. Welcome." Although the brief greeting was delivered like an orator beginning a speech, at least it wasn't unfriendly.

Adilah Abdul-Salaam reached out to hug her and Ayo final exhaled. "Welcome to our home, my dear! I've been waiting to meet you and I'm so glad you're finally here."

Ayo took an immediate liking to the stylish woman. The top of her head reached her husband's shoulder. A pale yellow scarf covered all but an inch of auburn hair that Ayo suspected was her natural color. It contrasted with the deeper gold of her knee-length tunic and matching pants. The color went well with her honey-butter complexion and lightly glossed lips. Tiny gold stars dangled from her ears.

"As-Salaam-Alaikum, Bilal. And what are you children up to?" Her eyes twinkled when she tilted her head up to meet her son's kiss. "And that means you too."

"Wa-Alaikum-As-Salaam. As soon as I can get these little ones off my neck, I'll introduce everybody." The twins protested but when he tickled their chubby legs, they slid down his body and ran to their mother. He took Ayo's hand and drew her closer, wrapping one arm around her shoulders. "This is Ayodele Montgomery. Ayo, these are my parents, Latif and Adilah Abdul-Salaam." Bilal swept the three of them in the beam of his smile.

Before she could answer, Kamilah ran to her grandmother, wriggling with excitement.

"Nana, Nana!" she exclaimed, tugging on the edge of Adilah's tunic. "Miss Ayo has a boy as big as Unca B. She said he would play with us, too!" The little girl turned to Ayo for confirmation. "Didn't you Miss Ayo?"

"Yes, I did, baby." When she looked up, Ayo felt a faint brush of apprehension. Did a fleeting frown replace the welcome Latif offered just a minute ago? Although not as exuberant as his wife's, it was a welcome, just the same. Strange—the only thing that happened between her introduction and Kamla's excited announcement was the mention of her grown son. How much had Bilal told them? Or left out? *Stop being paranoid. Everything is going well so far.*

Adilah gestured to the porch and took Ayo's hand. "Let's sit on the porch and enjoy this warm weather while we can." She smiled over at Ayo. "Before you know it, we'll be shivering in boots and coats."

The simple act meant acceptance. Ayo relaxed, putting the nagging unease aside.

When they took seats across from Bilal's parents, Ayo lifted the basket from the bag near her feet. "My mother told me to always bring a gift to the host and hostess, so I put this together for you all."

"Mommy! Miss Ayo has a basket!" Both girls bolted towards Ayo. In one smooth, obviously practiced move, Zahirah stuck out both hands and grabbed each girl in mid-flight. They spun around to Bilal, pleading with wide round eyes. He cut a furtive glance over to his sister. One perfect eyebrow arched. It was a stare full of warning and a good amount of teasing. Throwing up his hands, Bilal gave in. "Listen to your mother, little ones. Or we'll all be in time-out."

Laughing at both her children and grandchildren, Adilah accepted the gift from Ayo. "Bilal told us that you made soap, but it didn't really register until this minute. Oh my goodness!" she exclaimed, rummaging through the fragrant contents. She halted her excited ramble long enough to look up, waving her hand to beckon Zahirah. "Come here and look at this. Look, Latif."

Leaning over to Bilal, Ayo pointed to Latif's soap. She still wasn't comfortable with him, still not sure that his sudden coolness was real or imagined.

Latif lifted the amber and frankincense bar to his nose and inhaled. His eyebrows rose. A mixture of surprise and appreciation crossed his face. "Thank you, Ayo. Very nice." His expression settled back into a mask of reserve. "You have to love what you do to put this much obvious attention to your product."

Ayo brightened at his praise. Maybe she misjudged his reaction. She sat forward, launching into an explanation of her craft.

"Oh, I do. It's a wonderful, creative process. It's almost like baking." Ayo's smile grew. She gestured with her hands, turning to include everyone in her animated description of the joys of soap making."

"Do you have help?" Latif continued to hold the bar close to his nose. "Frankincense, right?"

"Yes to both questions. I have a part-time assistant who's a full-time pre-med student. She handles the packaging and labeling, but the formulation and production is mine alone. I could never hand over the creation of my products to anyone."

Zahirah joined her mother in poring through the basket. "Ayo, these are wonderful," she exclaimed. "A whole lot different from the soaps CVS sells, even the ones they have dressed up to look like these."

Bilal had been right. Her case of nerves was for absolutely nothing. Ayo turned to beam at Bilal when Latif clasped both hands at the knee of his crossed leg. He turned the full force of his gaze onto Ayo. "Have you always made soap?"

Ayo stiffened. It wasn't the question; it was his tone, indicating more than simple interest. More than that, she disliked the expression of judgment and skepticism that came with the query. Ayo plucked at the end of her blouse, forcing herself not to twist the fabric into a rumpled ball. Her stomach clenched, bringing back the pain that had been temporarily dulled by the medicine and the welcome she had received. This conversation was going somewhere, but not in the direction she had hoped. Instead, it seemed poised to freefall into disaster.

What's it to you? Ayo thought before taking a mental deep breath, biting back the question that itched to burst out. Instead she looked straight into his eyes. If he thought he could intimidate her, he was dead wrong.

Ayo tilted her head. Her lids fluttered. She was one blink shy of a full-on eye roll. "No." Taking her disdain down a notch, she measured her words. "I started my business nine years ago. Before that I was a research associate for Randall, Cooke and Associates. I'm sure you've heard of them." *If you haven't, then you're not as black and bad as you think!*

He didn't open his mouth, replying instead with a haughty, affirmative nod. "And you have a grown son? You must have been just out of childhood when he was born!"

Ayo's skin was on fire. She sucked in small, shallow breaths, the kind used to temper the pain of childbirth. If she could keep her mouth shut for just a second, the swarm of international curse words would stay behind her trembling lips. Through the red haze of anger, Ayo didn't see Bilal launch out of his chair towards his father. "What in the hell is wrong with you?" he shouted. "Don't you dare talk to her like that!" She didn't hear him for the roaring in her ears. She was just as oblivious to Adilah and Zahirah's simultaneous gasp of shock. Latif was all she could see.

Ayo raised her head, glaring at Latif with pure loathing. She spoke slowly and carefully, hoping the effort would keep her from shouting. "Yes, Mr. Abdul-Salaam, I'm forty-two. So let me give you a timeline. I graduated from high school at sixteen. I was married at twenty and widowed at twenty-two after a brief, but very happy marriage. Brief only because my husband was a photojournalist who was killed covering a story. Are you getting a better grasp on my life now?" She kept her gaze fixed on him, daring him to say another word.

"You're forty-two?" he exclaimed. Latif's brows shot up. He stared at her and back to Bilal in disbelief.

"Dad, I said stop and I mean it!" Bilal's outstretched hand clamped down on his father's shoulder. He was ready to spin Latif around until Ayo jumped between them, unaware of anything except that man who had just become her enemy for life. She ached to curse him out. But there were two innocent children who could dash into the room at any time. And two women who were in no way responsible for their arrogant, ill-mannered husband and father.

Ayo's chin lifted. She spoke in a voice just above a whisper but as sharp as broken glass. "I have my own business, my own home and my own money. So I think I've done well to have been such a young mother." Her head tilted; one hand crept to her hip. "Don't you? But whether you do or not, Mr. Abdul-Salaam, it's irrelevant now, because I never intend to speak to you again!" Gasping, Ayo snatched her purse. Pain exploded in her side but pride kept her from doubling over.

On her way out of the door, Ayo trained a face full of misery to Zahirah and Adilah. Her voice broke. "I am *so* sorry." The rest of her words got caught behind a sob. There was no way she would break down in front of that man. She swallowed hard and ran out of the door, leaving Bilal to catch up.

"Baby, wait!" He reached to pull her into his arms but she jerked away and ran, swiping her face with both hands. At the bottom step, she stumbled. Although she had a head start, Bilal's long strides covered the distance. He reached out and caught her before she fell.

"Baby, nothing!" She twisted out of his arms. Instead of allowing him to seat her, Ayo jerked her door open, plopped down and slammed it shut. Sobbing now, Ayo glared at Bilal from out of her window before turning away from his stricken face. The running, stumbling and slamming had brought on a new surge of pain, this time causing her to gasp out loud.

Bilal ran around the car and jumped in. He leaned over to gather her close. She shook his arm away. Bilal blinked. "He was dead wrong, but why are you angry with me?"

Ayo ignored him and stared straight ahead. She folded both arms across her chest and tapped out a staccato beat on the floor mat with the flat part of her shoe. If he needed an answer to that question, he was more clueless than she imagined. And what did that say about his purported feelings for her?

"For bringing me there in the first place! You led me into an ambush! That's what you did! And you lied! Cool people?" Ayo swiped at her tear-streaked face. "Maybe your mother and sister, but definitely not that man. And why didn't you tell them all about me and Kedar? Was my son some kind of secret you wanted to keep?" Ayo's voice raised until it was a bleary stream of words and tears. She twisted in her seat to face him. "So what? I'm not young enough? Not *Muslim* enough?"

Bilal ran one hand through the length of his hair. "Oh, come on Ayo! They knew from day one that you aren't Muslim!"

Ayo trembled from anger and another stab of pain that fueled her second attack. "And why didn't you say something when your father insulted me?"

Bilal's head swung in Ayo's direction. He braked to avoid the hitting the bus that was just inches from his headlights. Instead of following the flow of traffic, he swerved into the extreme right lane, pulling into the vacant lot of what once was a gas station and parked next to a bank of grimy, crippled pay phones. A pulse throbbed in his temple. "So you didn't see me get up? You actually believe I sat there with my hands folded? What did you want—for us to have a fist-fight? You were doing pretty well for yourself, by the way!"

Ayo whirled around so hard, the seatbelt dug into her shoulder. "Oh, I see, throw her to the wolf, her teeth are just as big!"

Bilal's eyes stretched so wide they resembled saucer-eyed cartoon drawings. His face crumpled; in his struggle to swallow the choking laughter, he looked like a man in the throes of agony. It burst out anyway, in dry heaves, drawing his shoulders up and down with every strangled gasp.

Ayo's mouth dropped open like a trap door. "What in the hell are you laughing at? Does male madness run in your family?" Whatever pain she felt had been replaced by a surge of sheer anger.

"I'm sorry," he stammered. But when he looked over at Ayo, the laughter started all over again. "Nothing about tonight is remotely funny, but when I looked over at you, all I could see was a lit fuse sticking out of the top of your head, ready to blow." Good thing the lot was empty. Some Good Samaritan might think he was having seizures and call 911. "I'm sorry, baby, but…" He couldn't finish the sentence. Instead he dropped his head on the steering wheel until the tremors passed.

His laughter was fuel to a flame and Ayo raged like wildfire over dried brush. "No, you're not. You're not sorry at all since you think it's such a big joke. So you either take me home or I'll get out right here and catch a cab!"

For the rest of the way, Bilal struggled to keep that image out of his mind. Ayo sat stiff as a rod of iron, staring straight ahead. There were two sounds in the car—the tap of Ayo's nails on her purse and snorts of laughter that Bilal just couldn't choke back down his throat.

On Manchester Road, Bilal parked a few spaces behind her Sequoia. Before he could get out and around to open her door, she had pulled up the latch and was on the street, her heels clacking an angry beat on the sidewalk. Bilal sprinted to catch her.

"Ayo, wait!" An urgent whisper kept his voice from carrying down the quiet street. Lights were on in every house on the short curving block; Manchester Road was not the kind of neighborhood that took kindly to loud, verbal showdowns. Inside, they got no farther than the foyer before she whirled around to face him.

"The only reason I didn't leave you right there in the middle of the sidewalk is because I have never caused a scene in public and at forty-two," she spat out, fashioning two fingers into imaginary quotation marks, "I don't plan to start."

Bilal stood with his arms folded, coolly regarding her tantrum. His face remained impassive, except for the pulse that jumped in his jaw.

"You talk a good game—progressive? With a father like that? I know exactly what would happen. As soon as you had me roped in, your foot would come right down on my neck." Ayo lifted her head and rolled her eyes. "Or at least you'd try."

She'd had her say, and as far as Ayo was concerned, it was over. She spun on her heel to walk away until the chill in Bilal's voice rooted her to the spot. He leaned up off the wall and took a step forward. The softness in his voice magnified the anger that blazed darkly from his eyes.

"Game over now, Ayo. I'm done with this. All the way over here, you steamrolled me, and didn't listen to a word I said. But before I walk out of this door, you're going to hear every word I have to say." One smooth eyebrow raised. "And without interruption."

Ayo's mouth gaped open. Each word from his mouth sounded like a slap. "The first time you made that comment about Muslim women,

I was cool, and I thought we got past it. But here you go again. I don't get you. I was so happy when you told me what you've learned about Islam. So what happened between then and now? And how could a woman trained to separate fact from fiction allow something so uninformed to come out of her mouth? I don't know why my father was a jerk tonight, but it's not because he's Muslim. If he worshipped a rock in the back yard, would you blame his behavior on the rock?"

She couldn't fit one word in between the scolding that sprayed her like ice water. "You know what I think? You'd rather be pissed off than consider that you just might be wrong! Maybe I was the one who was wrong." Without another word, Bilal pulled open the door. It slammed behind him before she could get her mouth open.

❧

Bilal jumped in his car and gunned the Chevy back across town to Brookland, nearly running the light as it switched from yellow to red. Idling at the intersection gave him time to reign in his anger. Not this time, he told himself, pulling out of the U-turn that would take him back to Brookland. If he confronted his father now, no telling what he'd say. He did know that it would be impossible to take back.

A gold-trimmed red Cadillac pulled up beside him in the next lane. Its female passenger stared, and then jerked her head away, but not quick enough to escape the sharp eye of her companion. When he leaned over to scowl at Bilal, the man's heavy jowls shook.

"Hey! What are you looking at?" he shouted "You can't find a woman of your own? I guess not, with all those naps hangin' off your head."

Bilal tilted his head down for a better look at the loudmouth in the old-school ride. "It figures," he snorted. The man's head barely cleared the back of his seat. With his narrowed eyes and trembling, flaccid jaws, he reminded Bilal of an angry little bloodhound.

"Go on home, Hush Puppy," he growled. "Look at you—acting like you can beat somebody. Your feet can barely reach the pedals! I'll bet you have to stand up to put on brakes!" As soon as the light turned red, the needle jumped to 45 and stayed there until he broke the speed down to 20 before turning onto his tree-lined street.

The Chevy lurched into the driveway, churning up a spray of gravel. Its heavy metal door slammed like a gunshot in the still night. From the porch steps he could hear the phone ringing and remembered he'd left it upstairs instead of in its cradle in the kitchen. Bilal's heart thudded—could it be Ayo? It better not be his father. Bilal took back the thought. Latif would be the last one to call; apologies were not the man's strong suit. Inside the house, Bilal's locks bounced against his back when he took the polished steps, two at a time. It was still ringing when he grabbed the receiver off his desk. He sat down hard on the suede and satin comforter and smiled, only slightly.

"Salaam-Alaikum—I should have known it was you."

"Wa-alaikum-As-Salaam," Zahirah replied. "If ever we needed the greeting of peace, now is the time! That was some showdown, wasn't it? I have never seen our father behave so badly!" Remnants of shock were still evident in Zahirah's voice. "But Ayo handed it right back. Now I see what you mean about her not being a pushover. When I got home Kalil was back from the hospital. I told him all about it, and he reminded me of his own ordeal at the hands of Latif Abdul-Salaam."

Bilal got up and paced, wearing a track in the pile of his carpet before coming to stand in front of the deck's sliding glass doors. A full moon illuminated the back yard. "Yeah, but with Kalil, it was that 'I've got a shotgun and I know how to use it' attitude. But tonight was different. After I took Ayo home, which by the way was another disaster, I was on my way back over there but I caught myself. Soon, though, he and I are going to have a real man to man." He sighed deeply.

The last thing he expected to hear from his sister was a sudden onset of giggling.

He left the doors and began his pacing again. "I don't know what you could possibly find funny about tonight!" What in the hell was going on? Everybody he cared for, with the exception of his mother, had apparently lost their mind.

Zahirah caught her breath and broke into another round of laughter.

"Look Zahirah, I don't know what's up with you, but I'm not in the mood for this. I'll talk to you later."

Before he clicked the off, she pleaded. "No, no, don't hang up B! I want to tell you what Kamla said to Dad. The girls came into the room right after Mama and I both had given him a piece of our minds. She looked up at him and said 'Grandpa, why are Mommy and Nana mad at you? Were you naughty?'"

Bilal fell back on the bed. A big burst of laughter temporarily replaced the tangle of disappointment and anger. "Man, I would love to have seen that. What did he say?"

"He stared at us with that King Latif look and said 'No, I wasn't baby. But some people think so.'"

Bilal shook his head. "That's Latif Abdul Salaam for you."

"Don't I know," Zahirah responded. "I love our father, but he needs a reality check. And B, I know you didn't think it mattered, but knowing our father, maybe you should have told him more about Ayo so he would have fewer questions to ask."

"'Tell him what? You remember what Cedric said? I'm a grown-ass man. She needs no explaining and I sure don't need his approval to be with the woman I'm crazy about. If anybody needs checking, it's our father."

"I see your point, but I just feel so badly for her. But she sure was enough for him."

"And me too. She chewed me up like ground meat all the way back to her house. Then I got mad and blew out of there like a bat out of hell." Bilal massaged the furrowed space between his forehead. "What a mess."

"Oh, B I am so sorry. But from what I saw of the two of you together, I hope you'll make it up. So what are you going to say to Ayo?"

Bilal hesitated. "I don't know. At least not yet."

Chapter 7
🕭

$\mathcal{A}$t seven a.m., it was hour two of Ayo's get-over-Bilal day. She sailed ahead at full throttle, boosted by caffeine, adrenaline and *I Will Survive*. The thumping disco bass pounded the walls of the entire first floor. Thank God for a corner lot and soundproof walls. The last thing she needed was the police banging on her door telling her to turn it off or take a ride downtown.

Her hands couldn't find enough to do. Any other year, the hot pinks, pastel greens, orange sherbets, and hangers full of white clothes would have long since been put into storage. She'd been distracted this season by the unexpected arrival of a man in her life. Now it was eight a.m. and time to put those memories away along with the clothes that triggered them. Ayo's mouth trembled when she zipped the peachskin and lavender silk into a dress bag and hung them at the far end of her closet.

Jerking handfuls of dresses from the stainless steel rod, Ayo tossed them in a colorful mound in the center of her bed. They began to slide off, but she threw more on top anyway, moving on to haul out a load of skirts and blouses.

After the last armful, Ayo pulled the phone from the breast pocket of her shirt. She stared at the tiny screen, knowing full well that it hadn't rung. Besides the fact that she checked it every five minutes, there was no way she couldn't hear a phone that had become a part of her anatomy an hour after Bilal left her sputtering in the foyer.

The housekeeping fervor quickly fizzled. What next? It was eight-thirty in the morning, but Ayo plumped a small village of pillows against her headboard, arranging them in a long comfortable cushion for her back. She climbed on the bed with a soup bowl of butter pecan ice cream, ready for a western marathon. *Buck and the Preacher* followed the *Magnificent Seven*. She loved western movies and their music. They made her see blue skies, white clouds and wide open spaces. Harry Belafonte, Sidney Poitier and Yul Brynner kept her company until she shoved aside the remaining clothes and fell asleep in the small space that was left.

At ten o'clock she woke again, groggy and sick to her stomach. The combination of coffee and half pint of ice cream created a roiling witches' brew in her belly. "This is worse than a hangover," Ayo moaned with both hands over her volcanic stomach. After a huge burp she dragged herself to the bathroom where a hot, fifteen-minute shower smoothed some of blurred edges of her mental and physical malaise.

Downstairs, her day began, again. *I Will Survive* had long since played out, replaced now by *La Vie En Rose*. It was the worst time to be surrounded by Edith Piaf's French warbling of starry-eyed love but she couldn't help it. When the phone rang, Ayo's heart lurched, until she saw Justine's home office number displayed on the tiny screen.

"Hello," Ayo sighed. Through the speakerphone, Ayo heard the rustle of papers behind her friend's cheery greeting.

"Well, hello yourself! You sure sound like you could use a break! I definitely need one because I've been reading this same release over and over again, and the words have become one non-stop sentence! So how about some roti in a about an hour?" Justine didn't miss a beat. "And then you can tell me why you sound like Eyore."

"Oh no you didn't!" In spite of her gloom, Ayo burst out laughing. "How could you compare me to Winnie the Pooh's sad little donkey friend?"

Justine huffed out a laugh. "Because both our children made us sit through endless repetitions of *The Blustery Day*. My recollection is just fresher than yours," she chuckled. "And this morning you sound like a sorry ass!"

"You hush!" Ayo giggled. "But I'm glad you called. I needed to hear a friendly voice." It was true; Justine may have gone overboard on the matchmaking, but the two women had seen each other through their best and worst times, and Justine's shoulder could always be counted on. A little of Ayo's gloom gave way to humor. "By the way, have you ever thought about becoming a TV psychic? Miss Cleo left a void that's yet to be filled!"

Justine's laugher pealed through the phone. "Let's take my car, though. It's hard enough to find a space for a little one. With that big monster Sequoia, we'd have to park behind God's back and still walk ten blocks!"

Justine's love of West Indian food saved the day. If she hadn't called, Ayo's would have been spent staring at the phone, willing it to ring. She changed into slim jeans and a thigh-length, high-collared white shirt. She clasped a chunky necklace of blue and amber stones around her neck and slipped on an armful of silver bangles. Her heart might ache, but today the rest of her was pain free. She sprayed herself with "Ayo's Ambrosia" and pulled her fingers through her hair, turning the twist-out style into a cloud of springy spirals.

An hour later, she and Justine were on their way to some of the best Caribbean food in the city. From the car speakers, Ruby Dee's elegant voice transfixed them with the audio version of *Their Eyes Were Watching God*.

"First we eat, then we talk," Justine proclaimed as she pressed hard on the gas with a blue slip-on Ked. It matched the pastel blue yoga pants and short-sleeved tee that had become her favorite at-home work attire.

Fall was temperamental. Today's low seventies could drop snarling into the fifties with little warning, but today every door on uptown Georgia Avenue was propped open, taking advantage of the spectacular weather; beauty parlors, mom and pop stores, carry-outs and the few new upscale hopefuls to the Avenue.

Outside the Caribbean restaurant, customers spilled onto the street under the awning painted in the red, black and white of Trinidad's national flag. A collection of colorful paintings depicting island life covered one wall of the small restaurant. An array of bright flyers and postcards announcing weekend dances and concerts fanned out along the sill of a large wide window.

Inside, Desmond Thompson, former cricket player and long-time fixture in the Caribbean community, held court under a picture of himself swinging his mighty bat in a pivotal match against England. Tall and strong, Desmond's sharp, handsome features and black satin skin made him a standout, even after retirement from the game he loved. Before he ever stepped foot on a cricket pitch, Desmond's father taught him to cook. Now, though the tools of his trade had become home cooked food, fresh baked bread and coconut rolls, his muscle had never turned to fat.

The two women ran the gauntlet of unabashed admiration to where Desmond stood. A wolfish grin replaced his animated conversation. "Dah-ling, how yuh goin'? How yuh keepin'? Lookin' *good*, yuh know!" The big man's gaze swung between them like a pendulum. Reckless eyeballing, her father used to call it.

Ayo pursed her lips and laughed. "If you could pull your eyes away long enough for two roti, I would be eternally grateful."

"Of course, dah-ling! So whatcha want–chicken or wild meat?" Desmond's eyes danced while his bold stare rolled over Ayo. The double entendre could have been the words from a suggestive calypso.

"Chicken—I don't eat game, foreign or domestic." Ayo shot back, bantering with her admirer.

Desmond took one step closer to Ayo, towering over her, and lowering his voice to a sexy whisper. "Who say I was talkin' 'bout game?"

Ayo shook her head and laughed. He had extreme flirting down to a science. "You need to stop, saga-boy!"

"Come on now, Ayo." Desmond clutched a large fist to his chest and whined in a dramatic show of hurt. "How yuh could say dat?" His thick brows lifted. "Me ain' no playboy, yuh know." Trailing a wicked laugh behind him. Desmond disappeared into the kitchen. Fifteen minutes later, he came back and handed Ayo a bag bulging with much more than two roti. "Some pan bread and something sweet from de bakery for you and yuh frien'." Desmond winked. The lip-licking grin re-appeared. "Is on me."

The street brimmed over with its special blend of all-day, all night energy. They passed a hair salon with its door open to the late summer weather, filled with women waiting their turn to be made beautiful, ready to fill the city's clubs like bouquets of fresh blooms. On either side of the street, African and Hispanic carry outs served up food to people wanting a taste of home or something new. Ayo stopped in front of a grimy Asian carryout whose faded paint had once been blue. She pointed at the dog-eared piece of cardboard that advertised *scraple, grits and eggs*. "Look at this," she chuckled. "Along with a visit from a health inspector, they need a dictionary. Or a black person to cook and spell."

"Huh," Justine countered. "They might not know how to spell scrapple, and would probably never touch the stuff, but you'd better believe they learned how to cook it. Speaking of food, I can't wait to dig into that roti. Desmond's is some of the best I've tasted." She let out a girlish giggle. "Not to mention the added benefits."

"*Now* what are you talking about?"

Justine threw back her shoulders and gave a small shimmy. "There is no better boost for a woman's ego like a roomful of West Indian men!"

"True dat," Ayo quipped. "Remember the time in Kingston when that man called you posturepedic?"

"Uh-huh. And I was ready to lay him out until he said my body was like a soft mattress he'd like to lie on all night! Ah, our Caribbean brothers. They have a style all their own." Justine stopped suddenly and grabbed Ayo's arm. "Wait a minute!" She turned back. Desmond caught her glance and sent the two women a grinning, flirty wave.

"Did you and he ever—"

Ayo reached over and playfully plucked Justine's arm. Her twists flew back and forth with the motion of her head. "Do you ever stop?" She laughed. "But the answer is no, no and no! He was never one of the two men in eighteen years, as you call them."

Justine's eyebrow arched when she looked over at the brown shopping bag. "Just checking, because that wild meat comment was hot. And so is he," she murmured. "Talk about a play on words! And I know that stash was more for you than for 'your friend.'"

Ayo threw up one hand and sent a beseeching gaze into the sky. "Is there ever any end?" She pointed a finger at Justine. "Now come on and drive. We've got some eating to do! And speaking of wild meat let me tell you this story." Just thinking about it made Ayo laugh. "Listen at this. When Karen's husband Trevor was in Trinidad last summer, he went to a wild meat party up in the country. He recognized the armadillo, possum and the wild boar, but he had never heard about cousin. He said he didn't want to look like a Yankee, so instead of asking what kind of meat is called cousin, he took it."

"What in the hell is cousin? I know Trinis have a slang for everything, but I've never heard that one."

Ayo gave Justine a dead-pan stare. "Monkey."

If there was any way Justine's cinnamon skin could have turned pale, that image would have been the trigger. Her mouth opened and shut. "Good Lord," she mumbled, pressing a hand against her mouth. When the moment passed, she reached for her water bottle, gulping down a long non-stop guzzle.

"I know," Ayo shook her head. "That's way too wild for me. But I don't eat muskrat, or coon, either and I grew up around hunters." Pursing her lips in a teasing grin, Ayo turned back to Justine. "You okay? Or are you thinking about Tarzan cooking Cheetah and having him for lunch."

Justine's eyes widened like saucers. "Will you stop!" Her stricken expression was too much for Ayo. She doubled over, covering her mouth to hold back the whoops of laughter.

"Okay, okay," she sputtered. Too bad it was at Justine's expense, but Ayo was feeling better by the moment. She leaned back against the seat and enjoyed the ride, glad again for her friend's unwitting intervention. Unhappiness got exactly what it needed—fresh air to blow it from the corners of her mind. When she got back home, she'd be better able to deal with a relationship that appeared to be over as quickly as it begun.

As it always did, day or night on Georgia Avenue, traffic moved briskly. Ayo loved her part of DC, generically referred to as "uptown."

Tucked between Georgia Avenue and Sixteenth Street, it was lovely, convenient to good food and easy transportation. Capitol Hill had its own lively cachet, with trendy restaurants, small boutiques and the landmark Eastern Market, but if she hadn't found her home on Manchester, Justine's vibrant Capitol Hill neighborhood would have been at the top of Ayo's list.

They sat on the raised backyard deck, next to railings fashioned from tree limbs that had been casualties of a springtime thunderstorm. Justine brought out paper plates, a roll of paper towels and two ice cold Heineken.

"Roti and beer," Ayo chanted. "Better than chicken and beer any day! And speaking of game, anyway, let's eat what we got and enjoy it! At least, I'll try." She had put up a good fight, and getting out of the house was the best thing she could have done, but sadness was worming its way back into her thoughts.

Two beers and two empty plates later, Justine spoke up.

"Let's get to the reason for your long face. So what happened?"

Ayo spilled out the whole story. "So that's the end of that. Game over," she sighed, repeating Bilal's hard words.

Justine's exquisitely groomed brows wrinkled. "Why? I thought he was everything you wanted. It's almost as if you're pushing him away."

Blinking, Ayo lifted her chin. The napkin became a wrinkled paper ball in her hand. "He's the one who stormed out! So what else am I to think?"

"His father sounds like a jerk, pure and simple. And it has nothing to do with Islam." She stared at Ayo. "Why did you throw that in the mix?"

"Because I don't want it to keep popping up every time."

Absently, Justine pushed both bottle caps around in a small circle. "It has nothing to do with Islam, and you know it. You're using it as a smokescreen to hide the real truth. Deep down inside, you know it. You're afraid."

Ayo's head jerked up. "I admit I might have gone overboard, but are you kidding? Afraid of what?"

Justine leaned back and leveled a long stare at her friend. "Of losing him. So you make a pre-emptive strike, and if you're in charge when it ends, it won't hurt so badly."

Ayo dropped her head in her hands that had suddenly turned cold. "Please, Justine."

"No, Ayo, it needs to be said, once and for all. When Maurice died, you nearly lost your mind." The memory of her friend's despair softened Justine's tone. "I was there, remember? I saw you teetering on the edge for a very long while." Justine reached across the empty plates to touch Ayo's hand. "I was mostly teasing with the matchmaking, but I'm serious now. You have to stop putting up these defensive barriers and live your life."

"I am living my life," Ayo protested. "I love men, but I don't need one to satisfy everybody but myself." She looked up quickly, not wanting her friend to take the remark as a personal attack. "And I don't mean you," she interjected quickly. "And I don't mean Magda either. You two have got my back and my front." She smiled briefly, but it was gone as quickly as it had come. "I mean the business-minders who have all manner of men in their beds just to say they have one. And think I should, too."

Justine patted Ayo's hand again. Her eyes and her smile were soft. "Oh, I know you didn't mean me. I expected at least two years before you got over Maurice's death enough to venture out in the world. But that leaves eighteen, and it is a long time. I know you haven't been celibate all that time, but you've never let anyone get close. Now you have a man who is everything you've wanted and instead of enjoying him, you're throwing up a roadblock."

"I don't mean to," Ayo murmured. But Justine was right, no matter what rationalizations she gave herself. Every time a man showed more than a passing interest, it wasn't long before the roadblocks went up, and the man was out of her life.

"Then live your life in the same way you did when you met Maurice."

Ayo sat still. "What do you mean?"

"Think about it. You met him by chance and he turned out to be the love of your life until now. Within a year you were married and living in Trinidad."

Ayo looked down at her hands folded in her lap. "That's true," she murmured.

"Same thing with Maracas Bay. You were fooling around with something you read in a book and before you knew it, you had a successful business up and running."

"Yes, but a business requires a lot of thought and planning. I don't think that applies," Ayo countered.

"I didn't mean that one day you got the idea, and the next day you were in the red. I meant you didn't sit down and say to yourself 'I want to start a business,' did you? You didn't do market research, you didn't write a business plan, and it just fell into place. Am I right?"

Ayo was silent.

"Look, I didn't mean to upset you…"

"No, no," Ayo spoke up. "I was just lost in the idea of what you were saying. I never thought of it in that way."

"So think about it. And put pride and fear aside. Call that man, apologize and let him love you."

When Justine dropped her home, Ayo's spirits were as high as a kite in March wind. Just in case, she sat down at her desk and checked both her phone and email messages. Nothing, at least from Bilal. Earlier today she would have been deep in despair. But Justine's advice was the kick Ayo needed. Before she called him, a shopping trip for clothing and food was definitely in order. When he knocked on the door, she'd meet him with something sleek and classy, and a meal that would knock Granny's bacon-in-the-drawers remedy back into love-potion history!

Singing the first song she could manage since he walked out of her door, Ayo drove to The Secret's Out, a newly-opened boutique that had women all over DC raving about its clothing. A mix of clean lines, Afro/Bohemian chic, and spectacular, custom jewelry, the shop's elegant offerings promised something for everyone. Ayo stood in front of an antique display case, admiring a silver cuff that reminded her of South African tribal jewelry.

"I need to get something really sexy." Ayo looked around to see who owned the sultry voice that belonged in a smoky blues club. She was a knock-out—petite, curvy and in this day of weaves and bone straight hair, her scalp-skimming natural brought all eyes to her already outstanding looks. But the too-tight jeans and tight t-shirt baring way too much cleavage cheapened her beauty. "Because the next time Bilal sees me, he won't see daylight until the morning after. Lawd, he makes my kitty purr. No, I take that back," she giggled. "When I look at Mr. Fine-ass Salaam, that thing growls like a full grown female in heat!"

The words hit Ayo like an open-handed slap. She dropped the cuff back onto its velvet cushion and quickly closed the display. Hurrying down the circular stairway and onto the crowded sidewalk, a million confusing thoughts careened through her head. Bilal and that woman? She was certainly beautiful, but Ayo couldn't imagine them out in public. But half-dressed and blatantly sexy didn't matter behind closed doors. Had she been stupid and overwhelmed by a combination of raging hormones and pursuit by a man that for the first time, she didn't want to resist? Couldn't resist? Ayo's mood plummeted. By the time she parked the Sequoia, all she wanted was the sanctuary of her home and desperately to get back to her life as she knew it before Bilal.

At home, Bilal paced. His latest appraisal report had been mailed.

Sloan's fine art auction was two days away. He needed something else to work off his frustration. Too bad he didn't box. Without that option, he decided to lose himself in the process of turning something battered and discarded into a thing of beauty. He could work up nearly the same amount of sweat. Besides, he loved his work.

From the first day he witnessed a fine arts appraiser sift through and catalog the treasure left behind by his grandmother, Bilal put his economics degree aside. The detailed follow-up report had him hooked. He loved the entire process—the photographing, the research that allowed him to separate the wheat from the chaff of fake reproductions, and the satisfaction of informing a client that his old piece of junk was really a collector's item worth hundreds, if not thousands of dollars. He owned an impressive collection of reference books on glassware, pottery, and furniture from every design period. Restoration and reproduction were natural progressions. His long client list was a testament to his expertise.

Outside, Bilal dragged a garish gate-legged table into to his garage-turned-workshop. It sat in the backyard between two apple trees. The only drawback to their sheltering shade was the soft mush left by ripe fruit droppings. But thanks to the spread of its branches, even on the days when D.C. wore humidity like a damp shroud, the room remained cool with only the aid of large round floor fan. At the moment it whirred like the rotors of a prop plane, sending the sweet woody scent of fresh shavings into the air.

Furniture in various stages of repair and disrepair took up one side and the entire back of the spacious room. To prevent a layer of dust from settling in his hair, Bilal shoved his locks under a knit cap, groaning at the amount of work it would take to get the wretched piece in good enough shape to begin restoration.

He was grateful for the distraction it offered. He spent half the morning glancing up at the clock and the other sanding off the two inches of cheap red and black lacquer the previous owner had slapped on in an attempt to give it an Asian look. The detailed work helped fill the hours until his arms burned from exertion. By the time the table was sanded down to the pale golden wood he and his clothes were sweaty and reeking of solvent. In the unfinished laundry room, he pulled off his paint-flecked work shirt and pants and stuffed them into a plastic bag. It was hard to get the eye-watering smell out of a room once it had been invaded by the scent of chemical stripper.

Inside, he headed for the shower. In case Ayo called, he took the phone with him to the bathroom. And even if she didn't, it was okay. He had gotten her back once, and *Insha'Allah*, God willing, he could do it again.

Chapter 8

❧

"Are the girls ready? I'm getting dressed now, and I'll be over to pick them up in an hour." Leaning over to pull on a pair of soft-soled Rockports, Bilal spoke to his sister on what she called his *Star Wars* speakerphone.

"Right now they're coloring with those nubs of crayons they refuse to let me throw away! 'Unca B brought them for us!'" Zahirah mimicked her daughters' outrage when they caught her trying to slide the bare chunks of color into a small garbage bag.

"Stop mocking my babies," he laughed. "I'll get them a new box today. And if you don't mind, I have to make another run while I'm out, so we'll be back later than I originally planned."

"I'll bet I know what run you're making," Zahirah teased.

"Girl, stay out of my business!" Bilal shot back. "You think because we're twins, you can read my mind? Stick to pill-pushing, ZZ Top, and have my girls ready. Unca B has a treat in store for them."

Zahirah sent back a sharp volley of her own. "If you don't stop calling me that, I'm going to start calling you BB gun! Have you seen them? They look like the Amish on drugs!"

"Slow your roll, sis," Bilal chuckled. "I give; I can't have you mad at me too!"

Bare-chested, he searched through the tall tower of alphabetized CDs for a John Coltrane selection. Next to the collection, two Beanie Baby kittens trained their soft brown gaze out into the room.

Bilal smiled affectionately at the stuffed toys and the pictures beside them. He'd taken Kamla and Kamilah downtown to the Museum of Natural History. Once he could pry the twins away from the giant elephant in the large circular lobby, they toured the sea life exhibit and went on to the gift shop. He was enchanted by the Beanies; their sweet expressions reminded him so much of the girls. He bought four—one for each of them, and two for himself, to sit at the corner of his desk devoted to his family. Bilal smiled again. There was plenty of room. One day the space would be dominated by pictures of his own wife and children.

To Coltrane's classic *Greensleeves*, Bilal pulled on a teal blue T-shirt over a pair of soft indigo-colored jeans. He stood at the mirror and pulled his locks back into a leather tie. Reaching for a small gold bottle, he tilted the top against his finger and dabbed a drop of the rich fragrance on his skin.

On Carroll Avenue, Zahirah and the twins were waiting outside. Kamla and Kamilah bounced up and down on the plant-filled porch, looking like tiny gardeners in their blue-denim coveralls. A pouf of thick curly hair stuck out from the semi-circle in back of their matching baseball caps.

"Salamma-laykum, Unca B. Where we going?"

"Wa-Alaikum-As-Salaam, my precious girls." He smiled mysteriously. "Just wait and see." He grabbed Zahirah, pulling her into a one-armed hug. "We'll be back some time after you get home." Bilal winked at his sister. "Don't worry Z—"

Zahirah pulled away and balled up her fist. "Don't you say it, Bilal!"

"Mommy!" The girls shouted.

"See?" Bilal swaggered, pointing both forefingers down at the horrified twins who were two quivering lips away from a full-fledged wail. "I got protection!"

"Go on before you need it." Zahirah slapped his arm, and bent to kiss her daughters, brushing her hands over their soft brown cheeks. "It's okay, babies. We were playing, just like we did when we were kids," she assured them. "And make sure Unca B behaves himself," she told them with a twinkle in her eye.

At mid-morning on a weekday, few people were in the giant toy store. Bilal plopped both girls into a large shopping cart. Kamla and Kamilah whipped their heads from side to side, craning their necks to stare up at the bright floor-to-ceiling array of toys. Giving the wide-eyed twins a conspiratorial grin, Bilal braked to a sudden stop and swung his gaze up and down the wide open aisle. "Here we go," he whispered. Gripping the handle and leaning into the cart, Bilal's long legs picked up speed. He propelled himself forward like the pusher on a bobsled team.

"Wheeee!" the twins screamed, as they careened down the long aisle.

An hour later they left the store, loaded down with bags of crayons, coloring books, a huge bucket of brightly colored Duplo blocks and two tiny Super-Soakers. *Zahirah's gonna get me.* A short chuckle escaped his lips. The little water cannons would never make it out of his big back yard.

After loading the front seat with their stash, Bilal buckled them in and tore two sheets of paper from a pad. He handed one to each girl. "Can you draw a picture for Mommy and Daddy?" They loved to color, and it would keep them busy on the ride to his second stop of the day. Before he could stick a handful of crayons in the cup holder between their seats, Kamla spoke up. "Can we ride in the air? Please?"

He shook his head. "Uh-uh, baby girl. I can't watch the traffic and make sure you're safe at the same time." Grinning, Bilal reached over and plucked the bill of her cap. "Besides, a bird might poop on your pretty hat!"

"Ewww," they shouted in unison.

He loved them dearly and indulged them often, but even he had his limits. There was no way he would drive through city traffic with the top down, and two rambunctious four-year-olds unattended in the back seat.

"But Unca B," Kamlah insisted. She leaned out of the open window and pointed up to the cloudless midday sky. "There are no birds up there."

Bilal laughed out loud at her determined efforts. Maybe that's why he relented. Besides, they were worn out. He had seen them rub their eyes and try to fight sleep. The fresh air and motion of the car would have them knocked out before he pulled out of the parking lot.

Just across the DC/Maryland border a stalled Metrobus brought traffic to a standstill. All around him, irate drivers blew their horns in frustration, but he paid no mind. He daydreamed, lost in thoughts of Ayo. How perfect it would be to spend a beautiful, sunny day just like this one with her and their own children.

"Hey! Hey!" He heard the shout but paid no attention to the urgent voice somewhere out on New Hampshire Avenue. Nothing was moving; whoever was making all that noise might as well save his lungs. Bilal drummed his fingers on the wheel. At last the cars on his left inched forward. Next to him, the driver's wild gestures jolted him out of his daydream. "Hey, brother man! Turn around—look behind you!"

Bilal spun around. The sight chilled him as if he'd been plunged naked into icy water. Kamla and Kamilah had twisted around in their car seats. Completely unbuckled, they kneeled, waving to the car behind them like tiny beauty queens.

Bilal inhaled a terrified breath. He swallowed the shout that wanted to barrel its way out of his chest. But he couldn't—if he startled them, they might tumble out across the trunk. He offered up a quick prayer of thanks that traffic had come to a complete stop. And a promise never again to drive top-down with Kamla and Kamilah.

It was now or never; the time for gentle coaxing was over. Bilal twisted into a half turn, reached back and slapped the seat behind him. On soft leather, the sound cracked like a slap on bare skin. "Kamla and Kamilah Ahmed, turn around right now!"

Kamla and Kamilah jerked around and bounced down into their seats. Four little saucer eyes stared. Their rosebud mouths froze open in shock. Then it started; a long, open-mouthed, one-note wail that ended only when they stopped to catch a shuddering breath.

In front of the house, Bilal dropped his head on the steering wheel. It was the longest ride he'd ever taken, and definitely not the way he planned to show up. When he unbuckled the twins from their seats, they had no more tears, only sniffles and baleful glances. If he weren't so upset, the sight would have been hilarious. Knocking hard on the door, he made ready for a less-than-grand entrance.

ॐ

Creation was the cure for what ailed her. The calculations clicked in Ayo's head even before she sat at her desk and pulled out the purple folder that held bits and pieces of inspiration. Choosing virgin coconut, jojoba and a combination of shea and almond oils, Ayo went to work. Armed with a calculator, she played with the portions until the combined fractions of each ingredient added up to 100 per cent. Two batches later, both had to be thrown out. They both smelled divine, but one was thick like cold butter and the other the consistency and color of runny oatmeal. She re-worked her formulation until the first successful test batch of Coconut Cloud sat cooling on the corner of the counter, next to five small jars for her friends who doubled as Maracas Bay guinea pigs. Ayo smiled; it was a small step on a journey that could have been a lot longer. Three hours had passed, and she hadn't thought of anything other than another success in the making. *Close call, Ayo.* Now if she could just keep it up, she'd be over Bilal in no time.

When she heard the sound, Ayo jerked her head up from the bowl that smelled like coconut in heaven. Who was banging on her door like a bounty hunter? She wasn't expecting a visitor, especially one with a knock like that. At the door, she squeezed one eye over the tiny hole and jumped back. Why was he here? But when she swung open the door and saw two sniffling, knee-high visitors, her jumbled emotions were swept away by surprise.

"Miss Ayo!" Kamilah pointed up at her uncle. "Unca B hollered at us!" Ayo stared at the twins and up at Bilal, who looked like he'd been carjacked and rescued after a day in the trunk of his car.

Ayo hustled them all inside, turning her attention to the girls. "Come here, babies," she cooed. "Let me wipe your pretty faces." Ayo retrieved a wad of folded tissues from her apron pocket, kneeled in front of them and patted their cheeks dry.

Bilal spoke in the extra-cheery voice adults used to placate children. "Why don't you two go out into the back?" A long hallway ran from the front of the house, ending at a door that opened onto the back yard. The girls brightened when they spotted the porch and large grassy yard. Halfway down the hall, Ayo called out to them. "But make sure you stay in the yard." The only way out was a latched fence, but she wouldn't be surprised to see one of tiny dynamos hoisting the other up to unhook the gate. On the way out, their heads turned in the direction of the sweet orange scent wafting from the soap kitchen.

"Let me lock this other door. There's too much stuff in there that could hurt them. I know it smells good, but the lye and essential oils would burn them badly." At the end of the hall, Kamilah turned back. "Is Kay-dar here?" she called out.

"No baby, he's away at school." Ayo smiled and touched her finger to the tip of Kamla's nose. "But you know what? When he comes home, I'll make sure you get to play with him, okay?"

Kamilah's head bobbed up and down. On their way outside, the two girls bounced the rest of the way like twin rays of smiley-faced sunshine.

The door banged shut, leaving Ayo alone with the reality she tried valiantly, but too hard to avoid. Who was she fooling? Her earlier resolve to forget him was suddenly so ridiculous. The early morning ice cream must have chilled her brain into a frozen mass of delusion. Her eyes skimmed the swell of muscle under the short sleeves of his blue shirt and his long legs under the loose denim jeans. But why was he here? The other night, there was finality in that slammed door. And why did he bring the two little girls with him?

Bilal jerked his heard towards where they could hear shrieks and laughter. "Just so you know, Kamla and Kamilah are now pint-sized versions of Thelma and Louise! Those two need a bodyguard! Or maybe I'm the one who needs protection when I'm out with them! I'll tell you all about it." Bilal's bemused expression changed into a serious stare. "But first things first. Can we go outside? Right now they need a constant eye kept on them."

Ayo stopped at the kitchen door, searching for something to delay the inevitable. And for the opportunity to gather her strength when the words fell from his lips. "Go on out. I'll bring you some lemonade." In spite of the sharp clenching in her stomach, her lips curved up at his flustered, bemused expression. And the knowledge that two beloved little girls could bring him to his knees. "You look like you could use a drink."

As long as she took, she could have picked the lemons from a grove somewhere in Florida. Finally she pushed open the door with her hip, carrying a tray with a pitcher and two glasses. She set them on the low bamboo table between them. Settling back against the green and yellow striped cushions, Ayo felt like a prisoner awaiting sentence.

"We need to talk." Bilal's expression gave nothing away.

Ayo swallowed. Finally. Whatever he had to tell her, she promised herself to handle it. She led him into the conversation with a joke. "So you brought back-up, huh?"

He turned and looked straight into Ayo's face. "You think I need back-up?"

Ayo stood suddenly. She took a deep breath, trying to control the tremor in her voice. "Can we go back inside?"

Her wavering voice brought him to his feet, leaving his half-full glass to sit in a moist circle. At the door, Bilal turned and called out. "Kamla and Kamilah, stay close to the porch where we can see you."

"Look Unca B! We're making a hairstyle!" Kamilah shouted. They tried valiantly to brush the long fronds of ornamental grass, but the curvy plants were taller than the girls. Halfway through their determined attempts, the slender stalks sprung back into their faces, tickling them and sending them into shrieks of laughter.

Good for you, Unca B, she thought. *Always on the job.* Ayo stood just inside the door and crossed her arms over her chest. She didn't want to hear bad news at the table where they shared their first meal.

"Let's sit down." Bilal pulled out a chair for Ayo before he took his own seat. He propped both elbows on the table and rested his chin on folded hands.

"Why do you think my father behaved like a jerk?"

Ayo blinked rapidly. It wasn't the opening she expected. "You know what I think." Her soft voice trailed off.

A half smile appeared, and then disappeared just as quickly. He looked at her a long time. Under the table, his foot rocked back and forth on its heel.

"I see...so you're certain it's because he's Muslim—right?" Bilal took his hand down and laid his palm across the back of Ayo's hand. She held off the rejoicing, although her shoulders felt a little less like cement blocks suspended in mid-air.

"Let me tell you about Latif Abdul Salaam. If he had bacon and beer for breakfast every day, he would still be the man you saw. My sister's husband Kalil is a lifelong Muslim, and my father put him through some hard paces."

"So what exactly is his problem? Is anybody good enough for either of you?"

Bilal dropped his head back. His Adam's apple pulsed from the laughter rumbling up from deep in his chest. "That's breaking it down to its least common denominator, for sure. But no, that's not it. With Zahirah, it's because she's his daughter. Men can be hard on the man who wants to take their little girl away, can't they?"

Ayo shook her head, remembering her first-hand experience with overprotective male relatives. The Mansfield clan raised their girls like hot-house flowers. None was allowed to date until she was sixteen, and even then it took a bold and brave young man to approach a Mansfield girl, especially during Magda's teen years. The rumor of fathers on porches with shotguns was a strong deterrent to dating.

"Dad is definitely not a laugh-a-minute brother, but I've never seen him go stone crazy like he did that night." Bilal's eyes hardened at the memory. "My mother filled me in," he continued. "First of all he thought you were in your early thirties. And when Kamilah talked about Kedar being as big as me, he was shocked that a woman your age had an almost grown son." Bilal held up his hand. "At that point he figured you must have been around fourteen when your son was born."

Ayo blinked rapidly. "I guess I should be flattered that he shaved ten years off my age, but he acted like I was spoiled goods!"

Ayo dropped her gaze. She pushed the salt and pepper shakers back and forth like a pair of square dancers circling each other. She took a deep breath, but couldn't look up. "Anyway, that's all well and good, but at this point, what difference does it make?"

Bilal frowned. "What do you mean 'at this point?'"

"Did he act the same way to your other woman?" Ayo snorted. If she could pepper her pain with the heat of anger, she might be able to get through the hardest part without crumbling into a sorry heap in front of him. "But I take that back. If she was dressed the way she was when I saw her, she might not have made it past the front door!"

"What other woman? The only woman I've taken to meet my parents is you."

"Oh come on! Is this the 'I didn't have sex with that woman' defense?"

"Look Ayo." Cold anger crept into his voice. "I told you—I have no idea who this phantom is or where you saw her. And I'll say it again—just once—I don't have any other woman."

Ayo wanted to cry. She hadn't been insecure since her curves developed a style that made her happy and turned heads. But the woman she saw yesterday was young and spectacular, and truth be told, Ayo was hurt, inconsolably jealous, and wrestling with the resurrection of an uncomfortable swipe of insecurity. Still, she lifted her head and looked into his eyes. "The one who said, and I quote: 'Because the next time Mr. Fine-ass Salaam sees me, he won't see daylight until the morning after.'"

Half his body stretched across the table. "Say what?" Unless he was the consummate actor, Bilal was genuinely shocked and confused. Raking both hands through the length of his hair, Bilal shook his head. "This week keeps getting crazier by the day!"

Ayo's hard line stance cracked a little. "I will say one thing–if it's true, I can understand why. The woman I saw was what my male cousins would call a petite brick house.

Bilal's eyes narrowed. "What did she look like?"

Ayo got no further than a description of the woman's hair. Bilal shot up from his chair. Under normal circumstances, the sight of his long legs planted wide apart directly in front of her would have been incredibly sensual. But there was nothing normal or usual about the transformation that took place. A pulse at the base of Bilal's throat throbbed wildly. One first clenched while the other hand dug deep inside his jeans pocket. Ayo took in a sharp breath. She had never seen him look so completely dangerous. With the tiny phone finally in hand, Bilal punched in a number.

"Z, I'm on my way back with the girls. Something has come up. Since I don't know how long it will take, I'd feel better bringing them back home. But I have to deal with it right now."

Ayo didn't know what to do or say. So she kept quiet and sat still while he called to Kamla and Kamilah. "Come on, baby girls," he told them, kneeling down to their level after they trooped in, dragging their dolls behind them. "I've got to take you back to Mommy for a little while, but I promise to come back so we can have ice cream and a tumble in the play yard at McDonalds." Their little faces crumpled, but a kiss on each forehead held off the tide of tears. "I promise," he repeated, gathering them both in his arms. With the girls finally comforted, he turned his attention back to Ayo. His expression had softened, but only a little. "Don't leave, and while I'm gone, don't jump to any more conclusions. I'll be back as soon as I can."

It was not the time, Ayo decided, to assert her right to go anywhere and do anything she wanted. Besides, the Feminine Manifesto held no answers to the questions she needed to have answered.

࿔

On Eleventh Street, Bilal pulled the Chevy into the last metered spot on the street. His brain was on fire, but he held himself in check out of respect for his friend and the boys he mentored as a volunteer.

He ran upstairs to Mark's office. Three walls of windows looked out on Eleventh Street. On the other, a glass-front cabinet held trophies, plaques and certificates earned by Midtown boys in academic and sports competitions. Bilal rapped his knuckles on the door.

"Hey, B! What's up?" During the school day or on Midtown Academy business, Mark wore the school uniform of white shirt, blue blazer and khaki pants. His free-form Afro was tamed down and a tiny stud sat in his pierced ear, but off the clock he wore an ear spear and let his long thick hair loose in wild splendor. Bilal's reply was slow in coming, causing Mark to take a longer look. He leaned back in the blue upholstered swivel chair. "Dag, bro—you look like you want to kick somebody's ass!"

"If she was a man, I would. But I need to speak to Arlena right now." He held up both hands. "And I promise I won't go off."

Mark's brows eased up. "She must have really ticked you off this time. Go ahead, bro." He chuckled. "I know you won't make Midtown the lead story for the six o'clock news."

Bilal nodded and hurtled down the steps to the administrative office. His fist thudded once on the copy room door. "Arlena."

The first time Bilal saw Arlena McCall, he had to will his eyes not to pop out of his head. An intern at Midtown, she had been referred by Mark's fraternity brother, who was also her department head. Petite and voluptuous, that day large earrings dangled from her ears. Thick lashes topped her large brown eyes. The seductive beauty of her full mouth was heightened by lips that were glossed moist and natural. Arlena had both brains and beauty. After a few years out of school, she returned to complete her degree, holding down a three-point-nine average while working full time in a downtown law firm.

His plan to ask her out ended the afternoon he saw her standing under the awning that sheltered Midtown's entrance. One foot was propped flat against the brick wall. She'd removed the sweater she'd worn inside, revealing a tight pink t-shirt. Over her outstanding breasts, the P-word stretched in bold white script, superimposed over a preening black cat.

"You know I can't go a week without getting some," she brayed into a cell phone. "And that last dude was so lame I could have read a book over his shoulder!" Bilal gave thanks on the spot that he'd seen the real Arlena before he found her out over dinner.

Arlena turned, and a sultry expression crept across her face, replacing the small frown. One of her eyebrows peaked. "Well hello there, with your fine self. Did you come to finally claim your prize?" She purred out the words, gazing at Bilal from half-closed eyes that took a slow, suggestive stroll up his body. She rubbed both hands down the front of the only pair of slacks she must have owned that didn't look painted on. After the day Mark forced her to wear a paint-smeared art smock over the crotch-cutting jeans she intended to flaunt, she found a whole new way of dressing, at least when she was in his building. "And by the way," she smirked, "I saw you the other night at that reception. So what were you doing—breaking grandma out of the nursing home for a charity date?" Her smile mocked him. "How commendable."

"Shut up!" Bilal commanded. The heat of his anger exploded like a nuclear blast.

Arlena's glossy mouth fell open. "What's wrong with you?" Her sultry expression turned surly and suddenly fearful. She took a quick step back, bumping her body against the whirring copy machine. "Why'd you come storming in here like a madman?"

"Because I'm tired of you chasing me like a sex-crazed bounty hunter. I don't want to hear your name and mine in the same sentence. Haven't you got the message? I don't want a woman whose body is like a vending machine—anybody with fifty cents can get some. Except in your case, no coin is necessary." Bilal shook his head; he'd be a hypocrite if he judged her, but at least he knew the meaning of thanks, but no thanks.

Arlena leaned off the machine and crossed her arms. "Very funny, Saint Bilal. Isn't that what you are—some kind of Muslim saint?" Arlena's sly giggle blew a gasket in his brain. He wanted to shake her, but she would probably mistake it for foreplay.

Bilal's jaw clenched. "By no means am I a saint. I'm a full-grown, red-blooded man with the utmost appreciation for a beautiful woman. But I like my women sexy and subtle."

Arlena rolled her eyes and flipped a red-tipped hand in his direction. "You need to stop acting like you're too good. Why would you turn down something that will have you blowing up my cell and banging on my door at midnight? Because that day will come, and you know it."

Bilal turned to her with a hard, dark stare. "Arlena, cut the bull. If I wanted you, I would have had you already." His mouth twisted into a mocking smile. "Oh, and about Grandma? She's everything I've ever wanted in a woman. Who knows, when you grow up, maybe you'll be just like her."

☙

Bilal pulled into the circular driveway on Carroll Avenue. Bounding up the steps, this time he could care less about the planters on his sister's porch. And neither could the girls. The screen door burst open. Kamla and Kamilah streaked out of the house, latched themselves onto each of his knees, and sounded out a duet. "Unca B, you came back!"

Grinning down at his wriggling nieces, Bilal placed one large hand on top of each curly head. "Didn't I promise?"

Zahirah stood behind them, looking down at her children and back up at her brother. He couldn't read her mind, but knowing Zahirah, she had a boatload of questions.

"I'll explain later," he told her. "I've got another promise to keep this afternoon, and it won't wait."

It was if a great weight had been removed from her chest, allowing her to breathe deeply and lay down the armor she'd placed around her heart. While the girls resumed their attempts to tame the resistant wild grass, Bilal and Ayo sat next to each other at the kitchen table. The adults could see and hear the children, but the girls couldn't see Ayo's hand held to Bilal's mouth while his lips brushed the softness of her palm.

"I didn't expect to see you sitting in the same place," he murmured against her skin.

"Well, you said don't move. And from the look on your face when you stormed out of here, I didn't dare," Ayo teased. She laughed gently, letting out as much of her joy as she dared. Inside, she was giddy. She wanted to throw up both arms and celebrate. She was his woman. And he cared enough to make sure there was no mistake in her mind. Actually, Ayo felt sorry for the woman she now knew as Arlena. To be on the receiving end of that towering rage was definitely not a good thing. Ayo wondered—was he as passionate in bed? This time she did laugh out loud. What was it that Magda said—from famine to feast? But what she heard next stopped her erotic wandering in its tracks.

"I didn't finish telling you about my conversation with Mama. After she told my father what she thought of his bad behavior, she reminded him that when the Prophet Muhammad married Khadijah, she was fifteen years his senior."

Married? For Ayo, every sound in the house faded to background except the words from Bilal's mouth.

"Dad told her that was then and this is now. He knows just how much I want children. He's afraid that if I make my life with an older woman, odds are it won't happen. What he fails to realize is that it's none of his business." Bilal shook his head again. "My father has trouble with boundaries."

Ayo gave no thought to his father's issues. Bilal's words captured all her attention, each one more astounding that the other. Make his life? Children? That meant marriage for her, and she'd bet any amount of money it meant the same for Bilal. Where was this conversation going? Where was the relationship headed?

"Well, what—"

Bilal leaned forward and gently pressed his hand over her lips. "Let me finish. I need to say this, once and for all, I hope. In the best of relationships, people disagree and sometimes they argue, but I don't want Islam to be the foundation for every one we have." He laid a warm hand on her cheek and smoothed back the twists that had fallen free from her upswept crown. He cupped her chin, raising her face to look deeply into her eyes. This time his tone was less than a lecture, and more like a soft caress.

"And here's what I need from you. I need you to believe in me and what I feel for you. Hear me out before you jump all over me. And most of all, understand that I will never fail to defend or protect you. Never. I'm a Muslim, but I'm also the man that cares for you deeply. You have to figure out which one is more important."

Ayo's pent-up tears flowed freely. Her bravado had been a shaky fence that was no guard at all against her true feelings for this man. Two wet splotches appeared on the sides of his shirt where she pressed her face. She looked up at him through spiky, waterlogged lashes.

"I'm so sorry," she sobbed. "I jumped to so many conclusions. Before you took me to meet your parents, I thought you would have already been asked and answered the usual questions—you know, 'how old is she, how many husbands has she had? Does she have a pack of bad kids'?" Ayo's laugh quivered. "I just assumed that you told them ahead of time. But I shouldn't have taken it out on you." Ayo sighed deeply. "You were right about me. I've been by myself for a long time. I need to remember that life does not revolve around Ayo Montgomery."

"Mine could." Ayo stared up into his clear brown eyes. Her mouth opened but no words came out; the Mansfield gift for a swift comeback had utterly failed her. Instead she let him hold her tight against the strong beat of his heart. "You hear me?" He rubbed his cheek against the softness of her hair. "You can count on it. And you can always count on me." With one hand, Bilal tilted her damp face up to meet his smile. "Are we cool now? Are we back to being Bilal and Ayo?"

"Oh, yes," she sniffled. "I was so miserable that night. I didn't get to sleep until after midnight and when I woke up at four am, I felt like I'd slept in a sandstorm with my eyes wide open." She didn't tell him about the ice-cream overdose; even now, it was too nasty to recall.

Elation surged through Ayo, a joy so profound it was almost physical. The honeymoon phase was officially over. The journey to the sweet and steady part of their relationship had just begun.

Ayo hadn't noticed it until Bilal pointed to the pink backpack. "Hold on a second. I think have something in here for you." When he bent over to withdraw a tin of Queen of Heart's Tea, Bilal's hair parted, and Ayo let out a shriek of laughter.

"What's so funny?" He leaned half way up to peer at her. The outburst brought a quizzical smile to his face.

"This is too much, even for a man as progressive as you," she sputtered, pointing at his unbound hair.

Bilal's confusion deepened. "What are you talking about?" He stuck one hand in the back of his head, bringing a handful of hair around to rest on his shoulder along with two pink butterfly barrettes that had been nesting in the coils. "They must have done it while we were stuck in traffic! My hair is so thick I didn't even feel it. What will they do next?" He turned and bent his head to look outside through the kitchen window. Kamla and Kamilah were seated at the table, engaged in an animated conversation with their dolls. They spoke to the brown-skinned figures and turned the doll's response into a high-pitched version of their own voices. He chuckled again. "You never know with those two, as you can tell from today's road trip. And a trip it was," he added, "literally and figuratively."

"No kidding," Ayo chuckled, shaking her head.

He turned, watching the girls run toward the house. "Look at them," he spoke tenderly. "*Insha'Allah*, I look forward to the day when I become a father and have my own. But I'll have to be a husband first."

It was the second time he hinted at a more permanent union. He turned away from the window to gaze intently at Ayo. "In Islam, it's said that when a man marries, he has fulfilled half of his religion." She took his words in stunned silence. From believing they were over to hearing the word "marriage" and its implications, not once, but twice. "The Qur'an describes a husband and wife as garments for each other–protection, comfort and warmth." His lips curved. "Sounds pretty good; I can't think of a better definition. Can you?"

Ayo took it all in stunned silence. Could their relationship eventually lead to marriage? And a child? For Ayo, the sweet longing ache for another child had never really left her. After Kedar's birth, motherhood was still unfinished business, but when her husband died, she tucked away the desire in the farthest corner of her heart. She didn't want the baby-mama life, even if the man was loving and responsible. If she cared for a man enough to have his child, he would have to be her husband, not her live-in lover. Since there had been no husband-worthy candidates, Ayo put that urge away for good, but now? She could still have a child with a couple of years to spare. Her mother was two months shy of forty-five when Ayo was born. Aside from her screwy periods, she was in excellent health. She had to be. Every doctor she'd seen found nothing wrong.

Their attention turned to the kitchen door that banged shut behind Kamla and Kamilah. Both girls stood in front of Bilal and patted his knees.

"Unca B, Unca B! It's time to eat. We're hungry!"

"Okay, little ones." Bilal's grasp swallowed up the twins tiny hands. His eyes shone down softly on the children he proclaimed to be the most precious little people in the world. Until his own, Ayo thought.

"I promised you, and we'll do it."

Kamilah turned, sweeping Ayo in her beseeching gaze. "Miss Ayo, you wanna come too?"

He turned to Ayo. He answered the question in her eyes with a smile. "It's still Ramadan, but children don't fast until they're past puberty. And I'm happy to see that you even noticed."

The day was suddenly so beautiful, Ayo itched to drop everything and jump in the car with them. Instead, she gestured behind her to the soap kitchen where a counter full of jars waited to be filled.

"I wish I could," she said sighing, "but I started a new project this morning. The jars have to be filled soon or my wonderful concoction will have to be melted and mixed again." She bent to smile and gently touched the tip of each girl's nose. "Can I get each of you to eat a spoonful for me?"

Their little heads bobbed up and down. "Yes, Miss Ayo!" Bilal smiled down at them and handed a pink and purple bag to each twin. "Okay, ladies, now wait for us at the front door. Not on the porch, but at the front door, okay?" He pronounced each word in the new, no-nonsense voice they'd never heard until today.

Kamla and Kamilah blinked. "Okay, Unca B," they chimed softly before darting down the hall, dragging their packs in one hand and clutching the dolls in the other.

Before he and Ayo walked to the front, Bilal pulled her to him again. This time his voice was soft and husky. "And now for you," he murmured, "Ramadan ends in a couple of days. Will you have dinner with me at my house? I've told you how I feel. Now I want to show you."

Chapter 9
❧

Bilal grabbed at his chest, crushing the smooth front of his shirt into a crumpled ball. His neck bent back, causing coils of hair to fall around his shoulders. His other arm dangled like the limb of dismembered puppet.

"B, what's wrong?" Zahirah dropped the jar and rushed over to grab her brother. Pungent yellow powder spilled across the tiled floor.

"This is the big one Zahirah! Don't you remember Fred Sanford?" He grabbed a dishtowel from the counter, waving it from his hand like a flag of surrender.

"Fool, I ought to slap you right here in this kitchen," she gasped, leaning both hands on the counter. "He was having a heart attack, not a love Jones! And with that rag over your head, you look like one of those sweaty, wild-eyed TV preachers!" Zahirah glared at him and rolled her eyes, but her short-lived annoyance ended in a spurt of laughter. Today her dark brown hair had been swept into a French roll. A white chef's apron covered her oversized red shirt and blue jeans. Both hands were covered with garlic, onion and cumin, and stained yellow from curry.

"You're lucky my girls aren't here. They'd never let you get away with it! How come you didn't bring them?"

"They're with Kalil. He's home today." A droll smile creased her face. "And I'll bet he's letting them get away with everything they can think of, or they've tied him to a chair and taped his mouth shut."

"Payback time, huh?" He gave her an affectionate hip nudge. "They're just following in your footsteps. Remember the time Dad had to climb up to the tree house and bring us down when we were about to go Tarzan on him?"

Zahirah giggled and Bilal pointed at her, raising both eyebrows. "Uh, huh, I see you do remember."

"I give," she chuckled. "But even though my little ones don't stop whirling and turning until they drop in their tiny tracks, I love them so much. I do remember what life was like without them, but now that they're here, Kalil and I can't imagine anything else. You just wait..." Her voice trailed off.

An indulgent smile transformed Bilal's face. "I can't," he whispered. "And tonight might be the first step."

"Wow, B! Already?"

"You know I'm crazy about her. And I sure wouldn't ask you to do all this for an ordinary date." He pointed to the pots simmering on all four burners, full of the hot, spicy foods he knew Ayo loved. The dense, warm aroma of curry hung in the air.

"I love to see you happy. You've been grinning since you got home. And speaking of home, I'm out." Zahirah gathered up her scattered spices and seasonings and placed them in a portable wicker rack. "I'll be back for my pot sometime this week. Since it can't go in the microwave, I know you don't know what to do with it," she teased.

"But I know who will." His eyes twinkled. "She's a boss with the pots and pans." At the door, they kissed each other's cheeks. "As-Salaam-Alaikum, B. I'll see you later. Have a wonderful evening, my bro."

"Salaam, Zahirah. I will. And thanks for helping me make it happen."

"You're welcome, and you owe me." She pointed her finger at his chest, winked and was out of the door.

ॐ

And as often as she'd seen the classic film, it still held her captive. No raw, graphic video could compare to the sleek sensuality of the scene—Carmen Jones perched on a chair with one long caramel leg extended while her lover painted all ten of her perfect toes. A heavy warmth pooled between her thighs and raced upwards, sending an erotic message to every nerve in her body. Before, when Ayo ached for man's touch, she let the feeling rise and fall like a sudden fever that spiked and broke. But tonight the drought would be officially over. She sighed, enjoying the sensation of cool goose bumps on her skin meeting the heat between her legs, delighting in the feel of the pale lavender silk and lace against her skin.

It was part of the special lingerie that she collected. Each time she bought a set, she laughed at her inability to resist, saying they were made with a man in mind. She'd never worn any of them, regarding the lacy silk as collections, just like her seashells and glassware. On one shopping trip when she bought seven sets in shades from pale purple to midnight black, Justine predicted, "One of these days you'll find a man who'll make you want to wear a new set everyday." Today she took them out of hiding, ready to put them to the good use for which they were intended.

Ayo smoothed her hand over the surface of her bed. She wouldn't see it until some time the next day, if then. She snorted, remembering Arlena's boast. Liar. I'm the one who'll keep him in bed until the next morning. Selecting an extra set of underwear, she rolled them into a ball that fit tight in the bottom of the purse. On top, she placed a small folding toothbrush. Her lips parted in anticipation. It was all she needed.

෧

Upstairs Bilal turned to the transformation of his bedroom. He wanted Ayo to see his family's pictures—a photo of his parents on their wedding day, and one of them in Nation of Islam when instead of Abdul-Salaam, their last name had been X. And another of Latif and Adilah, dressed in white robes, on their pilgrimage to Mecca. Then there were pictures of him and Zahirah as children and at their graduations from high school and college. And of course, the two little girls held more than their share of space. But that could wait; they'd have plenty of time. The blood ran warmer in his body. What he wanted more than anything was to bring her to his bed, for her to feel in the flesh what he held in his heart.

When he and the room were ready, Bilal opened the doors to the bedroom deck. A band of pale gray-blue smudged the edges of the golden day. It was almost time. He punched in Ayo's number. When she didn't pick up, he left a message. "This is your humble servant and very expectant host," he whispered. "And I'm yours until the very end. It's almost dusk, baby. I'll be there soon."

The blood ran even warmer in his body as he imagined her sensual laughter when she heard his message and the promise it offered. Before he grabbed his keys and let anticipation propel him out of the door, he stacked the CDs with the eclectic mix of music he had heard in her house. As the night progressed, the tempo would slow, from the heart-thumping bass of Gregory Isaac's *Rumors* to the soaring, sensuous saxophone of Gato Barbieri's *Europa*.

Outside, Bilal looked up at the sky. Right on time. He'd be there at sunset, with the Chevy's top down, playing a song she loved.

෧

On Manchester Road, the last layer of gold had shrunk to nearly nothing. Instead of striding to meet her, he leaned on the open car door and etched the moment in his mind. Ayo stood framed by the porch light's glow, in pale purple, a color that wherever and on what ever he saw it, always brought her to his mind. The dress wrapped in front and appeared so soft that one touch might melt it from her body. He branded the sight in his brain so that years later, when his locks were sprinkled with gray and her hair became a silver cloud, they would sit together on this same porch, holding hands and rocking together with the memory of this night still fresh and alive in their minds.

"Hey," Bilal whispered, finally walking towards her, with nothing but his woman in his sight. This time tomorrow, she'd be his in every way. And he would certainly be hers. He held out his arms for Ayo to step inside the circle. "I keep saying it, but every time I say it, it's true," he whispered. Sliding his fingers through her hair, he leaned down for a kiss that was a scorching preview of what would come later. "You're even more beautiful." Wrapping one arm around her shoulders, Bilal held Ayo close to his side on their walk to the car. The Chevy was his special occasion car, and nothing to date was more special than this night.

Inside, notes from a soaring trumpet stroked her ear. "*Stardust!*" she exclaimed. "You remembered!" Ayo sighed, leaning back against the soft seats. Bilal drove with one hand on the wheel and the other covering her hand. Earlier, he'd promised her the perfect evening. It was that already. He was everything she convinced herself she'd never find again. "I was about to ask how you could improve on perfection, but I take that back."

He took his eyes briefly off of traffic. What he wanted to say required looking into her eyes. His voice was soft and husky with anticipation. "I promise that by the end of the night, we'll have answered that question for each other. More than once, my sweetheart. And believe me; perfection will have a new definition." Bilal raised her hands to his lips, but the brief kiss was interrupted.

"Now see, that's what I'm talking about. Go on girl!" The two women who grinned and waved at them could have been a few years older than Ayo. One wore a stylish headwrap and long silver earrings. Her companion's silver locks were in the infant stage, standing up from her head like nubby horns. "If I had a fine man who courted me like that I'd wake up smiling every day!"

Ayo waved at the women, threw back her head and laughed. "Tonight, the entire world is cheering for us!" With such a beautiful beginning, she'd wake up smiling every day from now on. And not just from the sex, but from all that made Bilal a man more than worth the wait. For him, she'd wait eighteen more years.

Before they turned onto the street that looked like a slice of the country set down in the city, she didn't know what to expect. He'd told her that his house was a work in progress, but even its present state, the stately Victorian took her breath. "Look at this yard!" she exclaimed. "You must feel like urban landed gentry back here. Got any horses or fox hounds in the back?" Ayo teased. "But seriously, it's beautiful."

Bilal's arm still circled her shoulders. "It wasn't when I found it," he told her on the walk up the steps. "It was a dilapidated, fire sale property. But it was structurally sound and I knew I could bring it back to life."

"You're a miracle worker, that's for sure. You should name it Phoenix."

Ayo's admiring words settled over him. "Thanks." His lips curved up in a slow smile as warm as her praise. "Glad you like it. The owners hoped to open a bed and breakfast, but they abandoned the plan along with the house. On top of that, they owed a boatload of taxes. They were so relieved to get rid of it that they accepted my offer on the spot—no negotiating, no haggling—just took the money and ran." Bilal chuckled. "When I handed them the cashier's check, I thought they were going to break out in a happy dance right there in the lawyer's office."

Bilal's outdoor furniture was nothing like she had ever seen. Ayo ran a hand along an updated version of the famed Ashanti stool. "Did you make these pieces?"

"I did," he bowed modestly.

Inside, they walked through three bare rooms painted in a shade that reminded her of fine beach sand. Details of the gleaming hardwood floors, crown molding and brickwork surrounding the fireplace and mantle stood out even more in the stark, immaculate emptiness.

"Even unfinished, this house could be the star of one of those before and after shows."

"You're going to make my head swell," Bilal chuckled. "It still needs a lot of work. I've made four of the rooms livable. I plan to work room by room and by next summer this old girl will be an even grander version of her original self."

A small room on the eastern side of the house struck her by its austere beauty. The walls were a shade darker than those of the living room. Facing each other on separate walls, poster-sized silver frames held documents written in decorative Arabic script. A rectangular window took up another wall and looked out over a small pond. She recognized the Qu'ran resting on an ornate holder. The only other object in the immaculate room was a cream and red patterned rug.

Bilal stood beside her in quiet pride. "This is my prayer room. It's bare for a reason. Here, my only focus is on Allah."

"Which is Arabic for God," Ayo smiled, recalling her crash course on Islam. "Since my series of both feet-in-mouth, I've kept up my reading."

"Very good!" Bilal smiled broadly. "And since you've passed with flying colors, let's feast in celebration."

Arm-in-arm, they moved farther into the house. Bilal paused in front of white-curtained French doors and bowed with a flourish.

"Madam, your table is ready."

Ayo exhaled slowly. "Bilal," she breathed. The room rivaled any intimate bistro in which she'd ever dined. Two floor lamps stood at opposite corners. Tiny beads at the edges of their antique gold-fringed shades sent shimmering pools of light over the table set for two, where on the ivory tablecloth, Bilal had set cream colored plates over gold chargers. Adinkra-styled rings held their matching napkins and two thin flutes were ready for chilled sparkling cider. In the center, a clear glass cylinder held bamboo stalks and seashells. On the sideboard Dakota Staton's *Moondance* wafted from the Bose Wave player. The perfect song; it *was* a marvelous night.

Standing beside her, she heard him let out the breath he'd been holding. "I'm glad you like it."

"I love it," she replied simply. When she was seated, he drew her napkin from the ornate gold ring and placed it in her lap with a flourish worthy of a five-star server.

"Please let me help you with something." Ayo waved her hand at the exquisite table. "You've done so much already."

"Nope. Not tonight. But I can't take credit for everything. The meal is all Zahirah's doing."

"Oh, that's why I smell curry! There must be some Indian dishes back there!"

"There are. And I'll be right back so we can do it justice." Ayo twisted in her seat, allowing her gaze to follow him. Bilal was the blue-plate special and then some—masculine and gentle, tender and strong. He was a fascinating contrast—completely male but with a deep appreciation of fine craftsmanship and beauty. Each time she saw him, he revealed another layer—his love of both the old and new, his love of order and beauty and how much he cared for her. Here in his own element, it all came together.

The thoughts were still flooding her mind when he brought back two plates with a curried dish, rice pilaf, and a flat pancake-shaped bread. Ayo leaned over her plate and dug in, savoring the taste of curry and cumin, licking the spicy yellow gravy from her fingers with no sense of pretense.

When only a smear of curry and a few scraps of flat bread were left, they shared parsley and lemon juice to cleanse their mouths of the pungent spices. For dessert, Bilal brought out sherbet set in a scooped-out frozen pineapple. "At least I can claim a hand in dessert." Ayo giggled when he swaggered to the table and puffed out his chest. "I did this all by myself. I can wield a mean ice-cream scoop!"

"Keep this up and you'll have your own show on the Food Network," Ayo teased. Still laughing, she dipped her fingers into the small bowl of warm lemon-scented water in front of her. Before she withdrew them, Bilal grasped her hand.

"Here, let me." His voice softened. Stroking each finger with the warm moist cloth, he worked up and down their length, pausing to give special attention to the skin that joined her thumb and forefinger.

Her lids fluttered. "That's very nice," she whispered. "Do I get seconds?"

"Of anything you want." He gave the same bone-melting attention to her other hand, continuing farther up her arm, stroking from her palm to the bend of her elbow with the ball of his thumb.

She released the sigh that had been building since his first touch. "Oh..."

"Was everything to your liking?" he whispered.

"Everything."

"Is there anything else you'd like?"

Ayo tilted her face up to his. She couldn't pull her gaze away from the eyes that mesmerized her the first day she saw them flash, first in anger and then desire. It was what they both wanted, but she spoke the words out loud. "You. That's all what I want."

Suddenly, there was no time for the pale yellow sherbet that dripped over the edge of the pineapple and onto the linen cloth. Neither of them noticed. With his eyes still locked with hers, Bilal stood, bent over and brushed his lips slowly, back and forth across Ayo's half-opened mouth. Her voice caught between a sigh and a moan. She stood to meet him and leaned into the kiss.

They broke apart, rounded the table and stood face-to-face. How they got there was a blur, but at the bottom of the stairs Bilal stopped, pulling her to him and tracing the line of her lips with the tip of his tongue. Her mouth opened and she captured it, drawing it in, winding it around her own. Bilal tugged on the tie, her dress fell open. He bent his head to kiss the small pulse throbbing wildly in the hollow of her throat. His locks brushed against her bare skin. Ayo's nipples puckered, aching to push through the lacy fabric. He obliged their yearning with his fingers, grazing the tips into rigid peaks until Ayo sank back against his arm. Bilal traced a slow moving line of kisses from under her chin down through the center of her cleavage.

"Please," she moaned.

Wrapped together, they stumbled like intoxicated dancers, carefully picking their way up the stairs, leaving her dress in a puddle of silk at the bottom.

She stood near naked before him. Bilal's eyes devoured her, scooping her up from under hooded lids. He branded her with kisses, slow and sweet, hot and urgent. Sliding one lean leg between her parted thighs, he pressed against her slowly, circling side to side. They rocked back and forth against each other, enjoying the hot friction of flesh against fabric. Pleasure seeped through her pores, molding her face into a soft mask of desire. She trembled, reaching behind her neck.

"Leave the necklace," he whispered. "It's beautiful against your skin."

Ayo reached down and grasped the tail of his shirt, pulling it over his head. Her tongue found his nipples, and Bilal groaned—primitive and male. The sound triggered an erotic reaction. With her forefinger, she stroked the thin strip of hair that began just under his navel. Gripping the drawstring waistband, Ayo pulled and Bilal's pants slid onto the floor. Almost reverently, she took him in her hands, stroking slowly, exploring from root to tip, and feeling the tremors that shook him like small electric shocks.

Bilal gasped, pulling Ayo down on his bed. He slid his hand under the pillow, and tearing open the packet, slipped on protection. He teased her, working his hips in a slow, sinuous motion, sliding himself over her slick center until she lifted her hips, sheathing him in her creamy heat. Her breath caught; she called his name, but there was no pleasure in the cry that tore from her throat. Instead, pain like a lead-filled balloon swelled up inside her. Instinctively she pulled back.

Bilal heard her pleasure give way to agony. "Baby, what's wrong?" Alarm emptied every ounce of passion from his voice. "Am I hurting you?" Bilal panted against her damp temple. Gently, slowly, he withdrew from her warmth, leaving his senses in a state of agonized suspension, and Ayo poised between desire and pain. She tried to speak, but could only manage a pain-filled murmur. Alarm clanged its way into Ayo's thoughts. At her age, things went south and loosened up instead of clamping up like a vise. And the pain? It was worse than the time she lost her virginity.

Bilal gathered her close. "It's okay, sweetheart," he murmured against her damp cheek. "I've been waiting a long time to please you. I can wait a little longer."

Against him, Ayo's hair brushed against the pillow and his chest. When he withdrew, the pain receded. Nothing was going to turn this night into anything but joyful. "Oh, no," she murmured with a low, sensual, purr. "We'll just have to be creative. And I know already that you have good hands."

Bilal leaned up on one elbow, obviously eager to prove her right. His tongue darted around her ear while one warm open hand traveled slowly down the center of her body. "Shall I show you?"

Her back arched. "Oh, please do." Ayo opened like a flower to the first sun of summer.

He teased her, sliding his fingers over her slick center, bathing them in her molten, silky moisture. Ayo moaned and whimpered, thrashing her head from side to side. Her warm breath came quicker against his ear. Through a half-opened mouth, she stuttered his name, gasping as she shuddered against him.

Slowly catching her breath, Ayo leaned over him. Her hair brushed his chest and formed a curtain around his lower belly. "Your turn..."

Passion made him beautiful. Bilal's lips parted. A deep moan dragged from inside him. Tremors worked their way through his body, until a great gasp carried her name out into the moonlit room.

At three o'clock that morning, before they finally drifted into sleep, Ayo murmured against his chest. "You finished that conversation so very well. You certainly have a way with words."

Bilal entwined his hand in her hair. "You too, baby. But you know what I love even more? Your expertise with call and response." He laughed, sending a soft sexy chuckle out into the room.

Before dawn, Ayo shifted until she found the space that was hers—the place on his chest that fit her cheek perfectly. She inhaled sandalwood mixed with her perfume and the scent of sex on their skin. And he was creative, they both were. It was born from the heady mix of tenderness and raw desire they felt for each other. But how long would it last? What would happen when instead of easing gently, he wanted to thrust deep inside her? What would happen in the passion-drenched heat of the moment when he wanted her the old-fashioned way?

Her apprehension was blown away by his lips circling her ear.

"Remember the night we resolved our differences?" It came out in a soft, moaning stutter.

"You mean the night you realized that to resist me was futile?"

Ayo laid a gentle slap on his chest. "Cut the arrogance," she giggled. "Actually, you're right."

"I know it. And I knew that seeing you was a divine sign that we would be together. But what about that night?"

"After you left, and I was caught up in the rapture, I suddenly wondered if since you were Muslim you were also celibate."

Bilal's laughter blew into her hair.

"No, baby, I wasn't. I'm not."

No lie, Ayo chuckled to herself.

"But why would you think that?"

Ayo snuggled closer. "Autopilot. The same reason I came to my other half-baked conclusions."

Bilal shifted, leaning up on one elbow. She was taken aback by his sudden serious expression. "But I have to admit there was a time when I forgot my religion and my home training." His mouth turned down. "When I left home for college, for half that first year, I ran through women like a crazy man. Somebody described it as leaving them behind like crumpled gold foil in an empty box of chocolates." Bilal's gaze didn't waver. "But I began to feel ashamed of myself. It didn't take long for the dog days to be over."

Ayo blinked. Bilal's admission came as a surprise.

The intensity in his gaze softened. "Still like me?"

Ayo entwined her fingers with his. "More than ever. And one more thing. Kedar will be home next weekend. He's been telling me for years that I should get a life, so now that I've taken his advice, he'll be so happy. I can't wait for you to meet him."

And before that, I've got to go to a doctor and as Magda says, make sure my goods still work.

Chapter 10

❧

*S*oca pulsed through the bright, sunlit kitchen. It was the music of sun, sweat and rum. Ayo glanced outside and smiled. Two fat pumpkins perched on either side of the front porch, along with pots of marigolds and mums. An orange, gold, and green porch flag had replaced the pink-and-purple banner of summer. Two months ago, the tree had been as bright as green could get. Now it flamed like the Biblical burning bush. A few crisp leaves blew across the back yard. Although it was the opening act for winter and her least favorite time of year, Ayo had to admit that the scarlet and gold of fall was indeed beautiful, especially when the temperature was that perfect blend of short-sleeved days and cardigan sweater evenings.

The music formed a perfect backdrop to the scents of onion, garlic, thyme, and chive, the flavor foundation of a classic West Indian meal. Along with her waist, the ends of her calf-length burnt orange skirt moved in a sinuous wave, in time to the blaring horns. With one hand high in the air, she shuffled forward to the distinctive up and down beat. "This is called chipping," she grinned. Then Ayo bent forward, stuck out her butt, and wound her body down to the floor and up again. "And this is called winin'. But you haven't seen a real wine until you've been on the road on Carnival Tuesday! Those video girls ain't got nothing on a Trini sister!"

Bilal urged her on, clapping in time to the music and her moves. Glancing sideways at her rolling rear, he gave her a broad grin. "Or you either, baby."

"Oh no, I'm an oldie now," Ayo chuckled.

"But *such* a goodie!" Bilal exclaimed, kissing the tips of his fingers and flinging them in her direction.

"Glad you think so," she winked seductively. Then Ayo leaned up on tip-toes to kiss him. "I am so excited! I can't wait to see Kedar and for you two to meet. I'm just waiting for him to call me from the airport so I can pick him up." She twisted her mouth into a wry grin. "Of course, I always do better with the picking up than the taking back."

Ayo rinsed a basket of okra and wiped her hands on the towel stuck inside waistband of her skirt. "The food should be ready by then, and we can sit down and eat. I know he'll be starving. That boy should invest in a grocery store, as much food as he wolfs down." She caught Bilal's indulgent smile and stopped to catch her breath. He was used to her loving, animated descriptions of Kedar. Finally, the two men who meant everything to her would be under her roof, sharing a delicious home-cooked meal and with Kedar at the table, plenty of laughter was guaranteed. Ayo was happy. If the day got any more perfect she would explode into a million pieces of white hot joy.

Bilal stood over the remnants of chopped onion and garlic, scraping them into a small plastic bag. The tip of his tongue touched the center of his top lip. Today his hair was pulled back by a navy bandana. A short-sleeved, navy T-shirt capped the muscles in his arms. She loved him in blue—navy, teal, ice blue or turquoise—it had been far down on her list of favorite colors until she saw its variations on his milk chocolate skin. Ayo's lids dipped at half-mast; she never got tired of looking at him. Her erotic wandering came to a temporary end when Bilal pointed his knife to the bunch of dark greens topped with broad, veined leaves. "What's this called again?"

"Dasheen, but, I call it Trini collard greens," Ayo laughed. "It's used to make callaloo. After it's cooked down with okra and coconut milk, a lot of people use a swizzle stick to blend it together. Kedar's great-aunt Aunt Elvie showed me how to do it, but I, on the other hand, am more adept with the modern convenience of an electric blender." Ayo lifted the top off of a pot; the fragrant steam of good food cooking rose into her face. "Kedar loves his with crab, but since I forgot to pick it up, his second choice is pigtail." She looked up quickly. "But don't worry; I have a no-pork version for you."

"If it's as good as those greens with smoked turkey you made the other day, I can't wait." Ayo basked in Bilal's smile of appreciation; he and Kedar were neck-in-neck when it came to loving her cooking.

He drew her into a brief hug, but before his arm could slide from her shoulders, footsteps skidded to a stop behind them. Kedar stood framed in the kitchen door, gaping as if he'd stumbled upon a crime in progress. His hackles rose like a wolf whose territory had been invaded by a roving, renegade male.

"Oh my goodness, there you are!" Ayo dropped the towel, and clapped her hands, running over to pull Kedar into her embrace. "Why didn't you call me from the airport? But never mind, I'm just so glad to see you." Ayo's joy blinded her to Kedar's expression of shock and disgust.

Kedar's greetings had always been physical and boisterous. This time, instead of grabbing her up and swinging her around, he stood stiff in her arms. When she released him, Ayo frowned and pulled back. Kedar's gaze strafed Bilal, sizing him up and down with open hostility. *Oh, no, not you, too,* she groaned inwardly.

She forged ahead anyway, forcing a smile that felt more like a grimace, trying to ignore the waves of loathing that radiated from her son.

"Kedar, this is Bilal Abdul-Salaam." Her gaze swung between Kedar's scowl and Bilal's cool, impassive stare. The beginning of a major league headache throbbed over her right eye.

"I'm glad to finally meet you, Kedar." Bilal extended his hand, but the smile didn't reach his eyes.

"Hey." Kedar's response slid off the greeting like beads of water on wax. His fingers grazed the tips of Bilal's extended hand.

"Kedar!" Ayo felt heat rise in her face. *Has he gone completely crazy?* She felt like sinking through the floor or turning Kedar across her knee.

Kedar gazed at them with as much insolence as he dared. *Oh, no you don't.* She stared back, winning the contest of wills. Still bristling, he dredged up a revised, but no more enthusiastic greeting.

"Uh, hello." Kedar ground out the words through clenched teeth.

Ayo narrowed her eyes. Instead of a reprimand, she tried another tactic, hoping that if she ignored his sullen attitude, it would die from lack of attention. Another forced, bright smile replaced her grim expression. She gestured to the spread of his favorite foods. Maybe the sight would soften him.

"Kedar, the callaloo isn't done yet, but there's stewed chicken, rice, and macaroni pie. All your favorites. And I know you must be hungry because all they give you on the plane is some crackers and fake cheese." The rush of words sounded artificial and desperate, even to her own ears. She turned to see Bilal step back, out of the way of her futile efforts to coax Kedar out of his foul attitude.

"Uh-uh, not now. I'm tired." Without a backward glance or a word to Bilal, he bolted from the room. From upstairs hey heard the door slam like a battering ram. Ayo sagged against the sink.

"I can't believe Kedar! *My* son showing that kind of disrespect?" Ayo pushed herself away from the stainless steel edge of the sink. A deep frown wrinkled her forehead "I'm going up there." Ayo turned to follow Kedar but Bilal leaned forward and caught her arm.

"No, baby, leave him alone. Right now, it's best that I leave and when he's calmed down, you need to have a talk with him. Hearing about me was one thing, but seeing us together was a shock for him, especially for the first time to be with my arm around you. If you stay down here or go up and try to make him come down, either way he'll think you're choosing me over him. And you can't do that."

She shook her head. "No, Bilal. He's my child and he knows I love him. He'll come around."

Showing a slight frown, Bilal shook his head. "Ayo, I really don't think so, at least right now. But I know you have to try, so go ahead. I'll wait until you come down, just to make sure you're all right. Then I'll go. You need some time alone with your son. It's not the time for me to be here."

Bilal kept his tone neutral, but inside he seethed. It was the last thing he wanted or even expected, but his dislike of Kedar was swift and visceral. The stricken look on Ayo's face made anything but a polite distance impossible, and only because Kedar was her son. Anybody else who caused her that much pain would have a world of hurt on their hands. He pulled out a kitchen chair and straddled it to wait for the outcome.

When Ayo got to Kedar's door, the commotion and cursing she heard hit her like a fist to the chest. She wasn't naïve; she knew kids cursed when their parents weren't around. But the venom behind Kedar's anger stopped her cold. Trembling, she turned and went back downstairs.

In the kitchen, Ayo turned a sad face to Bilal. "You were right. It would have been like throwing gasoline on flames to say anything to him now. He's up there slamming his closet door and cussing up a storm. Now I see what you meant about confronting your father. I didn't see it then, but I understand now." A soft sob escaped her lips.

Bilal pulled her close, not caring whether Kedar was in his room or staring from the doorway. Ayo needed his arms around her. "Don't worry, baby. I got you," he whispered against her temple. "The people we love can really try us sometimes. Both of us thought that because we're happy, everybody we loved would be happy for us. Give Kedar some time, Ayo. You've been all his for a long time." *But he'll have to get used to sharing.*

She rubbed his knuckles across her cheek. "And thanks for not saying 'I told you so.'"

"I'd never say such a thing; you know it's not like that with us." Bilal laid both hands on her shoulders. "But listen—call me or email me, because I want to know how you're doing. And if you need me, I'll be here before you can hit 'send.'" He looked in the direction of the hallway before quickly brushing his fingers under her chin. "You hear me?"

After she watched him turn off her street, Ayo trudged upstairs. Behind Kedar's closed door, Jack White's licks slid up and down the scale like liquid silver. She had to give it to the White boy—he knew his away around a blues guitar. Blues had been the second part of Kedar's musical education. Today, instead of the Mississippi Delta, Manchester Road was the blues capital, at least in Ayo's world. In place of a history lesson, Kedar was due for a lesson in real life.

She found him slouched across his bed, engrossed in the hard driving beat that matched his mood. His laptop stood open. Shifting scenes of Jacque Cousteau's legendary *Calypso* scrolled across the screen, followed by Thor Heyerdahl's *Kon-Tiki* and Jean Michel Cousteau's *Searcher*. Ayo blinked back tears, remembering a day in late summer. Over chips and salsa, he brought it into her room, grinning happily and showing her his latest ocean-themed screensaver. The sweet memory of that day pierced her heart; she couldn't let that closeness get away from them, for either of their sakes. She knocked on the doorjamb to get his attention.

"Can I come in?"

"Uh-huh." He tapped the volume icon and sat up. "So where's Bilal?" He spat out the name like a bad taste coating his tongue.

"He left to give you and I time to talk."

Kedar snorted. "He did, huh?"

Ayo tapped her foot. "Kedar, move over."

He slid his legs closer together. Ayo perched on the edge of the bed and looked him in the eye.

"I know you're upset by seeing Bilal with his arm around me. It's not how I intended for you two to meet." When Ayo reached for his hand, Kedar flinched and jerked it away.

Ayo inhaled a sharp breath. Leaning forward she gripped his chin. "Kedar, look at me when I'm talking to you! You might be an angry young man, but you're an angry young man in my house, and I'm still your mother!"

"Sorry, Mami," he mumbled, squirming against the headboard.

Ayo relaxed, breathing out some of her apprehension. Her hopes rose when he didn't pull away. "Now talk to me."

He lifted his head. "I know you told me that you were friends with a man and you wanted me to meet him, but I didn't know it was like that." Kedar cut his eyes at her. "He was touching you."

Bingo. The touch. *That's easy enough*, she smiled to herself. "Meaning?"

"Well, I never saw a man put his arm around you like that. I know the difference between a friendly hug and a man/woman hug."

"I'll bet you do," she teased.

Kedar's mouth tightened. "Stop, Mami. I'm not playing, okay? And he looks younger than you. I mean you don't look old, but—"

"Kedar, what does that have to do with anything?"

"Look, you know how some younger guys try to hook up with older women because—"

"Speaking from experience?" As soon as they left her mouth, Ayo wanted to take those words back.

Kedar's mouth hung open. "Mami!" He dropped his head in his hands. "I don't believe you! It's bad enough that I come here and see you all wrapped up with that dude."

Ayo reared back. Her eyes flashed, but this time she bit back her own hot retort.

"Okay, Kedar, I was just trying to lighten the mood, but since you want it like that, let's be for real—or keep it real, whatever it is you all say. Most people get back in the dating world after the loss of a partner. But unlike them, it took me years later and by surprise, to you as well as me. It was the last thing I expected, but here it is. And there's nothing wrong with that."

"Okay, but when you told me you were going out with the man who did your appraisal, I was kind of glad, until I saw him. Remember, I wasn't here the first time he came. So I expected he would be somebody like Cousin Buck or Uncle Nick."

Ayo wanted to pinch herself to keep from laughing. If she let one giggle slip out, the fragile bridge she was building would be broken.

"What in the world do you mean by that? Old and safe?"

"Dag, will you give me a break? Please?" Kedar stopped, looked and her and exhaled. When he spoke again, most of the aggravation had left his voice. "I know Cousin Buck and Uncle Nick still hold it down, but you know what I mean, a man closer to your age!"

"Is that a guarantee that a man wouldn't hurt me? And don't forget your father was a few years older—I was nineteen when I met him and twenty when we got married. Is that different? There were people who thought that he had no business marrying a "young girl." And on the flip side there were men who were always nudging him in the ribs about his 'young t'ing.' Now think about it; and I don't want an answer for me. I already have one. Think about an answer for yourself–just try to come up with something that makes sense."

"Okay, Mami, I hear you. I don't have to like it, but I want you to think about something. You haven't been out there for years. I see Bilal's type all over campus. It used to be the light-skinned pretty boys, then the dark bald brothers—now it's the good-looking brother with the long locks. They got women chasing them from sunup to sundown." A deep frown furrowed Kedar's forehead. Contempt crept back into his voice. "And what is he anyway—some wannabe Rasta?"

Ayo shut her eyes and heaved a deep sigh. One step forward, two steps back. This conversation was like pushing a boulder uphill. "No, Kedar, Bilal is Muslim."

"Oh Lord." Kedar mumbled. "Next thing he'll be selling bean pies on the front porch."

Her hand shot up. "Okay, Kedar, that's enough!"

He lifted his shoulders. "Whatever." Then Kedar sat up, trading insolence for a stern lecture. "And Mami, one more thing—I know we're not super rich, but we have this nice house and we live well. Dad left us well off and you have your own money. Don't let him get up in here and take advantage of you!"

Ayo wanted to burst out laughing. She bit the inside of her jaw to prevent a burst of startled laughter from spilling out. From Rasta to gigolo. What next?

"Let me ease your mind, Kedar. Bilal owns his own home. He works for himself and is quite good at it. He has more business than he can handle. Because of that, as you all say, the brother is paid. And instead of a pimped out ride and an MTV crib, he has invested well, hence, more loot. Are you feelin' me now?"

Kedar cocked his head and stared. Ayo knew he wanted to laugh at her use of slang, but at that moment, staying mad was more important.

"And this is both the first and last word—no matter who or what happens in my life, nothing will stop me from loving you more every day. That's how it's been and that's how it will always be. Even though you're grown now and our lives will change, no one can take your place in my heart. Don't you ever forget it."

Out of everything else she'd said, she hoped those words made the most difference. Kedar blinked; his expression softened and a little more of the tension loosened.

Ayo stood, holding out her hand to Kedar. Now that the air had been cleared, the weekend she looked forward to with such anticipation could begin. "Come on and get something to eat. You must be starving by now."

Kedar shook his head. "No thanks, not right now."

❧

"Man, your lady can burn! You got any more?" Fishing for scraps, Mark scrounged through a container that turned out to be as empty as his plate. "When I called to leave a message about the volunteer meeting, I didn't expect you to answer," he explained. "I thought you were supposed to be over at Ayo's house." Today Mark wore a faded

Wizards T-shirt. His runner's legs were encased in a pair of Hampton track pants circa 1982.

The two men sat watching the spectacular end of the day. Over the trees in Bilal's back yard, the sun trailed a wake of red flame on its way west. He stalked the porch, leaving his plate of food uneaten on the table beside his chair. His short laugh was anything but jovial. "You can have mine. I'm glad you enjoyed it, but it was supposed to be eaten over there instead of over here."

Mark looked up. "I know, man. Exactly what happened?"

"In a nutshell, Kedar showed up early and caught me with my arm around his mother."

"Oh, so he freaked, huh?"

"Freaked?" Bilal raked a hand through his hair. He barked out a short laugh, in spite of the unfortunate scene in Ayo's kitchen. "Man, he was ready to blow, but Ayo put that 'boy have you lost your mind' stare on him."

"Uh-oh," Mark bobbed his head. "I'm a grown man, but I'm still well-acquainted with that look."

Bilal continued the recap of Kedar's near meltdown. "Then he turned from hot to cold. He refused to eat that wonderful meal Ayo cooked just for him. All morning she was like a kid at Christmas, cooking and laughing. She couldn't wait to see him." Bilal's mouth twisted. He pressed his whole palm over the pulsing spot on his temple. "She was so upset—I hate the way he treated her! It wasn't my place to say anything, but man, I was close to giving that young brother a good piece of my mind." Bilal gritted his teeth. "Not for me, but for Ayo. Next time, son or not, all bets are off."

Mark looked up. "You're not playing, are you? I mean, you'd go up against her son?"

"Not physically, of course, but I'm not going to stand by and let anybody hurt her. I had to set my father straight the other day."

Mark's brows shot up. "You took on the big man?"

Bilal nodded and sat down hard on the canvas-upholstered King's chair. "I did, but I cooled off first, and waited a couple of days. I waited until he and Mama had made their last *salat* for the evening, because prayer is no time for confrontation. And then I told him he had cashed in his one and only ticket to disrespect Ayo. But right now, I wonder what's going on over there. The last thing I wanted was to cause a rift between Ayo and Kedar. She loves her son so much."

Mark nodded. "You know you've got something on your hands now, don't you? A man child is very protective of his mother. And if I know young men, his imagination went straight to the image of his mother in your bed. Probably sent him straight over the edge." His earring shook when he tilted his head. "No joke, B. At school, I've come across almost every kind of situation you can imagine in the life of a young brother. And Mama's new boyfriend is one of them."

Bilal exhaled a long, weary sigh. His leg jumped like a jackhammer.

"I believe you. You should have seen him! He looked like he was just itching to kick my ass." Bilal snorted. "You know what? If I didn't know better, I'd believe that he and my father got together and cooked up this little revolt."

Mark stood up and collected both of their plates. "Listen, B, I need to get back to that report. Since you fed me, the least I can do is put these in the sink. And look, bro—I know it's hard to deal with the people closest to you when they're wrong and strong. But this is the happiest I've seen you. Don't give her up."

"No way, man, no way. Kedar and my father will just have to get a grip."

After loading the dishwasher, Bilal went upstairs, looking for something to distract him from what might be happening on Manchester Road. Ayo and Kedar may have reached a truce, which is what he hoped. Or they might be in the midst of a heated argument, which is what he feared. His thoughts spiraled downward. She had been Kedar's mother longer than she had been his lover. Would she have to choose? And if so, at the end, which one of them would claim victory?

෫

It had been the worst three days in recent memory. The day before his return, Kedar tried to get an earlier flight back to Florida, but determined as he was, he was just as unwilling to pay the hundred dollar re-booking fee to change his ticket. Ayo was torn; she didn't want him to leave with this barrier between them, but she couldn't stand him being home and treating her like something stuck to the bottom of his shoe. That morning, she found him with the phone to his ear, on hold with a cab company instead of carrying his bag to the Sequoia.

"Kedar, what are you doing? You know I'm taking you to the airport."

"I can get a cab." Tossing the words over his shoulder, Kedar shifted the receiver to his other ear. Before he turned completely away, Ayo's arm snaked out like a bullwhip. She spun him around with a hand clamped hard on his shoulder. "Kedar Maurice Montgomery, put down that phone before I throw it in the street! You've got one minute left and I'm at fifty-nine seconds already!"

Ayo slammed her purse on the foyer table. The gold-framed hallway mirror rattled. Under it, a bundled stack of mail hit the floor like a brick. Kedar sprung back with both eyes bucked like a deer staring down the barrel of a shotgun. Stretching one arm behind him, Ayo jerked the door open, sending the pineapple knocker clattering against the wood. Her other hand rested in a balled fist on her hip. "What? You don't think I'll do it? Pick it up again and find out!"

"Dag, Mami!" Kedar blinked and jumped out of her way.

"Dag, my ass! I'm about to show you some 'dag'. More than you can handle!"

"Please, please just shut the door!" Kedar begged, staring out into the street and back to his mother. At that time of morning, the leaf-strewn street was quiet and empty, but Ayo didn't care who was driving by or looking in.

She covered the last bit of distance between them. Thrusting her face an inch away from his, she jabbed her forefinger in the center of his chest. Kedar stumbled backwards.

"Keep fooling with me, boy, and the Lord is the only thing that can help you! Now you listen—I put up with your nasty attitude, even when you acted like you were raised in the woods instead of in my house. But as of right now, your reign of terror is over!"

Kedar stood frozen to the floor, blinking rapidly and still staring at the raging woman who had taken over his mother's body. His gaze shifted from Ayo out the wide-open door to the street.

Ayo's face and her head pounded. She reached around him and slammed the door hard. She burst into tears and ran from the foyer, allowing three days worth of tears, hurt and anger to spill over, smearing her mascara and making wide wet tracks through her carefully applied foundation.

Kedar's hard facade cracked from the shock of her explosive anger, but it crumbled into dust at the sight of his mother falling apart in front of him. He ran to follow Ayo and dropped down beside her. He grabbed her, looking confused and ready to cry himself.

Mami, *please* stop crying." His words tumbled out over her tears. "Please! See what I mean? He was here only a minute and already he's come between us!"

"I don't recall him being the one playing the ass," Ayo retorted. "You handled that role all by yourself!" Tears and mascara had glued her lashes together in wet clumps. Both hands were smeared black and brown from the residue of eye makeup and foundation. Kedar pried the twisted tissue from her hand and dabbed at her face, leaving specks of white lint on her damp cheeks.

She was nauseous from the band of pain that squeezed her skull. A dark room and a warm bed was what she needed, but first they had to make things right between them. And that included taking him to the airport. Now, more than ever, that ritual had to be continued.

"Now listen to what I'm saying to you. And don't brush me off with a flip 'whatever.' No one will ever take your love from me or come between us. I love you with every part of me—you *are* a part of me. I'll say it again—that will never happen." Ayo took a breath to calm her galloping heart. A wave of lightheaded disorientation set her off balance. "And as far as me getting hurt, nothing is guaranteed. It's how you deal with what happens to you. I'm a grown woman and it's a chance I'm now willing to take." The dizziness passed and Ayo stood up. "Now get your things and get in the truck. I'm taking you to the airport."

Kedar checked in at curbside, handing his bags to a smiling African attendant. They walked slowly past travelers lined up in front the of ticket counters stretching across the long, high-ceilinged hall.

"This is it, baby." At the point of no return, Ayo squeezed his arm.

Kedar didn't pull away, but his usual farewell tease was absent. "Mami, I never saw you heated like that. I thought you were going to cuss me out."

Ayo's eyebrow arched. "Kedar, I know plenty of cuss words and just because I know them, it doesn't mean I use them." She'd never shown that side of herself to Kedar, although he came closer than he knew to getting a taste of Ayo unleashed. "And don't talk to me about cussing. I was outside your door and heard bad words running out of your mouth like dirty water."

Kedar swallowed. "I love you. You're my mom and the best one in the world." To Ayo he was a heart-tugging combination of an almost grown man and the eight year old who yelled at a man to "stop looking at my Mommy!" What he said next made her feel like she'd been punched in the stomach.

"But if you plan on having him at our house on Thanksgiving, you'll have to count me out."

Chapter 11
&

It was *not* the most wonderful time of the year, as the song proclaimed it to be. She had Bilal in her life, who was everything he promised and more. But her relationship with Kedar had been strained to almost breaking. In a series of tense phone calls, she cajoled, negotiated, retreated and insisted until they came to a lukewarm truce.

"Okay, Mami, I'll come home the day before Thanksgiving. I'll have dinner with you over at Cousin Magda's. But I'm not staying. The day after Thanksgiving, I'm coming back to Florida." His words weighed heavily on her heart. Was her new-found happiness worth the loss of her son in her life? But he was practically grown. Should she sacrifice her happiness to appease her child who already had one foot into a life of his own?

Then there was the doctor's appointment she put off to complete and ship an order for a new client. Her body ached. Her assistant, Karina, was home on holiday vacation, and Ayo had to work alone. If she worked quickly, she'd be finished and sitting pretty by the time Bilal got there. Her heart sank when she heard the distinctive double-time knock on the door. *Busted.*

Bilal stood in the doorway and stared. Ayo's twists had been tamed by a navy and white bandana. She wore a faded T-shirt from a Mexican resort and a pair of loose tan coveralls. A roll of bubble wrap threatened to break loose from the tab of tape barely holding it in place. Packing peanuts poured out of a giant clear plastic bag. Six dozen jars, stamped with Maracas Bay's palm tree logo, took up the other side, along with the same amount of cigar-label banded soap.

"Ayo, this is crazy!" Bilal's soft leather jacket came open with one hard jerk of the zipper. He draped it on one of the high stools in front of the long workspace. A muscle pulsed in his clenched jaw.

Although she'd seen it many times, she still couldn't figure out how he managed to press that lush mouth into such a thin line of disapproval. "What's crazy?" Ayo turned away from taping up another box to level narrowed eyes at Bilal. "My determination to get this order out today?"

"You have a doctor's appointment! I came over to drive you myself. And here you are, not even dressed. And working in slow motion. I can see how much pain you're in! That's what's crazy!"

"Well guess what's even crazier! I'm not letting a few aches and pains get in the way of running my business. You of all people ought to know that." As soon as the defiant words left her mouth, Ayo sucked in a breath at the sharpness that sliced through her lower belly. "And besides, I need to get these gift packages ready for Sister Isabel's shelter. I do it every month and it's something I refuse to put off. They always get the necessities—deodorant, toothpaste—from other donors. And that's all very good. But when you're down and out, something pretty and utterly useless is a spirit-lifter, especially this time of year. Depression is a bitch," she mumbled.

Bilal cocked his head. She spoke with such conviction that he wanted to delve deeper into her emotional take on depression. Instead, he pulled at the sleeve of her frayed t-shirt and let the moment pass. He ran one hand down the length of her arm. "Look baby, I know you want to do well and give your zakah—"

"My what?" Ayo's head swung around.

Rocking back on his heels, Bilal laughed softly. "Sorry. Zakah means charity in Arabic. It's one of the five pillars—the duty of all Muslims. That's what you're doing when you give to someone less fortunate. Something like tithing, I guess. And it's great, but you've got to take care of yourself. It seems like you're in pain every day!"

"Not really," Ayo mumbled, easing her back to lean against the counter. When she grimaced, Bilal leaped forward. His mouth formed into a grim line. "Okay, that's enough. Come on, up you go." He moved behind her and placed both hands on her shoulder, propelling her towards the steps.

"But Bilal, all I need is to sit down, and I'll be fine." She pulled back, trying to halt the forward movement. Shaking his head, he moved swiftly to one side. He slipped one arm around her and continued to draw her forward. Her determination was no match for his strength. "Nope, what you need is to lie down. If sitting down worked, you wouldn't be doubled over like that. So come on; let's go."

"I don't need to lie down! I told you, it's not that bad."

"Not that bad!' Bilal tapped his forehead. "Who are you trying to fool? Look at you—you can hardly stand up! And think about Kedar. He's been upset since October, and if he sees you like this, he'll lose it." He turned a scornful glance in the direction of the jumble of packing supplies. "And if you would just organize that stuff, you wouldn't be running yourself ragged taking two steps when one would do."

Ayo gritted her teeth. It never failed; when she was tired and in pain, her tongue turned into a weapon. Raising one eyebrow, she lifted her chin and stared at him. "Organize it, huh? Since you're the king of everything in its place, why don't *you* do it? And what else do you suggest? Lay down every time I feel like it and let the business go to hell because I have a little ache or pain?" Her voice rose along with the sarcasm she leveled at him. "Are you going to take care of me if I turn into a wilting flower of womanhood? Bring me smelling salts while I languish on the verandah and drink mint juleps?"

Bilal's lids dropped to half-mast over eyes that flashed a dark amber warning. He took his arms off her shoulders and crossed them over his chest, meeting her defiant stare with a cool, unwavering gaze. "I know you're tired. And you're sick. That's the only reason you could talk to me like a stranger who offended you. So I'll let it go this time."

"Let it go? Who—?"

The soft steel in his voice cut the question in half. "I'm talking to you, Ayo. I'm crazy about you, but I am not a doormat or a little boy. So you can either come upstairs and let me *help* you take care of yourself. Or…" He let the word stretch out. "You can stand there with your lips poked out. Which one is it? Because if that's what you want you can sulk right here but I'll be on Blair Road while you're doing it."

Ayo fumed. This was new territory for her. She wasn't used to being told what to do by anybody. Or worse, reprimanded like a naughty little girl. Her first instinct was to stand there, just for spite. But what good would that do? She'd end up in bed, but she'd be sleeping alone. That was *not* what she wanted. Not after she had gotten so used to the warm circle of his arms and the scent of sandalwood in her sleep. Still, she had to hold onto a shred of control.

"I was going upstairs anyway!" Ayo spun around, leaving Bilal at the foot of the stairs. Her sandaled feet hit each step with a thud.

Instead of an angry retort, Bilal burst out laughing.

"What the hell is so funny?" Ayo demanded, whirling around, ready to blast him out the door with a few heated words. But as hard as she tried, she couldn't stop the smile that broke through her clamped, pouting lips. By the time they got to the bedroom, the smile had turned into hiccups of laughter. They tumbled on the bed. Bilal moved quickly, and with great care flipped her over and pinned Ayo's arms above her head.

"Okay, *I Am Woman*, I've heard you roar. Now where are your nightclothes?" Out of his mouth, the words were a sensual invitation to play. "I don't know because you never wear them to bed when I'm here."

Ayo arched her back, raising her mouth a breath away from his. "I start out wearing them," she whispered, brushing her breasts against his chest. "What happens next is your fault." A slow spread of desire competed against the pain. Closing her eyes, Ayo sighed deeply, praying it to win.

"Mine?" he murmured against her lips. "You know what's going to happen next if you don't keep still." Bilal's hands slid over the soft skin of her forearms. "Remember the night we listened to *Love Won't Let Me Wait*? And the half yard of silky fabric that that ended up in my hands instead of on your body? That's what's going to happen. Because we both know that pleasure can chase away pain. And now might be the perfect time to practice that theory." His mouth murmured the words against the pulsing hollow of her throat.

Ayo issued the challenge in a voice softened by the heat of his body pressed against hers. "So you want to play doctor, huh? Then show me."

Bilal's hand slid high on the inside of her thigh. When it met the edge of her underwear, he brushed his fingers across the soft cotton that Ayo suddenly wished were black lace. "Ah," he murmured, continuing his exploration through the tight curls covering her moist sweet spot. "I've got plenty to show you."

His remedy was already working. Ayo's voice caught on a sharp spike of pleasure. "Then show me with your clothes off. All of them."

Bilal's smile curved up slowly. His eyes pinned her in place with a potent mix of love, desire and a promise that by the time show and tell was over, she'd be more than satisfied. Bilal leaned off the bed and raised both arms, peeling off the black silk T and undershirt in one smooth move. Ayo gazed up under half-closed lids. She loved his body; the strength in his long arms, smooth sable skin over the muscles of his broad chest, his slender waist and taut, flat stomach. She reached for his belt, but Bilal stopped her hand.

He shook his head and smiled a sexy half smile. The coils of hair she loved so much brushed his strong, bare back. "Uh-uh, baby, I'm running this show." The belt slid out like a whip. Ayo's breath caught. His pants lay half-opened, exposing the ribbon of hair and the magnificent bulge straining for release against his black boxer briefs. She was wet and aching with anticipation. Answering her demand, he slipped the jeans from his hips and stood naked before her.

"Ah, the medicinal value of beauty," she murmured, leaning up to grasp his thick, heavy erection in her palm.

Bilal's breath hissed out. Leaning forward, his lips brushed her forehead. "I see you understand," he murmured. "And now, the medicinal value of touch."

With both palms on her thighs, he slid the textured fabric over her skin. The friction was delicious, especially the feel of soft cotton sliding slowly down her legs.

"Oh…" Ayo gasped, shifting back.

"Keep still, baby," he murmured, brushing his lips around the rim of her ear.

"How can I?" Ayo exhaled the words in a deep sigh. She had to have him. Enough of this improvising, no matter how pleasurable. Just this one time and if she could bear it, then maybe another time. Ayo leaned back, with her own offering.

A small frown creased his brows. "No, baby," Bilal insisted, "I want to please you, not hurt you."

Ayo wrapped her arms around his broad back and pulled him down. "You've had your chance. Now it's my turn to run the show," she chuckled softly, grazing his nipple with her lips. Bilal's body trembled. His breath came quick and hard. "And I want it to taste, touch and feel it all, from the beginning to the grand finale," she told him, sending a sensual invitation of her own. "Who knows? We might even need a curtain call."

Bilal reared his head back and laughed out loud. "You're something else, Ayo Montgomery." His voice grew soft and husky when he looked deep into her eyes. "And you're all I'll ever need." Slowly and gently Bilal worked his way in until her moist heat claimed every inch. They rocked together slowly; only once did she grimace, but with her face buried against his shoulder, he couldn't see it. Then pleasure claimed her, blotting out anything but Bilal poised over her like a magnificent sculpture come to life. He stroked harder, deeper and Ayo met each one in perfect rhythm until his name became one long sentence that she whispered, moaned and finally screamed out. When they could breathe normally, Ayo curled against him and sighed, enjoying his warmth and their mingled scents on his skin. She laid her palm on his warm heaving chest. "I'm going to need more of that remedy, you know."

Reluctantly Bilal broke away. "More. Later. I promise," he whispered, brushing his lips across her closed lids, her mouth and throat.

Bilal's glistening body was still magnificently naked as he rummaged carefully through her dresser, holding up with a long-sleeved, floor length soft cotton gown. Before she could protest, he was in front of her, straddling her legs and leaning over, placing both hands on either side of where she sat. No scent in the world was as wonderful as his, hers and sex. Ayo tilted her face up to meet his kiss. "No sexy for the rest of the day," he murmured. "Now raise your arms, baby." Bilal nuzzled against her neck, stroking the column with his mustache. He placed a mound of firm pillows between her back and the headboard.

To her dismay, he pulled on his boxers before placing both her legs across his knees. Next Bilal slipped a pair of thick, warm socks on her feet. "I know you'll kick these off, but right now you need to keep your feet warm. They're like ice. And one more thing—I'll bet you didn't take time through working—and let's not forget the fussing," he teased—"for little more than a big glass of Coke." A lopsided smile pulled at the corners of his mouth.

Ayo's earrings jangled like tiny wind chimes when she shook her head.

"That's what I thought. I heat food very well, as you know. I'll look through the freezer and find you something. And I'm warning you." His orders were delivered with an even sweeter kiss. "Don't sneak off that bed."

"I give, big boss man."

A broad smile broke out over his handsome face. "Ah, now that's what I like to hear." Then his expression softened. "Didn't I promise to take care of you?"

"You did," Ayo murmured.

Bilal brushed her hair back and held her face in both warm hands. "Then let me," he said softly. "Taking care doesn't mean taking over. It doesn't mean bossing you around; it means helping when you need me. It means taking up the slack when you can't." Before he stood up, Bilal kissed her softly. "And that's what I'm going to do right now. Right after I put on some clothes. You ought to be ashamed," he teased. "Got me butt naked before noon!"

Ten minutes later he was back, carrying a bed tray with a bowl of her homemade chicken soup and Coke over crushed ice. It was the perfect combination—something hot, light, and nourishing, chased down by the icy chill of her favorite cold drink.

The food was just what she needed, although she didn't realize it until the first warm spoonful hit her stomach. While she ate in contentment, Bilal stacked the CD player with music. "Good for the head, the body and the soul." He was so right. Arturo Sandoval's trumpet soared softly. By the time Dizzy Gillespie blew through *Night in Tunisia*, Ayo was tucked way down in the covers, half asleep.

"While you rest, I'm going downstairs to get some work done. I'll be back to check on you later." Ayo murmured a sleepy, contented response and sent him a half-wave from under her covers.

ॐ

Two days later, that same contentment was impossible. In a few hours, Kedar would be home. She prayed that seeing her in bed and Bilal in the house wouldn't send her son right back out the door. They had forged a fragile truce and cut a deal. She wouldn't protest his Friday-after-Thanksgiving departure if he would have dinner with her and Bilal in Annapolis. If anything could soften him, it would be dinner around Magda's table; a place Ayo had already declared a no-combat zone.

Consumed by thoughts of what would or would not happen, she didn't hear Bilal when he came back upstairs. He frowned at the untouched food and empty Coke glass.

"Ayo, I hope you own some stock in Coca Cola. And just so you know, after Thanksgiving, you need to make another appointment, because I'm taking you to the doctor myself. Nobody should be in this much pain so often."

She twisted around to find a more comfortable position. "I know, I know; and I'll go. As far as the Coke, did you know it was discovered by a practitioner of homeopathic medicine?"

"No, I didn't. But I do I see through your slick attempt to change the subject." Laugh lines crinkled at the edges of his eyes. "I know you're itching to spill it, so go on, Miss Wanna-Be Jeopardy champ."

Ayo sat up in the center of her bed to dispense the rest of her knowledge with a triumphant smile. "Somebody is always getting on me for my cola addiction, so I memorized his statement for just an occasion like this." She rubbed her hand across the moist, empty glass. "Anyway, 'it is the most excellent of all tonics, assisting digestion, imparting energy to the organs of respiration, and strengthening the muscular and nervous systems'."

Bilal rolled his eyes. "Whatever," he chuckled. "All I know is that you need a real doctor instead of—now what did you call it—a Homey the Clown physician?"

Ayo slapped his hand. "You need to stop!"

"It's not me, it's you!" he admonished. "Now lie down and get some rest before Kedar gets here. It's the first time you haven't picked him up from the airport. You know he's already worried."

Ayo grasped his hand and held it to her cheek. "Thank you for being concerned about his feelings, in spite of the way he treated you."

Bilal shook his head. "Don't worry about it, baby. I'm a big boy, and whatever concerns you, concerns me." Then his voice lost its tender edge. "But what I won't tolerate is anything or anybody that causes you pain." He bent to kiss her lips. "I brought my laptop with me, so I'll work from downstairs. But you call me if you need anything.

Okay?" Bilal turned off the TV and slid it behind the doors of the mahogany armoire.

An hour later, Ayo sat up, startled and confused, feeling like she'd slept through the night and into half of the next day. She got up and pushed back hunter green tab-topped drapes that had replaced her summer sheers. It was light outside, but she had no idea of the time. With her bladder almost ready to burst, Ayo tiptoed to the bathroom and back. When she climbed back into the bed, Bilal appeared at the door, as if he had radar or a built-in motion detector.

"I thought I heard movement." He came inside the room and sat on the side of the bed. "Feel better?"

"I'm getting there."

Easing himself behind her, he bent to brush his lips across the back of her neck. "Maybe this will help you. Lean forward a second." He kneeled, settling her back against his chest and applying gentle pressure with his thumb, up and down the center of her neck. With both open palms, he stroked under her chin and around each side of her face. The column of her neck felt like liquid under his touch.

"You have *such* good hands," she murmured. Ayo's lids fluttered. Her head lolled back against his chest. "I want more, but I know it will have to wait." She turned to look up at him with wide, pleading eyes. "But I'll settle for something else—can I please have some espresso?"

Bilal kissed the top of her head. He slid from behind her, rising from the bed. "I guess so," he laughed. "Since you asked so nicely. And since you seem to exist only on caffeine."

"Not only caffeine," she whispered, kissing the back of his hand.

At the kitchen counter, Bilal pulled a bag from the freezer. He measured the finely ground coffee into the contraption he'd finally learned to use. The mini espresso-maker had too many handles and looked like it belonged in Dr. Jekyll's lab. He didn't know how she drank the stuff, anyway. One cup had to be the equivalent of an entire pack of No-Doz. Bilal smiled while the brew bubbled. He loved Ayo's bright kitchen. It had a warm comforting smell. A hint of coffee always lingered behind the scent of whatever she had been cooking. He laughed out loud. He had never been happier. What they had was just a prelude to something so much better. And permanent, he hoped. Life was almost as good as it got, but the best would come when she was healed of whatever was making her so sick.

A sound behind him cut off his laughter like a hand around his throat.

"Where's my mother?" Kedar snarled. Narrowing his eyes, he scowled when he spotted Ayo's favorite hibiscus print cup in Bilal's hand.

It nearly crashed to the floor. Bilal choked back a retort. *Damn!* Why couldn't that young brother ever show up when he was supposed to? If Kedar had walked in a few minutes earlier, he would have found his mother in bed, melting against Bilal's chest. Kedar's scowl and the thought of their narrow escape destroyed Bilal's good mood.

Bilal took a deep breath. He didn't want to upset Ayo, but his earlier promise stood. Kedar didn't have to like him, but he would damn sure respect his mother, even if the lioness in Ayo came roaring out to defend her cub. So be it; Bilal could deal with the fall-out later.

"Kedar." Bilal nodded, leveling an unsmiling gaze at the younger man. This time Bilal withheld his hand, although he tempered his cool demeanor, and for Ayo put forth one last try at conciliation. "She's upstairs; she hasn't been feeling well and when I came over, she asked for some coffee. But I know that seeing you is what she really needs. Maybe you should take this up to her." *And watch your mouth when you do.*

Kedar's icy glance swept over Bilal. He accepted the cup without a word and sped up the steps to Ayo's room, unmindful of the dripping trail he left behind on the polished wooden stairs.

Ayo heard two male voices. *Oh, Lord, here we go.* I hope they don't need a referee. Pain had complete control of her body, and she couldn't move even if the two of them came to blows.

Kedar rushed into Ayo's room, sloshing a stream of coffee on her gold and green comforter. His smooth brows crinkled, followed by a stream of anxious questions. "Mami, how long have you been sick? Why didn't you tell me if it was bad enough to put you in bed? I *knew* something was wrong when you couldn't come to the airport. I would have come home earlier! Why didn't you call Auntie Justine or Cousin Magda?"

Ayo's stomach clenched. At least he didn't say "instead of Bilal", although it was the unspoken end of that sentence. *Are we ever going to get over this?* She put on a bright face anyway and broke into Kedar's rapid-fire barrage. "Hi, sweetheart! You're here early, and that's even better. But it's the day before Thanksgiving. I wouldn't think of calling anybody away from their own preparations to come over here. You know what's going on over at Magda's and Nick's family is coming up from Louisiana, so Justine has her hands full."

"Okay, but what about those orders you told me about? And since you've been in bed for two days, how did you eat? Mami, how come you didn't call me?"

She pried the cup out of his hands. "If I told you how I was feeling, you'd have been distracted from your school work, or worse, you'd come running home, and I won't have that."

"Mami—"

"Shh! Now listen. I know you don't like Bilal—"

"But Mami—"

Ayo slapped the covers. "Stop talking and let me finish! Since we've started this conversation again, we're going to end it, once and for all."

Kedar jerked back. His handsome face balled up into a disgruntled knot.

"Do you remember when I was sick like this once last summer?"

"Uh-huh."

"So you remember how I couldn't get out of the bed? And you had to heat up the food and run my errands?"

Kedar squirmed. "Uh-huh."

"So who do you think did all those things for me? And don't call him "the dude.""

"Bilal, I guess..." Kedar's voice trailed off. He shifted and dropped his gaze again.

Gently lifting his chin, Ayo continued. "Yes, he did all that, and more. We're past the 'impress each other' stage; actually we were never there. And since you're a man now, let me tell you something, for your own good. There are a lot more flamboyant but empty ways for a man to impress a woman other than struggling through rush-hour traffic in an oversized SUV to deliver soap."

Kedar's shoulders slumped. He looked down at the hands clasped in his lap. "You know what, Mami," Kedar spoke softly. "I called myself getting back at you by treating you badly, even though it hurt to see you so sad. I just didn't know what to do with all the stuff going around in my head, so I tried to be hard and mean. And for that I'm so sorry." Kedar lifted his head and gazed into his mother's eyes. The mix of emotions that battled across his face broke her heart.

"I know I acted like a jerk last time, but I just didn't trust him. I told you I would try, but when I saw him in the kitchen like he lives here, I couldn't handle it."

She leaned over to touch his face. "I love you, baby, but you'll have to. I'm your mother, but I'm a woman and entitled to a private life. And the two can co-exist. You'll see."

"Okay, okay." He was clearly uncomfortable with the thought. "This is still going to take some getting used to." Kedar's eyes hardened. He leaned forward. "And I won't back down on him or anybody else hurting you. I'll be watching. But right now I'll go downstairs and call a truce. Anybody who would do this for you at least deserves my thanks."

When Kedar left her room, Ayo's eyes rolled toward the ceiling. She fell back against the pillows. "At last!" Now she had to call Magda.

Instead of Annapolis, she, Kedar and Bilal would be eating Thanksgiving dinner on Manchester Road, even if the meal turned out to be five wings, mambo sauce and fried rice.

"I'm sorry you're sick. Ayo, I wish you would go get another opinion," Magda fussed. "I mean it. Take some time off from your soap making and take care of yourself. Please?"

"I will, Magda. Right after the holidays." She didn't want to talk about that right now. "Listen, I know you cooked for an army and I'm sorry we won't be there."

"Oh, don't worry about that—you know we always have a houseful—a couple of our neighbors and some of Buck's employees will be here."

"You mean your neighbors from next door?"

"CNN? Oh hell no!" Magda snorted.

"Uh, Magda, who in the world is CNN?"

"Colored News Now. She's a one-woman neighborhood watch—watching everybody's business. If I invite that woman into our home, before the night is over everybody in Annapolis would know not only how many patterns of china I own but where I keep my thongs. That heifer is the world's worst gossip, and she will never put a foot on my property again!"

"Oh Lord, Magda—shut up!" Ayo cut her off with a shriek. She hoped it hadn't carried downstairs to alarm Kedar and Bilal. That's all she needed, for both of them to come running and fight over who would take care of her first. "Please don't say anything else," she pleaded. "I'm getting ready to wet myself!"

Magda's laugh eased into a mellow chuckle. "Hey, I have an idea. Why don't you send one of those men over here early tomorrow to pick up some food? Then you won't have to eat Chinese takeout for dinner, or one of those terrible grocery store Thanksgiving disasters with the tough turkey and cardboard mashed potatoes."

Ayo sat up. "That's a perfect solution! I hadn't figured out what to do. I didn't know what would happen with the two of them in the same room. Looks like we made a breakthrough today, though. Thank God," Ayo sighed.

"For real," Magda said. "So what happened?"

"Kedar saw how well Bilal took care of me and decided he'd at least give him a chance. They're downstairs together right now." She leaned forward in the direction of her open bedroom door. "I haven't heard any shouting or any furniture being knocked over, so I guess they're both still standing."

"Girl, don't even joke about that. Anyway, you stay in bed and let your two fellows dote on you. I'll talk to you tomorrow. Love you,

Ayo."

"Love you too, Magda."

ॐ

Bilal tensed when he heard footsteps. *What now?* This time, when Kedar came into the kitchen, an outstretched hand preceded him. *Al-Hamdu Lillah, Praise God.* Bilal spoke a silent prayer of thanks. *One down, one to go.* His father might be a harder case. Bilal hoped Latif would come around, but if he didn't, it was his father's problem. Bilal's life with Ayo would still go full steam ahead to whatever future they chose together.

"I hear you took care of my mother."

Silently, Bilal nodded.

"I appreciate that." Kedar ducked his head. "Look man, I'm sorry. You know, when I started school in Florida, I would tell Mami that she should get out more often. But when she finally did, I didn't like it at all."

Kedar looked like a sinner, confessing a string of misdeeds to his priest. "I was jealous and afraid that you would take her love from me." He was contrite, but only to a point. He leveled a long warning stare at Bilal. "Or worse, that you would hurt her."

Bilal unfolded his arms and smiled at the clearly remorseful young man. At Kedar's age, there had been a time or two when Bilal had worn that same expression. "She's your mother, so you've known her longer than me, but I do know that nothing will ever replace you in her heart. You should hear the pride in her voice when she talks about you." Bilal raised a brow over twinkling eyes. "Even about your diving." If Kedar could try, so would he.

Kedar brightened immediately. "She did? Man, I'm so sorry. I was a real jerk for the way I've treated her. And you."

"Apology accepted. And understand this—I would never hurt Ayo. Never."

Kedar chuckled. "But she might hurt me; man, that last time she got right up in my face! Told me I acted like I was raised in the woods. Even though I'm twenty years old, I know I'd better check myself, because Mami ain't no joke. My mother is the sweetest, kindest woman in the world until you go too far. And then John Henry himself couldn't drop a hammer harder than Ayodele Montgomery."

Bilal couldn't hold back his laughter. "Don't I know. I've already seen her swing that hammer!"

Kedar stared and laughed out loud. "Are you kidding?"

"Oh, no; my brother, I assure you that I am not." He shook his head, chuckling at the memory of the first day he stood in this kitchen.

Kedar's expression changed abruptly, as if he'd just remembered something important. "Uh, Mami told me that you're a Muslim. I guess you know she's not going to be walking behind you."

Bilal gazed at Kedar before speaking. If this was the end of their issues with each other, now was the time to put his feelings on the line. "I don't want her behind me. I want her beside me."

The next day, instead of an elegant sit-down dinner in Magda's dining room, the three of them enjoyed an impromptu Thanksgiving picnic. Squat orange candles filled the room with the scent of fresh pumpkin pie. Removing her luxurious bedding, Ayo spread a cotton quilt over the fitted sheet. The dresser became a sideboard, holding the same grand meal they would have eaten in Annapolis. Instead the three of them perched on Ayo's bed, dining and drinking from Chinette instead of Magda's bone china. It was perfect; she passed the day in a cocoon of happiness.

The men stayed glued to the television during the marathon football games. While they watched and cheered, Ayo read a book. She never understood football. How could anybody tell what was happening when they were always tangled up in a heap on the ground? At halftime of the second game, she held out a forkful of white potato pie in their direction.

"That's okay," she chuckled, "You two go right ahead. I'll continue to indulge myself in the medicinal value of Magda's cooking." Her mother's phrase came to her in its full meaning. "The Lord sent it if the devil brought it." No amount of plotting, planning or cajoling could have brought them together in this way, not even Magda's ice-breaking, heartwarming hospitality.

In the middle of the night, when Kedar was asleep and Bilal back on Blair Road, she woke up to go the bathroom. Ayo gazed around her room, recalling the day's unexpected joy. Before climbing back into bed alone, she laughed and whispered the words out loud into the soft darkness. "Three o'clock and all is well."

Chapter 12

Halcyon—prosperous, peaceful, golden—since late November, it was the perfect description of Ayo's life. The religious wars were over. One half of the family battle had been won, and it happened to be the one she cared most about. As much as she loved Bilal, she didn't give a damn about his father's opinion. Latif Abdul-Salaam could either get glad or stay mad. Since the "Great Thanksgiving Truce," she had even pushed pain and discomfort to the background and immersed herself in the joy that had come so quickly into her life. There was nothing left to stand in the way of her happiness. Not one thing.

Their plane streaked over a landscape that even in December was far different from that of the frozen northeast. The arm of her seat formed a barrier, but Ayo leaned into the curve of Bilal's arm and laid her head on his shoulder. He cradled her hand, releasing it only when a flight attendant stopped to offer them a snack. When she moved to the seat row ahead of them, Bilal rattled the miniscule bag of pretzels. "I know they're in there somewhere," he laughed. "All two of them!"

"You're crazy," she giggled. "I wonder what Kedar is eating right now." The words came with a smile instead of sadness, even though she was a thousand miles away from her son. For the first time in their lives, Ayo and Kedar spent Christmas apart. It had been years since the Montgomery clan gathered for a real Trinidadian Christmas. This year they flew in from all corners of the globe. Some had never seen Maurice's son, and his aunts begged Ayo to "let de boy come."

Ayo gave a wry grin. "He told me that if I didn't have you in my life, he would have never left me. Or he and I would be in Port of Spain together. Talk about a change! His about-face and this trip is a dream come true!"

Bilal shook his head and joined in her laughter. "You're not kidding! Two months ago, he declared war on me and my relationship with you." Now he and Bilal were on their way to a real friendship. Gazing at her tenderly, he stroked Ayo's cheek with the back of his hand. "I promise, if there's any dream you have, and I can make it happen, consider it done."

Dream was the right word to describe the magic that began as soon as Bilal finally grabbed their luggage from the slow-moving baggage carousel. Outside the airport, they spotted a tall blond man. With his deep, leathery tan he looked like a big-game guide from the Masai mara.

Instead of khakis and a safari hat, this man sported a flower-splashed tropical shirt and white cotton shorts. He held up a sign with the name Abdul-Salaam printed out in large black type. When Bilal strode over to make himself known, the man's look of surprise was almost comical. He looked up at Bilal, over at Ayo and back to his sign.

They held their breaths. Was he expecting a Saudi prince instead of a dreadlocked African American? One who, in spite of a two-hour plane ride, looked like he had just stepped off the runway at New York's fashion week?

"Hey there!" he drawled. The man stuck out his hand and replaced his momentary surprise with a smile like the Florida sunshine overhead. Ayo and Bilal looked at each other and exhaled a simultaneous sigh.

"I'm Stan, and welcome to the Palms, or at least to the Palms limo," he joked, gesturing to the Land Rover behind him. "I'll drive you to the Welcome Center, and then we'll board our motorboat for the island."

Untethered from her mooring, the teak-colored boat skimmed over the water. Ayo and Bilal stood at the railing, wrapped in each other's arms with their faces turned to the breeze. The sun was hot and high in a sky just a few shades lighter than the turquoise water surrounding them. Tropical greenery sprung from the nearby shoreline. Close to shore Ayo looked up at the seabirds careening and cackling overhead, remembering the word and its mythical meaning. Halcyon was also a seabird, blessed by Zeus with fourteen temperate days during the winter solstice to lay her eggs on the water. When she nested, her presence had power to calm the wind and waves and bring beautiful, balmy weather. These were Ayo's own halcyon days. The loose threads of her life had finally been woven together.

Bilal pulled her closer and laid the side of his face against her hair. "I've never been happier in my life," he whispered. Raising his head, he looked out over the horizon. "The best is yet to come. I can feel it, baby. And it's coming quickly."

Up ahead, the resort loomed like a movie version of the perfect tropical island. When they disembarked at the small dock, Ayo let out a small cry of delight. "This is paradise," she exclaimed. Bilal held her hand as Ayo's head turned from side to side on the walk through pathways thick with tropical vegetation.

"Here we are," Stan smiled broadly as he unlocked the door and set their bags inside. "And if you need anything, just give us a holler. And I mean that literally," he quipped. "As you can see, there are no telephones or televisions in our bungalows. We even have a no cell-phone zone. But don't worry, you're not on Gilligan's Island." The three of them laughed. If it were so, Gilligan would have never left. "We're here to make sure you have a wonderful stay."

When Stan left them alone, Ayo turned an awe-struck face to the king canopy bed dressed in luxurious white linens and draped from the ceiling with sheer butterfly netting. Bilal stuck a hand in his pants pocket and smiled with deep satisfaction at Ayo's animated expressions of delight. "I had a choice of Indonesian or Balinese, but I chose the British Colonial just for you." Ayo moved to stand on tip-toes and kiss him full on the lips. "It's absolutely wonderful. You'd think it was my birthday instead of yours."

"What's mine is yours," he replied with a mysterious wink.

She left him for a peek at the bathroom and out to the verandah with its view of the shimmering ocean. "Bilal come look!" she cried out. "An outdoor shower! Do you think we'll ever leave this room?"

Before she could respond, he was at her back, pulling her against him and fitting her body against his arousal. "Not if you don't want to," he murmured, grazing her ear with his lips.

That night, both in white, they walked barefoot to their beachside table. Ayo's halter-topped sundress swirled around her ankles, brushing against the tiny silver bells of her anklet. In his own crisp attire Bilal looked like the prosperous owner of a private tropical hideaway. Small lights and tall flaming torches embedded in the sand lit the way to tables set at the water's edge. Over the Gulf of Mexico, the sky split into streaks of crimson and dusky blue.

At the candlelit table Bilal gaze's blanketed her. He smiled, stroking the face of the antique gold pocket watch she'd given to him earlier. "Thank you again for this beautiful gift." Last month it had called to her from the display case of an Annapolis antique dealer. She placed a down payment on the very expensive timepiece and had it wrapped in hand-decorated silver paper for his birthday. "You know me so well. I love it."

"It was perfect for you and just like you, it's gorgeous and finely crafted."

"And now," he announced, leaving the sentence to trail off unfinished. Bilal reached across the table to lace his fingers through hers. With the other, he placed a tiny gold box in front of her.

Ayo's eyebrows rose. "What's this? You don't celebrate Christmas, and you know I wasn't expecting a gift. Besides, it's *your* birthday."

"Remember I told you what's mine is yours? Think of this as *our* birthday."

Ayo fingered the box. "Now I'm really confused."

Bilal's eyes twinkled. "Don't be. Just open it."

Before she could pry off the paper, the top and bottom separated in her hand.

Ayo stared again. "But it's empty!" This was becoming more mysterious by the minute. Knowing him there was certain to be a grand finale. She twisted in her seat, expecting to see a quartet of singing waiters advancing across the sand.

"Still haven't figured it out?"

Ayo sighed in exasperation. "You know I haven't. Come on, Bilal—you're making me crazy! Why is this box empty?"

"Well, he drawled, leaning back against the chair back, "It's part of a ritual—sometimes couples do it together, and sometimes the man does it alone."

In spite of the mystery, Ayo burst out laughing. Her eyebrow raised into a high peak. "Is this the prelude to some kind of freaky sex?" She covered her mouth to hold back the giggle.

Bilal leaned forward, grinning and playing the game with her. "Oh I see," he teased. "You can't wait. Your mind is jumping ahead to that big romantic bed, isn't it? Don't worry, we'll get there." Then his voice softened. "That box is empty because it's waiting for something to fill it. Remember what I said? Sometimes a couple chooses the ring together, and sometimes the man springs a surprise on bended knee. Isn't that right?"

Ayo kept her eyes on her plate. She restrained herself; it wouldn't do to scream out loud; at least not here.

"Only you should choose something you'll be wearing for the rest of your life. When we get back to DC I hope you'll pick out a ring to fill that box. A ring that says you'll marry me."

Ayo's chair wobbled in the sand when she leaned up and out of her seat. Tears sprung into her eyes as if they were cued, just waiting for the word to begin trickling down her face.

Bilal met her halfway across table. Candle glow heightened the dark flash of his eyes. "What are we waiting for? We already know where this is going. Marry me, Ayo. To have you as my wife and mother of my child would be the most perfect gift in the world."

Chapter 13

Their announcement pleased everyone but Latif, but to Ayo he didn't matter. She didn't even care if he showed up to the Islamic and non-denominational ceremony they planned for spring. The first big planning session took place at B. Smith's in Union Station. In the classic elegance of the turn-of-the-century dining room, they shared upscale renditions of southern favorites, passing plates of seafood over mixed greens, jambalaya, and lamb with mint jelly.

"I wore Mehndi for my wedding," Zahirah told her, after a sip of sparkling cider. "It's like a henna tattoo for the hands—just a little something beautiful and unusual. Actually I was given a Mehndi party the night before; it was a different twist on the bachelorette party. Believe me—no stripper police or firemen showing up at the door." She laughed out loud, a softer version of Bilal's own laughter. "It's more cultural than anything, and absolutely unnecessary, so please don't think I'm trying to foist something off on you." Zahirah winked at her future sister-in-law. "It's just that you look like a Mehndi kind of girl."

Adilah turned between Magda and Ayo. "I know that you have a wonderful reception planned for after the ceremony, but I hope you'll allow us to host a *walima*."

"What's a *walima*," Justine queried. "I'm all about learning new customs and cultures. I get it from my husband." Ayo smiled at her friend. She looked forward to the day when those words could fall from her lips with regularity.

"The *walima* is a wedding feast, but it's usually held a couple of days after the ceremony. At this rate, we'll be celebrating for a week. But it will take that much time to express our joy. You've made my son so happy," Adilah beamed. "He wants so much to be your husband. And you've seen him with our baby twins. What a wonderful father he's going to be."

Under the table, Ayo's hand went to her stomach. She rubbed a small circle over the space where their baby would rest. Ayo favored her future mother-in-law with a jubilant smile.

She held to that thought, even when the pain and bleeding had become worse. That day Ayo turned into a one hundred and forty-five pound ball of pain. In the middle of mixing a batch of soap, she doubled over. Raw soap was unforgiving; mold it now or hack it to pieces later. As soon as the bars were set, Ayo spent the rest of the day and night on the guestroom daybed, curled into a fetal ball and clutching a heating pad to her side. She tried everything to manage the flow of blood, even the thick, throw-back sanitary napkins that felt like a heavy stack of towels wadded between her legs. Dragging herself to the nearest drugstore, she bought a pack of Depends, but they were soon soaked and chafed like rubber pants against her skin.

The next morning, old man winter coughed out a nuisance snow over D.C.—not enough to keep people off the streets, but enough to cover the pavement with a gray slush. As soon as the sun went down, the cold mush would turn into a thin sheet of ice. One day without Coke was all the lesson she needed. When she heard the weather report, Ayo made an early morning grocery store run straight up Sixteenth Street into Silver Spring, bypassing the long lines that stretched from checkout to the milk cooler in the smaller Safeway on Piney Branch Road.

She pulled the comforter off the bed, intending to brave the slush long enough to hang it on the line. Fresh air was still fresh, even without the special scent that came only from the summer sun. The phone rested between her chin and the folded comforter in her arms. She put it down, answering without checking the caller ID.

Smiling, Ayo sighed out a greeting. Bilal's voice was a better remedy than all the painkillers she had popped that day. For two days he had been in Richmond, working on an appraisal for a family who had recently cleaned out the home of an elderly relative. "I miss you baby. I hope you're feeling better today."

"I'm okay," she lied in a bright cheery voice. Every ache and pain alarmed him and sometimes she felt like a burden. "And what's even better is my doctor appointment tomorrow."

"Good! I hope this one can help you. I hate seeing you so miserable."

Time to change the subject and take the worry off his mind. When she was with him he monitored her every whimper. When they were apart, his imagination ran wild. "How's it going down there?"

"The work is going well, but I wish I could talk some sense into a couple of the woman's family members."

Ayo slid back, propping herself on the mound of bedding. "What do you mean?"

"They don't have a clue about the value of the contents of their aunt's home. All they know is her rich employer left her some old furniture. But you should see it! The chairs have their original upholstered seats. And the china closet—oh man, what a beauty! Their aunt was old-school; she knew that rich people don't buy junk, and whatever they gave her would only increase in value." Bilal's chuckle held no humor. "One of her knuckle-headed nephews did some online research. He knows just enough to make himself a real pain–and sound like a real jackass. He wouldn't know the real thing from a reproduction if it coughed up sawdust and had a 'Made in China' sticker slapped on the bottom!" Bilal snorted. "And he's looking for a quick buck. But I gave his brother the names of some reputable auctions and dealers who will get them a fair price."

Ayo had heard that exasperation before. A few months ago, he showed her a picture of a beautiful Queen Anne highboy. The piece was six feet tall, made of well-kept wood that still gleamed with a soft patina. It had been appraised for $8,000. But the owner was impatient and strapped for cash. Instead of waiting for an auction house to sell the valuable piece, she let it go on eBay for the highest bid of $1,000. "Maybe one of them will take your advice. At least I hope so."

"Me, too, baby. And don't forget, the local genealogy society has set up two presentations for me. One is tomorrow and one the next day. I drove the Commander this time, and as soon as I'm finished, I'll run that truck on eighty to get back to you."

Ayo sat back, shifting the bedding off her lap. "Look out for those good-ole-boy troopers," she chuckled. "But I'm proud of you; your seminars have kept a lot of people from getting short-changed on their valuables." Her lips curved. "Even if they do take you away from me."

"Not to worry, my love. And if it's still messy like I've heard, we can sit up in my room and look out over my snow-covered estate," he joked. "I promise you I'll make up for every minute my body is away from yours." Low and soft, Bilal's voice took on a sensual tone.

"Oh, I know you will," she replied with a sexy chuckle, already imagining the heat they would raise in his bed. "If I have to deal with winter, what better place to watch the sunrise than in the bedroom of the king of the castle."

"And your future husband, my queen."

"You know how much I love hearing those words," Ayo laughed. The two cups of coffee and an eight ounce glass of Coke filled her bladder to bursting. She squirmed, squeezing down to hold on a while longer, but it didn't work. "But I have to go to the bathroom. Don't hang up though—we can still talk. Just hold your thought through the flushing background music."

"Go on, baby," he laughed. "I've got to go anyway—I was just taking a break. But I'll call you from the hotel—I might have a bedtime story for you." His voice lowered into a soft sexy growl.

She answered with a purr of her own. "I'll be right here waiting. I always like a preview of the real thing." She couldn't wait. The last time he returned from a trip, they spent the night exploring the slow grind as foreplay. And that was just the beginning. For days after, the mere thought caused a moist tug between her thighs.

"Oh, when I get back, you are going to get all of it. As real as you can stand. Forever and a day. And do what the doctor tells you. When you're healed, our lives will be golden. I love you, Ayo."

"I love you too." She certainly did.

Ayo ate one more bowl of hot, spicy soup and watched a travel show featuring the best of the Bahamas. She dozed right after a rider on horseback galloped along a stretch of pink sand beach.

An hour later, she woke up. Bilal's optimism was catching. Tomorrow she would have an answer. Thanks to Eileen, Ayo had an appointment with the doctor who her friend proclaimed to be a miracle worker. "If anyone can help you, it will be Yvette Broussard," Eileen assured her.

Ayo thumbed through the newspaper. There it was—the circular advertising flowers, grass seed, barbecue grills and plants was the first sign of the spring to come. Until that year, Ayo hated January, February, and even most of March. They were the coldest months and a big letdown after the fiery beauty of fall, the spooky excitement of Halloween and general goodwill that began on Thanksgiving and carried through Christmas and Kwanzaa. But this year she was engaged to marry the man she loved. A life of love and healing was on her horizon. June could switch places with January and Ayo wouldn't care.

&

Eileen picked her up at seven-thirty. This morning her friend's signature red came in the form of a classic Chesterfield coat. Her luxuriant natural hair was like a handful of raw, soft cotton swept up into a rounded dark brown pouf. A tiny gap made space between her top front teeth. Ayo told her that Trinidadians considered it a sign of a woman's sexual prowess; it meant she had "a bag of sugar down there." After Ayo passed on that little tidbit to her friend, Eileen stopped covering her mouth and let her smile shine out like a beacon.

The shine was a little less bright on that gray, slushy morning. When Ayo shut the door of the jade green Jaguar, Eileen shook her head. "I need coffee! Real coffee!"

Ayo tilted her head. "Eileen, what are you talking about? You love coffee just as much as I do. You always have a stash."

Eileen pulled away from the curb, blending into early rush-hour traffic. With a red-gloved finger, she punched a button on her dash, searching for Howard University Radio. "Yes, but when I pulled out that last can and saw decaf on the label, I nearly went ballistic! How about we get some coffee before your appointment?" Suddenly, Eileen slapped her hand on the steering wheel. "Oh, what was I thinking? You can't drink coffee before blood tests. At least not like we drink it."

"What do you mean by that?"

"Once when I was scheduled for an early morning blood test, I told the doctor I'd kill the technician if I had to wait until after it was over to drink my coffee."

Although she was in no mood for humor, Eileen's story made her laugh. "So what happened? Test or coffee?"

"She told me to drink it black, and it wouldn't alter the tests results." She took a quick look at Ayo. "So are you game?"

Ayo shook her head slowly. "No, not today. If I'm early, she might see me sooner. I need to find out once and for all what the heck is going on in my body." At the door of the medical office building, Ayo put her hand on Eileen's arm. "Thanks so much for telling me about Dr. Broussard. I was at the end of my rope."

Eileen lifted one shoulder. "Glad to help, my friend. I'm quite a helper-bee, am I not?" Her eyes danced with amusement. "I see I helped you in the man department too! Who would have thought that a simple referral would end up being the romance of the century!" Eileen chuckled. "But you go girl!" She waved to Ayo and sped away, no doubt looking for a scone and a double espresso.

࿔

This is good, Ayo told herself. Inside Dr. Broussard's office, sounds of the Jazz Café met her at the door. A dark-skinned woman sporting a salt and pepper Afro stood and offered Ayo a manicured hand. "Good morning. I'm Jeanette Washington." She handed Ayo a clipboard and pen. "Please fill this out for our records, and help yourself to some refreshments while you wait."

This is very good! Near the semi-circular grouping of upholstered chairs, a glass cart held a silver tea service and an assortment of caffeine free teas. Since she declined Eileen's offer of coffee, water would do for now, even though she would have liked the ginger orange tea; it would have put down the roiling waves that accompanied her on the drive here. She settled into the chair and after completing the extensive medical history form, Ayo found a travel magazine. The coral, turquoise and gold of the tropic setting made her smile. In a few months, Mr. and Mrs. Bilal Abdul-Salaam would be honeymooning on a beach just like this.

"Ms. Montgomery?" Dr. Broussard's nurse stood in the door leading to a corridor of exam rooms.

Ayo followed. In the cool room she disrobed and sat on the edge of the exam table, swinging her bare feet and rubbing her arms in the air-conditioned chill. With the exception of one anatomical chart, the walls were covered with water-themed art—calm streams, waterfalls, an ocean at sunrise. On the counter, along with tongue depressors and packaged gauze bandages, Ayo spotted a well-known lotion product. In spite of the serious circumstances that brought her there, she couldn't help herself. Reaching over, she held it up to read the ingredient label. *I need to bring her some of mine to replace this mess of chemicals.*

Ayo sat up when Dr. Broussard knocked on the door, waiting for Ayo to respond. Tall, big-boned and shapely, Yvette Broussard looked like a female athlete in her prime. A coil of goddess braids circled her head and instead of a white coat she wore a tan turtleneck, khaki Dockers and Rockports. Black cameo earrings hung from both ears, dangling against caramel colored skin.

"Hello, Ms. Montgomery. I'm Yvette Broussard." Her warm, confident smile put Ayo more at ease.

"I understand Eileen Waring referred you to my practice. Please thank her for me." She scooted forward on the wheeled stool and sat near the end of the exam table. "Now let's see what's happening with you and what we can do about it. First, I need some information."

Dr. Broussard took notes as they discussed Ayo's history.

"When did the pain increase from sporadic to every month?"

Ayo's recollection needed no prodding. "For the past year, just before each period I've had to spend at least part of a day lying down. I used to be able to work around it, but not anymore. And I spent three days over the Thanksgiving holiday in bed. Ever since then, it hasn't let up."

Dr. Broussard frowned and halted her slanted, left-handed scribbling. "What have your other doctors told you?"

Ayo sighed. "One told me there was no reason other than the cramps that some women experience; another thought it might be fibroids."

"The first thing I need to do is a pelvic exam." A smile pulled at the corners of her mouth. "Okay, now, assume the position." Turning to the counter, she pulled on a pair of latex gloves. Laughing, she held it up and unwrapped a plastic version of the old fashioned metal speculum. "The days of the internal application of ice are gone!"

Dr. Broussard began the examination. "I'm going to move your uterus slightly. Let me know if it hurts."

Ayo couldn't utter a word. A gasp of pain spoke for her.

"Does it hurt here, also?" Dr. Broussard pressed on Ayo's abdomen as she probed her internal organs. Ayo winced and raised herself slightly from the table.

"Yes…" She expelled the word in a short, pain-filled hiss. By the time the examination was over, Ayo was certain most of her female organs had been relocated to the middle of her chest.

Dr. Broussard patted Ayo's hand. "Okay, you can sit up now, and get dressed. I'll come back, and we'll talk about what's next." She gathered her notes and left with another reassuring smile.

When Ayo was dressed, Dr. Broussard returned, handing Ayo one of two foil-wrapped chocolates. "If you're anything like me, you need this right now. A little won't hurt."

After popping a square of the candy into her own mouth, Dr. Broussard resumed her seat on the stool. "Here's what I want to do. I want to perform what's called a laparoscopy. It's minor surgery—"

Ayo's insides clenched. "Oh no!"

Dr. Broussard leaned forward and covered Ayo's trembling hands. "Oh, please don't be upset. I know the word *surgery* sounds serious, but it really is minor. Laparoscopy is an exam of your internal organs. Once I get a look inside, I'll know whether to rule in or rule out endometriosis. Then we'll really know how to proceed."

In spite of Dr. Broussard's attempts to reassure her, a twinge of dread plucked at Ayo's hopes. She kept focused on the doctor's optimism to hold it at bay.

"I've heard of it, but don't know what it really is."

"You're not alone—a lot of women have been misdiagnosed, although they suffer every month. But many have no pain at all, although they still have endometriosis. And what makes it even more frustrating is the explanation like the one you were given—'I can't find anything.' Well, something is causing your extreme discomfort and I intend to find out. First, you need to know what endometriosis is."

"I sure do. I haven't had a name or a clue about what's been happening with my insides." Ayo bounced the back of her legs against the table until the motion got on her own nerves. Sighing, she pressed both hands on her thighs to still the nervous jiggling.

"In a nutshell, it's caused when the tissue that's supposed to be inside the uterus finds its way outside. It attaches itself to other places in a woman's body—places like her ovaries and fallopian tubes, the abdominal organs, outside the uterus or the bowels. Now this is rare, but sometimes the lesions can even find their way outside the abdomen."

"Lesion? You mean like an open wound?" Ayo jerked forward, dragging a foot of the paper sheeting with her. Were her insides an oozing mass of infection?

"Oh no." Dr. Broussard shook her head. The cameos dangled back and forth. "In this case, lesion means the cells attach themselves in places where they don't belong."

A childhood image of raw yeast dough came to mind. Ayo would pinch off a handful and stuff it into her mouth. Her mother teased her, saying that it would twist into a sticky maze around her insides and never go away. At the moment, the image was too disturbing.

Ayo twisted the end of her exam gown into a wrinkled knot. Frowning, she stilled herself and listened as Dr. Broussard continued her explanation. This was much worse than she imagined.

"So do the lesions cause the pain?"

"Your body reacts to the swelling and bleeding by surrounding the cells with scar tissue. During your cycle, it becomes swollen, and painful. And as it grows and the scar tissue increases, it can cover and bind the abdominal organs."

"Oh, Lord," Ayo whispered. "Can it be cured?"

Dr. Broussard looked Ayo straight in the eye. Although Ayo appreciated the doctor's direct responses, she also feared them.

"Mrs. Montgomery, endometriosis is a chronic condition, and sometimes it gets worse. I'm not trying to alarm you, but I want you to have a full understanding of what we're dealing with. When a woman has mild symptoms further treatment may not be necessary. With severe pain or infertility, treatment options include medications and surgery."

"Infertility?" Ayo clapped a hand over her mouth although the shout had already bounced against the walls of the exam room. "Are you saying that it can cause infertility? So if I have it, and it's been untreated, I could be infertile? That because I waited so long to get treatment, that there is no hope?" Ayo's voice rose with each question.

Dr. Broussard's forehead creased into a small frown. "I see that you gave birth twenty years ago. At this point in your life, is fertility still a concern?"

Ayo sobbed, oblivious to the doctor's question. "My mother was forty-four, almost forty-five, when I was born so I had no reason to think it wasn't possible."

Dr. Broussard snatched a handful of tissues from near the sink and handed them to Ayo. "Mrs. Montgomery," she repeated in a gentle voice, "You didn't answer me. Is fertility an issue for you now?"

Ayo nodded, swiping at tears that leaked from the corners of both eyes. "So what's involved in the surgery?"

Dr. Broussard leaned forward to answer Ayo's barely audible question. "Well one good thing about laparoscopy is that you can still wear a bikini without a scar." Ayo appreciated the doctor's attempt to lighten her distress, but it didn't work.

"I'll insert a lighted instrument through a small incision just below your navel to get a good look at your organs. And the other plus is that if I do find evidence of endometriosis, I can use the laser to remove the lesions while I'm in there. And if you're concerned about fertility, that treatment can be successful."

"And then what?"

"In seventy to eighty percent of women who've had the treatment, the pain is significantly lessened and much more manageable than what you've told me you've experienced."

"What about my ability to become pregnant?"

"We wait and see. Ms. Montgomery, don't allow yourself to give up until we know exactly what we're working with. There are those who will present you with statistics about the age of your eggs, coupled with what might be endometriosis. They'll tell you that there is little or no chance of you being able to have a child. But one of my roles is to give hope when there's cause for hope and that's what I'm giving you. I'm a basketball fan and I remember the 1978 championship games. The Washington Bullets were down, but Coach Motta told the fans 'The opera ain't over 'til the fat lady sings'." Yvette Broussard bent her arm and flexed her muscles. "And I'm not singing yet!"

A grim-faced Ayo looked up from her lap. "How soon can we do it? And can I go home when it's done?"

The doctor nodded. "Plan on day after tomorrow, for two reasons. One, I believe I have an early morning slot available, and two, because you can't eat and drink for eight hours before. I'm hoping you won't need an overnight stay, but plan on it, just in case." She stood to shake Ayo's hand. "Don't give up until I tell you, Mrs. Montgomery."

Eileen had been right about Dr. Broussard—she was a champion for her patients. Her holistic approach, from the décor of her office to the demeanor of her staff was meant to put them at ease, but on that day, she might as well have been a witch doctor. Nothing she said could remove the fear that fell over Ayo on the drive home. It was a fifteen minute trip crammed with a year's worth of dread.

At home, she dropped her bag on the floor and stretched across her bed. In the silence of her room, only one part of Dr. Broussard's observations stuck in her head. For the first time, Ayo was glad Bilal was out of town. He'd ask too many questions that she didn't want to answer right now. She turned the TV on to one of the outrageous afternoon talk shows. In the middle of a neck swerving showdown between two women, Ayo fell asleep.

When she woke up, the evening news had replaced the talk show. It was time to eat, but her appetite was dead. Her imagination took its place, galloping all over the bleak landscape of everything that could be wrong. When she finally let go of her imaginings, a tiny speck of doubt had become Mt. Kilamanjaro. She needed to talk to somebody. Justine and Nick ate early; her call wouldn't disturb their evening meal. She hit speed dial; when Nicole answered, Ayo smiled in spite of her growing dread.

"Hey, Auntie Ayo." Nicole hadn't crossed over into the full-fledged moodiness of puberty; still childlike, she was a younger, bouncier version of her mother. "I'll get Mommy for you."

When Justine picked up, all of Ayo's pain and fear came tumbling out. "Every now and then I would feel like my happiness was too good to be true," she confessed. "I hate to admit it, but I wondered if something was lurking behind just waiting to snatch it all away from me."

"What do you mean? What does this have to do with your relationship with Bilal?" She hesitated. "Or is there something else, Ayo?"

Ayo's voice broke. She sucked in a deep breath and began to repeat what she learned from Dr. Broussard.

"I mean, I'm in love, real love, after all these years. My son has finally accepted my relationship. I'm engaged to a man who cannot wait to be my husband and father to our child. And now I may not be able to fulfill one very big part of his dream. See what I mean?"

Justine's silence bothered Ayo. *She knows I'm right this time.*

"No, I don't see what you mean, but I don't like where you're headed with this."

"But—"

"Wait a minute, Ayo. According to what you said, Dr. Broussard didn't rule out the chance of having a child."

"Justine, I heard her say the procedure would relieve a lot of the pain. I still might not be able to have a baby. Look how long I've had this and didn't know what it was. And look at my age. That's a double silver bullet aimed right at my reproductive organs."

"Ayo, stop it! You've already accepted the worse before you give nature and the treatment a chance. Please don't jump the gun and start talking about not being able to have a baby. If you have to cross that bridge, cross it when you get to it! Have you told Bilal about the surgery?"

"He'll still be away. And no, I'm not going to tell him. Any of it."

Chapter 14

That night after her surgery, Ayo lay drifting in and out of sleep. Her thoughts bounced around like gobbling Pac-man ghosts. It had been years since she felt this kind of despair. When she finally closed her eyes, grief took her back to a pain as sharp as it had been twenty years ago.

It was the rainy season in Trinidad and Tobago. Inside a door near the runway at Piarco Airport, Ayo Mansfield Montgomery stood flanked by her closest and newest friends. She felt slapped awake, jerked from sleep and made to stand on legs too weak to hold the weight of her grief. But if she fell, Justine Lewis would catch her. Her other friend Neville was on the private jet due to land any minute. He was bringing Maurice home.

Just as the brilliant tropical sun broke through, the plane bearing her husband's body turned in a semi-circle and began its descent. Its wheels touched down, and the plane skidded to a stop near a hearse parked on the tarmac. The cargo bay opened, and the smooth polished casket was brought out. Ayo pressed a fist against her mouth to hold back a wail of despair. She hated Martin Perry, the petty dictator of the neighboring island of Meridia. It was his foot on the backs of his people that sent Maurice running to cover the turmoil on the tiny island.

"I'm a Caribbean man, not just a citizen of Trinidad and Tobago. I have to go," he insisted when she protested. "We didn't get rid of colonialism to end up oppressed by one of our own. And with my contacts on the island, I can tell the story better than anyone." If she hadn't given in so easily, he would still be alive. As it was, by the time she was twenty-two, Ayo Mansfield Montgomery had been a wife, a mother and a widow.

The dream jerked Ayo awake, pulling her back to the day when her life turned upside down. She pushed her way out of a fog that felt like a down straitjacket. Bracing her elbows, she tried to sit up but her head spun from the exertion. In slower motion, Ayo moved to the side of the bed. She sighed deeply, dropping her head into her upturned hands. "See you tomorrow, baby," Bilal had whispered. "Weather or not." Ayo stood up and stretched her arms high over her head. Her mood matched the dreary scene outside. Time to shower and force something into her stomach. She would need every scrap of strength she could muster to endure the next day.

❧

Ayo watched him from the big picture window. She could see his smile from where she stood. Modern day warrior king. That's how she described him to Justine. Today the description was perfect. Bilal's hair hung loose over the shoulders of a full-length black leather coat. It draped his broad shoulders and tall strong body like the ceremonial robe of a beloved, conquering monarch. Under it, he wore a pale gray turtleneck over black wool slacks. Soft black leather gloves covered his skilled hands—hands that turned a piece of plain wood into a work of art. Hands that brought her pleasure and tended her when she was sick. He wore the boots he bought on that perfect fall day in Annapolis, when he made her feel like Queen for a Day. "Anything you want," he told her, buying Ayo a spectacular set of candles scented for her favorite time of year—Grass, Salt Spray, Thunderstorm and Flower Garden. On Main Street he bought a sweater set he swore was made to match her hair and skin, and near the dock a hammered silver mirror from a shop full of Mexican handcrafts.

As soon as she opened the door, he swept her inside his coat into a long, tight embrace. She loved his scent; it was a blend of sandalwood, leather and masculinity. He inhaled, burying his face deep into her orange blossom-scented hair. "I missed you baby," he murmured, grazing his cheek back and forth against the soft spirals.

When she didn't respond, Bilal frowned and held her out from his embrace. "What's the matter? Or do I need to ask?" He thought she didn't take good enough care of herself. It was the source of a running disagreement, but nothing like the first argument that blew up between them when he found her struggling to fill an order. He raised her chin and spoke softly. "I'm not arguing, baby I'm concerned. I know how much Maracas Bay means to you, but your health is more important. Isn't your new medication working?" He knew that she'd seen the doctor, but all she told him was that Dr. Broussard had prescribed a different, stronger medication.

"I'll bet good money you've been getting up early and going to bed late. Your body finally crashed. That's probably why I couldn't get you on the phone the other day."

She returned his examination with a shaky smile. "No, that's not it. But we need to talk." She felt like Marie Antoinette on her way to the guillotine. But unlike the Queen of France, Ayo would have to live every day afterward with the results of her actions.

They sat in the same spot where on that unforgettable night, their journey began. Ayo closed her eyes, thinking back to the hot, tumultuous day he entered her life. His love was the last thing she was looking for, but he became everything and more than she ever expected to find. Fiercely protective, tender and passionate, he had been her strength, sometimes a compass, and always an anchor.

Ayo sat straight up, clasping both hands tight. The gesture erased Bilal's easy smile. Tensing, he leaned forward. When he tilted her face up to his, her resolve not to cry was lost. Hot tears spilled down her cheeks and onto his hand.

"Ayo, what is it? Come on, baby, talk to me!" The urgency in his voice made her falter. She wanted to tell him; she wanted to pour out all the hurt that had stolen her joy. And like the man he had proven himself to be, she knew that he'd move the earth for a way under, over, around or through whatever caused her pain. Except this time. Even his mighty love couldn't move this mountain. *Lord, help me.* Ayo sent up a silent prayer that her resolve wouldn't crumble.

"I need to tell you something."

"Okay," he said softly. "Go ahead, I'm listening." He shifted to face her directly. "And you already know whatever it is; we can deal with it together." He reached over to pry her hands loose, but she kept them locked together in a rigid knot. He shivered, as if an icy fingernail had been scraped down the center of his back. Moving closer, he leaned over to face her. "Just tell me. *Please.*"

Ayo trembled, dragging the dreadful words from a place of desperation. "I can't lie to you. It's not fair, and you'd find out anyway."

"What are you talking about?"

A steady trickle of tears tracked down her face. "I slept with another man."

"What did you say?" Bilal's eyes stretched wide. His whole body lurched forward. He looked like he'd been mugged from behind.

Ayo took a deep, harsh breath. Pressing both hands over her face, she pushed out the words through her fingers, words that were bile in her mouth. "While you were away, I slept with another man." Ayo dropped her head to avoid the shock and confusion that distorted his face. Instead, she squeezed her hands together, open and shut with such force that her nails dug half-moon dents into each palm.

"I don't believe you." Bilal's head turned back and forth in slow motion.

"It's true." Her voice could barely be heard. Ayo looked down quickly. Since childhood, that gesture had been the reflexive reaction to a lie.

When she looked up, it was her turn to be shocked. A sudden glorious smile wiped the mixture of horror and disbelief from Bilal's face. He was almost giddy with relief. Her misery lurched into fear. Was Bilal having a breakdown? He was way too happy for a man who had just been told by his fiancée that she had been unfaithful.

"Wait a minute," he blurted out. "I know what's happening! It's the medication. I'll bet it's too strong!" Tenderly, he brushed a finger across the tip of her nose. "My poor baby," he chuckled. "Your medicine has you talking straight out of your head." Bilal sank back against the cushions. "That's it," he repeated. She knew that look well—it was the desperate stare of someone grabbing at the last straw left.

Without doubt, this was the worst thing she had ever done. He'd never believe her, but then again, she'd never have the chance to tell him that the strength to utter such terrible words came from love. She took another deep breath and tried again, adding enough painful detail to make it sound real. "No, it's not the medicine, Bilal, it's me. While you were away, I ran into a man I'd had an affair with years before we met. We got together and one thing led to another. That's why you couldn't get me on the phone. And after that, I realized that what I really want is not a permanent relationship. It had been so long I'd forgotten that kind of freedom. And I want it back."

"No, Ayo." He shook his head slowly, unwilling to accept the words that twisted into him like a dull knife. "I don't believe you. You're not that kind of woman. And besides, you love me too much to hurt me like that. I know you do." Bilal latched on to any threadbare shred of hope he could find. Ayo breathed hard, as if she'd been running. The ugly words made her so sick she wanted to vomit. She had tried to hold back her tears, but the sight of his stricken face was too much. He was hurt, confused and in desperate denial. Dropping her hands in her head, Ayo sobbed.

Bilal pulled her forward with one hand pressed against her hair. Her cheek rested on his chest while his words tumbled out, one over the other. "'Here's what you'll do. Call your doctor tomorrow and ask her to rewrite the prescription for a lower dosage. I'll pick it up. I don't want you driving, because as loopy as it's making you, you could end up in an accident." The smile was back; it was small and shaky, but hopeful.

"I told you it's not the medication!" Ayo shouted, banging a fist on her thigh. "Can't you hear me?"

"I heard you, now you listen to me," Bilal strong voice squashed her retort. "And don't argue. Besides my love, the next thing you need is a good night's sleep. I won't leave you alone, but I'll sleep downstairs because you need to rest your body and clear your mind. In the morning we'll talk." With both thumbs, he brushed away tears caught on her lashes. The tender gesture brought on a fresh round of sobbing. "Don't cry, sweetheart," he crooned, with his lips against her forehead. "That's what 'for better or worse, in sickness and in health' means. They're much more than a few pretty words good for one day only." His smile returned. Bilal stood up quickly and shook his head. "If I was a drinking man, now would be the time. But I'll settle for some of that sweet lemonade that got me hooked in the first place." He winked and leaned down to kiss her. Before she could utter a word, he was out of the room.

In the kitchen, Bilal's breath whooshed out. He bent over and laid his head against the cool edge of the sink, trying to control the tremors that wracked his body. His thoughts careened like an out-of-control roller coaster. It *had* to be the medication. He was glad that she'd finally found a remedy for the pain that plagued her. He wanted her healed and pain-free, but not victim to a cure that drove her out of her mind. But tomorrow it would all be straightened out. *Insha'Allah.*

૪ં

Ayo slept until eight o'clock the next morning in a bed that looked like a fight had broken out under the covers. She bent over the bed, scrounging through the layers of linens for her robe.

Up until the time she spit out those dreadful words, Ayo thought she could handle Bilal's reaction. She had it all mapped out in her head. She would make her announcement, he would resist, she would insist, and it would be over. She should have known better. Not with a man who loved her as much as Bilal. Today was her last chance. She had to make it stick, for his sake as well as hers.

A couple of years ago, Ayo attended a wedding. From the time they walked down the aisle as husband and wife, the bride and groom told their friends they couldn't live without each other. Two years later the marriage was over. Ayo visited her friend and offered her a shoulder to cry on. The now ex-wife held up their wedding picture and wondered out loud. "How did we get from there to here?" Ayo feared it would be her fate as well if she didn't stick to her resolve. It was far better to create upheaval now in Bilal's life now than to ruin it later.

When she eased herself down the steps, the morning sun was weak, like a runny stream of yolk on a dull white plate. The scent of fresh coffee greeted her at the end of the stairs. "Oh my goodness!" She jumped back. Instead of still asleep on the daybed, Bilal sat at the kitchen table with an early morning offering. A plate of fresh fruit and a mini-loaf of fresh bread sat next to her jar of orange marmalade. A small container of oatmeal rested on the stove's warming tray. He must have made a trip to the Safeway's breakfast bar. Bilal was making it difficult, but Ayo was just as determined to swallow this bitter pill as swiftly as possible.

"Morning," she mumbled.

Bilal tilted his head to look up at her. His bland expression gave away nothing. "Hey, baby. I hope you feel better this morning." He gestured to her red and green hibiscus cup. "Sit down and get your motor running." He must have timed its preparation when he heard her moving around upstairs. "And by the way," he continued. "Just to make sure I was on the right track, I called Zahirah. She told me that it's possible to have an adverse reaction to prescribed medicine." He gave a dry laugh. "She told me about a woman whose dosage was too high; it had her out on the sidewalk, pulling up her dress and waving at the cars." His eyebrow lifted. "We can't have you making a spectacle of yourself out on the very proper Manchester Road, now can we?"

If I don't end it right now, I'll crumble and give in.

Ayo bent an elbow on the table and propped her head in the palm of her hand. Her voice was sharp and cold. "Didn't you hear what I said yesterday?"

Bilal looked up. The smile turned into a grim, desperate stare. His leg jumped, bumping up and down against the underside of the table. "And didn't you hear me? I told you I don't believe it."

Ayo shot up out of the chair. Her head pounded and her heart hurt, but she put on a performance worthy of every award the acting world could bestow. "Well, believe it! I screwed him. I liked it, and I'm going to do it again!"

Bilal slammed his fist on the table. Cold coffee spread in a brown pool over the bright yellow cloth. They faced each other, heaving like antagonists after the first round, egged on by pain, fear and anger. "Why this? Out of all the messed up things you could say, why did you pick this one?"

"Because it's true." Her flat delivery was no act. The after-effects of surgery and the will to keep up this heart-breaking deception drained her dry. The thermostat was set to 70, but the room felt like a sauna. Blood pounded in her temples. Reaching into her robe pocket, she took out a set of keys to Bilal's house. She removed them from the conch shell ring he had engraved with their initials in Key West. She held onto the shell, and without a word slid the keys across the stained cloth. Bilal stared. "Are you serious?" His hoarse voice rasped out the question.

Ayo jerked her head up and down. She was weak, lightheaded and dizzy and it had nothing to do with the surgery.

"Just like that? Well, Mrs. Montgomery, do this for me. Give me back the shell. Obviously, it means more to me than it does to you. And you find any and everything in this house that belongs to me and leave it in a box on the porch. That way I won't have to see you again. I'll be back in an hour—and don't make me wait!"

A half-hour later, Ayo dragged a covered plastic container to the porch. If it rained, even on the covered porch, a cardboard box would get wet. The least she could do was keep his belongings safe. Too bad she couldn't have done a better job with his heart, but if she'd known in September what she found out a few days ago, it would have never come to this.

Ayo shut the door and climbed into the daybed where Bilal slept, burying her face in the pillow, absorbing as much of him as she could. At dark, she was still in his space, still in the same robe she'd worn that morning.

❧

"What? What did he do to you, Mami? I'm coming up there to kick his ass! Didn't I tell you I wouldn't let anybody hurt you?"

"Kedar!" Ayo had to shout his name to make him listen. "Bilal didn't do anything. I was the one who broke it off. And he's in more pain that you can imagine. Don't ask me for any explanations; just leave it at that." Besides Bilal, Magda and Justine were the only other people who knew the real reason Ayo gave him for their breakup. Unlike Bilal, her cousin and best friend knew the truth.

"Have you lost your mind?" Magda tore into her with a cold fury rarely seen in the easygoing, nonjudgmental woman. "How could you fix your mouth to come up with that low-down lie? That man loves you—not your baby-making ability. If you weren't nearly as old as me, I would come over there and turn you over my knee!"

Justine had always been the voice of calm and reason, always willing to see an issue from every side. Not this time; her reprimand was sharp, swift and left no room for interruption. "Ayo, I know how you suffered when Maurice died. And you swore you would never endure that kind of pain again. But this is just plain ridiculous! Now look at what you did—you threw away a chance for real happiness based on some half-cocked notion that you can't have a baby. And since I'm your best friend it earns me the right to tell you that you're a damn fool."

Her voice shook, but Ayo held firm. "Justine, it was the only thing that I knew would drive him away. You know Bilal; if I told him I might not be able to get pregnant, he would have said it doesn't matter."

"And it wouldn't! Anybody, even strangers, can see how much he loves you."

"I love him too, and that's why he would have eventually worn me down. And I couldn't do that to him. Or me. I'd be waiting for the other shoe to drop—you know, the one that would fall with a thud when it was obvious that I couldn't conceive a child."

"And what gives you the right to decide how he should live his life?"

Ayo huffed out a sigh. "Look, Justine. I'm not a weeping, whining and flighty damsel who'd rather be a martyr than be happy with the man I love. This isn't the 'I'll run and let you catch me' game. I'm a realist, and at my age, I know that what a person is sure they can handle at the honeymoon phase can be a whole other ballgame when the reality of real life sets in. But make no mistake—he comes first. Bilal is what it's all about. He'll get over me eventually and find someone who can give him everything he wants. And I can't bear to lose anyone else that I love. Hell, you know I won't even get a pet."

One day, Ayo almost gave in. She was drawn to a pet store and the plaintive eyes of the tiny Jack Russell terrier called out. She went so far as to hold the warm wriggling puppy and feed it from her hand. But pets die, and when it did, her heart would break. As much as she wanted to bring him home, she left the puppy in his cage.

The only person who didn't call to lay her out was Zahirah. Only because she didn't have time, Ayo was certain. Before their breakup, Bilal told her that Zahirah and Kalil were in the middle of planning a trip to India. As for Latif, Ayo was certain he was somewhere deep in celebration.

A new routine had been set for her life. She still woke up before dawn and brewed a cup of coffee. But instead of working at her desk or in the soap kitchen, Ayo went back to bed. Around noon she mustered the strength to shower. Then back to bed where she cried until wet lashes fluttered against her palms like soggy birds trapped in a rainstorm. In the early afternoon, she made herself eat a bowl of soup and a half sandwich. She forced it down, if for no other reason than not to alarm her friends when she started looking like a scarecrow.

The first knock came on an afternoon whose bright beauty made her even more depressed. Instead of opening them up to the sun, Ayo had drawn the curtains closed and barely left the bed. It came again, but she ignored it and curled back under the covers. She couldn't remember placing an order for anything, but if it was a delivery, the driver could leave it on the porch. This time the pounding was rapid and insistent.

"Damn!" Ayo threw off the covers. "How many knocks does it take? Even a Saturday morning missionary eventually goes away!" She tied the loose robe around her waist and slipped her feet into the formerly white slippers. Before, she washed them every week. Now they had turned the color of old concrete. Ayo's feet hit the steps hard. At the door she peered through the peephole to get a look at her persistent visitor.

"Oh no!" Ayo slapped both hands over her mouth to squash the startled cry. If he heard her, he wouldn't go away until she opened the door. For a week after he picked up his things from the porch, Ayo didn't see or hear from Bilal. But then he began to call once a day, every day. Thankfully, the first time, she couldn't find the phone and he was forced to leave a message. "Tell me what hurts so much that you had to lie to me. I love you and whatever it is, we can work it out. Call me, baby." But she didn't. So he called her; over and over again. She was so afraid to hear his voice that she ignored the "unknown", "unavailable" and "private" callers and only answered numbers that came with the caller's name displayed.

She should have known he wouldn't slink off to lick his wounds. A man who loved her like Bilal Abdul-Salaam would fight to keep her. Wasn't that the kind of man she wanted? The sound of his voice made her want to throw open the door. To tell him everything and take her chances. But she couldn't.

"Ayo, baby; I know you're there. I won't embarrass you by banging on the door until your neighbors call the police." She heard the faint sound of his chuckle. "I just want to talk." Ayo crept back up the stairs and crawled under the covers. When she came out of hiding, the only light in her house came from the glow of the streetlight. After a week, the calls stopped. But he mounted a new campaign. Three mornings in a row, she looked out her bedroom window and saw the Commander parked at the end of her street. Ayo waited him out; he couldn't stay there all day. As soon as she thought it was safe, she ran to the Sequoia and sped off in the other direction. Instead of her usual route to the Safeway on Piney Branch Road and the Brightwood Post Office on Georgia Avenue, she drove deep into Montgomery County's Rockville to shop. After that near miss, she parked her truck in a tight space in the alley behind her house.

It crept up on her with small steps, until the morning she woke to find the full weight of her old enemy sitting heavy on her chest. *I'm back*, it leered. Depression smothered her like a pillow pressed tight against her face. Struggling against her bleak thoughts only magnified them. The business of Maracas Bay was the only thing that pulled her out of bed. Each day she worked past dark to avoid the sudden spells of crying that came at dusk. They drained her and made her head pound. She left her house only when the cupboard was truly bare or when Magda's pleadings finally pulled her over to Annapolis where she went through the motions, but came home just as miserable as she left.

A full night's sleep was impossible. Some sadistic internal alarm popped her lids open around two-thirty a.m. and made sure she couldn't get back to sleep until it was time to crawl out of bed. One afternoon Ayo sifted through the mail, separating junk from the pieces she needed to keep. A package of pain pills had come in a promotional mailing. She read the blurb with disinterest until the words "sleep aid" popped up. One night in desperation, instead of one, she took two of the tablets and fell into a welcomed, deep sleep. To her profound gratitude, it was seven in the morning when her eyes finally opened.

When the sample pack was empty, Ayo used the coupon to purchase a larger bottle. She took three until they couldn't keep her asleep past two-thirty a.m. The next night, Ayo stood in the bathroom and shook four of the chalky pills into her hand. It would be so easy. Until four became a handful. She looked long and hard at herself in the softly-lit mirror. Her hair had been her pride—who said black women couldn't grow long, natural hair? Now her twists were frizzy. Some of them had become unraveled. The smooth skin under her eyes had turned to dark bags. *Dead woman walking*. The words were like a warning, frightening with their accuracy. Without caring that the pills and paper would clog the toilet, Ayo tossed the whole thing and flushed it. In her room, she fell backwards on the bed and stared up at the ceiling. Tears leaked in a steady stream from the corners of her eyes. Soon the sides of her face, the pillowcase and the entire back of her neck were wet. It was five o'clock when she finally lifted her head out of the dampness.

On her second night without a pill Ayo lay desperately awake with a TV that had been on for twenty-four hours. Even so, she had no idea of what was happening on the programs that rolled from one into another. She flicked through the channels looking for distraction. It came with a stand of swaying palms and a pink sand beach. Ayo dropped the remote and sat straight up. The decision came to her like a clear voice carried through the still night air.

By four a.m. she was downstairs at her desk. She glanced at the radio and smiled, deciding not to turn it on. At that moment, quiet wasn't so bad. She scribbled a quick list of the steps necessary to put her plan into action. Turning on her computer, she went to work, clicking through the selections until she came to the tiny Bahamian island. She'd seen Harbour Island, known for its pink-sand solitude, on the same channel the year before. The cyber-travel agents worked quickly; Ayo's flight and hotel reservations were confirmed. This time next week she'd be slathered in sun tan oil.

Charged up by excitement and a surge of hope, Ayo made a list of her customers. Most of them had monthly standing orders, and their deliveries had just been made. She always worked a month ahead; soap didn't spoil and with the help of her assistant, the next month's orders could be wrapped, labeled, and ready to go in two days.

Although sunrise was two hours away, Ayo ran upstairs and pulled through her closet; ending up with a month's supply of summer clothing that was stylish and comfortable without screaming 'cruise ship.' In front of the mirror, Ayo grabbed a handful of hair and held it up. An hour of combing, parting and twisting later, her crown had been restored to its former glory. She laughed out loud at her expression in the mirror and the suitcases on her bed. Pumping her first into the air, Ayo shouted out into the room. "Okay that's it. I'm out of this camp!"

❧

"I'll be gone for a month, baby, but think about it, I'll be closer to you in the Bahamas than here in D.C. I need this, Kedar." Ayo sat at her desk with the phone cradled between her shoulder and ear, writing out bills and checking more tasks off her to-do list. The sun had come up, washing her office in bright gold. Knobby green buds on the azalea bush outside the window were a sign that spring was just around the corner. In more ways than one, Ayo told herself.

She braced herself for the barrage of questions that came along with Kedar's constant worry after her breakup with Bilal. One weekend he had shown up to surprise her. Magda and Buck told her about his calls, pleading for them to look after his mother.

"What about the house? And your orders?"

"Got it all under control, sweetheart. I'll prepay the utilities. You know they don't turn down money," she laughed. "And I'll have the mail held at the post office. Justine and Magda both have keys and Mr. Cheney has just retired from the Government Accounting Office. He's right across the street and home nearly all day, so he'll look out for the house too."

The silence on the other end meant that Kedar was going over his own mental list, making sure she hadn't left anything out. She knew he felt that her decision was a desperate one. For Ayo it was a beginning for peace and healing.

"Okay, then, what about the grass and the newspaper? You know that first spring growth turns the lawn into a jungle."

"I've got that on my list too. I stopped the newspaper and I'm going to hire a service to take care of the lawn while I'm gone. After you left last summer I had to fire Mr. Leroy."

"How come? I thought you liked the way he took care of the lawn and your gardens?"

"I did. Until Mr. Leroy decided that Old English 800 was a necessary part of a landscaper's equipment. I looked outside, and there he was staggering behind the lawnmower, cutting crop circles in my grass! Even before I got close, I could smell the liquor. I told him to let go of my lawnmower before he tore it up and to get his ass out of my yard. You know he had the nerve to come back the next week?" She chuckled at the memory of Mr. Leroy's drunken scrambling when she threatened to turn the hose on him. "I guess that was the end of you feeding him, too. I know he used to look forward to cutting that grass. It meant something good to eat when he was done. So did he stagger off hungry?"

"You know he didn't," Ayo chuckled. "Right after I waved the nozzle at him, I fed that old liquorhead." He was so drunk and looked so forlorn that Ayo dragged him inside and plopped him at her kitchen table for a meal of fried chicken, potato salad and homemade biscuits, even though he stank to high heaven of cheap liquor and sweat. "I had to. He'd end up in jail for walking under the influence!"

Kedar burst out laughing. "Mami, you ain't right. But I know you gotta do what you gotta do. Or want to do," he teased. "Like you keep telling me, 'Kedar, I'm a grown woman.'" Kedar mimicked his mother's tone as if he were her twin.

Ayo laughed out loud, and coming from the heart, it felt good. "Oh you got jokes, huh? But don't worry, okay?" She remembered one more thing to tell him. "Listen, Kedar. Justine, Nick and Nicole are in Louisiana. Just so she won't call you in a panic when she comes back, thinking I've done away with myself, I'll call her on her cell phone."

Ayo heard seconds of dead air before Kedar replied in a tone very different from their earlier bantering. "That's not funny, Mami."

It took her aback. "Oh, Kedar, I was just kidding! I may have been down, but I ain't crazy," she quipped. "Next to you, there's nothing I love more than myself. I'm going away to become Ayo again."

Three days later, Ayo sat on the balcony of her room at the Island Inn. As soon as the flight landed at North Eleuthra airport, Ayo felt the beginnings of peace she hadn't known in weeks. When her cab passed the yellow and blue sign announcing "Welcome to Harbour Island" and drove up to the pale pink eighteenth-century island home, Ayo knew she'd made the right choice. The online pictures didn't do the place enough justice. She fell in love on the spot with the elegant intimacy of the 20 room bed and breakfast. Her room looked over the sea and a group of palms that faced the talcum powder sand and water every color of blue imaginable. That second night she left the French doors open, exhilarated by the smell of the sea and the steady swish of the nighttime tide as it washed up on the sand.

On her first night the inn hosted a Bahamian barbecue on the beach. When the small band struck up a familiar calypso, Ayo jumped to her feet.

"Mrs. Montgomery, you move like you know that music." Pamela Phillips, co-owner with her husband Malcolm, and official greeter, came to stand by Ayo. Still moving, Ayo turned to Pamela, who joined in, clapping in time to the beat. Pamela's smooth brown cheeks creased into a broad smile. The two women's shoulders swayed together, and Pamela's mixed gray French braid swung in the middle of her back.

"Years ago I lived in Trinidad and sucked up the culture like a sponge." Music and dancing was good therapy. It had been years since Ayo danced to calypso outside under the stars. The memories of long-ago good times spurred her on.

"I'll say you did. You know all the words, too," Pamela pointed out.

"Don't I now! Wait until they get to the part about eating white meat," she giggled. "I still love calypso, and it's been too long since I've heard it live."

Ayo discovered that Pamela was the unofficial island griot. Under a palm tree, she shared her own love of history and research. The two women delved into an animated conversation that broke off only when Pamela tore herself away to attend to her duties as hostess. After the guests had retired to their rooms, Ayo stayed behind.

"I feel guilty for taking so much of your time. Please let me help you clean up." Inside the large pale blue kitchen, Pamela washed, Ayo dried, and Pamela's husband Malcolm put the dishes away. He kissed the top of his wife's head and offered a warning to Ayo. "You started something you know. You better watch out - she'll talk your ears off!"

"Oh, wait a minute," Ayo chimed in. "I come from a family of talkers and believe me, I can give as good as I get. But as I told Pamela, history is one of the loves of my life. Wherever I go, I want to know who, what, when, why, how, and what now," she joked. "Have no fear—I'll soak up as much as she can tell me."

The next morning, Ayo accepted Pamela's invitation for a crack of dawn cup of coffee. She wanted to hear more about the island called Briland by its residents. A daily ritual began; each morning Ayo met the pink-and- blue tropical sunrise with the one cup of coffee she was allowed, her journal and a seat at the end of the counter in Pamela's bright airy kitchen.

Days at the Inn began to feel like healing balm spread with love on a raw wound. Ayo wandered through Dunmore Town, completely taken by the tiny village with its bright red bougainvillea and palms. She loved the combination of tropical colors on Victorian-styled homes. They reminded her of pastries iced in white butter cream and decorated with lemon yellow or candy pink. "It's like New England set down in the Caribbean," she emailed Justine. She ate down-home at Ma Ruby's and splurged one night at the very exclusive Pink Sands for a different kind of Harbour Island experience.

One day an unexpected storm blew over the island, bringing rain and high winds, turning the palm fronds into flapping, ragged flags. The sea darkened and waves crashed into white foam against the sand. Ayo had always been drawn to storms. She pulled a chair close to the door to watch the dark gray beauty of the churning sky and rain. Her emotions moved with the waves, full of deep currents of both melancholy and hope. As all storms did, it gradually blew out to sea, allowing the day to turn back into brilliant sun drenched blue. In the same way, she'd find her way back to life. Leaning over in the chair, she rocked back and forth, hugging herself. A shadow of a smile flitted across her face. Who would believe that gray clouds and a stormy sea would bring her peace? Ayo remembered her mother's favorite phrase. *The Lord sent it if the devil brought it.*

Chapter 15
❧

No matter what time of day he slept—a daytime nap or in the middle of the night, his dreams were full of Ayo. He tried everything- going to bed early, working himself to exhaustion, but she always caught up with him on his final drift into sleep. Where was she? He had gotten used to her not answering his calls—they were a casualty of caller ID. On the one occasion he programmed his number not to show up, she hung up as soon as she heard his voice. But now, whenever he called either her cell or her home phone, he heard the voice he loved, but in a recorded message. Instead of driving down Fourteenth Street, he took a detour across Manchester Road, but each time, the big bronze Sequoia was nowhere to be seen.

Bilal filled every hour with enough work to force his thoughts away from the empty space she left. Later that morning, an unplanned gaping hole swallowed up the next day. "Mr. Abdul-Salaam, I am so sorry. Out of the blue, my mother changed her mind!" His client's contrite and apologetic voice poured into his ear. "She thinks I'm going to sell her silver. She doesn't remember telling me to find out how much it's worth!"

Against the desk, Bilal's pen tapped like the beak of an agitated woodpecker. Catching himself, he grabbed a pad from the slot above his desk to keep from scarring the polished surface. He pressed the phone's speaker button, leaning forward to rest his forehead on upturned palms. His hair fell forward, closing around the sides of his face, just as sheer misery had enclosed him since Ayo's shocking revelation.

"I understand, Mrs. Grant. Don't worry about it. It's happened before. Sometimes older people have second thoughts about letting a stranger near their treasured possessions." He hoped his neutral tone hid his own disappointment. "I know you've got a lot on your hands. How about I refund your deposit? No sense in adding insult to injury."

"Oh Lord bless you!" Mrs. Grant shouted. "I thought I was going to have to eat each one of those hundred dollars." The good deed made him feel better until he remembered a conversation he and Ayo had about tithing and good works. He sighed, remembering the early days and the ups and downs of what they laughingly called Islam 101. Bilal shook his head. Her memory came to mind, no matter what he was doing.

Near dusk, the setting sun hovered just outside the door, beaming a glare onto the computer screen and straight into his eyes. He switched it off, flipping through the leather appointment book he kept as backup in case his computer ever crashed. Somewhere inside he had tucked away a notice of an estate sale. If he was lucky, it would be tomorrow and he would be the first to show up. Instead, he found a yellow post-it note stuck on the back of one page, written in Ayo's slanted left-hand script. Whenever he came across something of hers, he didn't know whether to burn it in the backyard or make an altar from the bits and pieces of herself she left behind. Like last night. On his way to shower, when he reached into the linen closet, along with an oversized towel, a gossamer nightgown came out into his hands. It was pressed between two towels, left there from one of the times when she was in his bed, under him, from dusk to dawn. Bilal dropped the towel and went back to sit down hard on the side of his bed. He dropped his whole face into the fabric, searching for her scent behind the artificial fragrance of detergent and softener. Squeezing his eyes shut, he rubbed the fabric between his fingers, remembering the feel of her body under the silky garment.

Bilal's phone rang. He wanted to ignore it, but Zahirah was leaving for India soon.

"Hey, what's up?" Bilal took the phone and stretched out on his bed with the gown still in his other hand.

"You, Bilal."

Bilal shut his eyes. He should have known. It was Zahirah's turn to take up his mother's worried slack—showing up with a plate of food when she "just happened to be in the neighborhood" although the neighborhood was on the other side of town.

"Go ahead," he sighed. Let her get it off her chest, maybe it would be the first and last time he would have to deal with any more well-meaning commiseration.

"B, you and I have always been close. Even when we were kids, our disagreements were over and done in no time. Remember how we could almost read each other's thoughts? Don't forget that I'm a part of you, and when you feel pain, so do I. I'm not going to come over there and wring my hands like our mother would like to do," she laughed. "But I'm always with you in my heart. Even while we're in India, you won't be far from my thoughts."

The next morning, he stood at the door of his prayer room. In the upheaval that was his life, he had put aside the very thing that had always brought him peace. For the first time in weeks, Bilal entered the unadorned room and stood, repeating the *Al-Fatihah*, the opening to prayer, allowing its peace and beauty to flood his soul. "In the Name of Allah, Most Gracious, Most Merciful..."

How could he have forgotten this peace? There was no beseeching or begging, only submission and faith in the goodness of God. To him, it was the sole purpose of religion. And that realization gave him hope and fueled his never-ending determination to have the woman he loved back in his life.

He wouldn't press her about marriage. If she wanted, they could start slowly, even go back to the beginning and work their way forward. The first bright idea he'd had in a long while burst into his thoughts. Grabbing his phone, he scrolled through the speed dial numbers. Instead of a voice, he got a recording. *"Insha'Allah*, this has got to work," he told himself before he left a message. "I know I'm the last person you expected to hear from, but *please* call me."

Chapter 16

Out the sand, Ayo set up at her favorite spot, under the grove of palms at the edge of the beach. She had been on Harbour Island for nearly three weeks, immersing herself in the island's culture and small-town feel. In Dunmore Town she held long conversations with women who wove beautiful baskets at the small straw market, talking about their South Carolina Sea Island counterparts and their world-famous sea grass creations. The library drew her like a magnet. That day, however, all she wanted was to lie on the sand. It was still early, and some of the night's cool breeze still clung to the warm morning air. The beach sweeper had made its run, leaving two long tire grooves in the flat-packed sand. Blue and white beach chairs lined the water's edge, like elongated baby carriages with their hoods pulled back to display contented passengers.

Reaching inside her sand-dusted bag for a book, Ayo became absorbed by the story. A hundred pages later, she looked at her watch and answered the call of her stomach. She headed back across the sand, through the now familiar path up to the lobby. Near the desk, she glanced over to wave at Pamela. For the first time since Ayo arrived, her unflappable host appeared to be losing control. Frowning at a piece of paper near the phone, Pamela threw up her hands. Her husband grabbed the phone and another sheet of paper.

"I have no idea how we can serve this party," Pamela wailed. "And I can't get anyone else on such short notice."

Since the first morning Ayo sat at the corner of their kitchen table, she and the Phillips had become more than guest and hosts. They'd become friends, sharing stories over morning coffee. At night they picked up, with ginger beer for Ayo and rum and water for Pamela. They were obviously in a jam and if she could, she wanted to help. Putting her protesting stomach on hold, Ayo headed for the desk.

"What happened, Pamela?"

Pamela clutched the list of names in a death grip. Half of them had been slashed out by the black felt-tip pen Pamela brandished like a sword. Her eyebrows rose, sending a rippling frown up to her hairline. "Some Texans vacationing in Florida read about us in a tourist magazine and they booked us for a birthday party tonight. The seaplane gets in late this afternoon, but the woman we hired to cook for tonight is sick. Margie, our daytime cook, is attending her daughter's piano recital. I wouldn't even think of asking her to stay."

Ayo slid her bag and book behind the desk.

"What are you cooking? Caribbean or American?"

"Caribbean, of course. That's why they're taking the trip over." Her quizzical look brought a half-smile to Ayo's face. She grabbed Pamela's hand.

"I can help you. Give me an apron and put me to work!" If she hadn't been looking directly in their faces, she would have missed the fleeting glance of disbelief that passed between them.

Ayo's head bobbed. "Uh-huh, I saw that. And I know what you think. A Yankee can't cook Caribbean. But I've got news for you! I can throw down on some peas and rice. Let me cook you up a sample pelau, and if you like it, then we're in business. Do you have any seasoned chicken?"

Ayo ignored the "let's humor her" expression and followed them to the kitchen. Although it was as modern as Magda's, among the gleaming pans that hung over the stainless-steel cooking island, Ayo spotted Pamela's impressive collection of iron pots—the staple of West Indian cooking.

Pamela pulled open the refrigerator door and retrieved a bowl of chicken that had been soaking in garlic, chive, salt and pepper. Ayo found a box of rice and a can of pigeon peas. "Malcolm, I'll bet you a Kalik beer that you'll like it." She put one hand on her hip and cocked her head in his direction. "Might as well put it in the freezer now. I like it ice cold."

"We'll see!" Malcolm shot back a good-natured retort before returning to the lobby.

Turning to the stove, she turned a high flame under the big iron pot and coated the bottom with oil. When it began to sizzle and smoke, she dropped in a handful of sugar that caramelized, transforming itself into lacy brown bubbles. She whipped around, grinning at her skeptical host, pointing the long-handled kitchen spoon at the pot. "So far so good, huh?"

Ayo dropped pieces of chicken into the pot and stirred quickly, coating each piece. When it browned sufficiently, she added a lidful of water and turned it down to cook until it was time to add the long grain rice and peas.

Nearly an hour later, she called her guests to the counter set with two plates of steaming pelau accompanied by a bottle of D'Vanyas Junkanoo hot sauce.

"Okay, you nonbelievers, it's time to 'taste my hand.'" She wagged her finger at Malcolm. "And when you bring my Kalik, get one for you and Pamela," she winked. "But mine better be the coldest one in the fridge."

After the first forkful, Pamela and Malcolm peeped up from their plates. Ayo stood at the sink with her arms across her chest, battling to control her triumphant smile. "Well?" Their sheepish smiles were answer enough.

Pamela chided her husband. "Malcolm, give the woman her beer!" During her college years, Ayo made extra money working with Magda in her fledgling catering business. Like riding a bicycle, she never forgot the drill. Sipping her Kalik, Ayo set to work in earnest, gathering chive and onion, garlic and thyme for seasoning the pots of pelau that would take care of the crowd.

At eight on the dot, the party of Texans arrived by water taxi, sporting flower-splashed tropical shirts along with their ten gallon hats. The birthday boy's face was boiled-lobster red and from the looks of all of them, they'd gotten a good head start on the celebration.

The party soared into overdrive. Near the end of the meal, each man announced his gift. The last wobbling reveler stood and slurred out that his gift would be ten longhorn steer, ready for pickup as soon as they got back to the Lone Star state. A loud rowdy Texas-style cheer carried across the lawn.

Ayo stood watching at the kitchen door, dead on her feet, but exhilarated. At home she cooked every day, but here the simple, ordinary task had been made extraordinary by the setting and the circumstances. Instead of a sad, solitary tourist, that night she had become even more a part of the Island Inn family and Harbour Island itself. And back to becoming Ayo again. At least another half-mile on her way.

Chapter 17
𝕫✿

𝒯he adrenaline rush wound down. She was nowhere near as desperate as she had been, but in certain spots, the wall of her carefully constructed recovery had crumbled. What did she expect? It was impossible to love someone so much and have his memory die so quickly. She put up a strong front, but Bilal Abdul-Salaam still held every part of her heart.

Today it was conch salad. Every day she ate the spicy mix of chopped conch, tomatoes, onions, lime and hot pepper. The servers teased her, telling her of its aphrodisiac reputation and its ability to give a "strong back." Her thoughts flew to her lover; if the rumor was true, she and Bilal would be gasping for breath every day. Too bad it wasn't just as good for the other use of her female organs. If so she'd be healed by now and on the phone trying to get him back.

After lunch Ayo wandered past the reception area that was a cool invitation to lounge with a drink. Tall potted palms flanked either side of sea grass chairs arranged around a glass-topped coffee table. Overhead, the wooden blades of two large ceiling fans were a pleasant alternative to the chill of air-conditioning. When Ayo stepped inside, Pamela looked up from behind the desk and waved her over. "There you are! I've been waiting for you—come on into my office."

Ayo took a seat across from Pamela's mahogany Empire writing desk. A wall hanging took up half the wall. It was made from burlap that had somehow had been molded and formed into a painted mask. "That's really creative. I'd love to take something like that back home with me. Did you get it here on the island?"

Pamela's eyes twinkled. "No, I got it at the Bahamian Craft Village on Paradise Island. And you can get one there, too."

"Paradise Island?" Ayo had seen pictures of the island and its showpiece Atlantis Resort. "Uh-uh," Ayo kept her eyes on Pamela. The woman looked like she was about to explode out of her yellow tie-dyed shift. "It's not in the cards or the budget. Besides, I came here for the quiet and calm. No Paradise Island for me—at least not this time."

"Yes, this time, my dear. I have something for you!"

"Have you been hitting the rum early? Or are you trying to get rid of me?"

Pamela's pent-up glee burst out. She flapped an envelope in Ayo's face. "Yes ma'am, I am—not the rum, but the getting rid of!" She laughed again. "Listen, you pulled our fat out of the fire with that pelau, and Malcolm and I want to thank you properly."

"Oh no," Ayo protested. "You don't owe me anything. I should be thanking you. Serving that party brought back some good old memories—just the thing I needed to help me to take my mind off myself."

Pamela nodded. "I knew when you came here that you were dealing with some sadness. It's like a shadow over your sweetness."

Ayo drummed her nails on the arm of the rattan chair. "Oh, was I that obvious? Did I look like one of those maudlin heroines in the dreary English movies, moping across the dark and stormy moors searching for the dark and stormy hero?"

"Yep," Pamela chortled. "Malcolm and I pay close attention to our guests and more to our friends. Even when you and I were joking in the kitchen, I could see it." Pamela propped her elbow on the desk, resting her chin in her upturned palm. "So what happened?"

Sighing, Ayo shut her eyes briefly. The sun, salt air and the change of scenery had done her good. At least she was away from the scene of the crime and the reminders of what came before—quietly standing aside to watch him perform his sunrise prayer in a corner of her room; his bed, where he would lean against the headboard and cradle her between his thighs, his smile when she cooked up a big meal of all his favorite foods; the workroom that he had saved from terrible disorganization by taking one whole day and turning it into a clutter free space worthy of Martha's magazine. And she'd be lying if she didn't admit that his smile, his scent, and the depth of his love didn't come to her all times of day and night.

Ayo dropped her head. When she looked up, she met Pamela's understanding gaze with a rueful smile. "When I least expected it, I fell headfirst in love with a man." A ghost of a smile played at Ayo's lips. Nothing could dull the magic of those months. "It's safe to say he took me by storm. He wanted me and didn't stop until he had me— until we had each other." Her voice caught on the words. "On his birthday, he asked me to marry him. I couldn't wait to say yes. But it's over now."

Pamela's eyebrows rose. "Who broke it off? You or he?"

"I did. I did him a favor, although he doesn't know it yet. But in time to come, he'll thank me. Right now all he knows is that I hurt him terribly. And in spite of all that I said, he never gave up on us. That's why I'm here. Because I would have given in, and that would *not* be a good thing."

"So I guess he don't t'ink it's a favor yuh did him, eh?" Ayo's head snapped up. She had never heard Pamela speak in patois. Although she was, Ayo shouldn't have been surprised. Her sisters-in-law were "bilingual." Karen and Avril spoke the King's English better than the queen, but when it was time, those two could break it down with the best.

Ayo shook her head. "He doesn't know the particulars of the favor." She spoke softly.

Pamela gazed at Ayo before speaking. "So you all by yuhself is judge, jury, an' executioner?"

Ayo shut her eyes. Those words stripped her act of the love that fueled it, although nothing could have been further from the truth. When she didn't answer, Pamela spoke into the silence. "But I do know one thing—what's for you is going to find you, no matter how hard or far away you run. In the end it doesn't matter what you say or do."

"So they say," Ayo murmured. She looked up to see an impish smile crease Pamela's face.

"Look," Pamela told her, sliding the envelope across the table. "Here's something that might bring a little more sparkle back to your sad eyes. You've been on our quiet little island for three weeks. It's time for you to have a different kind of Bahamian experience."

What could she be talking about? Everything Ayo needed she found right here. "What..."

"Shush!" Pamela's warm smile took the edge of her command. "We won't take no for an answer and besides, it's already been taken care of. To thank you, and because we care about you, Malcolm and I reserved three days for you at the Comfort Suites over on Paradise Island." Pamela held up her hand. "Now don't interrupt, let me finish. It's like being at Atlantis without the pricey rooms. It's just across the street, and you'll have all the privileges of the resort just as if you were booked into one of those six hundred-dollar-a day rooms."

Ayo was stunned. She sank back into the chair and finally squeaked out two words. "Oh, Pamela."

"'Yes, Pamela' is all I want to hear." She used her no-nonsense voice, the same one Ayo heard her use on the staff when all other means of persuasion had failed.

"Yes, Pamela," she replied in a meek voice.

"Good." Pamela clapped once, signaling that the deal was done. "You leave tomorrow on the ferry. It's a two-hour trip and you'll be in Nassau Harbour around twelve-thirty. Okay? And from the harbor you can get a taxi to cross the bridge over to Paradise Island." Pamela waved her out of the room. "Off you go now. Get to packing."

The next morning, a taxi dropped Ayo off at the dock. When she heard ferry, she imagined something like the nine passenger vessel that traveled between Oxford and St. Michaels, Maryland. To her surprise, a sleek blue and yellow bullet idled in the harbor, holding passengers on both covered decks. Ayo snagged a seat next to the railing to watch the wake of the ferry as it surged through the Atlantic. Out on the water Ayo gave in to an unexpected sense of exhilaration. Whatever good came along, she planned to throw herself in its way and enjoy the high while it lasted.

The ferry docked in Nassau a little after twelve. Ahead of her, the towers of Atlantis stretched into the sky. The cab pulled behind a coral wall on the other side of Atlantis. Outside the Comfort Suites, the driver unfolded his lanky body from the driver's seat. He retrieved her bags and handed her a card. The sun gleamed off a tooth that matched his gold-rimmed glasses. "If you want to party across the bridge, I'm your man."

"Thank you," she replied politely, sticking his card into her purse. But no thanks. Partying was the last thing on her mind. Since she had gotten lucky, she intended to spend every day of her bonus trip on the white sand of Atlantis beach.

Ayo stripped off her traveling clothes, pulled on a black one-piece bathing suit and covered it with a sheer white sundress. Armed with a tote bag filled with a book, sunglasses and sunscreen, she dashed across the street, through the flower filled lobby of the Coral Towers and out to the far end of the maze of pools. She grabbed the last covered chair and staked out a spot on the Beach Towers pool deck. Servers clad in khaki shorts and tropical-print shirts threaded their way through the crowd of sunbathers serving elaborate tropical drinks and snacks. A server approached, wearing a crown of goddess braids.

"Drink, miss?" Just one, Ayo decided. A hotel guest near her ordered a Virgin Vice for his young daughter and a Miami Vice for himself and his wife. When the drink arrived, it looked like creamy glacier split in half by a long slide of red. "Oh, my goodness," she heard him moan with his eyes rolling up into his caterpillar eyebrows. What better recommendation could there be? "Miami Vice, please!" When it arrived, Ayo reveled in the creamy drink blended with just enough alcohol for a mild buzz. She looked up from a long slurp when she heard the scrape of the chair next to her.

"Oh hi! I just read that book and loved it!" If Tinkerbelle had a black twin, it would be this woman. Feathered black layers fell in wisps around the dark brown diamond of her face. Her full lips were painted the same red as her two-piece tankini. She offered Ayo a hand and a wide smile.

"I love it too. I couldn't wait to get my hands on this one. I've read them out of order, but who cares—the combination of romance and history can't be beat!"

"I guess I should introduce myself." The woman's voice bubbled. "I'm Regina Moore. My daughter and I are here from Chicago." Regina shaded her eyes and looked down the expanse of sand. "She's somewhere up the beach getting a temporary tattoo. I'm supposed to meet her. Would you like to walk with me?"

"Sure," Ayo replied, jumping at the chance. In spite of all her good intentions, the sight of couples brought on a sharp, melancholy ache. They were everywhere—strolling hand in hand through the marble columns of the Crystal Court, or hugged up together, taking pictures with their legs hanging over the seat of the giant golden Poseidon's Chair.

She and the bubbly, talkative woman walked down sandy steps to the crowded beach where sunbathers of all shapes and sizes dotted the fine sand like powdered sugar doughnuts, many with no regard for just how much flesh they stuffed into too little spandex.

"Come on over here when you're ready," Regina called to her daughter. The two women sat in the sand, digging in their heels. Out in the water, a parasail in the blue, black and yellow colors of the Bahamian flag hovered high above the waves. Overhead, they saw the dangling legs of a man waving down at a woman in the boat below him.

Ayo shook her head. "Not me. That is one brave man. If that's his wife, she must be fearless too. Or crazy. Look at her waving up at him!"

"I hear you. I can see the sights just as well from down here. But speaking of men, I saw a fine brother yesterday in the casino. At the baccarat table, at that—he must be loaded! Girl, if I weren't married, I'd have to introduce myself," she giggled. "He's tall and slender, mixed gray beard, good-looking in a rugged, real man kind of way! You know, one of those strong, silent types?" Regina's laughter that reminded Ayo of a silvery explosion. "And talk about class! None of that diamond pinkie ring mess." She leaned over to Ayo, twisted her mouth and waved her little finger. "Check out the rangs, baby," she drawled. Ayo fell back into her chair, howling at Regina's pimped out pronunciation. Finally the heat and a half day of traveling caused

Ayo's eyelids to droop. She stood and stifled a yawn. "I need to get a nap, but let's exchange numbers so we can get together later."

Regina dug into her bag and pulled out an envelope. She tore it in half and scribbled her number. Ayo took the other half and did the same. "Get some rest." Regina told Ayo. "I'll talk to you later."

As sleepy as she was, Ayo took a leisurely stroll through the marble corridors. Her credit card took a big hit in Coles of Nassau. She left the upscale resort-wear haven with a sheer white blouse and matching camisole, along with a pair of pale lavender sandals, each embroidered with a tiny palm tree. Since she spent very little on Harbour Island, Ayo considered the splurge a reward for good behavior. Back in her room, Ayo spread her purchases across the bed. Nothing like shopping therapy to chase away sleep. Or a touch of the blues. Instead of sprawling across the bed, Ayo showered and dressed in the casual, glamorous outfit, pairing it with lavender Capri pants. They were a perfect match with her new fly-girl shoes. She looked down, wiggling her pearl-polished toes in the glamorous sandals.

Between the pastel Harborside Villas and the Royal Towers, a stand of royal palms ringed the Atlantis Marina. Ayo stood at the earth-colored stone barrier, admiring the floating villas docked in front of her. But it was dusk, she was in the Caribbean and instead of soothing her, the beauty of the tropical dusk reminded her of the night she and Bilal became engaged. One of her favorite phrases came to mind- the one she used on herself when her emotions needed reeling in: *You better get a hold of yourself!*

"Beautiful evening isn't it?" Ayo spun around. Her self-directed reprimand was interrupted by a voice that was warm, rich and definitely African American male. His skin was the color of moist brown sugar. A slender salt and pepper mustache and beard followed his strong jaw line. Laugh lines crinkled at the corners of his eyes. This must be the brother Regina raved about. Ayo understood the attraction.

She smiled back. "Yes, it is. This glorious sunset over the water with the exception of the palms, it could be a summer night at home."

"Where is home?"

"Right now it's D.C., but home was originally Annapolis. And for a short time, Trinidad."

"Then you can't help but love the water." He stopped suddenly and held out his hand. "Please excuse my manners. I'm Paul Champion."

"Pleased to meet you, Paul. I'm Ayo Montgomery." The texture of his outstretched hand surprised her. It was more of a working man's hand than his elegant appearance suggested. "So you've been to Annapolis?"

"Oh, yes, I have. It's a beautiful part of the country." When he smiled, the lines at his eyes deepened. "I've sailed the Severn and the Chesapeake, over to Kent Island, down to St. Michaels, up to Chestertown through the Chester and Corsica Rivers."

Ayo was impressed. Her father had taken her fishing with him in a couple of those bodies of water. "You know the region well. I see you've been all over the land of pleasant living." The phrase sprung from her childhood memory. "Oh, now that really dates me," she chuckled.

The smile began at the corners of his dark eyes and traveled over the angles of his face. "You wear it well. Or as my son would say, you carry it like a soldier."

Ayo brightened. "Oh, you have a son too? I try to keep up with my son's lingo, although it changes weekly. But you know, our parents said the same thing about our slang. I try to remember that when I find myself horrified by something the kids say or do."

Turning to face Ayo, he leaned on both elbows against the brick wall facing the lineup of luxurious yachts. "Tell the truth!" he chuckled. "Gabriel just turned twenty-one and never fails to let me know he's legal now. My wife died when he was eight, and it's been just the two of us ever since. We've had some times," he laughed softly. Paul shook his head; his bemused expression transported him to a place that was the sole province of parents. "But now he's a Morehouse man and I could not be a prouder father."

Ayo smiled. She loved to hear men talk about their sons with the kind of obvious love and admiration that Paul had for Gabriel. Buck and Charles, Jr. had that kind of relationship, and although Buck accused Magda of rolling out a red carpet every time their son stepped outside his room, he was just as devoted.

Ayo's lips curved. "Paul and Gabriel Champion. You two sound like archangels, or at least members of the Justice League."

He threw his head back and laughed. "Gabriel is my brother's name. I named my son after him. And Mischief League is a better description for my brother and me. My mother said we had already gotten into all the trouble in the world and were going back for seconds."

Ayo cocked her head, shooting him a teasing question. "You sure we're not related? I have some cousins who must have made that second trip with you."

"Were they masters of the stall?"

"The stall?"

"You know," Paul said. "What does a kid say when he gets caught. What's his answer to 'boy what are you doing?'"

"He says 'huh?' That's it! To buy time until he can come up something that will save his behind!" Ayo clapped her hands. "And ask me how I know! My son Kedar got a double dose of mischief making—both sides of his family are certifiably crazy. Right now he's a junior at Florida Atlantic University, studying marine biology. My water child is also a master diver and now, of all the things he could think of, he's itching to become a rescue swimmer."

"That's an outstanding aspiration, especially for a young black man. I know it must be frightening for you, but I'll bet you're just as proud."

"I guess," Ayo sighed. "I try not to think about it too much. When I saw the coverage of Katrina, and those Coast Guard rescuers, I understood why. But the training is brutal. There are only 300 in the entire world. Maybe that's enough to put him out of the notion."

"How does his father feel?"

"I've been a widow for a long time. My husband died before Kedar was a year old."

Paul's expression softened. "So I see we have one more thing in common. We both survived the loss of a partner and raised a son. Sounds like we did pretty well, don't you think?"

Ayo's lips curved into a smile. "I'd say we did. College, on their way to adulthood with only a few minor bumps in the road—most definitely."

Suddenly, Paul stood up, favoring her with a slow smile. "Can I ask you a question?"

Intrigued, Ayo nodded. "Sure, go ahead."

"If you're here alone and have no plans, would you join me for dinner? I'm eating in tonight."

Ayo took a half step back. "Eating in? What do you mean?" She was on vacation and game enough to dine with him in public, but if he meant room service, she would have to pass. He looked like an upstanding citizen, but Ted Bundy must have looked the same way to his victims before he carried them off and killed them.

Ayo saw the tiny smile that tugged at the corners of his mouth. She couldn't care less. If Mr. Sophisticate thought she was too cautious, that was his problem. She was alone in a foreign country. Even in D.C. she wouldn't put herself behind a locked door with a total stranger. Before she could offer him a curt refusal, Paul leaned against the railing and burst out laughing.

"I wish you could see your face. You thought I was handing you a slick come-on, didn't you?" He choked out an apology. "I'm sorry, that's the last thing I intended!" A few more chuckles escaped during his explanation.

Some of her suspicion died away, but she was still confused. "Well, what did you mean?"

"Instead of in, I should have said on board." Paul turned and pointed to a yacht that was well past a hundred feet long. Under the name Trinity, another, larger name was lettered in bold gold script. Ayo turned to stare at Paul. "*The Black Star*! Is she yours?"

"Yep," he grinned. "That's my baby."

Good Lord! When Paul spoke earlier about the rivers he had sailed, Ayo never imagined a vessel like this beauty. *The Black Star* sat in the slip like a regal queen on her throne. "That is definitely not a sailboat!"

He chuckled, coming to stand closer, bringing with him the understated scent of wealth—warm, aromatic pipe tobacco and what she recognized as Clive Christian's X for Men. Ayo's nose hardly ever failed her. She could read the notes of a fragrance like a trained musician. The bergamot and Virginia cedar blended on his skin as if it had been designed with him in mind. She remembered the extravagant scent from a visit to a pricey boutique in Florida. If Paul was as wealthy as he appeared, $680 for a little less than two ounces was probably pocket change to him. Ayo couldn't wait to tell Regina to find a much better word that loaded to describe this man.

"I traded up," he grinned. "And I hope I've proven that I'm not a sex-crazed serial killer trying to lure you behind the door of my lair. So back to my question—will you join me?"

Above them, doormen, and taxi drivers waited outside. Hotel guests passed in and out of the hotel's doors. The marina was in plain view and next to *The Black Star*, the passengers on another yacht sat out on deck to watch the sunset. *Why not*? She was at an elaborate resort with an invitation to dine on a multi-million dollar yacht. More than likely, this would be her only chance for a peek into a lifestyle she'd never see again. And something to take her mind, however briefly, off the man she loved.

Ayo grasped the hand Paul held out to help her aboard. "I'd be delighted." She tilted her head in the direction of the next berth. "Besides, your neighbors are home, and somebody up there would see or hear me if I screamed or had to jump overboard."

Paul threw back his head. Rich warm laughter like honeyed butter welled up from his chest. "Since you put it like that, I guess I'd better be on my best behavior."

They mounted steps to the top deck. It was more luxurious beach house than boat deck, even for a yacht like *The Black Star*. On one side, it held a Jacuzzi, a stainless steel outdoor kitchen and white wrap-around banquettes. On the other side, six chairs upholstered in sky blue-and-white striped ticking were arranged around a gleaming blonde wood table.

Paul kept his hand under Ayo's elbow. "Would you like the grand tour?"

"If it's grander than what I just saw, I wouldn't miss it!"

If the upper deck displayed casual seaside elegance, the lower could have been a sumptuous palazzo on the Amalfi coast, filled with African and Asian art hung on cherry wood walls. Furniture in the cream and blue formal salon sat on silk carpets. She didn't bother to keep her awe in check. "You know, I feel like the country goose on her first visit to the city."

Paul's lips turned up into a half-smile. "I'm glad you like her.

On a lower level of *The Black Star*, two casually dressed men dueled it out in front of a video game console that could have come from the *Starship Enterprise*. They halted their furious clicking when Paul stepped into the salon. Both men stood.

"This is Captain Peter Nixon." Paul nodded in the direction of a tall, muscular man whose gleaming bald head was the color of Magda's apple brown betty. He turned to the other gamer, a shorter man wearing hoops in both ears and a skull-and-crossbones bandana over his cornrows. "And this is our chief steward, Billy Bennett, or Billy Bones, as we call him. That's because he's a walking encyclopedia on pirates—check the headgear. One day I expect to see the Jolly Roger flying from our mast!" Ayo joined in the three men's laughter.

Up on top, sunset bathed the marina and Royal Towers in an amber glow. Paul and Ayo dined on grilled lobster, Chateaubriand, conch chowder and an assortment of grilled vegetables and tropical fruit. From his onboard stock, he uncorked a bottle of what had to be very expensive champagne. Ayo never heard of Pol Roger, but it couldn't be a no-name, she chuckled to herself. Not with the display of wealth laid out before her. Paul poured the pale bubbly into two delicate flutes etched with a bold, masculine capital C. He stood and smiled, raising his glass. "Here's to the unparalleled beauty of a tropical night and to the beginning of a new friendship."

Just as Paul completed the toast, Captain Nixon and Billy appeared at the top of the steps. He waved the two men over. "Come on and get some of this food. I'm sure it'll go down good with NBA Live. It can be a consolation prize to the loser," he joked. After the two men retreated downstairs to their game, Paul told her more about his sailing companions and their yearly voyages.

Her own story was far less exciting but Ayo liked the way he paid attention as if she was recounting a tale as exciting as his. "I needed a break," she told him of the round-about route she took to end up on Paradise Island. "When I did my hosts a favor, they presented me with this extra special thank-you." The champagne loosened her tongue and she unfurled the story her life in the best Mansfield tradition.

"I used to be a researcher—I still am in my heart, but now I make bath and body products in a soap kitchen at home. The success of my business crept up and really surprised me, especially since it started out as a hobby."

"You make them all by yourself?"

"Pretty much," she replied through a forkful of butter-drenched lobster. "I have an assistant who helps me package and label my products, but all the formulating and mixing is mine alone."

He leaned over to refill her glass. "That limits the markets you can reach. Have you ever thought about having your products manufactured by a private label company?"

Ayo nodded and placed her fork at the side of her plate. "I thought about it, but it would require more capital than I have right now. And I can't bring myself to give over production to an anonymous set of hands. They just wouldn't have the same emotional investment in my products as I do. And I love the formulating, the mixing, the stirring—you know, the whole creative process."

Paul nodded. He wiped his lips and dropped the napkin back in his lap. "You should do some research; it might not be as costly as you think. And if you provide them with your formula, they can duplicate it." Leaning across the elegant table, he added more lobster and vegetables to her plate. "I understand how proprietary you feel. But if you'd let me, I'd like to offer you some advice. You're limiting your growth by not expanding your production capabilities." He favored her with a smile. "And as much as you love it, you're also in business to make money, right?"

Making money was a skill Paul Champion had obviously mastered. While he spoke Ayo's gaze strayed around the opulent vessel. She wondered if he had a decorator or if he himself had chosen the blue bordered monogrammed napkins or the ice and cobalt blue table service. Paul's chuckle pulled her back. "No, I'm not a drug dealer, I'm too old to play *any* kind of ball and I definitely cannot sing or dance."

"Oh no!" Ayo choked on a giggle. "Drug dealer never crossed my mind. Maybe international man of mystery?" Her eyes sparkled from his sense of humor and two glasses of pricey champagne.

"Okay, if you say so," he teased. "What I am in real life is the chairman and CEO of an investment banking firm. But let's get back to you and your business. Let me help you by giving you the names of some of my contacts in the cosmetic world. The first thing you need is a business plan. When you get back to the States, give me a call. I can get you started and show you how to make your business a real success. It can be a great legacy for your son, even if he never looks at a jar of cream." He handed her an engraved card with PAUL CHAMPION, CHAMPION INVESTMENT GROUP in simple gold letters. "That's the number I give to people who don't have to pierce the human shield to reach me."

Ayo was impressed and intrigued. They were almost total strangers. Yet he offered to drop the same kind of knowledge that would cost thousands of dollars for the time and expertise of a business consultant.

"This is quite a gift, because Lord knows I need help. I'm good at the creative end, the mixing and the fixing, but after that, it's a slippery slope. It's only because of accounting software that I haven't gone off into the abyss of not knowing where my money has gone."

Paul's gaze flickered over Ayo's face and the skin exposed at the top of her blouse. "If your own skin is a testament to your product, you should do well."

She lowered her lashes. "Thank you."

Night had fallen. Soft, subtle lighting flooded the marina and the bronzed mythical creatures that stood at the top of the towers. Atlantis was lit up for the night.

Ayo reached to stack their plates and gather the silver and crumpled napkins. Paul jumped up and pressed both of his hands over hers.

"Stop," he laughed gently. "Unless you're applying for a crew position and you want me to see how quickly you can clear a table."

Shrugging, Ayo sent him a sheepish glance. "I can't help it."

"Oh, I know what's going on with you. I and my brother had kitchen duty after each one of our large family dinners. Believe me, I understand." He winked. She liked his sense of humor and the way he used it to put her more at ease.

Paul reached for the jacket draped across the back of his chair. "Do you feel up to a walk through the casino? All of a sudden I feel lucky."

"I'd love to. I took a quick look on the way back to my room. There's a lot of action going on in there," she observed, glancing down at her clothing and back up at him. He wore the linen jacket and slacks over a tailored white shirt as if they were white tie and tails.

On a less masculine man, his gaze would be considered dreamy. But on Paul, the look he gave her through lowered lids was just a shade below sexy, open admiration. It was classy, not pushy. Ayo was glad she accepted his invitation. If she hadn't, instead of a delicious meal on this spectacular yacht with good company and conversation, she'd probably be in her room, crying into a drink and wasting Pamela and Malcolm's generous gift.

The casino throbbed from the clink of coins, the shouts of winners and pulsing house music from the nearby disco. A steady stream of gamblers and hopefuls moved from poker to blackjack and over to the sports book where they could bet on the horses and team sports. Ayo was amazed. What couldn't people gamble on? Paul's game was baccarat, and by the end of the evening, he was one hundred thousand dollars richer.

It was late. Ayo patted her mouth to hold back the yawn that stretched open behind her hand.

Paul stood immediately. "Tired?"

"Just a little. It's been a long day, a lot of fun, sun and a little champagne," she smiled.

"And a good day, I hope. Glad to hear the fun part." His lids lowered slowly, a repeat of the same gaze he'd given her earlier. Paul placed a hand at the small of Ayo's back, steering her from the path of an excited slots winner barreling towards them with two cups brimming with tokens. A lot of that money would never make it out of Atlantis, thanks to the eye-catching displays that stayed lit up well past midnight. Ayo stopped to marvel at the Lalique satin-finished sharks standing out among the glittering crystal creations.

Ayo turned to him. As tired as she was, high excitement kept her from complete exhaustion. "It was wonderful. I feel like Ayo in Wonderland!"

Outside, they stood at the top of the steps watching as the moon laid a carpet of shimmering silver on the marina's water.

"I can arrange for it to continue, if you like."

Here it comes. Ayo waited to hear him out, but the answer would still be no. Dining on board was one thing, sleeping there was another?

"What do you mean?" She struggled to hold back the challenge that was ready to burst from her mouth.

"You seem to love the water just as much as I do. *The Black Star* carries a speed boat in her hull, and I'd love to take you for a early morning sail."

She almost laughed out loud at herself. *See, Ayo, that's what happens when you think you're cute.* Thank God she hadn't given him an indignant brush-off. Still, she had to give it some thought. So far Paul had been a perfect gentleman, although being out on the open water with man she'd just met was a little different than being docked at the marina. And she had promised Regina they would get together.

"Can I let you know in the morning? I'm supposed to meet a friend and her daughter, but we didn't set a time."

"Sure," he smiled back, without hesitation.

Ayo glanced over at him and chastised herself. *What did you think?*

That he'd fall to the ground, because now he might not get a chance to kill you and throw your body overboard?

"I want to leave around nine, so I can be back by noon for a meeting with an Indian business associate who's down here on vacation. You have my numbers. Call me as early as you like—wherever I'm docked in the world, I love to see the sun rise from my boat."

"Ah, you're a man after my own heart. To me, the sunrise is God's promise of a clean slate."

At the door of her much less opulent lodgings, Paul took her key, and unlocked the door but made no move further inside. He smiled as if he could read her thoughts. Ayo relaxed even more, now that the evening wouldn't end with her having to push him away, however gently. He was a true gentleman—that creature rarely found in the twenty-first century.

"Thank you for a wonderful evening. It was unexpected treat."

"You're very welcome," she replied. "And you're right—it was wonderful."

She stood at the door, watching as he headed back to *The Black Star*. A little ways up the walk, he turned and stood, raising his hand. "I hope you'll join me. And I'll wait for your call."

The next morning, Ayo was up, awaiting sunrise. A half hour later, she called to accept Paul's invitation. She waited until eight-thirty to call Regina.

"Girl, you hit the jackpot! I found out who that man is. He is more than loaded!"

Even over the phone, Regina vibrated with gossipy excitement. Ayo imagined the perky brown pixie grilling hotel employees for the scoop on Paul. "I know. He's the chairman and CEO of an investment banking company."

"Uh-huh, but that's not all! He's one of the richest men in the world. And I don't mean one of the richest in the black world, either. I mean richest men in the world. Period."

"You're kidding! Well, that explains that floating mansion of a yacht and the baccarat game last night. Even before that, I could tell he had money. It's like a subtle whisper rather than a new-money shout—know what I mean? Well, well, well—more power to the brother."

"More power to you, too. Go for it!"

Ayo chuckled. "No, fairy godmother, I'm not going for anything but a little peace and quiet."

Regina sucked her teeth. "Ayo, you listen to me! How many brothers are out there like him? You'd better snap him up or next thing you'll see him on TV with some horse-faced white woman."

Ayo clapped a hand over her mouth to hold back the shout of

laughter. Regina was like Justine on overdrive. If the two ever met, Ayo wouldn't stand a chance. Both of them would be perched on each of her shoulders like winged brown fairies, dispensing a nonstop stream of relationship advice.

Later that morning Paul and Ayo watched while Billy guided the smaller *North Star* speedboat from *The Black Star's* hull. Once on board, Paul took the wheel. A carafe of orange juice for him and mimosas for Ayo sat between them in the cockpit "I never drink and drive," Paul winked. Ayo sank back into her seat and let one arm dangle over the railing. Donning a pair of outrageous cat-eye shades she'd bought on her first-day shopping spree, she peered up as the sun shone bright in a perfect blue sky. Gliding through turquoise waters, on a day that was otherwise something out of a fantasy, a thought of home stole into her mind. Even though she shook it off, Ayo felt the shadow of sadness cross her face.

She looked up to see Paul watching her. His expression gave little away, but any female past puberty knew when a man was interested. His lips curved into a barely perceptible smile. He reached over to lay his palm on her hand and just as quickly, took it away.

Ayo watched and waited.

"I came down here to handle my business, as our kids would say, and to catch a little R and R. A woman was the last thing on my mind, but I'd be lying if I said I wasn't attracted to you. However, it appears that your heart is still somewhere in the District of Columbia. Am I right?"

Obviously, nothing went past his eyes. He didn't get to hand out that simple, but elegant gold-embossed card by not paying attention. She dropped her head. "You're very perceptive," she sighed. "It's a long story, and talking about it will take away from this beautiful day. And I refuse to do that."

"I gathered as much. When you get past it, I hope I'm the first person you call. If that time comes, call me, wherever I am in the world. You have the numbers. And even if that day never comes, I hope we can stay in touch. You'll find that I'm just as good a friend as I am a lover."

At that, he stood, grinning like a mischievous schoolboy. Suddenly, the boat plowed through the waves. Ayo's high spirits increased with the vessel's speed. Leaning far back in her seat, she stretched out her arms and twisted from side to side in the swivel chair, enjoying the moment for all that is was worth. Where else would she being drinking champagne at eleven o'clock in the morning, feasting on lobster kabobs and tropical fruit salad?

Back on shore, Paul insisted on walking her back to the Comfort

Suites. This time she held the door open for him. Glancing at his watch, he shook his head. "I can only stay for a minute. Even though my meeting is informal, I still need to get cleaned up and be on time. But since you leave tomorrow, will you have dinner with me tonight? You get to pick the place."

∂◆

Ayo spent the rest of the day with Regina. The two new friends lounged under the towering palms of the Royal Baths, laughing at Regina's detailed analysis of what Ayo should do about Paul Champion and watching people shriek their way down the Mayan Temple slide.

"I hear you, but he's definitely interested. I would have had that man signed, sealed and delivered before I got back home. Anyway, how bad could it be? He probably travels a lot. If you found out you couldn't stand him, at least you'd be living in the lap of luxury and wouldn't have to deal with him every day."

Ayo slapped the armrest and shook her head, laughing at Regina's determined stare. "You don't quit, do you? And let me tell you, it is *not* all about the Benjamins!"

That night, Ayo's sundress was the same ice blue as Paul's tableware. She and Paul dined on the *North Star's* flybridge, watching dusk arrive in streaks of blue and coral that reminded Ayo of a swirled, layered desert. When he placed a package next to her plate, her eyes grew wide. Tiny sea shells adorned the ends of the silver bow. The exquisite packaging was a gift in itself.

Paul smiled down at her. "Go on, open it. And before your mind starts working, it's a strictly no-strings gift to thank you for two wonderful days."

Ayo chuckled at his explanation. She pried it open carefully. Inside, the Lalique shark rested among a froth of white tissue.

"Oh Paul! I don't know what to say, except thank you so much! It's beautiful!"

"Your pleasure and your friendship is more than sufficient. He looked down into her eyes. "And I mean it." His mouth twitched into a smile. "So we're cool, right?"

"Right," Ayo nodded, returning his smile, and grateful that he was truly a gentleman and would be a friend, even after they each left paradise. After dinner they stood at *The Black Star's* railing. Water lapped gently at the hull. The tall palms rustled in the tropical evening breeze. Ayo looked around, drinking in her last look at this part of paradise.

Paul leaned forward and looked over at her. "If you want, I can take you back to Harbour Island on *The Black Star*. What do you say?"

Ayo's hand rested on his arm. "Even though it's only been two days, you know that I have a word for every occasion."

He laughed out loud. "Indeed I do."

"Hush!" she chuckled. "But even I don't have any words to thank you for the wonderful time I've had. You've been a real gentleman. There may be another word, but to me it's the best description for you. You saw where my head was and didn't press me. But let's leave my magical adventure right where it started. At least for now."

Paul brushed his hand under her chin before he took both her hands. "I would love nothing more than to ease you out of that sadness. But I know it takes time—it has to. If it didn't, I'd know for sure I was a rebound. And I don't want that from you. I want you to come to me free and clear, ready to accept all I have to give."

Ayo shut her eyes and cupped both hands over her face. "I don't know what to say," she murmured.

Paul pried her hands loose. "You don't have to say anything," he laughed softly. His eyebrow peaked. "I can wish, can't I? But remember this—if you ever need anything, and I mean anything, or want more than friendship, just say the word. Wherever I am, I'll come to you or send for you."

Chapter 18

❧

$\mathcal{P}$amela poured herself just enough Coke to cover the bottom of a shot glass and topped it off with rum. She handed Ayo a glass of cold, tangy ginger beer. Taking her usual seat at the table, Ayo ran her hand in a slow motion over the dark circle of grain in its center.

"This is where it all started, with one taste of pelau." She took a quick sip of her drink and held it out for inspection. "Ah, that's good. But I'll have you know that for two days I drank only champagne. And I don't mean Andre Cold Duck, either!" Her mouth puckered from the strong, sweet taste of ginger. "Let me stop lying. I had one Miami Vice and a little champagne, because although I really have no business drinking at all, I couldn't help myself. *That door is shut already*. And when I get home, I'm looking up Pol Roger to find out why Winston Churchill's name was on that bottle!"

The next morning, when she woke up, the sun had been high in the sky for hours. Ayo took a quick shower and ran down to the beach, hoping that a covered beach chair was still available. Two hours into her lazy lounging, Ayo looked up to see a server headed in her direction. Shading her eyes, she frowned. He had just brought her a glass of ginger beer. Why was he coming back so soon? And running like somebody was chasing him?

"Mrs. Montgomery, you're wanted in the lobby." The young man stood over her, sweating and out of breath.

Ayo jumped up. Her book landed with a splat in the sand. Fearful thoughts gathered like sudden storm clouds inside her head. She stared at the young man as if he was speaking another language.

"Is it a phone call? Is it my son?"

"Miss Pamela just said to come. I think you have a visitor."

A visitor? Ayo relaxed a little, but her fear had been replaced by confusion. There were only two people close enough to the island to pay her a visit. Paul wasn't due to leave Paradise Island until the following week. As interested as he had been, even he wouldn't sail for two hours after seeing her the day before. At least she didn't think so. Maybe Kedar decided to come over from Florida. It would be just like him to show up to check on her. Although she kept in constant contact with her son, he was still convinced she was not at fine as she made out to be.

Wrapping a white parea over her suit, Ayo rushed through the path and up to the lobby. She swept the lobby with an anxious gaze, but saw no one she recognized.

"Ayo."

The sun beat down hot outside, but a chill prickled Ayo's neck. No. She shook her head, refusing to turn in the direction of that voice.

"*Ayo.*"

If she looked her hallucination straight in the eye, it would go away. Ayo turned. "Oh, no!" Her chest heaved in and out like bellows. She stumbled back, but Bilal covered the distance between them in two strides, catching her before the back of her legs hit the bench.

"Ayo, *baby*," he whispered, pulling her into his arms. Ayo burst into tears. She grabbed handfuls of his shirt and pressed her face hard against his chest, wetting and wrinkling the white cotton. Bilal slid one arm from around her, and with his free hand, dug through his pockets until he pulled out a crumpled airline napkin to blot her streaming tears.

Malcolm's wary attention on the couple was taken away by a whining guest whose loud voice broadcast a litany of petty complaints throughout the lobby. When he heard Ayo cry out, Malcolm's head jerked up. Swiftly rounding the desk, he rushed toward them, aiming a threatening scowl at Bilal. "What de hell yuh t'ink yuh doin'?" Malcolm's tone dropped from British-tinged English into a growling Caribbean patois, snapping Ayo out of her shocked silence. Before she could open her mouth, Bilal whirled around.

"I'm holding the woman I love–that's what I'm doing!" His voice took on a harder edge. "And what business is it of yours?" Although he was in a public place in a foreign country, Bilal appeared ready to take on a legion of Spartans and toss them all out into the crushed gravel driveway.

Ayo stepped between the two men before the terse words turned into a shouting match, or worse.

"I'm okay, I'm okay," she stuttered. "I know him, Malcolm. I'm shocked to see him, but I'm okay. And you know how much I appreciate your concern," she added. Her words were directed to Malcolm, but she couldn't tear her gaze away from Bilal. He dialed down the dangerous look to one of extreme annoyance.

"If you say so." Malcolm glared at Bilal and sucked his teeth long and hard, drawing out the Caribbean sound of disgust. "But I'll be right here if you need me."

Ayo shook her head as if the gesture could clear her vision. So much bitterness had been squeezed into the last hour they spent together that she never expected another civil word between them, let alone be close enough to kiss.

"I see you in front of me, but I still can't believe it. And how on earth did you find me?"

Bilal dropped his bag on the floor next to a rattan love seat. He sat and drew her down beside him. One twist had fallen forward and stuck to her damp cheek. He brushed it back and cupped her face in both hands. Automatically, her hands encircled his wrists, finding their familiar place.

"Kedar told me."

"Kedar?"

He closed her mouth with a quick, but gentle kiss. "First things first. I know I'm the last person you expected to see, especially after the way we parted. And I hated the way it happened."

Ayo's head bobbed up and down. "But why? Why would you come all the way to find me after what I said to you?" That lie stuck inside her heart like a fish bone in her throat. She would never forget the stricken look on Bilal's face when she piled on the hurtful words. And their toxic exchange in her kitchen had been one of the most heartbreaking moments of her life. She had seen him angry before, but that day his rage had been formidable and frightening.

"For the only reason a man in love can give. I came to get my woman back."

Ayo choked back a startled sigh. If she didn't know better, she'd say her dreams conjured him up, sending an unconscious message to the man she could not get out of her mind. Pamela's prophetic words came back: *you can run but you can't hide.*

Bilal's gaze bored into her. "For a one whole day, I despised you." He gave a self-deprecating laugh. "But you know that couldn't last."

Ayo opened her mouth, but he closed it with another kiss. "Let me finish, baby, let me get it all out." He leaned closer, touching her forehead with his own. "When I left your house that first time, I was finally convinced that you were telling the truth. During that time, instead of making *salat* five times a day, I didn't pray at all. And then I went back to the one thing that had always given me peace in troubled times. That day, after morning prayer, I decided that even if it did happen, I wanted to move past it and back to us. But outside the heat of emotion, I gave it even more thought and came to one conclusion." His unwavering stare bored straight into her eyes. "You're lying. There is nothing you can say to convince me that you were with another man." He paused, to catch a breath just brief enough to keep her from cutting in.

"I'm here for three days. For two days we won't speak a word about what drove us apart. Remember what I told you? About being my other half? So if you can convince me that you don't love or want me, on the third day, I'll abide by what you say and leave you alone forever. But I don't believe you can."

Ayo's mouth quivered. She leaned forward to look past the alcove where they sat. She couldn't fall apart again, especially in front of the guests moving through reception area. Or give Malcolm another reason to confront Bilal.

Ayo kept silent, trying to get a grasp on the thoughts that swirled through her brain like tumbleweeds in a high wind. Bilal knew her heart. He knew she was lying, in spite of the hard way she handed him the news. News she thought would keep him away forever. Now here he was, on this island, and in the hotel where she was trying valiantly to reclaim herself. And here she was wrapped in his arms, as if nothing had happened.

Her mind and heart waged a fierce, but brief battle. In the end there was no other answer to give the man who had put his life on hold and flown to find her, not knowing what reception he would receive. Ayo nodded, and whispered out the word.

Bilal's face lit up in a slow smile that spread across his face. He held her close, rocking her from side to side in his strong, familiar embrace. His chin rested in her hair "Remember the first time you said yes to me? Just like that night, it's the only word I want to hear."

Ayo broke away when she heard steady movement behind them. Lunchtime seating had already begun. Ayo heard his stomach rumble and in spite of herself, she giggled. She was glad for the break it gave to her topsy-turvy emotions. "Let's go eat. I know you want to make up for lost time. And then you have to tell me how you got in touch with Kedar." The scent of pepper, and spicy sauces coaxed another rumble from his stomach. Laughing, she poked a finger just above his waistband. "I remember that hungry bear."

Bilal stood and held out his hand. "That hungry bear is starved! Now that I can stop holding my breath and put some food in my stomach, I can't wait to chow down."

At the door of dining room, Pamela welcomed Bilal again, before turning her attention to Ayo. "Can I speak to you a moment?" She turned to beam at Bilal. "I'm sure you're ready to eat, and I won't keep her long."

"Sure," he smiled back, unable to take his eyes off Ayo. "I've waited a long time. I can wait a little longer. I'll just take a look at the menu."

Out of his sight, Pamela pulled Ayo into a corner between the lobby and restaurant. "What ah tell yuh 'bout runnin' and hidin'?" she whispered. Her eyes twinkled with wicked merriment. "And oh gosh, girl, dat is one fine man. Yuh crazy to hide from he!"

With her hotelier/hostess demeanor back in place, Pamela seated them in a private alcove looking out over the vibrant tropical garden. Behind Bilal's head she mouthed "this is your lucky day" to Ayo. Overhead, a swirl of white clouds stretched across the azure blue sky. When their meal arrived, instead of one serving, Bilal's stoneware plate was filled to the edge with broiled fish, peas and rice and fried plantain.

For the first time since she arrived, instead of enjoying the meal, Ayo shifted her food around the plate. Bilal, however, loaded his fork and nearly swallowed the food whole. They fell into the conversation as if they'd spoken just the day before. "I know you need to fill up the abyss that is your stomach, but in between bites, can you please tell me how you found Kedar? And how you convinced him to tell you I was here?"

He held up one hand. "Hold on." He swallowed a forkful of fish. "First I tried Magda, but the day I called she was out. I got desperate and called Kedar on his cell phone. Remember, he gave me the number right after Christmas? Anyway, I left messages for both of them and he called me back first."

"But what did Kedar say?" They couldn't have argued; if Kedar had become his enemy again, the conversation would have ended with a few curse words and a dial tone, just as quickly as it began.

Bilal took his attention away from the plate to lock his gaze onto hers. "That he doesn't know why we broke up. But he knows we're miserable apart. You know it too."

Ayo kept silent, suspended between joy and dread, waiting until the eleventh hour and the fifty-ninth minute of the third day.

ॐ

Bilal never made it to the room he'd booked in a hotel further up the beach. When Ayo opened the door of her room, the scent of orange blossoms wafted out and caressed him. Closing his eyes, Bilal tilted his head back and sighed. She carried her sweetness with her, and it triggered a flash of memories and emotions that were almost physical. The canopied bed and the sheer, billowing curtains were a backdrop to her beauty. She was lovely in any weather, but time on the island had been good to her. The sun had smoothed away the lines of anxiety that pleated her forehead and fanned out from the corners of her eyes when he last saw her. She bloomed like the gold and yellow-tipped bromeliads that graced the reception area. Earlier, he watched her rush up the walkway, wrapping a parea over her suit. The sun had darkened her skin to a glowing, creamy sheen and against the white translucent cotton, it was radiant. The twist-out cloud of springy spiraled hair stood around her face like the halo of a bronze Ethiopian Madonna.

Bilal's eyes devoured her. She didn't resist when he scooped her into his arms. He tugged at the tie, allowing the gauzy fabric to hit the floor. His hands slid under the straps of her suit and with one pull, he peeled it from her body. Ayo stood naked. She moaned softly, allowing his mouth free access to her body. He trailed it along on her neck-soft brushes with his lips, a long taste with his tongue. Gently sucking her earlobe, he circled the rim like the tease of a feather. Bilal began a long-awaited exploration of the sweet familiar places that held her scent—the bend of her elbow, the hollow at the base of her throat, the silky space between her breasts. Ayo gasped when his tongue took a long, slow circle around their brown edges, laving each damp, puckered nipple. She cried out, grasping handfuls of his hair, holding him against her. A blaze of heat surged through her body and turned liquid between her thighs. Ayo trembled in anticipation. His tongue brushed her navel and traveled downward to where her juices flowed. He closed his eyes and sighed. Her scent was a more powerful aphrodisiac than any perfume in the world. With the taste of her sweet on his tongue, he laid his cheek against her warm, trembling belly. "Even when you're not with me, I can close my eyes and call up your scent. I could find you blindfolded at midnight."

Hours later, hunger was the only thing that pulled them out of bed. On their way to dinner, Bilal took a good look at the grounds. *We could honeymoon right here*. How wonderful it would be to return to the place of their reunion. Or fly their families down for a destination wedding. Bilal ran his hand over the cherry side table, topped with pale pink and alabaster conch shells and starfish. Simple, elegant and natural. Perfect for an intimate family reception.

In the candlelight of their table, he watched her, loving her and deeply grateful that he had played his hunch. For whatever reason she made up that story, Bilal knew that Ayo loved him. It was that simple and at the same time, that complicated. Passionate, unpredictable, soothing, steady and constant—he had never experienced anything like her love and he wanted it back. The first day was almost over. He had two and a half days to make it happen.

❧

At first he thought the sound came from outside. He didn't want to, but he pulled his face away from Ayo's sweet-smelling hair and craned his neck. The noise was too insistent and artificial to come from the open windows where the only sounds should be birds calling and people going about the early morning business of the Inn. When he realized it was his phone and that it was also six-thirty in the morning, Bilal pulled himself completely away. He reached one hand to the floor and grabbed it. The sudden movement startled Ayo. Groggy and confused, she leaned up on one arm.

"Hello?" It was more a question than a greeting. He saw his apprehension reflected in Ayo's face.

"What?" Bilal bolted upright, gasping and shaking his head. "Oh no, oh no. Listen, I'll be home on the next flight I can get. No, I'm in the Bahamas. Yes, Mama, but I promise you, I'll be there soon."

Ayo spoke carefully, afraid of what she would hear. "What happened?" The disjointed conversation could only mean bad news.

His eked out the words as if he'd been running uphill. "Zahirah and Kalil are missing in India!" His voice broke. Ayo scrambled across the bed, pulling him into her embrace. "Oh my God, no!"

"I've got to get out of here. I've got to get home as soon as I can." Bilal bent over, picking through the jumble of their clothes on the floor, grabbing and stuffing them into his bag, dirty and clean rolled up together. The night before they pulled them off with no thought of anything but each other.

Ayo took over. "You go on and take a quick shower. Between me, Pamela and Malcolm, we'll get you out of here."

There was one seat left on the flight; even if she wanted to return with Bilal, she couldn't. Two hours later, he was at the North Eleuthra airport ready to make a connection to Ft. Lauderdale and then to D.C. Ayo stood inside with him, while the Inn's driver waited outside to take her back.

When his flight was called, Bilal pulled her closer into his embrace. They clung together, gaining strength from the comfort of each other's presence. "Thank you for getting this done for me. Just pray for me and my family. I love you baby," he whispered.

At that moment, in the midst of such a terrible crisis, what else could she say? "I love you too."

"I'll see you when you get home, I pray with good news."

He was gone, as quickly as he had come. She was sad and afraid for him and his family, but her own emotions were wound up in a huge tangled ball. The tragic news eclipsed everything, including the conversation they were supposed to have two days later. Her time was nearly up at the Island Inn. Instead of somewhere on the road to healing she was pulled right back where she was at the beginning.

Chapter 19

Bilal liked to fly. He enjoyed the urgent hustle and bustle of airports. He traveled with his laptop, and even the layovers that left hours between flights didn't bother him. Today, the wait was everlasting. He walked the terminal, barely noticing his fellow travelers or the shops that lined long corridors, offering everything from souvenir baseball caps to designer clothing. For the entire flight back to D.C., hope and fear battled for control of his thoughts.

As soon as the wheels touched the tarmac, Bilal was unbuckled and half out of his seat. He dashed off the plane and through the concourse, glad that this time he could bypass the creaking baggage carousel. Outside of Reagan National, the Ethiopian attendant waved him to the first cab in line. The cabbie looked up in the rear view mirror. "Sir, are you alright?" His cautious question was spoken in a thick Eastern European accent.

Bilal shook his head. "Sorry, man," he sighed, and halted the rapid-fire thud of his heel on the Bluebird cab's floor.

The ride took forever. Finally in front of his parent's house, Bilal raced up the steps and rapped his knuckles hard on the door.

When Latif pulled it open, Bilal drew in a sharp breath and took a step back. The stricken look on his father's face began a new ache in Bilal's heart. His gaze switched between his mother and father. They let go of each other only long enough to embrace their son and repeat the entire story they'd heard over a transatlantic call from Kalil's cousin.

"How could they be kidnapped in Mumbai?" Bilal whirled around to stare down the hall. If the girls heard his voice, they'd come running. Before he gathered his precious nieces in his arms, he had to hear all of what his parents knew.

Latif sat down, drawing his wife to sit beside him. "They weren't in Mumbai. They were in Bihar."

Bilal dropped in the chair and laid his head against the back. Squeezing his eyes shut, he massaged the space between them with his thumb and forefinger. "I remember now." He was lost in a recollection of Zahirah's excitement over the places she would finally get to see—Gaya, Patna, and the Mahabodhi Temple, the holiest site in Bhuddism. "How did this happen? Were they grabbed off the street? Who's looking for them?" His questions flew out rapid-fire into the room.

"Who knows?" Latif sighed deeply and shook his head. "Kalil's cousin Aziz told us that Bihar has a reputation for lawlessness. Visitors are advised to stay close to their hotels once they leave the tourist areas. Kidnapping for ransom is commonplace. Zahirah's obviously a foreigner and Kalil's obviously an expatriate. That equals big money in the eyes of the thugs who took them." Latif's voice broke. "I did some research on my own. I found some terrible reports in Indian newspapers. One gang demanded a million rupees from their victim's family. That's sixty-four thousand U.S. dollars." There were deep lines in his face that Bilal had never seen. "These people know that Kalil has family in India, but I'll bet anything that the US dollar is floating through their criminal minds. They must think we're all wealthy. That's why they haven't demanded a set price. They're trying to get as much from us as possible."

Bilal listened, but his mind had moved ahead to every and anything they could sell to bring his sister and brother-in-law home.

Suddenly Adilah stood up. "I can't hear this again." Latif gazed up at her and reached out. She squeezed her husband's hand. "And I need to check on my grandbabies." Placing her hands over her face, she breathed hard, straightened and headed towards the room where Kamla and Kamilah were oblivious to the distress of the grownups around them. Latif's eyes followed his wife's retreating back.

Bilal and his father moved onto the screened porch. "I've already spoken to Kalil's parents," Latif continued, "so all we can do now is wait for their family in India to hear from the kidnappers again." He sighed deeply. "Aziz tried calling Kalil's satellite phone, hoping somebody would answer, but no luck."

"That's been sold already," Bilal replied bitterly.

"Meantime, we've contacted the American Embassy. *Insha' Allah*, they'll be found. We'll just have to wait and pray. But you know I can't just sit here and wonder. I'm going to India myself. Since you're back, I know your mother and the twins are in good hands. I've booked a flight out of Dulles in the morning."

Bilal gazed out onto the lawn at the great walnut tree that shaded one side of the house. The tree house Latif had built for his own twins still sat perched on a sturdy deck in the branches. When they were kids, they'd climb up to the deck where he and Zahirah pretended to be lookouts for pirate ships. They tied bright bandanas over their heads and waved newspaper swords at imaginary buccaneers. She always loved adventure. In a couple of years, he and Latif planned to refurbish the twenty-five year old wooden walls and floor. Then the playhouse would pass on to Kamla and Kamilah. Thoughts of the future took him to the one bright spot in his life. Now that he and Ayo were back together, one day, their child would join the twins in their own tree-top adventures.

Bilal swallowed, blinking rapidly. "Kalil and Zahirah were supposed to be back home in a month. And the girls have a little calendar that they've set up to mark off the days. If they aren't at least back in Mumbai by then, we've got to figure out how to distract them." Bilal's nod underscored his affirmation. "But Zahirah is the other half of me. And I'm holding on to the feeling that she's safe and on her way back to us. Both of them."

By some magic known only to grandmothers, Adilah had gotten the girls in bed and asleep. She returned with a carafe of coffee, three cups, a small bowl of sugar and a tiny pitcher of cream, setting it on the low table in front of the couch where they all sat. Although it was only late afternoon, the night would be long.

Bilal watched his father. He didn't wave his faith like a flag, but it was as much a part of Latif as breathing. Each month he gave money to a training program for homeless men and ex-offenders. Fridays found him in prayer at the mosque on New Jersey Avenue or the Islamic Center in upper Northwest. He and Adilah had made their pilgrimage to Mecca. He made salat five times each day, but Latif had been worn down by the news of Zahirah and Kalil's disappearance. For the first time in his life, Bilal took the lead. His words flowed from the faith and strength he had inherited from his father.

He reached over to grasp his father's forearm. "First things first. I'll take you to the airport in the morning and wait to see you off. I'll hold the family together until you get back. We've had our moments, but you're my role model for manhood. I love you, Dad."

Bilal turned to his mother. He gaze softened when he looked at her, sitting beside her husband, winding the ties of her scarf around both hands. Her eyes were dry, but still red. He suspected she had no more tears left. Underneath her sadness, he saw the beginnings of hope. Adilah had always been the buffer between her husband and son's disagreements. Their clashes wore on her like sandpaper on silk. If anything good came from this ordeal, it would be the shift in their relationship from father/son to man to man.

"Now, for Kamla and Kamilah. I have the most flexible schedule, so I'll pick up the slack while you're at work and Dad is away. I'll take them to daycare and keep them with me until you get home."

Adilah sat up. "But what about your restorations? You can't work with those chemicals and watch the children at the same time. They'd be all over the place and into everything." A gasp escaped her lips. Latif's arm rested behind her; he pulled her closer to his chest and rested his head on top of hers.

"It's okay, honey. Just let it out; *Insha'Allah*, we'll get through it."

Bilal moved to kneel in front of his mother. Her small hands were lost in his large grasp. He leaned forward, touching his forehead to that of his mother. Her eyes closed, and sighing, she reached up to cup her son's face. For seconds, neither of them moved nor spoke. "Listen, Mama," Bilal finally whispered, trying to reassure her with his steady gaze. "I know someone who can help me out. He'll be glad for the experience; he's been certified by the American Society of Appraisers and just waiting for his credentials in the mail. He can do the field work and I'll do the research from home. As far as my restorations, I can fit them in when the girls are with you." Bilal brushed her cheek. "Don't worry, Mama," he said softly. "I've already got it under control."

Adilah sent a beseeching gaze to her husband.

"Listen to our son, sweetheart," Latif replied, speaking softly to his distraught wife. "Let him finish."

Bilal grasped his mother's hands. "I can and will work it out. Their well-being is more important than anything right now, except finding Zahirah and Kalil." Whatever it took to hold his family together in this crisis, he was ready and able to do.

He stood at the window. Outside, the sun had given up its last bright burst, softening into gold before disappearing completely into twilight. Bilal turned first to his mother. "Mama, can you get the girls?" Adilah nodded, and without a question, she headed for their playroom. The shift was subtle, but Bilal's position as leader and comforter had been made clear.

Then he spoke to his father. "At this time of day, I'm usually across town, but today especially, I'm glad that we can pray together." Soon, Latif, Adilah, Kamla and Kamilah stood together, facing east. Bilal, who had been named for an ex-slave, and the first man to deliver the call to prayer for the Prophet, began reciting in a deep, clear voice. *Allahu Akbar. Allahu Akbar. (God is the greatest, God is the greatest.)*

❧

He took a cab home, grateful that, instead of driving, he could ride and think. He reflected on the love his parents shared. He watched his father shelter and be a strong shoulder for his mother. Even through its rancorous moments, the bond of the Abdul- Salaam family had always been solid, but that night its foundation was unbreakable. Later, Bilal sat out on the deck, allowing the still dark softness to surround him, immersing himself in a sense of gratitude that he always found in prayer. He knew Zahirah and Kalil would be found. Ayo would be home soon and back by his side. He couldn't reach her cell, but a napkin still stuck in his pocket bore the phone number of the Island Inn. When they were connected, the strain in her voice alarmed him.

"Ayo, what's the matter?"

"I'm just a little under the weather, that's all." Her voice was weary.

He didn't like the way she sounded. On Harbour Island, her return to good health had been obvious. What could have happened between then and now? He made a note to ask his mother for the name of another doctor. When Ayo got back he'd take her himself. It was time for a third opinion.

The next day, more for his sake than theirs, Bilal took the twins out for smoothies. That afternoon, they sprawled across his bed with their crayons, a stack of paper, and coloring books. Kamilah proudly handed him a picture. Four brown stick figures stood joined like paper doll cutouts. "Look, Unca B. This is our mommy and daddy, and this is you and Miss Ayo."

He planted a kiss on his niece's forehead. Kamilah giggled when he tickled her chin. In spite of the cloud that hung over their lives, a broad grin spread across his face. When she came home it would be Unca B and Miss Ayo again.

℘

When the call came, Bilal took the shortest shower of his life. He pulled on a loose cream-colored linen shirt over a pair of jeans and stuffed his feet into a pair of black sneakers. Palming a drop of sandalwood, he ran both hands through his coils. Once off Blair Road, Bilal broke the speed limit. It had been too long since he had driven down her street without sadness trailing behind him. At the familiar turn, his smile began. Being apart from her had been the worst experience of his life, but now it was over. For good.

Seeing her at the door made his spirits soar even higher. He leaped two steps at a time to pull her into his embrace. "There you are," he whispered, smoothing his hands up and down over her bare shoulders. He tilted her face and looked deeply into her eyes. She was beautiful—in the bright red and green hibiscus print her tanned skin glowed. His eyes roamed over the woman he loved like a searchlight.

Her subdued greeting worried him. Something wasn't right.

"Ayo, what's wrong?" With his arm wrapped around her, Bilal led a silent Ayo to the living room.

Ayo twisted both hands together in her lap. "Have you heard anything more about Zahirah and Kalil?"

That was it—it was sadness; she was as worried as they were. When Ayo began to cry, Bilal drew her close. "I know, baby, I know," he crooned against her hair. "It's hard on all of us, but in my heart I know they're alive, somewhere. And having you back gives me even more strength."

By then Ayo's damp face was raw and chapped from crying. "But I'm not back, at least in the way you want. We're not back together." Ayo choked on the words. "You didn't believe me the first time, but now you have to!"

Every pore rose on his body. He felt like a human sacrifice—one whose heart had been ripped from his chest, but whose brain was left alive to wonder how it happened. After such a sweet reunion, how could she tell him that nothing had changed? Bilal's knees banged the low table when he leaped up from the couch. "So what the hell was all that about?" His outrage made her flinch. She squeezed her hands together so hard that blood pooled under her fingertips.

"I love you Bilal," he mimicked, in a cold voice that hurt her more than the heat of his anger. "Laying up in the bed with me. What happened—your stand-in screw took a day off when I showed up? Don't even try to call it lovemaking, because a woman who loved me wouldn't do this. If you knew we had no chance, why didn't you tell me so, right there in that hotel lobby?"

"Because I didn't know what else to do!" The words forced their way out through her sobs. Trembling, Ayo pressed both palms against her face. Her shoulders heaved. Her breath came out hard and ragged. "I know I shouldn't have, but I did what you asked," Ayo sobbed. "I waited, but you were there only one day. And when you got that awful news, how could I hurt you even more?"

Bilal stared down at Ayo. His face twisted into a sneer of contempt. He stuck one finger on his temple and twisted it back and forth. "I must have been crazy to go back for more lies and deception. But I'll tell you this. I'll never look your way again. And if by some unfortunate chance I do see you, I'll pretend I never knew you. And that is obviously the truth!"

Chapter 20

🍃

$\mathcal{S}$omehow he made it through his appointments. Attention to detail saved him; otherwise he would have mistaken the set of Flow Blue reproductions for the authentic and much more valuable syrup pitcher and soup tureen. The rest of the afternoon he spent out on his deck gazing at nothing. Every time he thought he had the answer, he came up even emptier than before. At six o'clock he came inside. *It's a good thing I'm not a drinking man.* Bilal remembered the day he made that statement. Right now, something straight and raw would put him to sleep and dull his raging thoughts. But only for a while, Bilal thought bitterly, before crawling on top of his well-made bed and falling asleep.

When he woke up, Bilal rolled over and looked at the clock. It was eight-thirty at night. A search through the refrigerator came up empty-not even a frozen dinner hidden in the back of the freezer. Hunger pushed him out of his bed and down Georgia Avenue to Miss Polly's. He stood in line outside the carryout that was no larger than the foyer of his house. A tiny woman who wore her hair blonde on top and cropped short and black in the back held court, serving up generous pieces of fried fish, creamy macaroni, greens and homemade desserts to fans from all over the city. Inside was like a hot grease sauna.

"Hey, baby," Miss Polly called out to Bilal. She stood on a stool to see over the counter lined with homemade sweet potato pie and blueberry cobbler. "You want the usual?"

"Just half this time, Miss Polly." The regular was a serving large enough for him and Ayo to eat through an entire day. He hoped Miss Polly wouldn't ask why. But the crush of sweaty humanity that squeezed inside her door commanded all her attention.

"Okay, baby." Out of breath, she moved down the line of steam trays slapping fish, greens, and macaroni into a white Styrofoam container. Bilal paid and slid past the knot of people at the door. His luck held out. There was no pink ticket tucked behind the wipers of his illegally parked Commander.

"Well, well, well—this must be my lucky day. Or night, as the case may be."

Bilal's shoulders dropped. He exhaled a hard, irritated sigh. What next? Flying monkeys on motorcycles? He didn't believe in luck, but there was something seriously out of kilter in his universe.

He didn't need to turn around. She slid up to him, and like her companion, Arlena left little of her body to the imagination. The mid-thigh red knit clung to her lush body and shoved her cleavage into the low-cut V. She caught the glance when his eyes skimmed her body and curvy legs ending in three inches of ankle strapped heels. A small confident smile flitted across her face. She stepped closer. Her friend followed, bringing with her the smoky musk of street oils that overpowered Arlena's lighter, feminine fragrance.

The other woman sidled closer, eyeing him from top to bottom. "Mmm," she mumbled, in unabashed appreciation.

"My car broke down near that new club and me and Michelle were trying to catch a cab to my house."

Bilal looked out onto the street at the stream of cars and back to the last woman he wanted to see. He frowned "What are you talking about? Look at all those taxis on the street. You shouldn't have any problems."

"Well, we've been having problems for a half an hour," Arlena protested. She stepped closer. "Can't you give us a ride?" she cajoled. "We're going back to my house. It's not that far; just too far too walk in these heels." She lifted one shapely leg and pointed it in his direction.

Bilal looked at the barely clad woman and her preening friend. They were looking for trouble and were too stupid to realize the kind of attention they attracted could backfire into more than they could handle. He wanted nothing to do with either of them, but he couldn't leave them there like bait. "No," he spoke in a voice that signaled an end to the debate. "I can't. But I'll help you flag down a cab."

For fifteen minutes he stood with them, holding his cooling food in one hand and sticking out the other at each passing cab. He glanced over at Arlena and Michelle. *No wonder the cabbies won't stop. They must think I'm a pimp!*

"Ain't none of them stopping,' Michelle protested. "You got a car. How long you gonna make us stand here?"

Bilal speared her with a sharp glance. The vein in his temple pulsed out of control. Her irritating voice was like a nail stuck through his shoe. At this rate, he'd be stuck with them forever. Better to get it over with and be on his way.

"Get in," he ordered. Michelle jumped in the back, carefully stepping over the bag of food. Arlena slid in the front beside Bilal as if it had always been her place to claim. She flipped her head around to stick out her tongue and grin at Michelle. Then she hopped up on both knees and sprawled across the seat with her butt stuck in mid-air. She whispered something to Michelle and the two women burst into loud raucous laughter. It grated on Bilal's nerves. He jerked away when Arlena turned back, grazing his arm with the red swell of her behind.

Bilal looked straight ahead, following the steady stream of traffic. They had driven far enough to reach "just up the street" long ago. His eye jumped. "Arlena, just where do you live?"

She shifted in her seat to face him and pointed out his window. "Turn left at the next light. Michelle lives right around that corner. You can let her out there." She sat back with a satisfied smirk.

Bilal jerked around to stare at her. "I thought you both were going to your house."

He sped up the one-way street and slammed on his brakes in front of bright green carpeted steps leading to a shingled row house. Michelle jumped out, leaning in the window to give Arlena's shoulder a playful punch. "See you later, girl," she drawled with an exaggerated wink.

Bilal forgot he had been raised as a gentleman. He whipped the truck around the corner and back down to Georgia Avenue before Michelle's foot hit the second garish step.

Arlena leaned back in the seat and stretched. Her hem crept farther up. Bilal gripped the wheel, keeping his eyes on the taillights in front of him instead of her smooth, bare thighs. She pointed again, this time to a well-kept two-story brick house on a large corner lot.

"It's right here. And now it's just you and me," she crooned, reaching over to brush a silky palm across his bare arm. "Come on baby," she purred, "give it up." Turning to face him, she tucked one leg under the other and slid closer. Her scent teased his nostrils, bringing images to his brain that pushed their way past his good sense. The part of him that throbbed between his legs wanted to pull her onto his lap and give her the screwing she had been begging for.

"You know you want me." The hand that had stroked his arm slid down toward his thigh. Her lashes lowered. She chuckled, low and sexy, pointing one long red talon between his legs. "Looks like you want me right now." She leaned down to look up at her lighted house. Shaking her head, she turned back to him. "Damn it! My little sister is home. Pull into the garage!" Before he could open his mouth, she slid both hands under her dress and pulled down a red lace thong, laying it on the seat, inside out for him to see the moist invitation. His groin tightened. Bilal groaned inwardly. Images of raw, urgent sex flooded his brain. His thoughts flew back to a time in his life when the Commander would have already been rocking like a low rider.

"When we get inside, you'll have to put this in your mouth," she drawled, opening her legs wide and filling the car with her earthy female scent. Bilal's pulse quickened. Arlena pointed between her legs. "You'll need it, because when I wrap this around you, they'll hear you hollering in the next block." Her voice lowered. She flicked her tongue against his ear. Bilal's erection reared, straining against the fabric of his pants.

"You won't even remember that old woman and her dried up stuff once you get a taste of this…"

Blood pounded through Bilal's head. Arlena's words were cold water poured between his legs, literally deflating the lust he fought against. "Arlena, get your ass out of my car!"

"Huh? It's okay, nobody…"

"Right now!" He stretched across the stunned, failed temptress. His arm pinned her to the seat when he shoved the heavy door open. "Her name better not cross your mind, much less come out of your mouth!" What had been so tempting now looked like a garish kewpie doll after the carnival had ended. She scrambled through the open door clutching the strip of lace and staring back at him in shock.

In the safety of distance, Arlena's face contorted. "That's your loss, you stuck-up son of a bitch! You think you're too good for me? You'd rather screw that old-ass woman? I saw you with her, looking like if she peed, you'd drink it." Like a two-headed coin, she flipped, running back to the vehicle with the thong dangling from her hand. She shoved herself against his window, lacing her fingers into a V over her crotch. Her tone dropped to the same seductive register. "You don't know what you're missing. But that's okay. I was watching you watching me. I know I'll hear from you again. Bet on that!"

Bilal waved one finger slowly, back and forth. This time his voice was cool, like a leg-breaker delivering a first warning. "Don't kid yourself. I'd rather stick myself in a live socket than inside you."

He shifted gears and pulled off with his tires screaming, leaving Arlena to stand in a patch of ragged grass that sprung from the sidewalk. At a red light near his home, Bilal dropped his head on the steering wheel. Damn! Anything could have happened, especially when she pulled off that thong and laid it on the seat. Right then he wanted to screw her just like she wanted it—hard, rough and quick. If she had touched him again, how long would it have taken him to pull away? Or in his state of high arousal, would he?

Bilal threw the whole bag of food into the trash. Upstairs he stripped off his clothes and for twenty minutes allowed the cool water to run over his head and body. The calming water prepared him for prayer, and when he spoke, the words poured from his soul.

"O Allah, forgive me, and have mercy on me, and guide me, and grant me security, and raise me up, and make good for me my shortcoming, and provide for me."

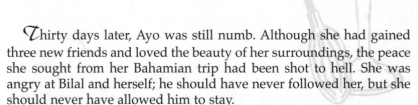

Chapter 21

$\mathcal{T}$hirty days later, Ayo was still numb. Although she had gained three new friends and loved the beauty of her surroundings, the peace she sought from her Bahamian trip had been shot to hell. She was angry at Bilal and herself; he should have never followed her, but she should never have allowed him to stay.

Although it was early, Ayo felt control of the day slip from her grasp. She couldn't focus, although she had a load of work to finish. Outside, she re-arranged the lawn furniture, but that was a pointless exercise in busy work. Inside, she turned to her drug of choice. A shot of caffeine was the kick-start she needed. At the counter, she loosened the drawstring around the small burlap bag of Blue Mountain coffee. It had come from Paul, along with the thick envelope of material he promised on writing an effective business plan. Ayo bent to inhale the rich warm scent of fresh coffee beans. She didn't care what anyone said—coffee did taste just as good as it smelled. But this morning she jerked her face away, nearly gagging from the scent.

"What? I hope I didn't catch anything from Eileen." They met the day before, and over lunch, Eileen complained about a nasty bug she caught. "It's the only thing that could keep me from this coffee," Ayo insisted out loud. She measured an oncoming illness by her inability to tolerate coffee. "Or maybe I shouldn't have eaten all those peanuts at 11:00 at night. They're probably just sitting there, digesting one by one and messing up my morning fix."

Ayo decided to try the coffee anyway. This precious blend begged to be brewed and savored. She poured the coffee into her favorite cup and carried it to the soap kitchen. Perched on the high stool, she looked around at the spotless workplace. Ingredients, utensils and packaging were ready to go. Still organized and put in place, just like Bilal had done many months ago. A tiny smile tugged at her lips. He'd be proud that she kept it that way. She shrugged off the thought. There was plenty more to keep her mind occupied. Thanks to the advice and stellar contacts Paul sent her way, she was ready for the big one—the largest order Maracas Bay had ever received. The one that would propel her from local to national attention. He'd even arranged to have her Pink Sand soap included in an A-list awards show gift bag. Ayo sighed. At least her business life was on solid footing.

She grimaced, setting the cup down hard. The coffee burned its way down her esophagus. It wasn't the heat. She'd laced the coffee with a general dose of milk, but when the liquid hit her stomach it solidified into a lump that radiated a slow burn throughout her system.

"If I put one more thing in my stomach, it'll stage a rebellion." But that didn't stop her from searching for the definitive cure for a massive case of heartburn Ayo tore open a container of Trader Vince's hot and spicy soup. She microwaved the contents and chugged the liquid in one long slurp. The soup blazed its way through the discomfort.

After a quick shower, she was ready to set up the production line that she and Karina would work through the next day.

Ayo fell in to her work cadence, stirring, bottling, and separating the jars and bottles for labeling. She looked up at the clock, surprised to see that it was nearly two o'clock, way past the time she would normally eat. But she had no appetite, and the burning sensation had returned, this time undaunted by the bubbles of carbonated water laced with lemon.

Ayo carried another glass of water into the guest room. At the edge of the daybed, she thumbed through a copy of a new beauty products journal. She shifted back against the pillows and instead of a short nap, fell into a deep sleep.

When Ayo jerked up and looked around, she was groggy and not at all sure of the time. A glance at her watch sent her into shock. She had slept for four hours in the middle of the day. Only because she had to, Ayo dragged herself into the kitchen and cleaned up in slow motion.

The next morning she woke up an hour later than usual with heartburn lodged in the middle of her chest. The smell of coffee turned her stomach upside down. Whatever caused her discomfort would have to be dealt with later. Ayo sent up thanks to the soap goddess that Karina would be in that day. The two-woman production team worked like one well-oiled machine. Together they could more than make up for the hours that were lost to sleep.

At nine o'clock on the dot, Karina bounced up the steps. A headband held her auburn-streaked afro away from the chocolate round smoothness of what she called her "moon pie" face.

"Hey, Ayo," she bubbled. She slid her army surplus bag off her shoulder, causing hoops that hung from four piercings in each ear to swing with the movement. "Ooh, what happened to you? You look like you couldn't catch up with the Sandman at all last night."

Ayo shook her head as they walked into the workroom. "Just the opposite, little sis. I got too much sleep." Rolls of labels, bubble wrap and boxes sat lined up to be filled and labeled for shipping. She gestured to the counter. "But since I got up early, I didn't get behind. It's a good thing, because I fell asleep around two yesterday and woke up at six. And you know that unless I'm sick, I never sleep during the day."

Karina glanced at the production schedule tacked up on the cork board. She turned from the list of tasks to look at Ayo. "Do you feel sick? Or are you just tired and sleepy?"

"No, I don't really feel sick, except I can't stand the smell or taste of coffee and you know how much I love hot caffeine. And I'm really tired and sleepy. The sleepy factor is new. If I was just tired, I'd chalk it up to getting up early and working 'til late."

"Have you felt this way before? Think back to whenever this occurred, and you can probably pinpoint the cause. If not, then you should make an appointment for a check-up. I might not be a doctor yet, but I do know the drill," she laughed.

Ayo listened with growing unease as Karina spoke. She put two and two together and was petrified at what four might turn out to be. But she couldn't allow it to distract her from work. The hours passed in an efficient blur until the order was complete. Halfway through, a terrible thought invaded her head. What if the fragrances made her sick? When the last box was taped, Karina left, urging Ayo to get a checkup if she continued to feel bad.

The little that was left of Ayo's appetite disappeared. She crawled into bed early, but this time sleep wouldn't come. Instead, Ayo sat up against the headboard. She wrapped her arms around her knees and rocked back and forth. "Oh no," she whispered.

Chapter 22

❧

*A*yo didn't need proof, but she wanted it, in spite of intuition and her body's signals. The wait seemed to stretch into the next day, even though Dr. Broussard's receptionist answered on the third ring.

"Hello, Mrs. Montgomery! How can I help you?"

"Is it possible to see Dr. Broussard today?"

Ms. Washington was unfazed by the urgency in Ayo's voice. "I'm sorry," she replied with her usual pleasant lilt, "but Dr. Broussard is in surgery all day. She'll be in the office tomorrow. Is this an emergency?"

To me it is. But to claim a pregnancy test as an emergency would be absurd and lose her some of Dr. Broussard's unending good will. "No, but can I please make an appointment for first thing tomorrow morning?" Ayo gnawed on her thumb, resisting the impulse to chew the nails off each finger like kernels of corn on a cob.

"Just a second." Ms. Washington put her on hold and returned a couple of seconds later.

"How about 9:30?"

"I'll be there when the door opens."

Ayo sank down on the daybed, wanting more than anything to take a nap. It had been a long time ago, but she remembered each step- for three months, she'd be dogged by heartburn and fatigue. She'd crave spicy food and something cold and carbonated, drunk straight down until the bubble inside her stomach popped. She'd be sleepy all the time—either knocked out cold or slogging around like a slack-jawed extra in Night of the Living Dead. And magically, on the first day of the fourth month, she'd sail through the following five months like the model for a perfect pregnancy.

Ayo tossed the phone, letting it bounce off the bed. She dropped down onto the rumpled comforter, leaning forward to rest her head on her knees. *Why did I let love get the best of me? I am too old for this!* The answer to that rhetorical question was clear. The man she loved had come to claim her. What woman could resist the lethal combination of vulnerability and unconditional love?

The drumbeat of a headache began. Ayo pressed one hand over her eyes, as if she could push back the pain along with the reality of what her life would become. And what about Kedar? What could she tell him now? Do as I say, not as I do?

Her eyes drooped. If she fell asleep now, it would be too late to cancel the plans she and Justine made for the next day. Her friend had enough skill to head that secret agency located in Langley, Virginia. She'd pick up on Ayo's distress in a heartbeat. After one probing question the whole sorry story would come gushing out.

Right now all she wanted was to lie down and let sleep blot out the turbulence in her mind. Her head spun when she leaned across the bed, fishing for the phone that fell between it and the wall.

"Hey, Ayo!" Justine chirped. "I hope you've got your shopping shoes ready."

Ayo shook her head. She couldn't stand perky today. "Listen, Justine, I can't make it tomorrow. I feel like a wrung out dishrag."

"What's wrong? I know there's some kind of virus going around. I hope you didn't catch it. Eileen said she felt like somebody beat her nonstop for the two days she was in bed."

"Maybe that's what it is," Ayo mumbled.

"Well, okay then," Justine hesitated, dragging out the sentence. Ayo cut in quickly, unwilling to give her perceptive friend the chance the probe and pick.

"But I need to lie down now. I don't mean to cut you off, but I'm worn out." A screensaver bounced across the monitor. Ayo stared at it without really seeing the brilliant maze of designs that formed, disappeared and reformed. This time tomorrow, what she already knew would be confirmed. A long 18 hours away.

A sudden thought pushed sleep away. Ayo leaped up and grabbed the phonebook from the bedside table. Under the heading "Pharmacy" she searched for a CVS far enough in the suburbs and far away from her neighborhood. The last thing she needed was to have anyone she knew, even in passing, see her purchasing a home pregnancy test. She grabbed her keys and purse and drove the Sequoia around the edge of the newly-developed downtown Silver Spring, across East-West Highway, and finally onto Old Georgetown Road, miles away from the brand-new Georgia Avenue store.

Even though she knew it was unlikely, she scanned the large, bright store for familiar faces. A hysterical thought crossed her mind. Suppose one of her neighbors was also on a stealth shopping trip? In spite of the serious nature of her mission, Ayo stood giggling in front of the counter displaying products for the act of love and its possible aftermath. All of the pregnancy tests with their cute acronyms looked the same to her. She picked up two brands to compare their claims, finally selecting the package with the clearest explanation and simplest directions.

At home, Ayo's sandals slapped at her heels as she ran up the steps. She pulled the kit from her purse, letting the empty bag fall to the floor. On her way to the bathroom, she ripped it open, leaving a trail of torn cardboard crumbs behind her. Her hand shook, but she followed the instructions to the letter. When a colored line appeared on the testing stick, Ayo slumped down on the toilet seat and wept.

What a mess she had made of their lives—hers and Bilal's. Instead of falling back on the faith she claimed to have, and her doctor's advice, she became a fearful know-it-all. How could she tell Bilal? And would he believe her? The lie had done her in; he'd laugh in her face, believing that the child belonged to her phantom lover. Instead of a bride, she would be a single mother.

Baby mama. Something she swore she'd never become. In spite of the absolute terror she felt, Ayo couldn't ignore the tiny swell of tenderness that came with knowing that Bilal's child was growing inside her. She cried and laughed, and cried some more. She gave up Bilal for nothing! How ironic—with failing female organs, there was no way in hell she should be pregnant. How could this have happened? *Whatever is supposed to happen is going to happen.* Tenderness aside, her life would never be the same, and neither would those of the people she loved the most.

Chapter 23

A loose red top floated over her white drawstring pants. At least her feet hadn't started to swell. On their way to the Sequoia, Justine cast a curious glance at Ayo's choice of clothing. "Gaining weight, aren't you?"

Inside the SUV, Ayo's heart thudded. If her hands weren't on the wheel, they'd be plucking at the hem of her tunic. Her answer was part evasion and part truth.

"Uh-huh. You know I have a deadline for a repeat of that first large order. Every time I get a case of nerves, I pop a cupcake."

Justine's inquisition ended. "Oh, that's right. But you need to be careful. If you don't watch out, somebody will be calling *you* posturepedic!" Their shared laughter soothed away some of Ayo's anxiety. When the time was right, they all would know. Just not now.

Although Justine had no idea, sharp cravings sent Ayo up to Capitol Hill's Eastern Market. Her pregnant body made its familiar demands—the refusal to digest meat and a craving for fresh fruit. Even on that misty, overcast Sunday morning, the streets and sidewalks were crowded with vendors and customers. There was something for everyone under the green awnings of the old railway station and out onto the triangle of sidewalk that jutted into North Carolina Avenue. Silver jewelry sat beside exotic blooms and green stalks of bamboo. Two tables of slender black incense in every fragrance imaginable shared the sidewalk with handcrafted quilts, art deco furniture, and soap.

Loaded with pineapples, peaches and grapes, Ayo and Justine negotiated the crush of shoppers. "Good thing I found a space right behind the market," Ayo grinned over at Justine. "Otherwise we'd have to pay somebody to lug this load." Ayo gripped her shopping in one hand and fished for her keys with the other. When she looked up, the sight branded itself into her brain.

"Oh, no!" she choked out. Ayo stumbled back, grasping the bag as one handle tore and slipped from her grip.

Justine's turned to see what caused Ayo's outburst. "Oh no is right," she whispered.

Bilal held Kamilah's hand, and next to him, a tall, graceful woman held onto Kamla. A pale blue scarf wound into a twist at the back of her neck. It matched the cloud of ankle-length cotton swirling around her ankles. Turquoise wedge heeled sandals exposed perfect toes painted dark gold. She was the epitome of bohemian sophistication, with the easy, willowy grace of women who walked with baskets on their heads. The woman bent, planting a kiss on the forehead of the giggling little girl. The four of them stopped at the door of popular Hill eatery known for its lavish, all-day Sunday brunch menu. At the door, Bilal held it open and placed a protective hand against the woman's back to guide her inside.

"Come on, Ayo," Justine urged, grabbing Ayo's arm and pulling her towards the Sequoia. Pedestrians shoved their way around the two women who stood like stone statues, cemented in place like life-sized sidewalk artwork. The keys shook in Ayo's hand. She jabbed at the button, unlocking and locking the door before it finally opened.

"Give me the keys," Justine pleaded in a soft voice, prying them from Ayo's hands. Choking on her tears, Ayo tossed the bag in the back. Fruit rolled onto the floor and under the seat. Inside, she bumped her head against the seat back and sobbed into her hands. The stares of patrons at Bread and Chocolate's outdoor café made no difference. At the traffic light on Pennsylvania, an MPD patrol car slowed beside them. The officer on the passenger side trained an inquisitive stare up into the Sequoia. "Oh, lord," Justine breathed, watching from the corner of one eye. When the light turned green, she pulled away as quickly as she could.

Justine kept one eye on the cross-town traffic and the other on Ayo. "I know you're hurting. And for once I don't know what to say, except this whole thing has been painful for both of you."

"He didn't look like he was hurting!" Pain thickened her voice. She swiped at the tears clouding her vision. Twice Bilal accused her of seeing the world only through her eyes. He was right. Why else did she delude herself into thinking he was alone and as miserable as she had been? It didn't take him long to find a replacement. She was probably younger; definitely baby-making age. Latif Abdul-Salaam must be beside himself with glee.

In front of her house, Ayo bent with one hand scraping under the seat until each piece of the bruised and battered fruit had been found and tossed into the torn bag. The flurry of motion made Justine's efforts useless. "Come on, Ayo," she pleaded. She put one hand on Ayo's shoulder. "We've been though some rough times before, and one of us never let the other go through them alone. So let's go inside. I'll make you something and we'll talk, if that's what you want."

Inside, Ayo dropped the ripped bag on the counter. Justine rushed forward to catch the bruised fruit before it splattered into the floor. By now it was good for nothing but yogurt and a blender.

"I know you mean well," she sighed. "Aside from Magda, you're the best friend I've ever had. And I say that because she's family. She has to care." Ayo managed a small flash of humor. "But I need to be by myself. I could use a double shot of rum, but I'll settle for a tall Coke and to lay my body down on some cool clean sheets." Ayo's alarm bell sounded. The last thing she needed was for Justine to ask why she wouldn't swallow the brain-numbing drink.

After Justine's reluctant departure, Ayo turned into a masochist of the worst kind. Instead of putting the morning's scene out of her mind, she tortured herself, replaying it over and over. Her imagination spun out of control and hurtled fast forward to a wedding, one in which she was not the bride. She pictured him and the woman standing before their family and friends. She made herself crazy conjuring up an image of their wedding night. But her frenzy didn't end there. Ayo ran into her office and grabbed the phone book. *I don't believe I'm even thinking about this.* Frantically, she pushed her hand across page after page, finally locating the instructions. When she dialed, her number would show up as "unknown caller." If Bilal answered, she'd just hang up.

"Hello?" Instead, a woman answered. Her soft voice was warm and confident. She was in her place and knew it. It was the confirmation Ayo both dreaded and needed to hear.

Chapter 24

ᔓ

*B*ilal moved through his days like a detached observer to a series of someone else's heartbreak. Zahirah and Kalil had not been found. Sunday brunch had been good, though. His mother had called in unexpectedly and brought the twins to his house. Because the little girls loved breakfast food, he decided a late morning brunch was in order. Monica Walters was immediately charmed by the children. "We're gonna eat pancakes," Kamla announced before grasping Monica's hand and pulling her inside. In their company, the day turned out to be a very pleasant distraction from his misery, until he and the children returned to Brookland.

Latif appeared broken. "Can I talk to Grandpa for a minute? I promise I'll play with you as soon as we finish talking." Full stomachs and the promise of a romp with Unca B was enough to placate Kamla and Kamilah. They pounded down the hall to their playroom without a look back at the adults.

Bilal took a deep breath. His mouth moved in a silent prayer for strength to endure whatever his father would say. "Just tell me, Dad. Just say it."

"Son, it's not as bad as you think, but it's bad enough. Kalil's cousin got word that the kidnappers upped their ransom demand to two million – not rupees, but United States dollars." Latif's powerful shoulders slumped. "Our only hope in this outrage is that kidnappers are usually too greedy to kill Zahirah and Kalil." He croaked out a short, bitter laugh. "After all, dead people bring no ransom. Would you believe that some of these criminals even take payment plans?" Latif's voice raised and broke. "But they come back and kill you if you don't pay up!" It was painful for Bilal to see cracks in the armor his strong, proud father had always worn. Of one thing, Bilal was certain: by now, a lesser man would have broken completely.

"So tomorrow I'm going to begin the process of liquidating my real estate holdings," Latif continued. "I'm well-known in this business, and I'll do everything I can to push the deals through. Along with the money that Kalil's family is pulling together, *Insha'Allah*, our combined efforts will buy Zahirah and Kalil's freedom."

After the latest disheartening news, Bilal gathered the girls in his arms. "Mommy and Daddy have to stay a little longer in a place where it's hard to use a phone. But they want me to tell you that they love and miss you. They'll be home as soon as they can. So right now, I'm taking you home with me. Grandpa has some business to take care of." In the absence of their parents, Kamla and Kamilah clung to him. He wondered—did they share a bit of the same bond with him that existed between him and their mother?

While they waited for Adilah's return, Bilal pulled out cans of brightly-colored Play-doh. "Can you make something for me while we wait for Nana?"

"I'm gonna make a bowl for Unca B. You make a plate," Kamla ordered her sister.

Kamilah's faced turned into a tiny storm cloud. "I don't wanna make a plate. You make it!" She puffed up, jerking both arms across her chest.

"Hey, hey," Bilal bent between them, cajoling in a soft voice, "Why don't we all make a ball and bat like the kind you play with in T-ball? I'll make one too." For an hour Bilal played peacemaker and sat between the twins, rolling out the red clay. His efforts pleased both girls; they fashioned their own lumpy replicas and the truce held. An hour later, he sent them to wash their hands. How hand washing turned into hair-pulling, he didn't know. But when they emerged like two irate wet hens with mushroom clouds for hair, Bilal burst out laughing. "We can't let Nana see you like that!" he chuckled. "She'd put us all in the corner. Go get your comb and brush." How difficult could it be to put two big braids in their hair? By the time they had wiggled and twisted their way through his clumsy attempts, each girl ended up with a part as crooked as a bolt of lightning and one braid twice as large as the other.

"Nana, look!" When their grandmother arrived, Kamla stood in front of Adilah, turning to show her Bilal's handiwork. "Unca B combeded our hair!" The word came to a full stop with an extra syllable added for excitement. In spite of his uneven results, Bilal stood proudly with the child-sized comb and brush in his hand.

"Oh, Bilal…" Adilah's voice trailed off. Her mouth twitched at his hesitant expression. "Son, I appreciate everything that you're doing. But please, let me take care of their hair."

Bilal looked at the twins and back at his mother. He let out a low chuckle. "Okay, okay, I get the picture."

"I'm glad you do," Adilah pointed to his handiwork. "Because that looks like practice for macramé 101." She looked up at him. "But what happened? I combed their hair this morning."

Bilal stopped laughing and shook his head. "I don't know, Mama. The girls have their little fights, like all children do, but I've never seen them go at each other like that. It started with the Play-doh and ended up in a kitten fight in the bathroom." Bilal tried to make a joke of the incident, but it bothered him.

"Kitten fight—that's cute." Adilah gave a dry laugh. "I know you're worried, but don't worry too much. I believe they've picked up on our fears about their parents. They don't know what's happening, but they're aware that something is wrong. And their little brains can't process it, so for them, it comes out in fighting. People show pain in weird ways. You think you know the reason for a person's strange behavior, but it turns out to be something entirely different."

He felt it coming while his mother spoke. By the time she finished, the idea had streaked through his mind like a comet and struck him hard with its simplicity. He had wracked his brain, searching for every imaginable reason for Ayo to break their engagement. It wasn't religion; those issues had long since been resolved. And it wasn't her son; he and Kedar had made their peace. Or his father; whose displeasure they ignored. It was so obvious that he had been oblivious. Shock and hurt blinded him to the timing that should have set off an alarm the first time she uttered those awful words. Right after her last doctor visit. The girls' little brawl went right out of his mind. "Mama, what could cause a woman to have periods painful enough to put her in bed?"

Adilah Abdul-Salaam raised her head, leveling a long, keen look at her son. "It could be a number of things," she answered slowly. "Fibroids, endometriosis, or simply what is known as dysmenorrah—painful periods. It can be an ongoing condition, or brought on by age". She looked at him sharply. "Is Ayo the reason you're asking? I do remember you telling me about her problems, but I thought she'd been helped by her last doctor."

Bilal nodded. "You know I've been racking my brain trying to figure out why Ayo left me. It was so sudden, I knew it was more than she told me." He had never told anyone the reason Ayo gave for leaving him. "And the more I think about it, her health has to be the missing piece of the puzzle. Nothing else makes sense!"

"So what will you do? If she won't talk to you, how can you find out?"

"I don't know. But it ain't over 'til it's over, and believe me, it ain't over yet!"

Chapter 25

$\mathcal{A}$yo and Magda sat in Ayo's backyard, shaded by a khaki-colored umbrella. The years favored Magda Malone, turning her into a graceful beauty with only a few strands of gray laced throughout her chin-length bob. At fifty-two, she was petite, still chic, and still deeply in love with Charles "Buck" Malone, the preacher's son who captured her heart at sixteen.

Near seven o'clock; the sun gathered itself for a last bright burst, bathing the backyard in orange and crimson light. The end of the golden day was in direct contrast to Ayo's mood.

Magda stood up, pulling her shades down from their perch in her hair. A smile curved into dimples on her smooth maple sugar complexion "I've got to get back to Annapolis before I have to get a room at Motel Six and wait out the rush-hour traffic."

Ayo hooked her arm through Magda's. The two women walked around the flagstone path that led to the front yard. Some kind of vine had grown up where the blocks joined. The cloying scent made Ayo gag. Magda frowned and narrowed her eyes. "When I leave, you need to lie down. Maybe you should come on over to Annapolis for a change of scenery. I don't like how you're looking."

"Maybe another time, Magda. There are some things here that need my attention."

Ayo stood on the sidewalk and waved as Magda nosed the Infiniti from its parking space. She let out another long sigh. Magda was right. She had to set her life in order. Bilal or not, baby or not, she still had a business to run. Kedar was practically a man, but until he threw that mortarboard up into the Florida sky on his graduation day, he was still her responsibility. Tomorrow morning when her mind was clear, she'd find the right words. It was time to tell the people closest to her that she was going to be a mother.

Bilal would have to be last. Until the situation with his sister and brother-in-law was resolved one way or the other, she would wait. He didn't need any more upheaval in his life. Although the thought pierced Ayo's heart every time she imagined them together, she was glad he had someone in his life to lean on through his family's tragedy.

A pile of mail lay on the floor; so much, the mailman must have stood there for five minutes feeding it through the slot. Ayo made a mental note to leave a box of cookies for him. He had served her street for years and made sure that if at all possible, she didn't have to trek to the post office to pick up the oversized packages that sometimes came.

She smiled. One of them was a slender package and a note from Paul. This time he was in Hong Kong. She opened the tube carefully. "Wow," Ayo exclaimed softly, carefully unrolling an exquisite length of lavender silk.

I remember the color you wore that first evening on Paradise Island. Here's another version that I hope you like. I'll be in D.C. in a few days. I'll call you and I hope you'll have dinner with me.

Paul's uncanny timing never failed—he had a way of calling or writing just when she needed her spirits lifted. The man who wanted to be her lover turned out to be a great and constant friend, lending his shoulder through email or cell towers, whenever she needed a cry.

"I'll tell him first," Ayo decided. Speaking out loud firmed her resolve to start breaking the news. Paul wouldn't judge, or criticize. And he wouldn't drop the corny "I wish it was mine" on her. Instead he would listen with that inscrutable looked she teased him about, and offer her any help she needed.

That was it! Halfway down the hall, Ayo knew what she could do. Had to do. Under any other circumstance she'd rather drink muddy water than talk to that man, but this was one time she was glad to contact Latif Abdul Salaam. She prayed that a secretary didn't answer his office phone. That meant screening and announcing her call. He'd never take it—Ayo was certain. But before she stepped into the lion's den, she had another, more important call to make.

Ayo glanced at the clock, sending up a fervent prayer that he was still in his office. Her hands trembled from excitement, apprehension and the secret she kept. When she heard Latif's cool voice, she swallowed and began.

"Mr. Abdul Salaam, this is Ayo Montgomery."

"Yes?" Behind his surprised response, the chill was unmistakable.

"I know you didn't expect to hear from me, so I'll be as brief as possible."

"You do that," he replied.

Blame it on raging hormones, but she couldn't help herself. Under any circumstances the man plucked her nerves like a ragged hangnail. "I can't catch a break with you, can I? First you didn't want me with your son. And now I'm not. So what is your problem with me now?"

"Look, Ayo—"

He was ready to hang up. Ayo quickly clamped a lid on her irritation. Nothing in this conversation was about their extreme dislike of each other.

"I'm sorry, Mr. Abdul-Salaam. Please don't hang up. This is urgent." She moved on quickly, knowing that her cryptic comment grabbed his attention. As fast as the words rushed out, he didn't have a chance to interrupt. "I have a good friend, a wealthy private citizen with business interests in India. I called him today and told him about Zahirah and Kalil. He agreed to put all his resources and contacts behind a search for them. However, in his position, he wants to remain anonymous to anyone but you and me." She stopped to catch her breath, to make up for the one she didn't dare take during her run-on explanation. It would have given him a chance to interrupt, or worse, to hang up.

"What—"

Ayo sped up again, and cut him off. "Please hear me out. I know you went to India yourself. No disrespect, but you don't have the clout or the money that he does. If you agree, I'll put him in touch with you, and you both can take it from there. He'll be in D.C. on Friday."

Latif's cool arrogance was replaced by wary interest. "What do you mean more clout? Who is this person?"

Ayo slumped over and heaved out a sigh. At least she had his attention.

"His name is Paul Champion. Do you know who he is?"

"Paul Champion! Of course I do! But you know him personally? Now I see what you mean by money and clout." Latif hesitated and Ayo held her breath. "And you've already talked to him?"

Now they were getting somewhere. "Yes, I have. I would never have called you if I hadn't spoken to Paul first. You must know I care about what happens to your family, even though you and I don't see eye to eye."

"Ayo, for once I don't know what to say or how to thank you." Ayo never thought she'd see the day when Latif Abdul-Salaam was anything but cool and controlled, but it had come. Instead of smug satisfaction, she felt an overwhelming sympathy for her old enemy.

"Mr. Abdul-Salaam, if you want to thank me, the only thing I ask is that you promise, *please* promise, not to tell Bilal that I had anything to do with this. He doesn't need any more distractions in his life, especially from me."

"Why wouldn't you want him to know?"

"Our time is over and he needs no reminders." *He's doing quite well without me.* "But enough of the past, Mr. Abdul-Salaam. Can I give

Paul your number?"

"Oh please do! Give him this number, my home and cell numbers." He repeated the numbers while she wrote. "Tell him to call me at any time of day or night. And listen, Ayo, I promise to keep my word. I won't even tell my wife because she will certainly tell Bilal. I'll just tell her that a person who cares about us put me in touch with someone who can help. I won't be lying."

Chapter 26
❦

At the door, Kamla and Kamilah clamored to stay with him. Any other time he would have relented. But not today. He had work to do. After sending the protesting twins home with his mother, Bilal ran up the steps, two at time. He dragged the chair in front of his computer. When the search engine screen popped up, he began in alphabetical order. Endometriosis was first. At the bottom, an arrow pointed right, guiding him to page after page of information. He clicked on each site, gave them a quick review and printed out the pages that seemed most promising. He repeated the same procedure with dysmenorrea and finally, for fibroids. Half a ream of paper later, he had enough information to keep him reading for hours.

The words jumped out at him, flashing like neon on a dark, deserted street. "The other well known symptom associated with endometriosis is infertility." That was it! Bilal felt a rush of hope so strong it lifted him to his feet. She was afraid she couldn't give him a child. It was so obvious. She lied to him, making up the one thing she thought would drive him away. And when that didn't work, she ran away from him, and lied again, to save him at all costs for the life he wanted. Or so she thought. But he didn't want saving, he wanted a lifetime of loving from Ayodele Mansfield Montgomery. No biological child was worth losing her. They could adopt. And when he caught up with her, and he would, he'd put an end to this charade forever.

With hope spinning through his thoughts, Bilal sat back to print out five appraisal reports. Even after the pages he had just printed, his brand new laser was a workhorse, spitting out in seconds what took minutes with another printer. The detailed reports would be finished in half the time and ready for mailing and delivery tomorrow. Loading more paper, Bilal shook his head. What did people do before computers and printers? He couldn't see himself laboring over a typewriter. A sudden thought cast a brighter beam over his over-the-moon demeanor. One of Ayo's prized possessions had been a mint condition vintage Smith-Corona, the kind that commanded hundreds of dollars on the auction market. Prehistoric, she called it. He chuckled at the thought.

Bilal stood at the door to his deck, lulled by the soft click of paper hitting the sides of the printer's tray. His daydreaming was cut short by the sound of strangled wheezing groan. Instead of a graceful glide through the rollers, the paper jammed into a tangled crunch. "Not now," Bilal groaned. He lifted the top and reached into the intestines of the machine. Instead of dislodging the piece of paper that jammed the machine, he snapped the carriage in two. Damn! He couldn't repair the broken part and the documents needed to be mailed tomorrow. His one saving grace was the large twenty-four hour drugstore further down Fourteenth Street. The twenty-first century pharmacy carried everything—from milk to garden fertilizer. For this one job, a cheap inkjet would do.

On the way back out through the automatic doors, Bilal chuckled to himself. Along with the printer, he came out with a paintbrush and a can of wood glue. He balanced his packages, trying to hold onto the big box that was slipping from his grip. He had to hug it, holding it in place against his chest with the loop of the bag wrapped around his wrist. He was a block away from the truck when a sleek car drove by. He gave it a long, appreciative whistle. A Mercedes Maybach was no ordinary car. If that was new money gliding down Fourteenth Street it was new money with good taste—no spinners, no amped up bass shouting "new money!"

He smiled at the driver's outline through the glare of streetlights. *Go on brother, with your bad self.* The woman beside him turned, just enough for Bilal see her face. His mouth fell open. He would recognize that hair anywhere. When she pulled it up, some of her twists invariably tumbled free down the back of her neck and at the sides of her face. While he stood, gaping like an idiot on the sidewalk, Ayo's smiling companion reached over to adjust the wrap that slid off her shoulders. Tilting her head back, Ayo clapped her hands in a gesture of pure delight.

"I don't blame you for staring, bro. That is one nice ride." Bilal barely heard the man who had come to stand and gawk alongside him. He didn't answer. Instead the block long-walk felt like a trek through wet cement.

Who was that man? How long had Ayo known him? Was he the one she slept with? Barely noticing street signs, traffic lights and pedestrians, Bilal found his way home. Inside, as he passed each light, Bilal switched it off, leaving darkness behind him as he trudged up the stairs. With the exception of the glow from the monitor, his bedroom was dark as outdoors. He stripped off his clothes and left them where they fell. Naked except for his briefs, he laid on top of the covers, hoping the absence of light would help him sleep and erase the image of Ayo and the man, clearly enjoying each other.

In the dark room he set the CD player to "repeat" and listened over and over to the wail of Gato Barbieri's "Europa." Ayo loved this tune. She said it soared like a musical prayer to heaven. It was the last thing Bilal needed to hear, but he couldn't help himself.

In his mind, he played the tape of the past year of his life—his futile, short-lived relationship with Katherine, the love he shared with Ayo and the heartbreak of her rejection and betrayal; not once, but twice. He rubbed a hand over his bare chest and looked down at himself. In the tumult of recent events, sex had been the last thing he thought of, but it might be just what he needed to take his mind off his problems. Sex that had everything to do with the flesh and nothing to do with the heart. Some unattached, sweat-running-down-the-crack-of-your-ass sex. It had been years since he wanted it straight, without the chaser of emotion; the feeling that failed him time and time again. The hour was late, but as he watched his erection grow under the sheet, he remembered a silky touch, smooth bare thighs and a scrap of red lace.

Chapter 27

Kamla and Kamilah came bursting into the house, dragging their grandmother behind them. "What are we gonna do today, Unca B?" Kamla eyes swept the hallway, looking for evidence of the fun she hoped Bilal had planned for them.

"I may regret this," he admitted to his mother, "but I bought a roll of white paper, and some paints." Laughing, he raised one finger. "Oh yes, and two little painting smocks."

"You're a brave man, Bilal Abdul-Salaam," Adilah teased. "I'll see you all later. As-Salaam-Alaikum, son." Her eyes were tender when she bent, gathering the girls against the front of her blue and green-swirled tunic. "As-Salaam-Alaikum, Kamla and Kamilah. Behave yourselves, you hear me?"

The ties of her scarf brushed against the twins' shoulders. When she released them, they squirmed in place, waiting for Bilal to break out the paints. "Salamma laykum, Nana," they chirped in unison.

After Bilal settled the girls on the kitchen floor with paint and paper, he sat outside where he could still keep an eye on them. He had some time to kill until Mark brought over an artist's sketch of proposed renovations to Midtown's aging building.

The clear, cloudless sky matched his reflective mood. He couldn't call it a breakthrough. It was more like wiping the corner of a soot-covered window, allowing a sliver of light to shine through. In the early morning quiet, he recalled the real meaning of Islam—that of submission to God. That morning, more than sex, Bilal realized that he craved peace. In his prayer room he surrendered, giving over all of his pain. He prayed for guidance and forgiveness. Prayer became his safety net, especially from the erotic dreams that kept him on the edge of sleep all night. It kept him from a decision he would have regretted as soon as the last gasp of pleasure was over. Now more than ever, he had no choice but to get over Ayo, but not like that.

In the early afternoon Mark and Bilal stood in his kitchen, leaning against the counter. Two sets of chopsticks clicked, diving in and out of their Chinese carryout containers. He left the girls upstairs, sprawled on his bed and engrossed in the antics Barney and Friends. Bilal folded the flaps over his food and pushed off the counter. "I haven't heard a peep for a long time. I'd better check. They're either sleep or up to something." He was at the top of the steps when the phone rang.

"You want me to answer it?" Mark yelled up the stairs.

"Yeah, go ahead."

Kamla and Kamilah were transfixed by the smiling purple dinosaur and his sidekick Baby Bop. Even more than Sesame Street, Barney and Friends was the one show that held the twins' complete attention from beginning to end. Before Bilal could turn back, Mark shouted. "B, B, get down here, man!"

Bilal turned quickly to the girls. "Stay right here until I come back. Don't move, do you hear me?" Since the near disastrous day in his car, the girls knew the tone Unca B used when he was not playing.

Bilal heard blood roaring through his head. He scuttled down the stairs, nearly missing the last two steps. He reached around the corner, grabbing for the phone even before he crossed into the kitchen.

"Here," Mark pushed the receiver in Bilal's hands, "just take it."

The last time he heard the catch in his mother's voice, it came from tragic news. Whatever she told him, he had to keep himself together in case Kamla and Kamilah came hurtling down the steps. He squeezed his eyes shut, bracing himself. Again. She spoke, and this time when his eyes flew open he shouted out loud. "*Al-Hamdu-Lillah.* Praise God!"

"Yes, yes!" His head nodded vigorously with each word. "I'll be right over with them!"

Bilal's smile was a bright as the break of dawn when he turned to his friend. "Zahirah and Kalil have been rescued!" The two men pounded each other's backs in a quick, celebratory embrace. "I've got to get over to Brookland right now!"

Mark gathered his briefcase and the over-sized drawing pad. Bilal followed him to the door. "B, call me when things settle down." Mark pumped Bilal's hand one more time.

Kamla and Kamilah's safety was the only thing that kept Bilal from flooring the Commander through town. Near his parents' street, a cluster of students from a nearby Catholic school held up placards advertising a car wash. He waved them off. Any other time he'd be glad to support their efforts, but today he had time for only one thing. In front of the house, he jerked into park, unbuckled the girls and ran up the steps with each girl flanking him like tiny queen bees.

Adilah met them at the door. She had been crying, but this time the red that rimmed her eyes was from tears of joy. She reached down to scoop up her grandchildren in a lingering, tight embrace, rocking them back and forth with her eyes squeezed shut.

"Nana, if you're happy, why are you crying?" Clearly confused, Kamilah stared up at her grandmother.

All three adults burst out laughing at the twins' puzzled expressions. "I promise to tell you all about it." Adilah's eyes sparkled. "And as soon as I talk to Grandpa and Uncle B, I'll do just that."

When the girls had been settled in their playroom, Latif began the tale of his daughter and son-in-law's rescue. Huddled around the coffee table, Bilal and his mother listened intently. "Here's what I know."

Before he could finish the sentence, Adilah cut in. She had regained some of her composure. She brushed her hands over the front of her color-splashed top and adjusted the scarf that had slipped from her head. Patting her fingers under both damp eyes, she took a deep breath.

"Bilal it's so wonderful! I didn't know your father knew people in such high places! He won't tell me who, but apparently somebody had enough power to cut through the bureaucratic bull and rescue those children!"

Bilal turned to his father. "Who, Dad?" Whoever he or she was, Bilal wanted to thank them in person.

Latif shook his head. "I gave my word that I would keep his name out of it." Latif's expression shifted. It was an uncharacteristic action for his father. Bilal suspected there was more to it, but now was not the time to press the issue. More important than the name was the knowledge that his sister and brother-in-law were free.

"I will tell you this. Money *and* muscle greased that wheel. And I understand that the kidnappers were "injured while trying to escape." Latif gave a short laugh. "As a black man, I never thought I'd appreciate hearing those words, but in the case of my daughter and son-in-law, I don't mind at all."

"Me either. I hope they got a good old third-world beat down, one so bad they had to call Amnesty International." Bilal didn't believe in settling his differences with his fists, unless there was no other choice. But all bets were off when it came to protecting his family. "Tell us the rest, Dad."

Latif stroked his silver beard, continuing with no small amount of satisfaction. "Our friend's contacts had eyes and ears everywhere. It didn't take them long to find out who was behind it and where Zahirah and Kalil were being held. And now the jail has five new guests."

"Good!" Adilah clapped once; a hard sound that signaled the end of their family's ordeal.

Bilal came to stand next to Latif. "When are they coming home? I can't wait to tell those two little girls. They'll be so excited, we'll have to tie them down," he chuckled.

Latif's laughter filled the room. "Now that's truth," he nodded. "They'll be home at the beginning of next week. And that's because our "friend in high places," as your mother calls him, is sending them home in his private jet."

Adilah stood, holding out her arms to her husband and son. Standing on either side of her, they each reached down with one arm and tucked her in the center. "Look at the two of you," Adilah beamed, turning from one to the other. Her silver earrings shimmered with the movement. "I am so proud of the Abdul-Salaam men. You both did every and anything you could to keep me from falling apart and to care for our little girls." The end of her sentence gave way to a sob. "Now I'm going to tell my babies all about tears of joy."

Latif leaned down to brush away his wife's tears. "While you do that, I have a call to make." He turned to Bilal. "Will you be here?" Latif reached out to embrace his son.

"You know it," Bilal replied, looking into his father's eyes. "I wouldn't be anyplace else."

૨૦

Ayo sat on the back porch, waiting for Justine's return call. It was time to start telling her friends. They would find out soon because she was rising like yeast. She still didn't know how to tell Kedar but his change in summertime plans gave her time to think. Last Christmas in Trinidad touched him deeply. When Karen and Avril announced a summer time trip, he jumped at the chance to return "home," as he referred to the land of his birth. He wanted to see Maraval's lush greenery again, and the home he shared with his parents for those short months before his father's death. All these years, Ayo refused to sell it; right now the hillside house was available for the use of the Montgomery family, but the beautiful, planters-style home was Kedar's birthright. One day it would belong to him.

Ayo snatched up the phone on the first ring. Now that her decision had been made, she couldn't wait to get the announcement off her chest.

"Hello?"

Instead of Justine, it was Latif Abdul-Salaam. Ayo held her breath until he began to speak. Her former nemesis sounded like a new man.

"Ayo, I just got the news we've all been waiting for. Zahirah and Kalil have been found! Champion's intervention did the trick."

Ayo's hand flew to her chest. "Oh, thank God!"

"Ayo, your actions glorified Allah. How can we ever thank you?

Without your help, who knows what would have happened." He hesitated. "Don't you think it's time to tell my family about your part in this happy ending? It's too great a deed to keep secret."

His voice broke, but this time Ayo wasn't surprised. Since his daughter's kidnapping, Ayo had seen more of the man who kept himself under a coat of strong armor in front of the world.

"Mr. Abdul-Salaam, I can't. Please understand." She wanted to see them all, she wanted to share their joy, but she couldn't be anywhere Bilal and his new love. And since she really did look like a setting hen, Ayo wanted to stay far from Adilah. Her nurse's eye would spot Ayo's condition as soon as she waddled into the door.

He hesitated. "It could be just me and my wife, if that would make you feel better. I insist, Ayo. We need to thank you."

She kept her voice light so that their truce wouldn't crumble. "Ah, but you gave your word, remember?"

He laughed. "Yes, I did, so I guess I have to honor your request. I may appear at time to be a hard man," He gave a rueful chuckle, "and for that I apologize to you. But I am a man of my word."

Ayo let out a sigh. "Thank you, Mr. Abdul-Salaam. There's one more thing I'm grateful for. Look at you and me. Who would have ever thought we could carry on a conversation without snarling at each another. I guess even more good came out of this than we imagined."

"*Al-Hamdu-Lillah*. And Ayo, if there is anything I can ever do for you, just let me know."

"I'll do that, Mr. Abdul-Salaam."

Ayo leaned back against the cushions. That day, it was the best news she could have heard. It wasn't the first time near tragedy or even necessity had brought old enemies together. "Talk about unlikely allies," she chuckled to herself. Ayo's eyelids fluttered. As far as Latif's offer of assistance whenever she needed it, that time was closer than he thought. Ayo wondered—would the battle lines reform when he realized she knew of her pregnancy throughout their recent contact?

Right now Ayo was tired. The high fence that ringed her property came in handy. She could fall asleep right there and even if her mouth hung open and she snored like a saw, no one would see or hear her. But before she drifted completely into sleep, the phone rang again.

"Ayo, I got your message, but I don't know when I'll be over." Justine words rushed out. "Nicole got stung by yellow jackets and she's swelling up. We were up at a bakery near the DC/Takoma Park line. I don't know if there's some kind of bush those bees are addicted to up that way, but they need to be bombed with a nuclear-powered insecticide! I've given her Benadryl, but I still need to take her to the doctor. Can I call you later?"

There was no point in being disappointed. Her belly wasn't going anywhere but up. "Sure, and I hope Nicole feels better. You know, you should get a bee kit. Especially if she's allergic to stings." Her tone brightened. "Oh, Justine, guess what? Kalil and Zahirah have been found. Bilal's father just called me. Paul's involvement did the trick."

Any mention of Paul sent Justine into feverish throes of matchmaking. She'd be a millionaire if she combined public relations with her passion for putting just the right couple together. Today Ayo didn't mind Justine's unrelenting Paul and Ayo campaign.

"Since you insist on staying away from Bilal, at least you ought to give Paul a chance. Looks like he'll do anything for you. And from what you've told me, he's just waiting for you to say the word."

Ayo had to laugh. "Justine, you can't see me, but you know I'm over here shaking my head. You won't leave it alone, will you?"

"You don't have to marry him right now, just give him a chance."

"*Right now*? Oh come on, Justine."

"Yes, I said right now! Work your way into it. I think you're set on one kind of love and sometimes that kind of heart-stopping romance comes only once. But companionship, mutual respect, and attraction—those things make a real relationship."

"Ask me how I know," Ayo sighed. "And the woman in his life will never want for his complete love, attention and devotion. For that reason, he deserves better than a rebound. You've heard me say it time and time again."

Justine surged full force ahead. "Ayo, you know how I held out on Nick. And now I don't know what I'd do without him. As for Paul, you couldn't find a better companion than him. And can we mention the money?"

Ayo burst out laughing. "Hush! I met a sister in Nassau who was even more of a matchmaker than you. If I was a masochist, I'd put us on a three-way call and let you two babble in each ear. Paul is a wonderful man, and he has proven everything he's promised, but this one stands out—he's just as good a friend as he would be a lover."

Chapter 28

The next day Ayo drove to a bookstore on the Takoma side of D.C. It was a community institution and one of two African American bookstores left standing in the city. There had been rumblings that it might close. Through a series of negotiations and fundraisers, the bookstore managed to stay open and even to thrive. Now it boasted a small café and coffee bar. It was one of Ayo's favorite places. It looked like a bookstore was supposed to, with a series of reading areas, floor to ceiling shelves and the unmistakable fragrance of bound books. She came in often to browse, sit and read in one of the deep chocolate brown chairs.

The day was hot and sunny, but DC's legendary humidity was still on the other side of the cotton ball clouds. Today cars filled the parking lot and lined the shady, old-town streets. Bright-colored balloons hung in front of the two story building. She hadn't kept up with community events, and was surprised to find that today was the store's annual children's day. Kids and their parents from all over the city attended the popular day-long celebration. The sign announced that a clown, a griot and a face painter would be on hand to entertain the children in the courtyard back of the building.

Ayo smiled at the high-pitched squeals of excitement. In a couple of years, she would be the mother of a toddler herself. Instead of planning a Mexican vacation, she would be arranging play times, and watching tapes of Gullah-Gullah Island, or whatever would be the must-see toddler show of the moment. Would she be the oldest parent in kindergarten? It was still hard to believe, but Dr. Broussard had been a godsend. More than from a physician's duty, her care and sound advice came from a bottomless well of good will. Ayo pulled out her list of the doctor's recommendations for over-forty pregnancies.

"Oh, I remember this," Ayo exclaimed out loud. It was an updated version of *What to Expect*, the book she consulted daily during her first pregnancy. She remembered the hormonal roller coaster she rode. At the book's end, when it described the nine-month's journey's end and meaning of the new life, Ayo burst into tears that lasted for many days. Rubbing her hands over its cover, Ayo gave a contented smile and placed it in her book basket. It was hard not to fill the entire basket, but reluctantly, she pulled herself away from the stacks. She stood in line leafing through passages that brought a nostalgic smile to her face. When Ayo looked up from the book, there was one more person ahead of her. She stuck a finger between the pages and shifted to reach in her purse for her wallet. A little girl's voice rang out.

"Nana! Look! It's Miss Ayo!"

Ayo breath caught in her throat. She whirled around to see Kamla and Kamilah wiggling their little hands in her directions. She couldn't ignore them, but she had to move quickly before Adilah leaned back and saw her. Fluttering a quick wave at the excited children, she slid out of the line. "I forgot my wallet," she stammered to the surprised clerk who had just seen her pull it out, prepared to pay. "I'll be back."

Ayo fled from the store. On the street, she leaned against the Sequoia to catch her breath. She had one foot inside when she spotted the Midtown van, loaded with boys and Mark in the driver's seat. Not him too! At least he couldn't see her belly hidden by the door. Ayo raised one hand to wave when her heart lurched. The smiling, aristocratic woman she'd seen with Bilal turned to face the children. She was laughing, apparently sharing a joke with the boys. Ayo felt a huge, hormonal crying jag coming on. In less than ten minutes, she had nearly run into Bilal's mother, his best friend and the woman who had replaced her in his life. Could he be somewhere close by?

That half-hour had been enough hide and seek for a lifetime. It was time to go home and stay hidden for a while. Ayo jumped in the truck and pulled off as fast as she could without causing attention from the police and anybody else she knew. That was close, she muttered, taking a deep breath. Behind her, she sensed movement in the back of the truck.

"Oh no," she gasped. She turned to see a pair of yellow jackets streaking for the front. When they hovered near her face, Ayo's free hand windmilled around her head. The pair tag-teamed her, buzzing in circles around her head like angry fairies. Ayo rolled down the window, coaxing them to fly out. Instead, they dove for her face. She shrieked and batted them away. With her other hand, Ayo jerked the wheel and slammed her foot on what she thought were the brakes. Instead, she hit the gas. The big vehicle leapt back into the lane and jumped the curb, crashing into a stop sign. The last thing she felt was the airbag as it exploded against her head.

る

She woke up in a small room next to a sleeping woman whose hospital gown splayed open, revealing a huge mound of pale naked behind. Ayo's shoes and purse sat in a grey plastic chair against the wall. A machine dispensing digital read-outs was hooked to some part of her anatomy.

A man in blue scrubs stood over her, making notes on a medical chart.

In the chilly room, she was gripped by a new sense of horror. "Where am I? Am alright?" Ayo struggled to sit up, but her body would not cooperate. "Are you a doctor?

His genuine smile calmed Ayo's fears. "Yes, ma'am; you and the baby are okay, but I'm not a doctor." His drawl came from way south of the Mason-Dixon Line. He held out the ID that dangled against his blue scrubs. "I'm Ralph, your nurse, and you're at the Hospital Center."

"Oh, Lord have mercy," Ayo gasped. The Hospital Center was the size of a small town, but if she wasn't with the twins, Adilah could have been on duty in this same ER. Then the hiding would be over and the explaining would begin.

Her outburst alarmed Ralph. His smile disappeared. "Are you in pain?"

"Oh, no," Ayo gasped. "I'm just shocked to find myself here," she explained.

"Good! You had me scared for a minute." His voice reminded Ayo of hot biscuits and sweet King Pot-Rik syrup.

Ayo was kept under observation long enough to make sure she had suffered no real injury. Even if she could have driven herself home, the Sequoia was crashed on an Aspen Street curb. As soon as she got home, she'd call a tow truck. Here, a cab could always be found, cruising the hospital's circular driveway. On her way past the nurses' station, Ayo waved to the desk clerk. Just before the elevator doors parted, she heard one of them whisper "Her husband sure was cute. He's probably outside to pick her up."

Ayo whirled around. Who could it have been? And why did they think he was her husband? But a ride home and a long sleep in her own bed was more important than what was certainly mistaken identity.

❧

When Mark trudged up the steps with his head down, Bilal felt unease slither down his back.

"Something must be wrong, man. Come on out back and tell me what's happening."

Mark dropped into the cushioned chair, under the spot where the branches of an apple tree cast a cool shade over the porch. Bilal leaned forward, resting his hands between both knees. He trained an intense gaze on his friend. "Talk to me. You look like you've been robbed!"

Mark shut his eyes briefly before beginning. "B, you know I hate news carrying. So you know if I'm here, it's something I saw with my own eyes."

Bilal felt even more of his well-being slip away. Whatever it was, if it brought Mark to his door looking like a pall-bearer, it had to be bad.

Bilal sat up straight; this was not a conversation for a casual slouch. Mark plunged ahead. "I was leaving the bookstore with Monica and the kids when I saw Ayo's Sequoia." He looked over at the growing apprehension on Bilal's face. "It was crashed into a stop sign on Aspen Street."

Bilal's misgiving turned to pure terror. He lurched forward, grabbing Mark's arm. "Where is she? Is she okay?"

Mark held up one hand. "Hold up, let me finish. A police officer was still there. She told me that Ayo had been taken to the Hospital Center."

Beginning to pace, Bilal raked a hand through his hair. "Oh, man…Mama had Kamla and Kamilah today; otherwise I know she would have seen her. She would have told me." Bilal's voice shook. He jumped up to stalk the space between the railing and where Mark sat.

Mark nodded. "Anyway, to make a long story short, I had Monica drop me off at the hospital and drive the boys back to Midtown."

"Come on, Mark!" Bilal demanded. "Stop dragging it out! Please–I need to know!" Bending his head, he ran both hands front to back through his hair, holding them in place among the thick coils.

The urgency in Bilal's plea ended Mark's rambling. "Sorry, man. I'll get to the point. I guess I looked so upset when I ran up to the nurse's desk, that they assumed I was her husband. And here's what they told me: that my wife and baby were okay. She was being examined, but I could see her shortly. I was so shocked, I didn't know what to say. I kind of stammered that I'd be back, and then I split. B, I know you two have had a lot of upheavals. I know you're doing better, but you still love the sister. And if she's married, you need to know. That way you can put it to rest for good."

Bilal stood expressionless, like a mannequin of himself. *This must be what it feels like to be shot in the back. One minute you're standing up on two feet, the next you're sprawled face down in dirt and gravel.* For a long time he didn't speak. When he did, his words came out in a whispered monotone. "That must be the man I saw her with." He gave his friend a blank stare.

Mark let himself out, sensing his friend's need to be alone. Zombie-like, Bilal made his way to the porch. Ayo, married? And *pregnant*? She was supposed to be his wife and the mother of his child, not some super-rich brother who couldn't love her half as much as Bilal could. And still did. Would this man feed her Manhattan clam chowder or hot and spicy soup when she was sick? Would he massage her slowly, from the top of her head to the soles of her feet? Did he know she couldn't sleep with socks on? Or how much she loved coffee, coke, sunrise and spring? Bilal played the words over and over in his head until dark and insects drove him back inside.

Before, Bilal had been furious, nearly compromising his principles and acting like a fool. This time he was too numb for rage. He loved Ayo deeply, and in spite of every hurtful word and disastrous turn in their relationship, somewhere in the back of his mind, he held onto hope. Now he had no choice. He had to give up the idea of ever being with her again.

≀▲

Bilal wasn't ready to tell his family about her marriage. He stayed away, claiming a backlog of furniture restorations. It was true that he had more clients than he'd soon be able to handle. He was glad to join in an as-yet informal partnership with Randall Jamison, whose time and skill had stood him in good stead during his family's crisis.

Zahirah and Kalil had taken the girls to Disney World for a Friday to Sunday trip, allowing him to escape his sister's psychic scrutiny. He prayed five times a day, needing an anchor to keep him from anywhere near the edge he'd nearly fallen over.

When his emotions were settled enough he resumed frequent visits to his parents. To his mother's joy, a relaxed camaraderie continued to replace the tension that had existed between Bilal and his father. One late morning, on his way back from a client's home, Bilal decided to stop by his father's office with an impromptu invitation for lunch. When he pulled into the parking lot, Bilal slammed on his brakes, staring at the car next to Latif's pearl gray Lincoln Town Car.

There weren't that many coincidences and that many Maybachs in the world, especially with the vanity tags CHAMP. Why was Ayo's husband parked at his father's building? What in the hell was happening to his life? If he got one punch to the gut, he would have to be committed. But before they carried him away with his arms tied behind his back, he was going to get some answers.

Latif's secretary opened her mouth, but he gave her no time to utter a word when he strode past her desk. Without knocking, Bilal pushed open the door. His father was in conversation with a man who looked like he had everything life had to offer. And that included Ayo. His gaze raked over the man whose wealth was made more obvious by his understated elegance. Bilal knew clothes; more than tailor-made, the suit bespoke Savile Row. From the time cloth is selected to final fitting could take four months and cost at least $5.000.

He ignored Latif completely and trained his eyes on Paul. "So you're Ayo's husband? What are you doing here?" His resolve to hold back his anger was lost in an eruption of pain he had convinced himself was under control. Bilal turned to his father. "I thought we had made peace with our differences. But I guess you're so glad she's finally out of my life that you invited him over for congratulations. Or to give them a wedding gift. Although my man looks like he can buy anything he wants." He halted his rant long enough to stare at his father. "Wait a minute! How do you two know each other?"

Bilal's confusion rose when, instead of responding with a sharp reprimand, Latif returned his son's angry gaze with the smile of a man holding a secret. "Bilal, I'm going to leave you to speak with Paul alone. He has the answer to every one of your questions."

Chapter 29

❦

"*K*edar, someone is at the door. I'll have to call you back....Yes, I promise."

Kedar was still in Trinidad, and even from that far away, he didn't buy her insistence that everything was fine. He claimed to detect something unsaid lurking behind their conversations. Her evasive answers weren't doing the trick. He pressed harder and harder until the urge to blurt out the whole story was so great she was glad for the knock on the door. On her way to the front, the loose white sundress swirled around her calves.

When Ayo peered through the peephole, she didn't know whether to satisfy her shocked curiosity or run upstairs and hide until they went away. She stood uncertain at the door until it was obvious that running away would only delay the inevitable. Whatever brought the two of them together at her door would surely bring them back. It might be time to deal with Bilal, but what alignment of the planets brought Paul there with him?

They got as far as the foyer when Ayo faced them. She leaned against the console table and stood up just as quickly. The white cotton draped across her stomach, and if he looked closely, she was sure Bilal would notice. Paul's enigmatic smile contrasted with the hope and amazement she saw on Bilal's face, far different from the hateful sneer he left her with.

"To say I'm shocked is the understatement of the year! Will somebody please tell me how you two even know each other? And why in the world are you both here together?" Ayo twisted her hands one over the other, praying that his gaze stayed above her neck. Paul's enigmatic smile confused her. It held a hint of satisfaction, of a job well done, but what it was, Ayo had no idea.

"I'll let Bilal tell you, since I only came to run interference. We both knew that, under the circumstances, if he showed up alone, you wouldn't open the door."

"What? Under what circumstances?"

Neither man answered. Instead, Paul squeezed Ayo's hand. "I'll see myself out and I'll talk to you later. You two have some catching up to do."

Bilal pumped Paul's hand. Each man slapped the other on the back. Instead of strangers they acted like old friends. "I can't say enough to thank you – for everything."

While Ayo walked Paul to the door, Bilal reveled in the scents and familiar surroundings; it was like coming home. When she returned, the sight of Ayo and the small bulge poking from her middle brought a rush of staggering emotions. "You're really pregnant," he whispered in reverent wonder, smoothing both hands over her stomach. "I can't believe it. But how? I mean, even in our rush to devour each other, I still used protection."

Ayo's eyes and her mouth opened wide. "He told you? Oh my God, this is all too much. I need to sit down and hear this from beginning to end."

She sat apart from him on the couch, aching to move into the circle of his arms. There had been a time when that was the only way they sat together. Her eyes devoured him—the strong jaw covered by the fine beard, his eyes the color of every dark gem imaginable, the hair sweeping his shoulders and the fragrance of sandalwood that would always trigger the scent of his warm skin and the feel of their bodies wrapped together. But those days were over.

Ayo cast her eyes down. "Yes I am. And until I went to Dr. Broussard to confirm my pregnancy, I couldn't figure it out either. Before I left for Harbour Island, I needed another prescription. It came with written warnings, but I was too crazy in the head to pay attention. All I wanted was to get away." She laughed ruefully. "There's an ingredient in the cream that breaks down latex. So there you have it." Looking up again, she let all the months of sorrow and frustration pour out along with her tears. "I've been so miserable," she sobbed, "All those lies and pain for nothing! But I told you the worst lie I could think of because it was the only thing that would make you stay away. And now I've made a mess of everything."

Bilal slid his fingers down her face, wiping her tears with his bare hands. "What do you mean?"

"I mean with you. You wanted to be a husband and father, not a baby daddy. And since you have someone else in your life now, that's exactly what you'll be. A man with a child from a previous relationship, as they say." She laughed bitterly.

Bilal rocked back against the back of the loveseat. He punched his knee and let out a loud whoop of laughter.

Ayo stared. Between her hormones, her hide-and-seek conversation with Kedar and seeing Paul and Bilal together on her porch, every bit of fear and heartbreak broke through like flood waters through a dike.

"What in the hell is so funny?" she demanded. "Don't patronize me. Just because you're happy doesn't give you the right to come over here and act like all is well with everybody else in the world!"

Bilal reached over to grab her in a bear hug. "Oh, my sweet baby," he chuckled rocking them both from side to side. "Do you know how much I miss hearing you fly off the handle? Now stop and listen to me. When I went over to my Dad's office, I saw Paul's car. It was the same one I had seen on Fourteenth Street one night with you in it." Before she could open it, Bilal laid his hand over her mouth. "I stormed into my father's office, ready to do battle with him for knowing the man I thought was your husband and with Paul for having you when I couldn't."

"My husband! Why in the world did you think I was married?"

He told her about Mark's experience at the hospital. Bilal shook his head slowly, as if the pain was fresh in his heart. "That day was the worst. Out of everything that happened, hearing that you were married was the absolute worst. It meant there was no way, no hope of having you back. But then Paul told me everything from the beginning to the end, including his part in Zahirah and Kalil's rescue. We had a long conversation and he set me straight on a lot of things," Bilal admitted. "He's a very good friend to you."

"That he is," Ayo replied. "But I saw you and the twins with a woman on Capitol Hill. You were going into a restaurant and you had your hand on her back!" She left out the part about her stealth phone call. It was too embarrassing to admit.

Bilal frowned. "You did?" Then he let loose another round of laughter. "You know, this could be a full-length melodrama! The woman was Monica; she's Mark's lady. She's relocating to the city to teach dance at the school for the arts. We were all meeting for brunch and she and I got there at the same time."

"Oh my goodness. I saw you, you saw me. And one and one made five!" For the first time in a long while, instead of tears, anger and harsh words, their combined laughter filled the room.

Ayo nestled against him, resting her head on his shoulder and pressing one of his warm hands over the swell in her stomach. She gazed up at the man she could never stop loving. They were back in each other's hearts and lives, and with the greatest gift they could give each other already on the way. Bilal closed his eyes and sighed deeply, drawing her closer. His lips moved against the curve of her cheek. "I'll never be without you again. And that's a promise, Ayo Montgomery."

And then Ayo remembered Justine's long-ago observation. It was true—her greatest life decisions had come on the spur of the moment.

Why not continue the tradition? It had always worked in the past. Ayo disentangled herself and slid her heavier body off the loveseat. She couldn't manage one knee; she needed both to hold her weight. "Strike while the iron is hot," her mother used to say. Grabbing his hands, she looked up into the face of the man she loved. "Bilal Abdul-Salaam, will you marry me?"

Epilogue
❧

"They are a garment to you and you are a garment to them." The day before, standing with Bilal before the imam, Ayo remembered the first time she'd heard those words.

Tonight, the balcony doors were open to the sounds of the sea. Vibrant tropical blossoms filled the room with their lush beauty and sweet exotic fragrance, complementing the vanilla scented candles placed throughout the room.

"I thought you could never be more beautiful than yesterday, but I was so wrong." Bilal's voice was softened by love, joy and wonder as his bride walked toward him, wearing nothing under the gossamer gown that molded itself over her ripe breasts and the swell of her belly.

From the king-sized bed, Bilal held out his hand. He drew her down onto the silky Sea Island sheets, settling her between his thighs and the warm circle of his arms. "This is where our lives began–again," he murmured into her hair.

"And the new life we created." Ayo snuggled back and smiled down towards her lap. The sight filled her with immeasurable joy; their hands entwined, both wearing matching bands and resting on the bulge that was their baby.

"New lives for all of us. From the first time I saw you, you've been in my heart and my blood. Even when you left me, I couldn't let you go. And now that I never have to, I promise to be your husband, your protector and your lover–all you'll ever need for a lifetime of love." Bilal leaned forward and brushed his beard against her cheek. "And my beautiful, beloved wife, this is just the beginning."

Author Bio

Niambi Brown Davis was born in Philadelphia, Pennsylvania, and raised on the Eastern Shore of Maryland. Niambi is the mother of three adult children.

For nearly three years she wrote for Bronze Thrills, True Confessions and Black Romance Magazines. She indulged her passion for sailing and travel by serving as publicist for the Black Boaters Summit and as a member of the National Association of Black Travel Writers. Presently, Niambi writes for Travel Lady Magazine.

A script for her first digital novella has been accepted and published by Arrow Publications, LLC. Aside from travel and writing, Niambi is an avid reader of historical fiction, and deeply involved in tracing the history of both branches of her family tree. Her day job is running the business of Sand & Silk/Soleful Strut, Niambi's own line of handcrafted bath and body products.